Déjà Vu: The Domino Effect

DÉJÀ VU

THE DOMINO EFFECT

JOHN GATES

Norfolk Publishing Group
800 Boylston Street
Boston, MA 02199
www.npgbooks.com
info@npgbooks.com
editorial@npgbooks.com

Déjà Vu: The Domino Effect
A Norfolk Publishing Group Book

NPG Ebook edition/December 2020
NPG Paperback Edition/April 2021
NPG Trade Hardback Edition/April 2021

Hardcover: ISBN 13: 978-1-950457-02-1
Paperback: ISBN 13: 978-1-950457-01-4
Library of Congress Number

This is a work of fiction. All the names, places, and incidents are a product of the author's imagination or used fictitiously. Any resemblance to people or place is completely coincidental.

Cover by Victoria Cooper Art

Interior design by Chris DiRusso
www.chris-dirusso.com

John Gates Fan Mail: j.gates@npgbooks.com

1

The Dream

Keep Running....Whether Keith Richards was running away from or towards something, he didn't know. Nor did he recognize the surrounding buildings. The surroundings were unfamiliar. Although Keith was in a vast city, he had no idea which one. *Keep running, Keith*, the familiar voice in his head urged. *Move your ass!*

He knew enough not to slow down and definitely not stop. From whom was he running? To where? Question after question flooded his mind. *Damn, what did you get yourself mixed up in this time?*

He gripped something tightly in his hand that felt familiar, comforting, yet somehow terrifying—he glanced down and saw a black semiautomatic handgun. He was sure it was a 40 Cal. His preferred round. *Run.* A round, he knew, had just been fired. The gun still warm. None of this surprised him. Who did he kill now? Everything appeared strange. The buildings, the weapon, and the city seemed off. He questioned his memory.

He exited a short alley into a busy square. The buildings were tall—yet still unfamiliar. People were everywhere. Some stared at him and, more importantly, at the gun in his hand. The sidewalks were packed, and cars jammed the streets. *Run!* The voice again. His voice. He obeyed and pushed through the crowd.

He stayed close to the building and switched his gun hand to the left. Healthy and ambidextrous. Though, he preferred his right hand the best. Concrete exploded an inch above his head. They were getting closer. The sidewalk was too jammed packed for him to shoot back. Sure, if it were him doing the chasing, he would not have taken the shot. He picked up the pace.

Frantically, he ran—he bumped into people, knocking some down, as he shoved his way through the dense human forest. Concrete exploding above his head nagged at him. It bothered him to no end. He never heard the shot. Professionals were chasing him, ones with suppressed guns.

Lost and confused, Keith didn't know what to do except to get out of there. He went across several traffic lanes with an overwhelming sense he needed to make it to the other side. Cars honked their horns. A car missed him as he cut in front of it. Something was desperately wrong, but...what...he didn't know. The cars, something about them, wasn't the right. He couldn't place it. *Stop thinking and run!* Something still nagged at him. He couldn't recognize any of the cars. Not a one.

A street sign came into view, and he needed to go down the narrow street. But why? Keith pushed himself even harder, his legs burning as he banged the corner at full speed—and he came to a full stop. The landscape changed. Now, complete darkness surrounded him. A hooded figure came out of nowhere, materializing from the darkness itself. Two guns aimed at him, as the assailant unloaded both weapons—

Keith woke with a start! Cold sweat covered his body, which made him stick to the plastic mattress. He gulped air as if breathing for the first time and looked around the room, confused as his eyes adjusted. *Damn, another nightmare.* Safe in his cell. Home sweet home. Keith sat up, grabbed the notebook, and wrote down every detail of the dream before it faded. A habit since he was twelve.

Over the years, he learned only to write down—the dreams—the ones that always came true. These dreams differed from the others. They faded fast. Soon he'd lose all memory of the dream—zero recall. Without a doubt, this was *one* of those dreams. The cars still bothered him. Shit, he wasn't getting out anytime soon. *Like never.* The only way he'd be leaving prison was in a pine box.

After Keith finished writing down his dream, he looked at his watch, seeing it was 5:30 in the morning. He decided he would stay up. Count an hour away. He got out of bed and turned on the TV, and decided the best use of the hour would be to workout.

He thought about his life as he did his cardio. It pushed him to work out harder. Seven years had passed since he had been on the streets. At the beginning of his prison bid, he was as wild as they came. He fought all the time and over the stupidest shit. He even stabbed a few dudes. His careless attitude kept him in a maximum-security prison for four years. He was just glad he never got caught for the stabbings. *Shit, if he had, he'd still be up at the Max.* Shit out of luck. The atmosphere at the Max made it hard to implement change. He tried, but the GED he got while there amounted to the only good thing that came out of that place.

He'd been at the current facility for three years. The place was worlds apart from the Max. He had no intention of going back. Unless he overturned his case, he would die at the facility he was at now. If only he could change his past, as he did himself over the past few years. He recently received a bachelor's degree in sociology through Metro College. The college, through alumni donations, covered the tuition for the classes at the prison. Professors held courses in the prison's school building.

Although still feared by many who had seen him in action, he calmed down. A lot. Peaceful even. Keith had realized his attitude needed to change, so he did his best to change. Now, he was able to think things through—even through the toughest of situations. It was new to him to be able to react without violence. Something, 20 years ago, he wouldn't have been able to do.

He took a break from his workout and picked took a sip from his water bottle while plugging in the hotpot to heat water for tea. Green. Something on the television screen caught his attention. Breaking news. Six teenagers got gunned down, and they had one of the gunmen in custody. The alleged killer's picture popped up on the screen. A baby-faced kid of about 20 appeared and brought Keith back to his own situation. Right back to the crime.

2

Crime-2005

The block he lived on was as live as the city itself. He looked out the windows again. The blue and red glow of the flashing lights from the cruisers was gone. Police always patrolled his neighborhood. He couldn't get away from them and loved it when he would go to his friend's whiter neighborhood. Keith could smoke trees on the front porch and relax with his friends. Not a cop in sight. He let the blinds snap back as he moved away from the window. It looked like everything was clear, at least for the moment. The police would be back.

He made a call on a cellphone as he sat on the couch and stared at the coffee table—one item in particular that rested upon it called for his attention. An all-black 40 caliber handgun. The line connected at the same time he picked up the burner. He pulled back the slide to make sure a round was in the chamber, then ejected the mag and added another round. He smiled at the thought that most people would say clip, showing their ignorance of what a clip was. Automatic handguns, shit, assault-styled weapons to too all had magazines. But every day, he'd hear motherfuckers call it a clip.

"What's up, Ty," he said, still handling the handgun. "What happened?"

"Those motherfuckers got Jay," Tyson said. "They ran-up on him as he sat in his Escalade, dawg. They lit him the fuck up. He's dead, fam. Dead. What are we gonna do?"

"We ain't gonna do shit," he said in a flat tone. "You're gonna chill, and you make sure everyone else stays cool as well, ya heard?"

"Yeah, I heard, but what—"

"Don't worry, I got you," he paused, thinking this would go a lot smoother if Tyson stayed out of his way. "You're sure it was them, right?"

"Yeah, Tony saw it all go down."

"Alright, dawg. Let me call you back at you, but relax, son. I'll take care of it."

"Okay, okay, fam. That's why you're around, right? I'll let you go, one."

"One," he said and hung up.

The game always fucked shit up on a motherfucker. Although this time, it had helped that Dougie was a half-ass stickup kid who was nothing without his guns. And Keith knew it was him and his boys who killed Jay.

He tucked the 40 Cal into his waistline and went into the spare bedroom, heading for the closet. After moving a few stacks of shoeboxes, he slid the back-wall panel to the side. The space beyond contained a four-foot safe. The safe contained all kinds of things: Jewelry, money, and guns. It was the latter that he was after. He grabbed another 40 Cal, several mags, and a box of ammo.

After closing the hidden stash spot and putting back the shoe boxes, he tucked the 40 Cal. The burner. Handgun. Whatever the fuck you want to call it into his waistband on the opposite side as the other. He then grabbed the seven mags and put them in his jacket pockets along with the box of ammo. Just in case.

Twenty minutes later, Keith stood in front of the triple-decker he knew Dougie and his boys hung-out at—Kelly's place. Dougie was an ignorant cat, who besides being ever self-important, never tried to better himself, even though he had been locked up for more years than he'll ever get to spend on the street. Dougie was a stickup kid with no mindset to be anything else. As far as he was concerned, Dougie had no future, and he would help that along if he could—or die trying.

Dougie and his friends, on most nights, hung out on the back porch. He hoped that's where they were at the moment. Before walking up the driveway, he checked himself to make sure he had everything he needed. Locked, loaded, and ready to go.

He moved down the driveway as silently as his 252-pound frame would allow. As he neared the back of the building, he heard voices. People were chillin on the porch, and he hoped to God it wasn't the rare occasion the upstairs folks used the back porch. One voice rose above the others. Loud and boisterous. It quelled his concerns. There was no doubt in his mind that person was Dougie.

He pulled out both burners from their concealment and stepped out around the corner towards the porch. Quickly, he walked to the porch as he raised both weapons and unloaded. *The crew had no chance.*

Dougie was among the first dead. One person survived—the person who testified against him. If it weren't for the motherfucker, he would have never got caught. There was a time he wished he made sure they were all dead. But not anymore. Now, he was a different person. Something that he once thought impossible.

He had to work hard at it, but in the end, he changed his focus—to something more substantial. *Life.* His own ways of doing things had nothing to do with living life. It was more like chasing death.

3

The Last Subject

The secure facility, which included the lab, looked unassuming. The five-story brick structure built during the Cold War held many secrets. Most of the offices within the building were legit businesses. The government facility located on the subterranean levels was accessible only through one business. The Sleep Research Clinic contained the only elevator that accessed the subterranean complex. SRC was the only business in the building that the government controlled. The building itself was owned by a big tech company that had no idea that the subterranean complex was there. SRC had a 99-year lease so that it would remain a secret for generations.

Dr. Reginald Bell entered the elevator. There were no floor-numbers displayed or buttons—just a circular pad. Dr. Bell tapped his ID card on the circular card reader. The elevator descended with barely a notice. The Complex began five stories below the surface. The elevator doors opened to the control room. Dr. Bell nodded to a couple of colleagues getting into the elevator as he exited.

He glanced around the anteroom. The glassed-in space provided additional security. The elevator already scanned biometrics and his body on the way down. In the anteroom, he had to pass through another body scanner, and security would check badges, bags, and hand wand for weapons.

He approached the glass door, slid his card through the card reader. After the light blinked green, he passed through. On the other side of the door, he handed his bag to the guard, who searched its contents. He also had to empty all his pockets, and they X-rayed his bags and belongings. He walked through what looked like a metal detector but was another body scanner. He waited for another green light before he grabbed his things and continued on to the lab.

A woman with brown hair and blue eyes hidden behind glasses approached Dr. Bell as he entered the lab.

"Here is the lab report I called you about," Dr. Jennifer Jenkins said. "The data is promising."

Dr. Bell flipped through the pages of the document. It had been 10 long years, and they were making some serious progress. The subject's file before him appeared more than promising. The subject was perfect in every way, right down to his genetic makeup. He was also a decorated soldier who served in Iraq in 2004 and was now on the Boston police force.

The subject arrived shortly after Dr. Bell, who had his assistants prepare the subject for the test. Dr. Bell hoped they resolved the issues. This would be the fifth subject they tested. The first one died immediately. The second and the fourth both went crazy. The third subject completed the task, but after several diagnostic tests, they determined subject three had very realistic dreams. Though it took longer, he also succumbed to a psychotic break. It had been six months since the last test.

A glass petition divided the room, and a chair reminiscent of one in a dentist's office sat in the middle of the other section.

The latest subject sat in the chair, waiting for the procedure to be started. Dr. Bell walked over to the control panel. He checked various screens that held the subject's vitals and other important data for the project. One crucial component was brain wave activity, which his dedicated assistant monitored. Everything looked good. Dr. Bell was satisfied.

Dr. Bell glanced over at the patient in the chair. The man appeared to be asleep. Two technicians were in the room with him, standing by the chair.

"Okay, inject the CTE," he said.

The CTE, also known as the Chemical Traumatic Episode compound, would mimic stress levels present during a traumatic event that activated unique brainwave patterns.

"His vitals look good, doctor," an assistant said.

Dr. Bell nodded to Jen, who then gave the order to proceed.

Dr. Bell watched as the patient's body reacted to the CTE. They pumped a cocktail of fluids into his body to help induce a deep state of sleep. He entered REM, and his levels reflected the dream state. As the CTE compound took effect, his vitals jumped. If he didn't watch the screen, he would have missed the bounce.

The subject's vitals rose in slow increments to that of a conscious person. They were close; he could feel it. He looked at the screen, monitoring brain activity. Scrutinizing every ebb and flow of the waves. He smiled. The pattern began to change. Different parts of the brain lit up and turned bright pink. The designated color that the computer program used for the parts of the brain that activated during the transition. The subject's brainwave activity resembled that of a youth.

"It's working. I can feel it."

Jen agreed.

The room filled with excitement. The promise of a successful test. Unfortunately, the excitement was short-lived. The bright pink color turned dark as if death had taken over. The darker colors showed inactivity; the darker the color, the less activity. They scurried around the subject and ministered fail-safe protocols. The man's heart rate continued to rise at an exponential rate, as did his blood pressure.

"Something's wrong," Dr. Bell said. "Inject him quickly. Bring him back. Now!"

The technicians tried; Jen went to assist. They waited as the numbers dropped. Steadily at first before they plummeted.

"He's entering cardiac arrest. Start lifesaving protocols," Dr. Bell ordered.

Ten minutes later, they pronounced the subject dead, and it sent them back to the beginning. Dr. Bell was sure the project would shut down with two deaths and three other subjects experiencing severe psychotic episodes. The data said they were on the right track, but they missed something. He needed to solve the problem before testing another subject, even if the research took years to find the missing piece to the puzzle. Time would be relative if they solved the issue. Something had been overlooked. They were too close to stop now. He had to find the answers.

4

Bloodwork

The artic breeze that swept the prison yard made Keith Richards shiver. Snow covered the ground, making it slick. The weather had been brutal so far this season. Snowfall records were being broken. Every year the weather got stranger and more volatile. He was a firm believer in climate change, but the Earth getting colder on the surface challenged his perception of global warming. Keith smirked at the thought. *What did he care about global warming or erratic weather changes?*

The only whether that concerned him was the kind that closed the yards at MCI-Norfolk, where he'd most likely spend the rest of his days. He did, however, believe the Earth used the weather to protect itself. It's what happened during the last ice age, and that was what will do during the next.

Most of society wouldn't expect that a man walking around the prison yard serving a life sentence would contemplate such things, but he often did. Even before he started college there at the prison, he contemplated things that were not usual. However, he found many of his fellow prisoners, inmates, cons did. Though for him, his curiosity intensified after he started studying for a college degree. Something he never thought possible. It felt good to graduate with a bachelor's degree. The only positive accomplishment besides straightened himself out. One thing that he found interesting about prison was that there were many college-educated people behind those walls. But he wasn't one of those people. No, people would think a thug like him had no intelligence at all. *No hope to change.* Hell, Keith didn't think he had intelligence or could change, but he did.

It wasn't until he met a Jewish man named Bob, with who he'd been cellmates for a short time. Yes, in Massachusetts, your cellmate can be of a different race or ethnicity. Bob told him he was an intelligent person and could have gone far in life. Only a matter of choice. Keith didn't believe him at the time. But that was the seed that led to change.

Listening to people or taking advice was never his strong suit. No, he preferred to do things on his own. Keith took it as someone talking down to him because bad decisions were the only decisions he came up with. He understood they meant well, but bad decisions were easy to make. He always wondered why that was the case, but he never found an answer. Bob had been instrumental in reducing his violent streak.

Bob liked to debate as much as Keith. The two men agreed that debate was paramount to understanding. Debating meant you had to possess a lot of information on the subject to surmise outcomes. To have neither of those things would make for a foolish argument and eventual loss. Though Bob and Keith debated and had heated arguments, they remained friends and cordial. To say Bob pushed his buttons would be an understatement. Bob always took up the opposite side of the argument. He could argue things he didn't believe in and make you question your own stance.

If Keith went to him for his opinion on something, Bob would shoot it down without question. Keith feeling some kind away, fought back. Later, Bob revealed he did this on purpose to see if Keith had thought out the business plan or whatever idea he had. He helped to make him a critical thinker. Someone who valued truth and data as much as opinion and feeling, which most people used in a debate.

Bob tried to prepare him for the future. Not that he had one, but he was grateful to the old man for helping him out. Bob moved to another facility, and they lost touch. At least, he left Keith with a valuable tool and mindset. *Nothing's set in stone.*

There were many people in the yard. He walked laps, whether sun, rain, or snow. The only time he didn't do laps was when the officials closed the yards because of inclement weather. He heard fast, evenly paced footfall, but years of prison life told him it was only a jogger. He stepped closer to the fence to give the runner some room by creating some distance.

Keith looked around the yard as a snowy wind blew into him. He saw no one in the yard that he wanted to engage in conversation, so he continued to walk. With his walking time almost up, it gave him an hour of free time before having to go back in for lunch. He got lost back in his thoughts as he pushed forward and picked up his pace, as he did at the end of every walking session.

He approached the front of the only building that looked out of place with the rest of the MCI-Norfolk complex. The square concrete building looked sterile compared to the 1920s-something, cottage-style housing units. The 8 Block was not his favorite place. While the rest of the prison looked like a private school, the 8s reminded him of the Max. He spent 11 months in unit 8-2 in cell 119 when he first arrived three years ago.

He looked at the phones lined up outside the unit, but he had no one to call. He seldom used the phones, only on his birthday and Christmas. His family liked the calls, but he felt like he was intruding if he had nothing to say. He put himself there. Nobody else. Though like every other person yearning for human connection, the phones elicited some regret. Was he that much of an asshole that he had no one to call? No, he realized his real friends still wrote him from time to time and that the friends he thought about turned out not to be friends at all. Friends never lose touch, but he understood life was so much harder on the outside than one could ever imagine. Not to say what he had to deal with daily was any picnic, but he didn't need to worry about paying electricity, rent, or buy groceries. Though he fed himself, he didn't like the food they served much, so he went to canteen and earned money to pay for the canteen by hustling. He made fudge, bracelets, and even gave writing lessons.

Despite the lack of support from outside and the realization that all people only ever saw his worst side, he wasn't depressed or angry. He knew it was his own doing, and he paid the price for not being nice. However, he was proud of himself. Keith was the only member of his family to take college classes and graduate with a bachelor's degree in sociology. He understood how people worked and how systems affected outcomes imposed on society. He wanted to continue with his education and earn his Master's degree, but that would've had to be through the mail, and he didn't see the worth in that.

He turned right after the phones and headed for the quad, which was his favorite place. He had to cut between the Seven and the Eight buildings. The alley was one of two chokepoints in the prison. Usually, the yard guards known as IPS monitored the alleys that led to the quad. However, sometimes the guards were not standing watch. A year after he arrived, he got stabbed in the alley by someone he stabbed at the Max and got sent to the hospital. He came out of the alley and turned right. The only direction you could walk on the quad—counterclockwise. There were more people on the quad than in the West Field. The difference was everyone was moving. No stopping allowed on the quad. He said hello to a few guys he knew as he picked up his pace again after slowing down to get through the ally. The quad was paved, which allowed him to walk faster than on the dirt track. Someone called to him from behind. He glanced back and slowed his pace. He waited for the guy to catch up.

"What's going on, kid?" He said, giving his friend Jose Dap.

"Not much," Jose said. "Just another day."

They walked two laps around the quad, and they talked about everything and nothing. Keith liked the distraction. He had a medical appointment at 9:30. The appointment was for more bloodwork. Ever since he got stabbed, they took his blood a lot. Keith never liked dealing with the medical department. At least not if he could help it, but he had to go. It was mandatory. They announced movement over the loudspeaker.

"All right.," He said, "I got to go to this med appointment."

"I got you," Jose said. "Check you out later. Coming out in the afternoon, right?"

"Yeah, I'll be out for my afternoon walk. See you then."

Keith walked to the medical appointment.

5

A Promising Breakthrough

The computer monitors displayed six separate boxes. Data scrolled along the edge of each image. Dr. Bell scrutinized the data of the anomaly his team found. He prayed they found something viable.

"Um, what am I looking at?" he said, then pointed at the scrolling data on the side. "What's this diagnostic that's running?"

"Proteins," the technician Billy said. "The diagnostic is trying to figure out which protein this one is." He pointed at the screen to a box with the sequence code. "These are the protein levels and blood types of the past five subjects. The one subject that has made it to the past and back had high levels of an unknown protein. The other subject that made it but died coming back also had the protein but low levels. A protein we didn't know to look for until now. We discovered the further the subject who got to completion of the transformation had the highest levels of this protein."

"All right, I can see where this is headed," Dr. Bell sighed. "Now you gonna tell me the presence of this protein is very rare."

"Most of the population doesn't have this protein in their genetic makeup, so finding a subject with high levels of this protein will be next to impossible."

"We did put out a medical search," Billy said.

"Did we get any hits?"

Jen and Billy looked at each other. "Yes," Jen said, "but unfortunately, they are not viable candidates for the project. One is a 10-year-old boy in Minnesota, and the other is a psych patient who is committed to the hospital."

"Yeah, they don't sound very promising." Dr. Bell said as he looked at the screen. Its data flowing. "Find me someone and find them fast."

"Yes, sir," the team said. "We'll get right on it, sir."

Dr. Bell left Dr. Blake with the technicians. They had a lot of work ahead of them. He left the lab to go to a meeting. He hoped to bring good news to this meeting. He guessed they had to settle for promising information because that was all the Board of Directors were going to get. He entered the conference room. Six stern faces looked up at him as he entered. He was late as usual. They were not happy.

"Dr. Bell, it's great to see you again." The man at the far end of the table said. "Tell us, do you have any good news?"

"We made a promising breakthrough," he told him as he explained what his team just finished explaining to him. He even told him about the boy and the lunatic. Hoping the rarity of this protein would extend the program and not kill it.

To his surprise, they were interested in possibly using the two found subjects, at least for testing purposes. They were especially interested in the one residing at the psychiatric hospital. Sometimes Dr. Bell wondered what the government wanted with such science. Technology like this could be helpful in the right hands but devastating in the wrong ones. He didn't understand why they would consider using a subject with severe psychiatric issues.

After the meeting concluded, he was glad to get back to the lab. There had to be a test subject out there somewhere. A perfect candidate. His bosses told him to find anyone, and if they couldn't, they would use the psychiatric patient. He had severe reservations, so he informed his team to find the best candidate as quickly as possible. The government even gave them access to all medical data, which they could issue a search for anyone whose bloodwork showed high levels of the protein that they now called Xchrm3.

Though he hoped the board of directors wouldn't use the lunatic, he realized that nobody in the lab would care if the subject died. He wondered if this was how the board thought as well, but if it was successful, he feared the lunatic couldn't be trusted.

6

More Blood Work

The holding area of the medical department was cramped. Other prisoners waited for their appointments. Besides the medical staff's incompetence, waiting in an overcrowded holding cell took the number one spot. 15 to 20 guys crammed in a room no bigger than 10' x 10'. There were just too many guys. A problem waiting to happen. Although he chuckled now and then when someone would come in, and their enemy was inside the holding cell. No handcuffs or shackles.

The guy would always stop short at the door upon seeing their enemy, which was funny since it was an open camp. There was no protective custody (PC) there. Everyone could see everyone if they came outside. Usually, in this instance, name-calling would replace actual fighting, but violence occurred every once in a while. *They were in prison, after all.*

The other thing he disliked about medical—some men would never get seen, so you'd wait an hour or more for nothing.

The CO called his name and let him out of the holding cell.

He entered the room they were using to take blood. A nurse directed him to sit in a chair next to the desk. Keith sat and wondered what was going on. He hoped nothing was wrong. For the 30th time, they took his blood. Something had to be up, but no one would give him a straight answer.

"This is the thirtieth time someone here has taken my blood in the last year," he sighed. "Is there anything wrong?"

The nurse looked at his chart. "No, it looks routine."

"It doesn't seem like it's routine. Twice a month for almost a year now. Does that sound like routine to you?"

The nurse looked at him in a strange way before drawing his blood. Keith noticed she took four vials instead of the two they usually took. When the nurse finished, she told him to stay put for a moment. She left the room and returned with a severe-looking woman. Keith had seen her before. One of the nurse practitioners. She never had anything good to say.

"Good morning, Mr. Richards," she said. "I am Arlene Proctor, the nurse practitioner. Jane here said you expressed some concerns about us drawing a lot of blood from you over the last several months."

"Yes, almost twelve months. Is there something wrong with me?"

"The tests showed some signs of concern. Nothing conclusive. But we're going to send you to an outside hospital for further testing, and that's what the blood is for."

"When am I going?"

"I can't tell you the exact date," she grimaced. "But you should go within the next couple of weeks. If not sooner."

"All right," he said, thinking why he really hated dealing with these people. He strongly felt that they were severely inept. They never gave you God damn straight answer. He saw a blessing in all this and was glad to know if he'd be going somewhere else. Maybe then he'd get some answers. The only place he'd hate to go would be the Shattuck Hospital. It had to be the worst place on Earth. "Where're you sending me?"

The nurse looked inside a folder she held in her hand. "Looks like you'll be going to Boston Medical Center."

"Oh, okay," he said as he stood, recognizing the appointment was over. "Thank you, can I leave now?"

The head nurse said he could, so he left the office. Hundreds of questions rushed through his mind as he walked down the hallway to leave. He had many questions. When he got back to the block, he looked around before pulling the front door open. Shit, the medical staff had him thinking too much about the negative possibilities. All he remembered was walking down the hallway to leave medical and then climbing the steps to his unit. Strange. *Very strange.*

7

Hospital Tests

Dr. Bell sat behind his glass and steel desk when Jen rushed into his office. Smiling ear to ear. "Doctor...we found him!"

He looked up from his paperwork. It had only been a couple of weeks. Dr. Bell was impressed with his team. They never seemed to disappoint him.

"You found a viable candidate?"

Jen handed him a folder. "Yes."

The folder contained the potential subjects' complete history and criminal record. Of course, there had to be a catch. The man was locked up at MCI-Norfolk for murder. He had to run it by the directors, but they were willing to use a person with severe mental illness so that it might be a good day after all.

He looked back up at Jen. "Let me see if I get him cleared," he said, picking up the phone. "I'll come by the lab when I'm through."

To his surprise, the conversation with his director was painless. He gave the go-ahead in less than a minute. It had to be a governmental record. Dr. Bell went to the lab to inform his team.

"We got permission to make contact."

The team erupted in joy. They danced around the lab. High-fiving each other like kids on the schoolyard playground.

Dr. Bell retreated to his little corner in the lab. His office away from his office. The end approached. He could feel it. It had been a long journey since the beginning. He could remember vividly getting laughed at during one of his lectures by his peers. Ten years melted away. Time waited for no man. In the beginning, he just thought of it as free money. Something he could do until it dried-up. He wasn't sure if other researchers thought of it that way, but he did. The only thing he cared about was proving his hypothesis. If they could manage a successful test and repeat it a few dozen times—the process would be known as the bell theory of time travel. The first concrete theory of time travel. Not that he could publish it or anything, since it was a secret government contract, so the money would have to do.

The only thing needed now was to get this man, Keith Richards, on board. Dir. Harrington said he could offer the man anything, even starting his life over. Literally, Dr. Bell thought. Wouldn't that be something?

He leaned back in his chair and smiled because life was good.

•

The ride to Boston Medical Center was quick. Two quick. A car which he found unusual had taken him. He stared out the windows and enjoyed the view. Everything looked so strange to him. The city he grew up in looked unfamiliar in many ways. The cars. They were the strangest things to him. Buildings that weren't there when he was out. It had been seven years since he had been among the cityscape of Boston. Though he watched the news, TV shows, and movies that showed new cars and stuff related to Boston, it wasn't the same as seeing the city in person. It elicited strong emotions.

After they arrived at the hospital, they brought him up to a private room. Keith asked no questions, but he wondered what was going on. The private room was not standard procedure. Not for a day visit. Was he staying more than a day? He thought he'd be going to the examination room in Emergency.

None of this made much sense to him—a nice private room. Still chained at the waist, he took a seat in a chair by the window. It wasn't the best view of the city, but he could see the downtown skyscrapers.

"Why did we come up here?"

"Don't know," the guard said, "it's where they wanted you."

"It just seems like I'm about to get bad news."

"I don't know, but the room looks nice," the guard said, smiling. "But I could take you back if you want?"

He knew the guard was trying to be funny. "Nah, this is way better than my cell back on the block."

The guard laughed and shook his head as he stepped outside the room.

The guard came back into the room moments later with three people. An older man with glasses and two younger folks. A man and a woman.

The older man looked at Keith. Noticing the chains, he turned to the guard. "Can you please remove those restraints, please?"

"Well—"

"Don't give me excuses. Please remove them."

"It's your life," he said. "You know what he's in for?"

"As a matter of fact, I do," the doctor said. "But you weren't supposed to tell me, were you? Besides, he'll be staying—we're admitting him."

Keith listened to the two men talk. He knew it. There had to be a reason they gave him a room. Shit, there had to be something wrong with him. Something serious. He looked at the doctor. Reading people had always been a strong suit. The doctor would have answers to his questions.

The guard removed the chains and stepped back into the hall where he waited. He heard the door lock. There was nowhere to go. Not that he wanted to go anywhere. No, he was content. He had always been optimistic. Something good would come his way. He didn't know when, but it would come.

The doctor turned to him and explained all the tests that they were going to do. They explained to him he had high levels of a rare protein that affected less than 1% of the population. They brought him in so they could examine the rare protein in person. It was connected to important research that could potentially save thousands of lives and change the course of history in the process.

Keith didn't care because he got a vacation out of it. A day away from the prison was a good day. The food was way better than what they served in prison, and the room and views were incredible. The doctor sure knew how to make someone feel at ease.

They began testing him the following day and would take several days to complete the test. There were cardiovascular tests, stress tests, sleep tests, and a diagnostic for this or that—things he didn't understand. There were so many physical tests he felt like they had recruited him to play football or something. By the end of the fifth day, it drained him. Exhausted.

The doctor and his two assistants came in and told him he would test anymore. That they had enough data and that he could relax. Keith got comfortable in the bed and turned on the TV. Doctor's orders—time to relax.

8

The Offer

The hospital was a buzz of activity. A nurse came into his room twice since lunch to see if he needed anything. He asked her if he could get some ice cream. She asked him what flavor he would like, but he told her it didn't matter. They were nice to him. At first, he struggled to believe it was real. Normal people usually weren't nice to him. She left the room and returned moments later with a brown bag containing a bunch of ice cream cups—ten Hoodsie Cups of various flavors. He supposed it was everyone they had.

Since he arrived at the hospital, he was very happy. He smiled a lot more than usual and felt normal for once in his life. Needed. A productive part of society. If he could change his past, he wouldn't hesitate one moment. He chuckled to himself at the thought. Time travel. If only.

Keith finished the last of the Hoodsie cups when Dr. Bell came into the room. He looked over at him. "So, what's the verdict? Am I going to live?"

"Yes, you most certainly are," Dr. Bell said, stepping closer to the bed. "Keith, I have a serious question to ask you?"

"What's that, Doc?"

"Well, how would you like to be involved in a research project?" Keith blinked at him in disbelief. "One that could let you physically walk the streets. No promises, but you may even be able to start your life over."

"Don't play with me, Doc," Keith said, sitting up. "There's no way they'd let me participate in any kind of research project. I'm a murderer, Doc. Shit, I'm doing life. I'll die in prison."

Dr. Bell smiled at the honesty. "Just answer the question. Would you volunteer if you could?"

"Sure, anything not to go back to prison, who wouldn't in my position."

"You have a point," Dr. Bell said, handing Keith a clipboard and a pen.

"What's this?" he said as he quickly perused the document. Grateful for his college education. A couple of years ago, he wouldn't have understood a word of it.

"A voluntary release form and NDA."

Keith finished reading it and looked up. "You're serious. You guys really want me to be part of this program?"

"Yes, all you do is sign the form. I will need to get it cleared by my directors, but I'm confident they'll give you a go."

"I am a bit concerned. It explicitly says this experiment has a high mortality rate. How high is that risk and no bullshitting?"

"There were five subjects before you, and two died."

"What happened to the other three?"

"Severe psychosis," Dr. Bell's said. "Those that got the closest to what we're trying to achieve had the same protein, but not at nearly the level you have. Your body makes this protein at a very high rate."

"Those some serious risks," Keith said, "but I could get shanked in the yard on any given day. Life is not guaranteed to anyone. I'm in."

Keith handed back the signed release form and NDA.

"I do have one more question. What is that I'll be doing?"

"Well, you signed the NDA, but I'm not sure you're going to believe me."

"Okay, what is it?"

"Temporal displacement."

Keith smiled ear to ear. "You messing with me? Time travel, really?"

"Not at all. The research is for the government, and I've been working on it for about 10 years. We're close."

"So, you guys made some kind of machine that sends you to the past?"

"It's complicated. However, you're sent back through a dreamlike state. Okay, it's more like brain waves send you back through a dreamlike state."

The minute Dr. Bell said dreams, Keith froze. He stared at the doctor for a moment. It hit him hard, like a lock in a sock. His own dreams came back to him. Strange surroundings and cars. He already knew he accepted the offer and was successful.

"Are you okay?" Dr. Bell said.

"Yeah, I'm good. A dreamlike state. I like it, so when do we start."

9

The Arrival

It was a beautiful day. Not that Dr. Bell could see the outside. He was several stories underground. It was still a beautiful day. He mused at the thought because all he could see was concrete, glass, and steel. He was in a delightful mood. He had not been this happy in months, years even. The new test subject would arrive soon, so he'd been going through a series of computer models.

According to the data they collected from the subject over the last week, he was in perfect physical condition and had extremely high levels of the protein Xchrm3. It made him very optimistic, but he was so sure the last one would make it.

Jen poked her head into his office. "Dr. Bell, the subject has arrived."

"Good...good," he said with a smile on his face.

"Doctor, I've been wondering about something," she said as they walked to the lab.

"Well, go on, Jen. You know I value your opinion."

"It's...it's...well, it's the subject," she said, wrinkling her nose. "Have you read through his file? The man's a monster.... He murdered several people and showed no remorse." She opened the file that she had been carrying and pointed to it. "Look at this. In his own words, he says 'they had it coming' and here 'they got what they deserved.' I know he's passed all the physical tests, sir. But what if we succeed and send him back and he murders again—"

"I read this man's entire file, but you have not, have you?" Dr. Bell snapped. "I'm well aware of what the man has done in the past. But I'm positive you stopped reading when you found out his admissions showed no remorse. You know what this man has accomplished despite believing he would never see the outside again? It's in the file, so you should know."

Jen stared at him blankly. "I read the complete file," she said with a bit of irritation in her voice.

"Do you know what his accomplishments are? Go on, tell me."

"I don't know what you mean by accomplishments. This guy has been violent while in prison."

"Now, I'm sure you overlooked some things," Dr. Bell said, stopping in the hallway. "Yes, when he first got locked-up, he was a complete menace. On the street and in prison. He spent four years in the maximum-security prison at Shirley. He showed how violent he could be there. There are infractions for not obeying the rules and fighting his way through his sentence. Violence was his way of life. The way he solved a problem until four years ago."

"Wait, what happened four years ago. I don't remember any—"

"Let me finish," he said, pointing to the file. "Four years ago, they moved Keith to the medium-security prison where we found him. Before the move, despite the hostile environment in a maximum-security prison, Keith received his GED."

"Good for him," she said, crossing her arms.

Jens reaction surprised Dr. Bell. He wondered if there was something more going on here than a concern of the subject's past. She had no reservations about using the man with severe psychiatric issues. He had to look at her file later to make sure there's no conflict of interest.

"You're right," he said, ignoring her sarcasm. "After he arrived at the medium-security prison, he enrolled in college classes through Metro College. Also, since arriving at the facility, he has received no infractions. Zero. Like a switch got turned off." He took the file from her and flipped to the pages. "Here are his transcripts from college."

She took the pages as Dr. Bell continued. "He just received his bachelor's degree, and look at his GPA."

"He has a degree in sociology," Jen said, confused. "How did I miss that? A 4.0 GPA, are you serious? He made Dean's list every year. Okay but—"

He raised his hand as they walked again. "Look, give him a chance. It's either him or the man with severe psychiatric issues."

"I'd rather that patient," she said. "It's obvious this guy has psychiatric issues as well. It's great that he has been doing good for the last four years, but his lack of remorse concerns me."

"Okay, we'll have him do a complete psychological assessment. Will that you satisfy your conscience?"

She nodded with slight hesitation. "Yes, I believe it would."

•

Keith entered a room that was half glass. On the other side of the petition sat a chair. His escort called it the lab. He stared at the chair on the opposite side of the glass. He knew he and the chair were going to get very acquainted. He looked around the room. There had not been one window since he got off the elevator. He found it interesting since the building they pulled up to was a brick glass and steel building. Lots of windows. They had to pull into the garage and then take an elevator to get to this level. He couldn't tell if the elevator went up or down. However, the absence of windows told him it was down.

He turned from the glass petition when the doctor and Jen walked in. Keith liked them. They seemed like decent folks. And he needed to know how decent folks acted like, so he could emulate them. He walked over to the doctor, shook his hand, and then Jen's. The shadow crossed her face. Keith instantly recognized the look. Jen had finally read his file.

"How was the ride?" Dr. Bell asked. "I hope it was pleasant."

"This where we'll be working?"

"Yes, it is," Dr. Bell said, "now let us tell you what we expect of you."

Dr. Bell and Jen explained the procedures they had to go through. They told him they were also going to run a few more tests, including psychological evaluation. Keith wasn't surprised. He would have felt something wasn't right if they didn't do one. Like a murderer was who they wanted. Once they covered everything and satisfied, he understood, they showed him to his quarters. They then took him on a tour of the facility: cafeteria, the gym, restrooms, and first-aid.

After, he sat at his desk and took in his quarters. Kieth had every luxury a prisoner wished for in their cell: television with cable, a phone (not that he wanted to call anyone), and a digital radio. The place, though it reminded him of prison, was a lot better than a cell.

10

Test One

The first week was a blur of various tests—some physical and some mental. Keith also had to see a psychologist for an hour each day. To him, that was the hardest part. He had never been one to discuss his emotions. He knew what most everyone wanted to know. Why was he so violent? He knew the answer, though most professionals dismissed it. Keith was a product of his environment. Coupled with cognitive distortions of self-worth and self-image among a plethora of other issues. His parents tried their best, but it wasn't good enough.

They were strict even though they ran through the streets. It made him rebel early. The only upward mobility he saw in his neighborhood was through selling drugs. At the time, he thought he would amount to nothing and could never make it to college because he wasn't smart enough. He was wrong, but this came about through his feedback from the surrounding people, including his parents.

In junior high and high school, his grades were terrible. He dropped out in the 10th grade. Yet, his grades for college were perfect. He put in the work. Professors and others encouraged him. He felt like he belonged. Though, still an outsider in a rich man's world. He learned to chase fulfillment and not the dollar bill. He enjoyed learning new things. The project was a new chapter in Keith's life story. He glanced at the wall clock, which read 6 o'clock.

He woke up early again, still on prison time. Count would be in a half-hour. Every day for the last four years, he'd awoken at the same time. He now saw the benefit of a schedule. It felt good not to be in prison. It didn't matter that he couldn't leave the Complex, that it was, in fact, a prison in of itself. These people treated him with respect, and he wanted to give it back. Try his best. Do his best. They had shipped all the stuff from prison. All his belongings. He piled most of the boxes up in the corner, which were left virtually untouched. Maybe he'd do it later, after the test. It was the big day. He was nervous. He could die. However, with the knowledge of his dream, he was confident dying was not in the cards. In three hours, he'd know for sure.

·

The team moved into the underground complex, so they could work around the clock if they needed. Although it had only been there a week, Jen felt more comfortable with their pick. She wished she never read that damn file. She was a young girl when her cousin got killed by an act of revenge. She knew how it consumed people, chewed them up, and spit them out. For the first time, she realized that there was more than one victim when someone got killed. The more she learned about Keith, the more she saw that different influences would have produced a different outcome in his early life. She started to believe Keith deserved a second chance. She wished she wasn't so harsh on him in the beginning.

·

If not being able to sleep was a good thing, Dr. Bell should be on top of the world. He got very little sleep. Maybe four hours, but he was ramped up and ready to go. He wanted this to go smoothly. No more deaths or hospitalizations. Although at first, he thought using a prisoner would ease his conscience, but then he met Keith. He liked Keith's sense of ease and curiosity. During all the tests, he asked question after question. He wanted to know how everything worked. He wanted to learn new things and was willing to put in his share of the work. The man gave his complete confidence to Dr. Bell. At the same time, Dr. Bell was fully aware Keith could kill him in an instant if he thought he needed to. The psychologist had said as much, but he also said Keith was stable. He was in no danger of getting into any kind of trouble.

•

Dr. Bell walked into the lab with ethereal, complete confidence. Test time. The technician strapped Keith into the chair. Dr. Bell spoke into the microphone one last time.

"We're going to be successful...believe me. I just know it," he smiled. "All right, let's begin."

The technicians injected Keith with the CTE compound. He looked over at Jen, who was watching the monitor. He knew it was the one for his vitals.

"How's our boy doing? Good, right?"

"Yeah, everything looks good. His heart rate's falling steadily. Sudden drop. The CTE is taking effect." She smiled. "He staying stable.... Brainwaves are changing. There it is...the transition's complete. Should we wake him?"

"No, not yet...let the clock fully count down."

"60 seconds," the other technician said.

Dr. Bell smiled ear to ear. "All right, let's wake him up."

Jen signaled to the tech in the room to go ahead, and she injected him with a stimulant.... A few moments passed before Keith opened his eyes wide, trying to move, but the straps held him in place.

"Wow, what a rush," Keith said. "It worked...Dr. Bell... I went back to several hours ago, and I talked to you. And I told you a word that you told me before I got strapped in."

"Yes, you did," he said, "but we need to know what it was like and how long were you there?"

"It was 6:15 AM, and I was only present for a few moments. A couple minutes tops. It felt weird, like being in a dream that you could completely control. However, there was no doubt in my mind that it was not a dream and it was real. And me telling you the keyword proves I traveled back in time."

"It was a success, ladies and gentlemen!" Dr. Bell said, smiling.

11

First Month

The Complex as Keith started referring to the underground installation, especially the two levels that occupied the SCP, which Keith referred to as the Second Chance Project, buzzed with excitement over the first successful test.

He mused about the initialism of the project. After the first jump, as the team called it, they told him the program's name was SCP, but nobody would elaborate what the initials stood for. The team began calling SCP unofficially the Second Chance Project since Keith kept calling that in hopes of getting the real meaning, but it worked well enough for him. Dr. Bell told him the original program was a collaboration between the government, several archaeologists, and several sociologists. Still, the program had deviated a lot since the program began 12 years ago.

The more controversial part of the project was the idea that they could change events for the better. The founders and the current directors believed if done right, the future could be brighter.

The governmental involvement in the project made Keith wary. He saw nothing good come out of anything when the government was involved. Better energy options turned into bombs that had destroyed cities.

There were only a few people working out in the gym when he first arrived at 6:30 AM. Only he remained. He was so consumed with his own thoughts; he didn't even see them leave. So much for prison teaching him to be aware of his surroundings. They vanished into thin air, but that didn't even happen with time travel, it turned out. Nope. Instead, you rode the waves of time through your subconscious back to a younger version of yourself. He still didn't understand it.

It wasn't so much different from the dreams he had that came true. The dream state always heightened those dreams. More dramatic and terrifying than the actual events when they occurred. He found it interesting that he remembered the dreams when they occurred, so he kept the dream books.

He completed his workout and headed to the locker room. Losing time concerned him. He was usually aware of his surroundings, so he wondered if the blank spell was the upcoming test scheduled to take place in a few hours. He wasn't so sure, but the plan was to send him back as far as they could, so the blank spell probably wasn't that. He made four trips over the past four weeks. One per week, they told him. They didn't want to tax his mind. They so far could only send him back a couple of weeks.

The trips back had been easy. So far, the most common side effects had been a sense of feeling like a stranger in his own body during the trip. Kinda like his brain knew he didn't belong there. The more trips, the easier it became if you can count four as being more. He didn't think the jumps would ever feel real to him, but only time would tell. The hardest part was coming back.

After rudely pulling him back to the present, he would be disorientated. Like being on a plane for too long. Jet lag. Images flooded his mind. Minute changes to the timeline, according to Dr. Bell, who theorized that his presence alone had the potential to change the past. By doing things out of the ordinary, his mind had to catch up to the changes made. Maybe when he jumped back, he interrupted something his past self was doing. Keith didn't really buy that part. It had only been four jumps, but every time he woke from his sleep. Always in the morning. They wouldn't know for sure until he jumped further back and had more jumps under his belt.

After he took a shower and changed, he went to the cafeteria to get breakfast. Bacon and eggs sounded good to him. His stomach growled in agreement. He was eating his breakfast when Jen and the tech Billy came over.

"Can we sit with you?" Jen asked.

"Sure, why not?" He said, making a sweeping gesture with his arm. "Sit at your own risk."

Jen laughed while Billy looked scared. Intimidated. Keith picked up on it like a predatory beast waiting to attack. He could smell it in the air. Jen, on the other hand, had no such fear. At first, there was contempt, but now Keith believed he and Jen were becoming friends. He needed friends with an excellent moral compass. He never really had them. She would do just fine. He thought about the word friend for a moment. Trusting people was never a strong suit, so he never thought anyone could truly call friend or that he would ever have such a person in his future.

Billy asked him something, but he didn't hear what he said.

Keith blinked. "I'm sorry, I was thinking about something... what did you say?"

"Ah...nothing...really," Billy said, pulling his chest inward and lowering his eyes. Shrinking into himself. "I asked...how are you doing?"

He had to smile and did. "Oh, I'm doing good. Can't wait for the jump later."

"Jump?" Billy asked.

"That's when I called the trips backwards. Don't know what else to call it. And don't say traversing temporal displacement. That's a mouthful, and I thought one of you told me it was called a jump. Maybe not, I guess."

"Jump," he said, feeling the sound of it. "I like it. It reminds me of an old TV show."

Jen shook her head. "It could have been Dr. Bell; it sounds like something he'd call it. However, are you ready for this?"

"Yeah, I'm looking forward to it," Keith said, studying her. "Why? Is there something wrong?"

"No-no," she said. "We had no one take this much CTE compound, so we don't know what effects it will have on you physically and mentally. You have been our only successful subject. Uncharted territory."

"Isn't the whole project uncharted territory?" Keith replied, thinking about his dream book. "We won't know till we know. But I think I'll be alright."

"The optimism is great, but I'm worried about the consequences. The further we sent you back in these four jumps alone, the more disorientated you were when we pulled you back. I'm concerned, that's all."

"Jen, I know the risks involved," he said coolly. "I'm well aware that I could die. However, it's been a success so far, so we should ride the wave all the way."

"There has to be a limit—"

"And if it goes bad, at least my life added to the advancement of society."

"I didn't know you felt that way."

Billy sat there in silence.

"I just know that all this is something great, so I'm excited. Aren't you? Come on; you must be. Billy is, look at him."

Jen and Billy were obviously elated about the project's success. Unfortunately, it was the first time they got to know a subject. Over the last month, Jen discovered Keith was a kind, caring human being who helped out with whatever was needed, even if it was just an ear to listen. Not to mention the man was truly intelligent. All her preconceived notions from the start were becoming the excessive negativity of a person who was taught to think criminals couldn't change.

It was kind of absurd, seeing they were all about change, through manipulation, when you thought about it. Jen knew what her genuine concern was. Dr. Bell might believe the story Dir. Harrington sold him about the project, but Jen had her reservations. Jen believed that they only told Dr. Bell things needed to get him on board. And she just hoped the powers-to-be, known as the board of directors, didn't have any hidden agenda. She didn't want Keith caught up in the middle of an internal struggle.

They finished their breakfast and headed to the lab. Dr. Bell and Dir. Harrington was in the middle of a discussion when they walked in. Both men stopped talking. It must've had been a sight to see for the two older men because they walked into the room laughing and joking like there was no chance of death.

"I assume you're ready," Dr. Bell said, glancing at the wall clock. "You're early."

"We're excited, sir," Jen said.

Billy and Keith agreed.

"I wouldn't want any other way," Dr. Bell said. "Take your stations. Keith come over for a second?"

Keith walked over to the two men. "This is our benefactor and director."

"It's a pleasure to finally meet you," Dir. Harrington said, offering his hand.

Keith shook his hand. "Likewise, sir."

There was something in the man's eyes Keith didn't like. The man was all smiles, but something lurked behind the surface. As he could smell Billy's fair, he could sense this man's deception. Instantly, Keith knew he neither liked this man nor trusted him.

"So, are you ready for the big test?" Dir. Harrington said.

"Jump," he said. "Yeah, I'm ready to make this jump."

"Good luck, son," he said. "I've heard nothing but good things about you. Keep it up, and we'll see what we can do about your current situation."

"Thank you, sir," Keith said, rolling his eyes a bit. "I've got to go get ready, but it was nice to meet you. Are you staying for the jump?"

"Yes, I am."

"That's good. I only wish there was more for you to see besides me unconscious in a chair." He said before passing through the petition to the chair.

Dr. Bell and Dir. Harrington walked over to Jen and Billy. They watched through the glass as Keith strapped into the chair.

Dr. Bell leaned over to the microphone. "Are you ready, Keith?"

He gave the thumbs-up sign

"All right, you have the green light. Administer the CTE compound."

The two techs in the room with Keith both injected the compound. Pressing the injection guns to both arms. He could hear the sound of escaping air. The techs nodded thing was a go. A counter started counting down from 60 seconds on one of the displays. When it hit zero, Dr. Bell spoke. "How's our boy doing?"

"Everything is perfect," Billy said, still excited.

"He's on his way, sir," Jen said.

12

First Long Journey

Keith opened his eyes and sat up in a darkened room. He glanced around the room to determine the time period. The digital clock lit up the darkness displaying 6:15 AM. A fuzziness clouded his mind. The room shifted as his vision came into focus. He swung his legs over the bed, but his toes just reached the floor. The room continued to spin. Once his head cleared, he knew how far back they had sent him.

"Damn, they sent me way back," he whispered to himself.

He stood while still glancing around. With no conscious thought, he reached up and pulled the string to turn the lights on. Light washed over the entire room, which blinded him for a moment. He recovered and took in the small confines of the room and all its contents. As he scanned the room, he noticed items that were long forgotten: the drawing table, magazines, action figures that would be worth a fortune. The walls of the room were the focus. Graffiti art traveled around all four walls. The continuous piece his uncle had painted for him. His name and favorite characters. He wondered how far they sent him back. His mirror hung on the back of the door.

He stood in front of it. An innocent-looking boy stared back at him. Shit, he must've been about 11, if that. About the time he started recognizing he had two types of dreams. Also, that no one else he knew had them—none of his friends or family members. The year the dreams started, they consumed his thoughts.

A calendar hung on the wall: June 2001. He just turned 11, so there would be no notebooks chronicling his dreams. Memories long forgotten forced their way to the front of his mind. To fight for the present, which was his past. He remembered the mission.

After the amusement of seeing himself as a child in his old home wore off, he had a sense of the tasks he needed to do. He wasn't there to play around after all. Part of him wouldn't mind sticking around for a while. He had to make sure things got done within a couple of hours. A rough calculation of the time he would have in the past. He knew his parents would be asleep in the other room in the apartment. His father was a very light sleeper, so Keith would need to be as quiet as possible. He crept out of the room, walked through the living room straight into the kitchen, where the phone hung on the wall. A cordless. He picked up the phone and dialed the number he had to memorize. When the line picked up, a robotic voice to leave a message after the tone.

"Delta-21-10-five-B 16-bravo," he said into the receiver before hanging up.

It made no sense to him, but Dr. Bell handed him the code several days before asking him to commit it to memory. Dr. Bell told him they could track his progress by using it. He wasn't sure how it was possible, but he didn't question it. He headed back to his bedroom but realized he had to pee in the worst way. Welcome to youth. He crossed the kitchen to what passed for a bathroom, but more resembled a hallway with bathroom fixtures and a door.

He did his business, washed his hands, opened the door, and got startled by his father, who was standing there.

"You're up early," his father said, "you wash your hands?"

"Yes, sir," Keith said, still afraid of the beast from his past. "Couldn't sleep, so I got ready for school."

"You hungry?"

Keith nodded.

"All right, I'll make you something...when I come out of the shower."

The shower turned on, and it dawned on Keith his father was getting ready to go to work. It was rare to see his father in a good mood, and he was grateful for it, but he had no current memory of it. Something lost to time. The terrible memories filling the void. The whole thing was odd because there were very few moments when his father acted like one. Keith went back to his room and got dressed. He lay on the bed thinking about memories themselves. How some stayed and others were as fleeting as dreams. His dad opened his door and popped his head and to see what he wanted for breakfast. His father said he was already making bacon and eggs, so Keith told him he'd have that as well. *Is that why I like bacon and eggs?*

After they ate breakfast, his father patted him on the head, bent down to kiss him on his forehead, and told him to be a good boy. He watched his father leave the apartment with mixed emotions. He didn't remember this side of him, but he liked it. He wished he saw more of it. Maybe that way, the times he was nice wouldn't have fallen into the waste bucket of forgotten memories.

He went back to his bedroom. He looked at the clock and became surprised to find more than an hour had passed. He wondered how long it would be until they pulled him back. Time didn't run linear between the two timelines, so he wasn't able to use the current time to determine extraction. He had yet to pass the max time. He wondered what he could do for the next hour now that he completed his task.

They told him he would have approximately two hours for this trip. When the max time came during the previous jumps, he was ripped from the past no matter what he was doing. He wondered how that could be, considering he always woke up from the bed sleeping. Not once had he been at a desk, though he'd been ripped from the past from sitting at his desk during the last test. Every time you'd arrive, as confirmed by this jump, it would be 6:15 AM, but going back was different and could happen at any time. Usually, he'd feel dizzy, and pressure in his head would form like the beginning of a migraine. Things would then blur together into blackness. In one moment, he could be running in the next, waking up in the chair. It felt like being woken from a realistic dream.

He sat on his bed staring at the things in his room, especially the walls. He really liked the graffiti art. It was a cool room. He put his hand to his head as he felt dizzy. The room distorted and contorted into a kaleidoscope of images. *About time.*

13

The Code

He opened his eyes wide—images fluttered forward. His head ached. When it stopped, he closed his eyes, but even they were sore. The pain became exacerbated by the lab's bright lights, so Keith didn't attempt to move. Afraid pain would explode throughout his head again. A disembodied voice asked him if he was all right, again. He believed it was the second time the voice had asked. He looked forward through the glass at the concerned faces beyond and smiled. "I was 11, but you should know that, right?"

The technicians unstrapped him. He stood on wobbly legs. The rush of images that overtook him was incapacitating. Something felt different-wrong-but he figured it was just another side effect of the jump. Maybe it was that butterfly effect he'd heard about, but he wasn't sure. Images collided with his memory. It was strange. As if he now had two sets. He hoped it wasn't something that happened every time after a long jump.

The world stopped spinning; he wasn't sure when it started, but it stopped. Billy, Jen, Dr. Bell, and Dir. Harrington waited for him outside the glass petition.

"You were how old? Eleven, you said?" Dr. Bell said, grinning. "That's amazing."

"How long did it take before you got pulled back?" Billy asked.

"Over an hour. An hour and twenty minutes, maybe. Something like that," Keith said as he made his way to the couch that was in the main part of the lab. He looked at the poor people before him. His head still spun. He focused on director Harrington and Dr. Bell. "I made the call, so you know where I was, right?"

"What call?" Dr. Bell asked.

"The one you told me to make once I arrived. You said it was to track my whereabouts and in the past." Keith pointed at the director. "He gave me a code to memorize."

"I didn't give you any phone number," Dr. Bell said and then looked at the director. "Did you give him any such number?"

"No," he said, "I only met him today, remember."

"All right? I'm not imagining it. He told me to call this number," he said, rattling off the phone number. "You also gave me a code. It...was...Delta-21-10-eight-B 16-bravo."

"Hold on," Dir. Harrington said, then asked him to repeat the phone number and code to write it down. "All right, I'll check this out. Sit tight. I'll be right back."

Dir. Harrington left the room, and they all stared at Keith.

"So, what was it like?" Dr. Bell said.

"It was truly amazing. Surreal but amazing."

14

The Board Meeting

It was 80° outside. Summer had arrived, and people were out in force enjoying the day. It was always a cool 70° inside the Complex. Dr. Bell got called into a board meeting. The long journey test had been a remarkable success. After briefing Keith, they discovered valuable information.

The further Keith jumped, the further apart the time calculation. By doubling the time, they could adjust the estimate for the length of a jump. Five minutes in the chair equaled roughly 10 minutes in the past. However, five minutes in the long jump took one hour and 20 minutes. Dr. Bell knew he could use this information in conjunction with the amount of CTE to predict how far in the past a jump could go and for how long. It was a beneficial breakthrough.

"Dr. Bell...Dr. Bell," someone called.

He looked up. "Sorry, gentlemen. I was thinking about something."

"Anything important, doctor?" Thomas Crane said. The liaison to the White House.

"It's...about test subject, Keith. Upon returning from this long jump, Keith's body and mind went through severe trauma," he looked around at the table, and the directors, "My team and I are afraid the trauma could...well...possibly send him back to his old ways."

"Is he showing any signs of concern?" Dir. Harrington said.

"Well, no," Dr. Bell said, "Keith is still the calm, cool, and collected person he's been throughout the program. The crashes he experienced when he came back result from his memories of the present catching up to the changes made in the past. His presence alone changed the outcome. Do a task, and it can be very debilitating. We are not changing anything yet, but every jump, the crashes have gotten worse."

"Let me get this straight, Doctor," Dr. Reginald Lewis said. "You're afraid once he changes his past by going places, he rarely went that this could cause the stress levels to rise when he comes back initiating these crashes?"

"I'm concerned it could cause unrepairable damage to his mental health. Every time he comes back, he has two sets of memories, and it takes an indeterminate amount of time for them to intertwine and for the present one to get overwritten by the fresh memories."

"You think he's going to be violent because of this?" Dr. Reginald Lewis said. He looked at Dir. Harrington. "Tom, I'm concerned about this development. And I know the president will be as well."

"Look, we think there could be an X number of jumps that make it, so the catch-up never happens, and the memories stay separate from every jump after that. I'm afraid we could make him schizophrenic. If we change something small, but it has an exponential effect on our present, we can lose the subject. No more trips."

"Do you have any suggestions to potentially quell this from happening?" Dr. Harrington said.

"If we can allow him to furlough when he comes back, it's possible that it will quell the episodes. Put him up in a hotel. Keep him under surveillance. Whatever. If he is able to stay relaxed and excited to do his job, I think he will habituate to the timeline conversion."

"Doctor, you're afraid that he's gonna be violent, but you want us to him let him go out into the public," Dr. Richard Tennyson said.

"No, we're trying to prevent the violence from coming back. What I want is for you to give Keith some of that freedom you keep dangling before him. To you, he may be a subject, but if I'm, to be honest, he was to me too until I got to know him. Let him have some downtime away from the Complex so that we can experience the changes for himself. Not limited to the Complex."

The six men around the table glanced at one another. They all nodded to director Harrington.

"All right, we'll let him go for this weekend coming in the following weekend after every jump."

"Thanks, Dir. Harrington and board," Dr. Bell said.

"I have some rules and guidelines," Dr. Harrington said. "However, I want him Geo tracked with a subdermal implant. No tracker, no furlough."

The one dissenting voice, who still voted the allow it, spoke up. "Doctor, though I'll go with the majority, I don't see why the subject would need a vacation. He's gonna get plenty of that during the jumps."

"The jumps are more like a dream to him and not reality."

"Dr. Bell, no need to explain," Dir. Harrington said. "The board voted, and I gave the order, so he's going on furlough this weekend and every weekend when he returns from a jump. And if we get to where he's able to do multiple jumps in a week, we'll revisit this weekend only."

"Thank you, gentlemen, I really appreciated it, and I know Keith will as well."

The board meeting was dismissed, and Dr. Bell rushed out of the room. He was proud of himself for recognizing Keith as an individual. A good person who got derailed from the path. He could hardly believe he got the board of directors to agree to let him have a furlough. Then he remembered the code and the phone number. He turned and headed back into the room. "Dr. Harrington, did you find out what the number and code were all about?"

"Yes, it's nothing. By Keith calling that number in the past, he's made it obsolete. How do you think we knew to pick you, doctor?"

Dr. Bell nodded as director Harrington turned on his heels and walked away. He had a mission of his own and turned the other way off to Keith's quarters. He had some good news to bear. On the way, he contemplated Dir. Harrington's answer to his question. It made little sense. They would still need to give Keith a note to give it to them, so something was amiss. Did they forget it was his research? He got them to this point. Distrust of Director Harrington began to set in.

15

The First Mission

The weekend had been a blur of traffic, skyscrapers, and the luxury hotel. It surprised Keith they put him up in a penthouse suite. He'd never stayed in one before. It was weird to be free. No shackles of any kind. Of course, there was the subdermal tracker under the skin at the base of his skull. Placed there to deter any attempt to remove it. The tiny Intruder itched from time to time, reminding him it was there. He went clubbing and hooked up with a fine and intelligent woman on Friday. He pretty much stayed in the hotel room until Sunday. The weekend was one long good time, which was something he needed. He explored the city a little and saw some changes. He wished the time didn't go by so fast.

Monday came, and he trudged along the murkiness past skyscrapers and people rushing off to work, but a jump wasn't real to him. Although it should be, it wasn't. He was there in the body of his younger self, but it was hard to describe. *The jump just felt off.*

The board had pushed up his next jump. Give him a little and take a lot. He wasn't ready. He dreaded what would happen when they pulled him back, but this was his new job, and he was as curious as they were. The goal was to send Keith back a year before he got arrested. He was doing a lot of shit back then, and the temptation to leave himself a note to get out was high. It was tough knowing that he could've gone to school and been something. Prison didn't need to be in the equation.

The jump would be the longest time he had so far spent in the past. He'd have 24 hours to complete his task. To him, it was 24 hours of changing unintended things. Little things that would all come crashing to the front when he returned. More phone numbers along with codes. He also had to pick up a package from someone and deliver it.

Keith wondered why they needed him to pick it up and deliver it when he knew they had plenty of spies in the business to do these kinds of things. However, imagine the best spies were from the future and used the younger versions of themselves to be spies. It could change the game. A kid at a baseball game could watch a mobster who was there to watch his kid play. He would never know he had been surveilled—*kinda scary.*

Keith made the phone calls and delivered the codes. Now, he had to pick up the package and deliver it. He wondered if the team would remember this time.

Dr. Bell had told them that because Keith used the code, it changed the past and altered the present, which was why the code no longer needed to be used, but he could see plainly on the older man's face that he didn't fully believe it. Neither did Keith. He knew that wasn't the reason and hoped these codes would tell him. It was in his nature to be suspicious of everything.

The mission sent him downtown to pick up the package. The person handed him a brown paper-wrapped package and an envelope. The envelope was for Keith, and it contained a round-trip ticket to New York City and a fake ID. For this mission, he was Charles Bernard Shaw, who lived just outside the city in a small town called Hingham. The ID was flawless, and he was sure they had it made at the RMV.

As he walked down 51st St. in New York City, he looked for a specific address. He walked past a light pole with a bunch of music stickers all over it and got an overwhelming sense that he'd been there before, except this was his first time he'd been in New York City. He wondered if he jumped here again, but farther back. It could also mean he dreamed it, and he had the dream book in his backpack, so he'd look it up later. He looked around and got disorientated.

The buildings appeared to close in around him. The surrounding buildings became more familiar with every step. Images of him running from something—someone—with a gun gripped in his meaty hand jumped through his mind. He recalled the dream. It had to be a dream and not a jump. When they would come through, they were never as bad as the dream. He wondered if he should tell them about the dreams and his notebooks. The images left as fast as they came. He made it to the address a few minutes later. The grayish brick and stone building loomed over him. He took a deep breath and let it out before entering.

Twenty minutes later, he left the building. It had been the longest twenty minutes of his life. Uneventful but distorted images flooded his head. Every minute there, he waited for something to happen and still did as he walked away from the building.

He stepped into the street and hailed a cab. Several cars later, one finally pulled over. He told the driver to take him to LaGuardia Airport. He sat in the backseat staring out the window like a little kid on a family trip. Everything so new and exciting to him, despite it being a year before he went in. Everything looked normal, except for the murkiness he couldn't explain. The package and its unknown contents entered his mind. He wondered what he had brought to New York City and why. He looked away from the window and down at his hands. The murkiness subsided, but just a little bit. Everything in the car became clearer. The longer he stayed in the past, the more his conscious mind became one with the body of the past.

The trip back to Boston was quick. It wasn't until he landed and headed back to the apartment that he relaxed. None of that dream came true. The only thing from the dream he saw were the buildings. He shook it off as his vision blurred and the world spun. They pulled him back to the present.

He braced himself for what he knew was to come. However, nothing could prepare him for the onslaught of images. His eyes went wide before he slumped into the chair—sensory overload.

In the control booth, Jen, Billy, and Dr. Bell frantically watched.

"What just happened?" Dr. Bell said.

"The download," Jen said. "It was too much."

"He crashed," Billy said, "bad."

Two technicians in the room with Keith got to work. They wasted no time. They took him to his quarters. He was still resting when Dr. Bell and Jen left his room and headed back to the lab.

"You believe it was what?" Dr. Bell said.

"Sensory overload," Jen said. "His body couldn't take that kind of assault from the images, so it shut down."

"I think we should hold off any more jumps, for now," Dr. Bell said. "Unless there is some way, we can prepare Keith for that onslaught of streaming images."

"I've been working on something since he told us about the download, which I've been calling it, and ultimately it would involve a simulation where we would bombard him with sounds and images that would hopefully diminish the crash, but it's only a hypothesis."

"It's worth a try," Dr. Bell said. "Get to work."

"Yes, sir, I'm gonna need the computer technician Tony to help with this."

"Yeah, no problem."

Jen headed to the computer lab to grab Tony and get to work. She was confident the two of them could develop and implement a computer program that would act like white noise and cancel at least diminish the download.

16

Chillin with the Homies

The room was dark. Keith lay on his bed and had been for most of the day. Pain in the form of images exploded through his mind. Like he was swimming in a mental pool with pictures that came to life. Somehow, he'd change the past, or more to the point, jumping alone changed it. Dueling realities floated before him. Confusion set in. Unable to discern the current reality.

He lay there in the darkness as he struggled to focus. He wondered what was in the package. How could its contents cause so many changes? Although he crashed hard, he still felt like his mind and body were adjusting to the download.

Although Jen designed the prototype for preconditioning, she pushed him to try it, anyway. He recovered quicker than the last jump. It seemed to relax him. The simulated images didn't have nearly the same disorientating effect—he saw them as just pictures. However, they did something on a subconscious level. It quelled the pain for some time, but the prototype was just that, and the relief didn't last long. He remained hopeful that this procedure would help the download go more smoothly after future jumps.

They postponed all jumps for three weeks. They used this time to prepare Keith's minds. Physically he was in top shape, but he now got frequent headaches followed by images of a dual reality. He started meditating on his own to help himself focus. Meditation helped him in prison to focus and redirect his energies into positive things like school and to better himself. In this situation, it helped him sort out the images between current reality and past realities.

The room was neat, with sparse belongings and metal furnishings. His quarters in the Complex. He got up, flipped the light switch. White LED lights flooded the room. He turned on his television to watch the local news on Fox 25. He waited for the hot pot to boil water and then made tea. He drank it while watching the news program. After the program ended, it was time to work out. Later that day, he would have another jump. He had not fully recovered from the last one, but the powers-to-be wouldn't heed Dr. Bell's warnings.

•

No phone number, codes, or packages. Nothing. No plan. They told him to take a trip to anywhere he liked and had 48 hours to do it. They told him to have fun and explore the past.

They sent him back to when he was 18 years old, which allowed him to hang out with homies that were long gone from this earth. They had drilled him over and over, not to change anything too big. He knew one of his friends would die the next day, but he couldn't do anything about it. He affected things because he'd do some things differently, like have a conversation with someone on a deep level instead of yelling and screaming at them like he had the first time. All the while trying not to change anything. *It was not easy.*

He understood that if you save someone's life that had died in his current timeline, it could drastically change his future and put him and others in danger.

They considered this jump a gauge test. He was supposed to do nothing out of the ordinary, and when he got pulled back, they would use it as a baseline to compare the download and its subsequent crash.

Although they said that he could go anywhere he wanted, Keith hung out at home and relived it all over again. He had a heightened memory while in the past. It allowed him to remember everything that happened...thought for thought... and...word for word. The memories of the last jump pushed forward to the front of his subconscious.

In short, he knew what was gonna happen before it did as long as he stayed within the original timeline. Any deviation had the potential to stop that ability—then he'd be alone. On his own. Making it up as he went along. He had a feeling a crash from that download would kill him.

It was weird that he knew what he would say before he said it. He'd also learn about events before they happened. While in the past, he constantly had to decide to say what was in his head or something else. However, he didn't have that problem when he deviated from the plan, like when he went to New York. The things he said and did there he had no idea about. No seeing into the future once you deviated from the timeline.

Most of the time, it was just bullshit that meant nothing. Keith knew there would come a time when the advice he gave led to someone's death. He wasn't sure that he could let that happen. How could he let one of his homeboys die again based on something he said? He was afraid he would react differently if that happened but needed to let it play out if it occurred during this jump. Keith just didn't trust he could.

He wondered if he should go somewhere else, especially remembering that one of his homeboys would die the following day. He snuffed out a joint he smoked, and went back into the house. His house. The only apartment he ever had by himself. Not long after that day, he would be imprisoned until SCP found him. There is one thing that you couldn't change. They kept telling him—it was death.

The car honked his horn. He looked out the window and saw his homeboy, Adam. He hated the damn thing but said hustlin was the only thing he knew. He confided in Keith that he hated how it made him feel and how it brought violence out of him. It made him a different person. However, today he was smiling and having a good time. A few people came over to chill.

There were always people in his house when he first moved out on his own. He was young and naïve and thought the door should be open to all his friends. The same friends never contacted him after he got locked up for doing something for them.

He always remembered Adam having a good time that day, and being able to relive it was priceless. However, it was painful to know that his boy sitting less than a foot away would commit suicide—and there was nothing he could do to help. Keith could only enjoy the time he had with him.

He pushed the gloom back into the recesses of his mind so that he could enjoy the rest of his day with his friends, especially Adam. He had been there almost 24 hours, the halfway mark. The team got better at predicting the length of time, but it wasn't set in stone. There was a margin of error. He could have another 24 hours, though it could be more or less, which of the three he didn't know.

There were several people in his house. They sat in the living room watching the Pats play the Bills. The Pats were up 25 to 1. He glanced around the room at the smiling face, except Pete, who liked the Bills and was getting clowned for it. The room spun as he placed his fingers at his temples. He hoped the rush of images and eventual crash wasn't too bad—but he felt it would be severe. He picked up his 40 ounces of old English and deliberately poured some out for his dead friends' past and future. *May in peace, may they rest.*

17

No Crash

The download has been quick and painless. Keith suffered no signs of a crash. It didn't make any sense. When he was kicking it with his friends, he gave them better advice that was backed by his education and life experiences. Adam still died, but it wasn't from suicide; he was murdered during a drug deal gone bad.

In the original timeline, Adam committed suicide, and the crew grieved. Six months later, Dougie and his crew set up Tony and took him out. However, the events and histories that played out before him differed for the crew and himself.

The course of Adam's life changed, but time got the death it was owed, and it claimed another one sooner. During the original timeline, Tony sat in his car waiting to make a deal that turned into his murder. This time he was with Adam, and they both got murdered. Set up by Dougie and his crew. Shortly after, they arrested Keith for the murders of Dougie and most of his crew. Three people survived this time, but the same one testified against him.

Keith didn't know what to make of it. The past changed, but it only affected his crew. The gravity of the implications pulled him down like cement blocks tied to a drowning man. He didn't know who to trust. Something wasn't right. He could feel it under his skin as it crawled and scratched at the surface.

Everything outside the circle stayed the same. There were no significant changes. At least none that affected his memory or his tiny piece of the universe.

Dr. Bell was elated that the download and crash had been next to nonexistent. They did several tests on Keith. They weren't sure the cause but assumed the mental preparation had played a part.

Keith became more comfortable during the jump. With all the different memories inside his head of the same event, the jump started to feel right, more so than the present.

Keith walked into the lab. There was no scheduled jump today, but the place was a beehive of activity. About 30 people were buzzing around the lab. He scanned the lab, looking for Billy and Jen. He found them working on something at Billy's station.

They hunched over a monitor when he approached.

"What's going on?" Keith asked, motioning with his head towards the monitor.

"Testing some new equipment," Jen said. "It's still in the beginning stages, but if we can get it to work, we'll be able to track you in real-time."

"How?"

"It's rather complicated," Billy laughed. "I wouldn't know where to begin."

"Don't sweat it," Keith said. "Have you all seen Dr. Bell? He wasn't in his office."

Jen looked around, surprised. "He was just here."

"Don't worry about it, I'll find him. You two look busy," Keith said, "so I'll let you get back to work."

He walked to the door.

Jen watched Keith head for the door and sensed something bothered him. "Billy, I'll be right back," Jen said as she followed Keith into the hallway.

Keith was about to turn the corner to the elevator when she called to him. He stopped and walked towards her until she caught up.

"What's going on, you okay?" She said, her facial features signaling concern. "You look like you need to talk."

"I do," he said, "that's why I'm looking for Dr. Bell. I need to tell him something about the last jump. And I don't know how because I have a strange feeling something isn't quite right."

"What are you talking about?" She said, grabbing his hand. "Come on, let's find a place we can talk."

She led them into the cafeteria. The place was bustling, so they took a booth away from the people that were already there.

"Okay, now, what's going on?" Jen said. "You look very distressed."

He started by telling her about the new advice he had given his friends—and the outcomes. He explained how in the other jumps where he did little changed so many things in the present that the download caused a crash. Painful and agonizing.

After each of those jumps, he had a total recall of every change since the first jump. He expected a more intense download and a devastating crash, but he got a minor download and next to no crash—a slight headache.

Keith paused and placed his hands over his eyes, and took a deep breath. "That wasn't even the worst of it. The only things that changed, at least as far as I can tell, related to my friends. My friend Adam still died, but not by suicide, and Tony still died, but not alone in his car a year later. I still got arrested, but six months sooner."

"I understand you're concerned," Jen said, "but I'm not sure about what? So, you didn't have a crash or a severe download despite some changes. I think it's the preparation."

"I'm not so sure," he said, putting his hands on the table a little too hard. "Jen, nothing. Yet, I see the changes of only my friends. Barely a download and no crash. Don't you see what this could mean?"

"Keith, you're suggesting that our present reality was changed and that it's somehow different from when we first met you. If that were the case, you would have a major download and crash. It would've been very severe. I'm not sure you would've recovered for months. We understand the math, but we don't understand the consequences. Maybe, it's just your mind trying to figure out what's going on."

"I know it's crazy, but it happened," he said, scrunching up his face as he got visibly upset. "You think it's my mind trying to catch up and figure things out. Yeah, then how is this possible." He pulled out his phone and pulled up an article about his friends' death. "This isn't what happened the first time."

"Okay, so your memories from the last jump changed. I get that," Jen said, putting her hand on one of his. "I still think it's some sort of side effect of the jump."

"A false memory where no memory should be?"

"We prepared you this time, that's all," she reassured him. "Maybe you'll feel better after you go on your weekend in the real world."

"Yeah, I'll be fine," he said, though afraid of what he'd find beyond the walls of the Complex. "Maybe your right. However, I broke protocol, and I need to tell Dr. Bell."

"Don't worry about that, you told me," she said and smiled. "I'll tell him. I want you to relax. You need to relax. Don't get so worked up. You have a jump tomorrow—if you feel the same way after, then will look into it further, all right?"

"Okay, he said, despite not feeling okay.

18

The Old Man

Keith entered the lab, which was filled with more people than usual, a couple more technicians, a person he didn't know, and the director. He knew they would add more technicians. They had mentioned it during the last weekly meeting, but there was a lot more than he expected. He headed for the chair. They gave him the mission slip the night before, and he had roughly 10 hours to commit it to memory. Another long jump with a mission attached.

•

He woke at 6:15 AM, right on schedule. The room remained decorated, as it was on the first long jump. It felt like home, seeing the graffiti art on the wall. Good times. The only thing new was different posters. Girls in bikinis and a giant Rakim poster. He loved old-school rap. He looked in the mirror. A boy's face stared back—but not as innocent as the last. A faint mustache highlighted his upper lip. His face was hard and cold—a child who desperately needed some love—at least a hug, damn. The lack of affection in this family was world renown.

He reached under his bed looking for the wooden box; he kept his valuables and found it. His memory was very attuned to this time. He made a note of it. He wondered if the first jump back carried over a couple of years since. Keith knew what he'd find inside the box. The beginning of his downward spiral to prison.

Keith looked at the contents anyway and shook his head. A bag of weed rested on the top of a bound journal, his dream book. Next to the book was a small .25 caliber handgun and a stack of folded money with rubber bands holding in place. There was also a pack of condoms and a hard-core XXX magazine. He grabbed the cash and Journal and then closed the box before putting it back under the bed.

Keith smiled at himself as he read and reread the last entry of his dream journal. It was dated a couple of weeks before he arrived. The last dream he had was of him not being quite himself. He had gone somewhere he had never been. Some kind of park in a big city. He stood under a short tunnel underneath the bridge and waited for someone. He hands the man a letter in this dream and walks away. Then everything blows up—the entire city blown to pieces. Debris rained down on him. The dream ended.

By the time he took a shower and got dressed, it was nine in the morning. He looked in the mirror. Pretty fly for a young guy. The clothes he wore were brand-new, and he knew he bought the shirt and stole the fitted hat and jeans. The crisp Adidas Shell Toes on his feet his mother bought for school. He looked fresh.

Downtown Crossing was busy, and he saw plenty of kids he knew. A lot of girls. Most tried hard to get his attention. He got some phone numbers, but he couldn't remember being chased down by females like that. A good thing, he thought. He'd probably have 100 kids if you knew girls were into him like that. It was bad enough being a clueless young man. He removed the phone numbers from his pocket and read the names. He remembered messing with two of them, so we kept them and threw away the others. It was for the best.

He headed into the corner mall's food court and bought some Chinese food since he had plenty of time to kill. He checked his watch and decided it was time to go. He finished eating and left. He had to meet someone at the statue on top of the hill In the Common. He made it to the statue in 10 minutes. Nobody. Not a person in sight, except some kids, but not adults. He sat on one of the benches and waited.

A woman approached the statue and took pictures. Keith waited a few minutes to see if anyone else would come up or she would leave. Neither of the two things happened. If she was his contact, he was sure she had no idea to expect a 14-year-old kid. He wondered what she was gonna think as he left the bench to find out.

"Excuse me, miss," he smiled. "Do you have the time?"

She looked at Keith, confused. "Yeah, 11:05 AM."

It wasn't the response he expected. He chuckled. The woman really thought he wanted the time. He watched as she looked around. Concern evident on her face. He could almost hear her thoughts. *Where's my contact?* I'm right here.

"Miss, are you sure that's the correct time?" He said, exposing his watch. "I'm supposed to meet someone; I thought you might be them."

The woman blinked in surprise. "Maybe…It's…broken," she said, pointing to a watch.

"Oh, that's too bad," he said and smiled upon hearing the password. "I need to use the restroom, but I'm supposed to wait here. Besides, Uncle Sam always liked the spot."

The woman, lost for words, just stared at him. The world's youngest spy, to her surprise. "My uncle liked the spot too."

"You weren't expecting a teen?" He said in a firm voice. "Well, nobody else would suspect me either, which is kinda the point. You have something for me?"

"Yes, I do," she said with a smile as she handed him the envelope, "and not in a million years. I'm not sure what's going on, but I've never dealt with a child before, and I'm not sure how I feel about it, so be careful."

"Don't worry, I will," he said. "Besides, I'm a lot older than I look."

He turned on his heels and walked down the hill towards the Boston Public Garden. He surveyed the park as he headed to the exit. There was no one around. He glanced back once to the hill. The woman was gone. He saw no one in that part of the park, not even college-aged frisbee players.

When he saw the FAO Schwarz giant bear statue, he went into the toy store. Once he was inside the store, he removed the envelope. The large manila envelope looked huge in his child-sized hands. After tearing it open, he emptied its contents: another envelope, some money, a picture of an elderly-looking man, and a map of the city of Lynn, just 12 miles north of Boston along the coast. He stuffed the items in his jacket pocket and discarded the envelope.

Two hours later, Keith was in Central Sq, Lynn. He stood on the commuter rail platform and stared at the map. He followed the map to a small park near the ocean. It was a pleasant park, not one that you would think would be in Lynn. It overlooked the ocean. A brisk breeze blew onto the shore. There were only a few people in the park. Teenagers hanging out and few adults. An elderly-looking man sat on a bench feeding the birds from a loaf of bread. He checked the man against the picture and sat down next to him.

"Can I help feed the birds?" Keith asked.

The man looked around. "Sure, I come here every day, at the same time, to feed them. They know me by sight now," the old man said, digging into the bag and tossing more crumbs to the birds.

Keith took some of the bread and fed the birds. The old man seemed to enjoy his company, so he talked with the man. Keith looked at his watch. The commuter train going back to Boston would leave soon, and he needed to be on it. He didn't want to get his younger self in trouble with his mom for being out too late.

"Well, I gotta go," he said as he removed the envelope.

"That's fine, young man," the old man smiled. "Have a good day now."

"I will, sir," he said, handing him the envelope.

"What's this?" The old man inquired as he took it.

"Don't know, sir," he said. "Just know I'm supposed to give it to you, is all."

"Oh, all right, thank you," the old man said, worry spreading across his face.

Keith walked away as evening approached fast; he pulled his jacket close to protect himself from the chilly breeze. The old man didn't appear too happy to receive the letter. Again, he wondered what mysteries those letters contained. Last time was a package; this time, it was a letter.

At that moment, Keith made a conscious decision to see what was inside the next package or letter. No matter what it was. He needed to know what he was delivering. Something wasn't right. He could feel it. The wind howled as its icy grasp swirled around him and sent a shiver up his spine.

The commuter rail train was late, which was a fortunate happenstance. Because if it weren't, Keith would've missed his only way home. When he arrived at North Station, he bought a soda at the newsstand and then headed for the exit back in Boston.

As a very little kid, his dad brought him to the old garden. He looked around for any signs of the old place. Unfortunately, it had already been torn down a few years prior. So much history lost.

A pressure-filled his head. He felt funny…weird. Pulsating pain emerged at his right temple, so he reached up to touch the spot. His vision swirled as it turned everything into a fun-house mirror. Keith knew what it was—the actual test. *Time to go back home.*

When Keith opened his eyes, he was in his room at the Complex. Confused, he looked around. Jen and Dr. Bell were there.

"Hey, he's finally awake," Jen said.

"About time, we were really worrying," Dr. Bell said.

"What, why-am-I-in my room," he stammered. His head, still groggy.

"You don't remember?" Jen asked.

"No, I don't remember."

"Well, you barely opened your eyes," Dr. Bell said before he paused, "when you went into cardiac arrest. You were resuscitated and remained unconscious until now. Do you remember the jump?"

Keith needed little time to think about the subject. He remembered everything except coming back. The images in his head were confusing. He knew there were big changes made to this future. Or present. He didn't even remember anymore. Damn, his head hurt. He shut his eyes.

"We should let them rest," Dr. Bell said.

That's right, let me rest, he thought. Seconds later, he was asleep. His mind, not yet ready to deal with the present.

19

Beautiful Sky

The sweltering Midsummer day sent Keith to the beach. He lay on the towel as he enjoyed the company of an intelligent, beautiful person. Kristin. Summertime at Revere Beach had always been crowded. He scanned the water and the beach through hazy vision. Whether it was from the heat or the jump, he couldn't tell. He'd become accustomed to the jump. And it now seemed to be a better place to be than the present.

After Keith delivered the last envelope, there had been a light download and the occasional crash that amounted to nothing more than a headache. Over a dozen jumps since, none with severe consequences to him or the timeline. He still thought something was amiss.

A couple of seagulls landed near him and Kristin, which interrupted his thought. He glanced over at Kristin, who opened the cooler and was making sandwiches for lunch. There had to be a reason the scavengers had shown up. Kristen asked what he wanted, he told her.

A moment later, he was back, lost in his thoughts.

Since the letter's delivery, Keith wrote down every jump in his journal as if it was a dream. The process awoke something in him. He noticed small things. Things that were hard to explain, like an errant memory with no jump attached to it. It prompted him to read all his journals. The ones he had with him since he began his sentence and those he read within the jump. He took time to read as many as he could.

He focused on those that started 12 years before they initiated him into the program. At first, everything looked consistent. However, once in a while, he'd come to an entry. One without a date, and that was something he never did. He had never noticed because he rarely read them after they came true.

Keith found six such entries, and he only covered the first few years. He knew they'd be more. He read and reread these passages over and over. They consumed him and still do. He wondered if he had left some kind of message to himself in these passages, but if he had, he couldn't figure that out.

"Keith, I'm talking to you," Kristin said. "Earth to Keith!"

He looked over at her, then smiled. "Sorry, I was thinking about something."

"About what?" She said, wrapping her arms around him.

Keith missed the human contact, and it made him feel good, so he lied. "You, of course," he said as he leaned in and kissed her. He couldn't remember why they had broken up, but he was sure it was his fault.

She handed him a sandwich and kissed him one more time before getting up to go to the water. He ate the sandwich while he watched her head to take a swim. When she came back, and he was done eating, she asked if they could leave.

They packed up their belongings, which didn't amount to too much. The usual beach items. He deflated a beach ball and stuffed it into his bag as Kristin struggled with hers. He closed up the bag and put it on his back.

The two teenagers trooped across the beach to the sidewalk and walked along the shore on the pavement. As they walked to her car, they admired the view.

"It's so beautiful, isn't it?"

"What's that?"

"The ocean and sky. Look at the colors."

He loved how Kristin would display her youthful spirit, which was so full of dreams. He then looked to the ocean and the horizon beyond. Beautiful indeed. Unless someone pointed it out, it was not something he would notice. He was too consumed with his thoughts to notice things around him. Jump or present, it mattered not. At that moment, he was consumed by the oddities he found, but in the past, he would not have noticed because his mind would have been on immature teenage things. He knew she was good for him, but he knew prison or death was in his future even then. He never realized how much he beat himself down. The jump oddities were trying to invade his mind.

"Yeah, you're right. It's beautiful, isn't it?"

Keith's vision blurred as the world spun. He glanced at his watch. *It's not time.*

20

Near Miss

The tiles of the drop ceiling came into view as Keith opened his eyes. Billy unstrapped him. Keith sat up and looked around. It was him and Billy on their side of the petition. He looked at the three people standing on the other side. "Why was I pulled back?" Keith said. "It wasn't time."

"We had a problem," Dr. Bell said, his disembodied voice echoing across the chamber. "We'll fill you in at the debrief."

Twenty minutes later, Keith sat in Dr. Bell's office with Jen and Billy. Dr. Bell was in the middle of a conversation on the phone but ended it. He looked up at the three people before him.

"All right, you're probably wondering why you here," Dr. Bell said as he continued. "They informed me today...we... lost an asset. Whatever task he was supposed to do, he never accomplished it. You get killed, so we pulled you out before it happened."

"How is it possible that you knew I would die?" Keith said, with a touch of bewilderment. "None of this makes sense." He looked over at Billy and Jen, who looked as bewildered as him. "I thought the missions were for the project. To better it. Now, I get the impression you left something out. Who do I really work for?"

"None of us knew this was possible," Dr. Bell said. "I just found out today. As far as who orchestrates the missions, the military, we get a large part of the funding from them."

"Which branch?" Keith asked.

"A branch with no official name or charter. They only answer to the president. You've been completing missions that originally failed. You also set up the network of people that would set this project in motion. Keith, you've been under surveillance since you were 10-years-old. The furthest we have a set you back."

"Hold up," Keith said, trying to process the information. "You're saying that during one of these trips, I somehow gave orders for this project to be set up and placed myself on surveillance. That's why I made the phone calls and delivered the packages? I thought doing those things helped solidify this program."

"Yes, you set up a line of communication," Dr. Bell said and struggled to continue. "Nobody knew why they were meeting you."

"I...still don't...understand," Keith said as he got up and paced the length of Dr. Bell's office. "How did you know to pull me out? There's no way you could've known, so please tell me."

A picture frame caught his attention as he paced. It was a picture of the team. Well, the people in the room at this moment. None of the other technicians were there. He didn't like what was going on and wasn't sure he understood it, but something wasn't right. He kept pacing as Dr. Bell spoke.

"I don't know the details," Dr. Bell said, "only what I was just told. Another project was set into motion with the first phone call you made during a jump to 1997. The furthest we've ever you sent back."

It confused Keith because the furthest they ever sent him back was to 1999. When he was 11-years-old, he assumed he hadn't gone back yet, but how could they know about it? He guessed a phone call would have been sufficient.

"Since that mission, your entire life has been under glass," Dr. Bell said. "You were left to live your life. Any change to your life and the project would never exist, so you became important to the government. There is even an unofficial file of crimes you never got caught for. I'm sure you wondered why and now you know. They made sure your life played out the way it had in this timeline so that the program could begin."

"I still don't know why you didn't tell us this," he said, raising his voice a bit.

"I know this will be hard to believe," Dr. Bell said, lowering his eyes, "but I wasn't aware of this. Not until today. None of it is important, right now—"

I'll be the one to decide that, not you, the military, or the fucking Director."

Jen couldn't hold back any longer. "Why do you think it's not important?"

"The only important thing, right now, is trying to find out who tried to kill you."

"That's the part I don't get. If you pulled me out, then I didn't die, so this other team that surveillances me would see me not die. It makes no sense."

"He's not wrong, Dr. Bell," Jen said. "The messages we get from the past to the director are on the timeline being altered or traversed."

Dr. Bell looked at Jen and then Billy and Keith. "This is what they told me, and I didn't question it, but honestly, I was a bit taken aback by all the other information. Billy, what do you think?"

"The only explanation could be an altered timeline. One where we get the information and then alter it. It could be right now we're still in the old timeline, but when we send Keith back, and he changes it—they don't kill Keith."

"The thing I don't get," Keith said, "is that no one tried to kill me. Not in the least. No picked fight. *Nothing.* Nothing up to that point was dangerous, so how do I know what they say happened is what happened. And what about the guy I was supposed to meet. What happened to him? A line of communication needs to be unbroken."

"In short, that's why we pulled you out," Dr. Bell said, taking a deep breath. "We're supposed to send you back. I will try to make it for the next day or so. It's the reason why I'm telling you everything right now. You deserve to know and decide for yourself if you want to continue. I know death has always been a potential consequence of the program, but I never imagined someone would kill you while on a jump."

"Come on, Doctor," Keith said, plopping down into the chair. "There's no way they'll let me back out."

"I can stop the program," Dr. Bell said.

"It's the military or some other unknown agency that runs us. I cannot afford you to be naïve. I have no choice but to do this mission because they won't allow me to stop."

"I guess what I'm asking then is when will you be ready to jump?"

"Scratch that," Jen started the stand-up and object, but Keith stopped her.

"No, it's all right," he said, then turned to Dr. Bell. "I'm ready right now, but I want to be sent back to the same day."

"You know we can't," Dr. Bell said.

"We don't know what the consequences would be," Jen said. "The data suggest that two beings cannot occupy the same space."

"Yeah, I get that," he said, "but it's the consciousness that is transferred to the past. I come in contact with my past self with every jump. Do we know what happens to the consciousness of that present? Does it come forward, or does it go dormant? *We don't know.* Maybe all that happens is That I push the consciousness out."

"The risk still outweighs the mission," Jen said.

"Then get me as close as you can."

"We can get you there the day before or the day after," Billy said.

"Only if you could get me to the time when you took me out, then it wouldn't be a problem."

"Unfortunately, big guy, that's the best we could do," Billy said.

"Let's do it," he said, already heading for the door. "Now."

21

You Must Stop

The sun rose above the horizon as Keith made his way to the meeting. He wasn't sure how Billy did it, but he got him there on the next day. He rushed to the meeting, but this time he would not be an unwitting pawn. He had his girlfriend drop him off downtown while she headed off to work. He said he had errands to do. Although he could walk to his destination, he took the T and switched cars and lines several times. It took longer, but it made it harder for them to follow him—survival instincts at full alert. *Not dying today.*

He felt confident, and the 40 Cal tucked in his waistband didn't hurt. His stash box under the bed remained, but the contents changed. Weed changed to coke. A few hundred dollars turned to stacks and no magazines.

He decided not to be easy prey this time. Being killed during this timeline was not an option. A few things still bothered him. He still didn't understand how bringing him back stopped him from being assassinated. It's not like his younger self disappeared. No, it was more to the story than he'd been told or more to the point that Dr. Bell had been told.

He believed Dr. Bell was ignorant of the actual mission of the project. It only made sense that some secret organization not on the books would want to control time travel.

Nobody told him exactly when he supposedly got killed. Just that he never made it to the meeting. He stared up at the building and made his way to the garden entrance, where the exchange was to take place. Keith even thought maybe the contact killed him, thinking he was some kind of thug trying to rob him. The scenario had to be considered, or the contact was the assailant.

Before he got on the last train, he used a payphone to set up the meeting. The gate to the garden was locked, so we had to go through the museum. Elizabeth Gardner Museum was an old estate and now a Museum that boasted fine works and antiquities. In 1990, an art heist made headlines because the thieves dressed as cops, and the works were never recovered or the suspects identified. He made his way to the garden. Grateful it was uneventful.

There was nobody in garden when he got there. Not a soul. Keith went back into the museum and watched the entrance for a half hour. He decided he waited long enough and found a payphone to call the number. The contact picked up on the second ring.

"I apologize, but I had to cancel the meeting," the contact said. "Go to the city of Malden and call me when you get there."

"Gonna take me a while to get there," he said, not liking the plan.

"Call when you get here," the contact said and hung up.

An hour and a half later, Keith arrived at the orange line station in Malden Center. He exited the train but stopped to tie his shoe. The one he untied on the train. He scanned the area. No one else got off of any cars that look to be interested in him. He left the station and crossed towards the police station, where it no longer stood in his present.

The afternoon sun started to lose its heat. The city wound down. He climbed the stairs to the police station and walked down the street, and turned left. Once he got to Oak Street, he took it past the high school until he reached the 7Eleven. He went inside the store and bought a drink and a bag of chips. When he came out of the store, he used the payphone to call the contact. He set up the meeting again, this time for 10 minutes at the movie theater in Revere.

A few minutes later, a black maximum pulled into the parking lot. A man in his late 20s early 30s got out and went into the store, bought a pack of cigarettes and drink, and came back out.

"Excuse me, Mister?" Keith said, walking towards the man getting Inti his car. "Are you headed down Oak Street towards Revere?"

"Yeah," he said. "Why, you need a lift?"

"Sure, I'd appreciate one, sir," he said with a smile.

"All right, hop in," the man said. "Just don't call me sir."

Keith thanked the man as he got in the car. "I'm going to Lynn," he said, in case anyone was listening. "Where you headed?"

"To the movie theater..."

Keith knew exactly where the man was headed because that's where he was told to go. When you come from the future, you have certain advantages. He recognized the man as soon as he exited his car. The man looked like the picture Keith memorized. He wasn't sure if it was dumb luck if he was, in fact, the assassin, but he would find out soon enough.

"Hey, thanks again for the ride," Keith said. "You see, I was supposed to meet someone yesterday at Revere Beach, but I had to cancel the meeting."

"You were at Revere Beach yesterday?" the man said. "I was there too and was supposed to meet a friend who never showed up."

"That's why I called you this morning to meet at the Museum."

"And now, I suppose."

"Someone's been watching one of us. I'm not sure which one or whom it is—all I know is we need to be careful. You have the package?"

He picked up a CD case and handed it to Keith. The case contained nothing special except a compact disk. Keith shut the case and put it into his jacket pocket.

"Just drop me off at the bus stop or store 24."

"All right, kid," the man said. "Be careful."

"Don't worry, I will, sir."

The man dropped him off it at Store 24 and continued to the movie theater. Keith crossed the street and waited for the bus to bring him back to the train station. He'd been there 10 minutes when a car pulled over and dropped off a man. Not an unusual sight for this bus stop, but he recognized the man from 7 Eleven. Keith sat on top of a traffic control box and watched the area.

Keith was careful not to look in the man's direction too much. He waited a couple of minutes and walked across to the store to see if the man would follow him. He bought a couple of items: bug spray and another soda. The man stood at the payphone outside the store. Keith looked around for the car. Not seeing it, he walked towards the man heading back to the bus stop.

The man hung up the phone when Keith reached about 5 feet away and turned towards him, but Keith pretended to read the bug spray's directions. He glanced at the man and turned away, paying no attention to him. He made it to the sidewalk. When a car came to a stop at the light, he looked up and saw it was green. The light was green. Everything happened fast. The man on the phone rushed at him, as the other one got out of the car.

Keith reacted with little thought and sprayed the first man in the eyes with the bug sprayer. Stopping the man in a fit of pain. Temporally blinding him. Keith took off and ran as fast as he could. The other man shouted for him to stop before he took up the chase. Keith didn't look back. He knew the area because he had cousins that lived there. After running a few blocks in a crude circle, he headed into the projects. He ducked behind one of the buildings and pulled his gun. Ready. His youthful body easily outran the man that pursued him.

A few minutes passed, and he heard the man calling for someone. He couldn't hear the name, but the man's voice became louder and clearer as he got closer.

"Come on, boy," the man shouted. "We're the police. We need to ask you a few questions about that man who picked you up. We think he's a drug dealer. Is that why you're running?"

Keith wasn't sure of the man's cover or what agency he worked for, but he still didn't believe the man. However, in case these men were just overzealous detectives, he stuffed the gun into his waistband and dashed across the street. The man spotted him and gave chase. He barely made it across the street when the guy started shooting. Keith could feel the hot air and piercing sound of the slugs as they zinged by him. He heard no gunfire, just the sound of the bullets that passed between them.

Silencer.

He ducked behind a brick staircase and pulled his gun. He didn't have a silencer, so he knew he was about to make a lot of noise.

The man turned the corner. "If you come out and give yourself up, I'll stop shooting...but you gotta stop running."

Keith remained silent. His more lethal instincts took over. He heard the man approach.

"Come on, kid," he called as he moved forward.

He was close—almost time.

"Dammit, kid!" He yelled. "I know you're back here."

The man's voice grew louder, but Keith still wasn't sure how close he actually was. He took a chance and peeked over the steps from where he crouched. The man stood a few feet away, listening and probably looking for potential hiding places. He had his back to Keith. Almost time. He could see the gun in the man's hand, and it indeed had a silencer attached to the business end of the weapon. He took a breath.

It's time.

He stepped out from his hiding spot. "Looking for me."

The man spun on his heels, raising his gun, but it was too late. Keith had already squeezed off two shots, which reverberated off the close buildings. He hit the man somewhere in his torso. The man collapsed to the ground, releasing his gun as he fell. It clattered to the ground. Keith quickly picked it up and stood over the man as he looked up at Keith. Agony filled his eyes. Tears, not fear.

"Why are you trying to kill me?" Keith said. "Who sent you?"

The man shook his head. "You don't understand...we must stop you," the man grimaced in pain.

"I'm not doing anything...why...me?"

"You know why?"

He could hear the sirens in the distance. He knew someone had called the police.

"The police are coming," he said, "so I guess I should kill you now, and then that will stop you from trying to kill me."

"There...will...be...others," the man said, gasping for breath. "we must stop you."

Keith heard enough and shot the man with his own gun.

Pfft. Pfft.

He made sure the man was dead and took off. "Others," the man had said. It weighed on him as he ran. This man spoke the truth, and he believed it was because the man had a partner. He wasn't out of the woods yet. He had to find out who was after him and why. *Why must he be stopped?*

He ran as fast as he could, cutting through backyards and abandoned lots. He made it to a small plaza, walked in the

Dunkin' Donuts, and bought a strawberry Coolatta and a cinnamon stick. He sat there and ate it while he cooled off. The sun hovered above the horizon on its descent.

He was there all of five minutes when two cops came in... One was a tall, scrawny white guy, and the other stocky black guy. Keith watched them, but they didn't appear to be looking for anyone.

"How're you doing, boys?" The woman behind the counter said. "Where'd you fellows' takeoff to a few minutes ago?"

"Over few blocks, there was a report of gunfire," the white cop said, "but we found nothing."

"Supposedly, someone got shot," the black cop said and shook his head, "by a teenager, but there was no sign of a victim. Nothing at the hospitals either."

The woman took and prepared their order. The two cops sat down near the window. Two booths down from Keith. He finished the cinnamon stick and left. The cops seemed to have dismissed it and gave up. He became puzzled because they should've found the body. The guy bled bad, so there had to be evidence at the scene. Keith finished his cinnamon stick and went to the bus stop.

He saw a bus coming his way, and it pulled over to pick him up.

He started his trek back to Boston. He took the longest way he could think of, which involved only buses. When he got home a few hours later, his mother was home and complained about something he didn't do. Some chore or something. She admonished him by saying, "those that don't do their chores will end up in prison." Though she wasn't wrong that he would end up in prison, he knew it had nothing to do with chores.

He saw the trash overflowing and figured that was the problem. Enhanced memory, not helping one bit. He took out the trash.

Keith entered his bedroom and sat on the bed. He took off his coat and tossed it beside him. He felt guilty that he went straight home and that his mom was there. He hoped in this timeline he didn't put her in jeopardy. It wasn't part of the plan to come back home. He was supposed to call another number and find out what he was to do next.

However, someone was trying to kill him, so the plan needed to be altered. He wanted to know why and wondered if the disk in his jacket pocket had anything to do with it. After a few minutes, he sat up, reached over for his jacket, and removed the disk. He didn't have a computer, but the kid across the hall did. He got up and went across the hall, but as he stood, he got dizzy. Quickly, he looked for a place to stash the disk for safekeeping. He slipped the disk into a book on his bookshelf as his room swirled together.

22

Something Strange Happened

Keith worried because he expected more from the download, and some kinda crash with all that happened. He didn't expect nothing. A blip of change. He looked around for any visible signs of change. Nothing.

"Everything okay?" Dr. Bell said over the intercom.

He nodded as he waited for the tech to release the straps. No, Billy in sight. Just two techs he didn't remember ever seeing. As he crossed through the partition, the first thing he noticed was their faces. They showed none of the concern that as before the jump. Nothing. He halted, saying anything until he found out what was going on.

Dr. Bell approached him. "How was the trip?" He stopped in front of Keith and looked at the tablet. "Did you find the problem?"

"What problem?"

Dr. Bell shook his head. "The one they sent you back to fix. You seem different lately. Are you sure you're all right?"

"Yeah, Doc," Keith exhaled, "I'm fine. But I don't think it was time to be pulled out yet."

"You completed your mission," Dr. Bell said. "This time, you didn't die."

"You know—" he said, then thought better of it. "Never mind. I'm tired. Can we get this briefing over with, so I can go lay down?"

"Oh, sure," Dr. Bell said.

It only took 10 minutes to debrief because Keith left everything out. He just told them he picked up and dropped off. Uneventful. Since they believed he made the drop, he went with it. He knew something wasn't right. He stashed the pickup in a book at his house, so it never made it to the drop. He expected to get help for it when he got back, but nothing. *Not a word about it.*

Something changed reality, but he didn't know how. This present was somehow different from the one he left. Once he got back to his quarters, he pulled out his journal and wrote everything down. After he finished, he read every entry, working backwards.

He found what he thought he would find. They were different, but he didn't know how it was possible. He had no memory of any changes—nothing in the download. There was no crash. No images that haunted him to death. He couldn't work out what he was missing. He continued to read the entries for clues. He hoped to find at least one.

23

Confused Reality

It had taken Keith three days to read through each journal. As he believed, he found not one clue but many. He lay on his bed and wondered what to do. The rest of the team thought the mission was successful—and happy he didn't get killed.

Keith believed they were on a different page. After the debriefing, Dr. Bell and Jen expressed serious concern. They told him he had to be more careful because they didn't want another freak accident—to kill him. If he hadn't been under surveillance, he could've died. Then there would be no project. They were a little confused on the how, but Keith agreed. He needed to be careful.

Records. The thought jumped into his head; he had full access to mission records, and they encouraged him to go through them. If he found anything, he'd add it to his dream journal.

The laptop he had in the room had limited access. The one in the lab he could use. He left his quarters and went to the lab. He saw Dr. Bell and Billy in the hallway. "Hey guys, I'm headed to the lab to go over mission files since I hadn't done so in a while."

"Good idea," Dr. Bell said, "I think revisiting the missions and committing them to memory will help you acclimate yourself during and after a jump."

Billy nodded. "Though I agree it could help, I'm not sure what it can do for you during and after a jump, but who knows. We don't know everything yet."

"Very true," Keith said, "I'll let you guys go so I can get to it."

A few moments later, Keith found himself in front of the computer. He started with the last mission but decided to start at the beginning. The first mission or test as they started out being called.

The details of the first mission were brief. All the missions were laid out the same. Each file contained a mission objective, a unique description, and an outcome. They recorded dates for each jump and the present time, as well as the date in the past. The mission outcome had two dates. When it got put into the system, usually in the past, and when they retrieved it in the present.

The first several missions contained nothing out of the ordinary. Unchanged. Around the fifth or sixth mission, the mission logs didn't measure up to his own recollection. Everything changed. However, he had no memory of the change—and that worried him. *How was this possible?*

Several alternate realities floated at the edge of his consciousness. With precise clarity, he could recall each one. It had taken lots of practice over the last few months. *Why was this will not there?* No matter how hard he tried—he just couldn't call it up. He slammed his fist down on the table. *What was he missing?*

After printing out three missions with the anomalies, he went back to his quarters. There he matched up the mission reports with his journal entries and intact memories. He believed he left himself clues—this he knew for sure—but what they were, he didn't know. It was like he needed to find a missing piece to the puzzle to unlock it. He didn't know where that piece was or what it comprised, but he needed to find it.

A single thought pushed its way to the front. Maybe the clues he needed to follow were in the past. He may have to wait for the next jump. In the meantime, he studied and compared the missions to his entries.

Keith was sure that it was his future self that had been dropping breadcrumbs. He toyed with the idea that maybe he changed the past, but why would he do that? He didn't know.

The one thing that didn't add up in any of it was his lack of knowledge of the change to reality.

He had been comparing injuries to the missions for about an hour when someone knocked on his door. He slid his journal and the loose sheaves of paper that contained his notes under his pillow. "Who is it?"

"It's Jen."

"Oh, come in," he called as he sat up in his bed with his back propped against the headboard.

"Were you just in the lab?"

"Yeah," he said, holding up the mission records. "I was bored, so I went over mission reports and make notes."

"Which missions do you have there?" Jen said, motioning to the papers. "I know that's not all the missions."

"The last three," he said, shifting over to make room for her to sit down on the bed. "They don't add up to what I remember."

"What do you remember?"

"Well, first off, I have no memory of completing the mission," he said. "I never made the drop."

"Maybe what you thought was the mission wasn't," Jen said. "All I know is you completed the mission, and we called you back."

"That's what upstairs told you?"

"If you mean the director, yes, it was him who told us."

"See, that's the problem," Keith said. "he told you guys to pull me back too soon, but you look at me like I was crazy, so I left it alone."

"You were under surveillance since the first mission. You know this, and that's how they know before we do."

"I understand how," he said, standing up to pace his small quarters. "I didn't understand who told you until you just now, so he also told you the time to pull me out?"

"Yes, after you jumped, he made a phone and then gave us the time to pull you out."

Something clicked in his head. The gears of intuition with slow determination turned. "At that exact time?"

"Yeah," she said, "if we didn't pull you back at that time, the accident...would...still have happened, and you would've died."

They kept referring to it as an accident. He was afraid to tell them that in the past, they knew it was a hitman. He wondered why that detail changed. It had to be significant enough for it to be erased.

Before Jen knocked on his door, he had no lead or suspicion, but now, he was sure it involved Director Harrington.

He found it too coincidental that Dir. Harrington ordered him to be pulled back at the time he hid the disk. It was important that during the next jump he found out what was on the disk. He hoped that his past self didn't discard it for some reason. Though he had no such memory, he no longer trusted the present or the other realities in his head. Someone found a way to make his memories not trustworthy.

"I suppose that's it," Jen looked at him closer. "Are you okay? You were staring off into space."

"Yeah, I'm fine," he said, trying to get his thoughts straight. "I was just thinking is all. It ain't nothing. Maybe I need some rest."

"Oh, all right," she said as she stood. "Well, I need to get going, anyway."

"I appreciate the help."

She stopped at the door and looked over her shoulder. "If you need someone to talk to for any reason, I'm just down the hall."

"Thanks," he said and smiled. She was a beautiful woman, but he needed to stay focused. If there were more hidden in her offer, it would have to wait. He had a disk to find.

24

1992

The gym at the Complex had a mat floor that was designated for martial arts training. He stepped up his game. Being in top physical shape wasn't enough, people were trying to kill him.

He found himself on the mat, looking up at the ceiling. The workout was grueling and had him drained. Top shape for a fighter took quite a lot of work. It's time to sharpen the skills. Although he had learned from a 3rd-degree black belt in Taekwondo who had since gone home, he never trained formally.

After he stretched out, surprised he was only a little tight, he got down to work. First, he warmed up with the basics. It didn't matter that he worked out an hour and a half ago. He moved on to hitting the bag, starting with hand strikes and kicks.

Several others were working out on the mat, so it wasn't hard to find a partner. After a couple of weeks, he led a small makeshift class. His abilities impressed some of the others but surprised no one. Once he finished his workout, he hit the shower.

Jen and Billy were in the lab and told him there would be a jump at noon. They were excited because they would send him back to 1992. The furthest jump so far on record.

Dr. Bell entered the lab a bit excited. "Keith, did they tell you? You're going way back. Hope you up for it?"

"I'm ready," he said, hoping the crash wouldn't be too bad. The further one went back in time; there was a higher potential for change. Little things could add up over time. A crash could be devastating. "I'm fine and ready, so send me back?"

"We got pretty good predicting your teens, but we're sending you further back, so if our calculations are correct 1992."

"1992," Keith said with a chuckle. "I'll be five years old. What's the mission objective?"

"Your mission is simple," Dr. Bell said. "Not unlike the first few. A simple phone call, and you're out of there. You have an hour to complete the mission."

"Sounds doable," he said, "but I'm a bit concerned about going back that far. Though I haven't had many crashes of late, I'm concerned coming back from this could debilitate, to say the least."

"Jen has a suggestion to lessen the crash upon returning." Dr. Bell said.

Keith looked over the Jen, who looked uncharacteristically stunning. She put more effort into her appearance. He always thought of her as a get-up-and-go person. Someone that had more important things to do than worry about wardrobe and makeup. He wondered what brought on the change, but he had no answer.

"I got the idea from something you already do," Jen said. "You were meditating before and after each jump. We tried to prepare you with images, and that didn't seem to work, but the more jumps you did, the more each crash's intensity diminished. I think it's the meditating, so meditate while you're in the jump, and maybe that will help."

"It couldn't hurt," he said, glancing at the clock. An hour to go, "I'll try it on the other side."

Keith went back to his quarters and mentally prepared for 45 minutes. When he returned to the lab to jump, he felt relaxed. Once they strapped him in the chair, they sent him on his way.

•

Keith opened his eyes and sat up in bed as a blue glow washed over the room from a nightlight plugged into an outlet somewhere near the bedroom door. He sat up and glanced around the unfamiliar room. He felt the memories from the time period trying to push forward. There were few memories from his childhood—only fragments. Soon he would have total recall. He hoped for a pleasant time. His earliest memories consisted of a Christmas when he was four years old, riding a horse for the first time, and sledding down a big hill behind the house where he assumed they lived. *Soon he would have more.*

Memories long forgotten entered his mind. The experience was incredible as every jump. His favorite part of the heightened recall of that time's present. It was also cool that he kept all his memories from his present so that he could work. Things would've gone completely different if he lost all his memories on landing. *Yikes, that would suck.*

As became his ritual, Keith scanned for the clock. 6:15 AM. He jumped off the bed and meditated for 15 minutes before being interrupted.

His mom walked into the room. "What are you doing? She said with her hands on her hips.

Keith cracked a smile. "Nothing, mama, just playing."

He could only imagine what his mom thought. He sat with his feet together in a butterfly position with his palms facing up at the ceiling and his forefinger and thumbs touching on both hands touch. Not to mention his back ramrod straight, as he looked forward with his chin up and eyes close. The sight had to make one hell of an impression on his mom. She probably thought he was crazy.

He bounded to his feet. "Mama!" He said as his mother left the room.

She stopped right outside his bedroom and looked back. "Yes, baby. What is it?"

"I'm hungry."

"Come on," she said. "Got to feed you when you want it, or else, you'll starve."

He was either a picky eater or just didn't care about eating. *Enjoy it while it lasts*, he thought. In a few years, he'd make up for his lack of hunger. He practically ate her at a house and home.

He sat at the table eating frosted flakes. They were his favorite because he liked Tony the Tiger. After his mom made his breakfast, she disappeared into her room. Although she said nothing to him, he knew she wouldn't come back out for quite some time. *Time to make the call.*

Watching the doorway to the kitchen, he picked up the phone and dialed the number. After an operator picked up, he gave them the extension in the biggest grownup voice he could muster.

Although Keith exhumed confidence and high articulate skill, he could detect doubt in the operator's voice, but she still patched him through—a woman answered the phone.

"Hello?" The female voice said.

"Blue-yellow-three-two-seven," he said.

"Okay. Beta 16," she said.

"Let the bird fly the coop," he said, sounding very much like a five-year-old.

There was a pause. Keith heard the rustle of paperwork. The woman came back on the line and didn't sound happy.

"Repeat that one more time, please?"

"Let the bird fly the coop."

"Let the bird fly the coop," she repeated and then laughed. For the first time, she realized she had been talking to a child. "How old are you, young man? And do you know who you just called?"

"Yes, ma'am, I do. Blue-yellow-three-two-seven. Next, let the bird fly the coop," he said, with the confidence of his 30 something-year-old mind. "My age is irrelevant. Please log the response."

"Yeah, I'm sure I will," the woman said as she laughed and hung up.

What the fuck. He hoped to god she logged in the entry. Somehow, he doubted she would log it in. He hung up the phone and went back into his bedroom, where he meditated until they pulled him back. He was in such a calm state when it happened; he didn't even know until he opened his eyes— and had the crash of a lifetime.

25

Major Crash

The tech rushed to Keith's aid as he collapsed to the floor. His eyes rolled up into his skull. The monitors in the control panel screamed in various tones. The cacophony of sounds merged into one high-pitched scream. *Flatline.*

They used a defibrillator on him twice. After they were able to get him stable enough for transport, they sent him to an outside hospital.

Dr. Bell, Jen, and Billy were mortified as they watched Keith be taken out on a gurney.

•

Keith awoke on his own accord. He found his hospital room filled with flowers and get-well cards. They all came from the Complex. Nobody else knew he was free. Nor would they care. The cards wished him a speedy recovery. Some even thanked him for his participation in the project and for adding to their life experiences. Keith wasn't used to such concern being expressed by others. Not at all. He could get used to it. It was good knowing people cared.

The cards and flowers were not all he found when he opened his eyes: Dr. Bell, Billy, and of course Jen were all there, sitting in chairs waiting for him to wake. From the looks of them, they had been there all night.

"Damn, think you all look worse than me!" he said. "And the way my head feels right now, it isn't good. Believe me."

They all stood up and approached his bedside.

"It's good to see you awake, big man," Billy said.

"Yeah, I have to agree," Dr. Bell said. "You had us worried."

Jen hugged Keith, not able to control her emotions. "Keith, you had us worried—the crash almost killed you."

Keith smiles but wondered if that wasn't the plan. Now, he understood and appreciated automated answering systems. You wouldn't have a problem if it were a machine. "Well, it's good to see great people around you when you wake up in a hospital," Keith said, adjusting himself a little in the bed. "Believe me... it's good to see you all."

"Now, how are you feeling?" Dr. Bell said.

"Line A freight train hit me," he said. "My head is swimming.... How...the...jump go?"

Another reality pushed at the edge of his memory. He used all of his strength to push it back. Not ready to see what changed. It impressed him by the ease it went away. It might've drained his power, making him sleepy, but it had to be done. He didn't know what to make of it. He looked around at his friends and realized he'd been staring off into space.

"I'm sorry, but I'm getting tired," he said, his smile waned. "Please tell me how the jump went? Was the mission completed?"

"We don't know," Jen said.

"As far as I know, you completed your mission," Dr. Bell said, "and whatever it was—I guess it was a doozy—because it knocked you on your ass."

Keith grinned. "It sure did." He shook his head. "It sure did."

Keith let go a hearty full belly chuckle. Everyone else laughed with him. He was alive, and that was all that mattered. Anything else was extra. He knew it wasn't over yet, because he was alive.

The crash made him more determined than ever to find out what the hell was going on. Why did someone want him dead? He looked at his friends, and the broad smile never left his face. "When's the next jump?" He laughed. "I won't let this minor setback stop the project. Hell no! Let's do this."

They shook their heads in disbelief.

26

Temporary Shutdown

Keith stayed in the hospital for 10 days. During his hospitalization, they poked and prodded him—a whirlwind of MRIs, blood tests, and cardio, this and that. He understood the tests were necessary, but he didn't have the heart to tell his friends that someone in the Complex wanted him dead. It had to be someone with access, but he didn't know who or why.

He also understood when he got back to the lab they would do more tests and probably put new procedures in place. Though this is what Keith expected, it was not at all what happened. Instead, the four found themselves in front of the Board of Directors being grilled about the incident.

"The mission at least was a partial success," Dir. Harrington said. "I believe I speak for the others as well; I'm glad to see Keith pulled through it with flying colors. However, the risks are getting out of control."

Keith shook his head as Director Harrington droned on. He had a feeling he knew where the speech was going. Whatever the real plan had been, Keith believed they accomplished it. The bureaucratic ass holes in front of him were about to pull the plug. He couldn't let it happen. No, not until he found out what the hell was going on. He sounded like a broken record. One that played in a continuous loop. He paid attention again after he heard his name.

"... Keith has done a phenomenal job. However, we suspended operations until further notice. You'll continue to live in the Complex until we decide the future of SCP. Any questions?"

The other members of the board sat stone-faced during the Director Harrington speech. Keith looked at the others: Dr. Bell looked defeated; Billy was absolutely crushed; Jen, however, was too indifferent. None of them seemed like they were going to protest. Keith couldn't help himself.

"Yeah, I have a question or two," he said as he stood up. "The mission was a partial success, you said. Why was it only partially successful?"

"Dir. Harrington looked over to one of the government officials. Not even Dr. Bell knew what the two men's positions were. Mostly because they never spoke during any of the hundreds of meetings he'd had with them. Keith watched Dr. Bell's interest peak as one of them spoke.

"You made the phone call," he said, "but it wasn't recovered for a couple of years or so."

"Oh, then shouldn't we try again. At least one more time. Aren't these missions I've been running for you a matter of national security?"

The two members looked at Director Harrington.

"In short, yes," Dir. Harrington said, "but it doesn't need to be redone."

"Why is that?" Keith said. "Now, I'm really curious. Are you considering it executed?"

"In a matter of speaking, yes," Dir. Harrington said with a pained expression spreading on his face. It contorted his facial features, making him look insidious.

"Well, if that's the case, why are you shutting us down?"

"We're not," Dir. Harrington said. "Well, not entirely. It's only a precaution. The project most likely will be up and running next month."

Keith shook his head. "Three weeks from now."

Dir. Harrington ignored him. "Until we decide the final outcome, everyone on the project must remain at the Complex. Things may change, and we may need to reactivate the program."

Keith nodded as if it satisfied him. Though he was far from being even the slightest satisfied, he sat back in his chair and let the alternate memories come forward. It wasn't something he wanted to do, but he had no choice. He took a breath and slowly exhaled and shut his eyes as pain initially spread through his head before it subsided.

Someone, Jenny, he believed, asked if he was okay. He nodded. He let his mind relax until the first and last realities showed side-by-side within his mind. He looked over at Jen, who was watching him. He didn't know what it meant, but Dir. Harrington had just lied. Reality had changed, and not for the better, and Keith knew what he needed to do. He had to find a way to do it.

27

Mutiny Talks

After the meeting, Dr. Bell was asked to stay behind. There were things they needed to discuss with him. Keith believed more than ever the disk held the answer. He felt bad for the team, especially Billy and Jen. They were the hands-on members of the team—the troubleshooters. Dr. Bell oversaw operations, but it was his theory they confirmed.

Keith believed they would shut the program down for good. Something major was about to happen, and they needed them out of the way.

The Complex became as small as a shoebox. No weekend trips or outside access. He felt he could convince Billy to do a jump on their own so that he could search for the disk.

Jen and Billy were eating lunch at the cafe with Keith. The noise level of the cafe rose to its height as the 12 tables packed with bodies. The three of them sat at a roundtable that afforded them to be alone.

He'd noticed early on that none of the other departments talked to them. Some did speak to him while he was in the gym, but nobody talked shop with him.

Billy stared at his food like a little kid pouting they wanted chicken nuggets. Jen tried to cheer them up by talking about anything but the project and its temporary shutdown.

He couldn't hold back any longer. "You know they're going to screw us, right?"

Jen looked at him. "How did you come up with that?" she said, ever optimistic. "What do you think they're going to do, huh?"

He didn't know if they were gonna do anything, but his instincts told him something wasn't quite right. He trusted his instincts. "I don't know, but I bet they won't let you leave the Complex. Something *is* going on. I don't know about you, but we should better be prepared for the worst."

Billy played with his food. He seemed nervous. Keith figured he just didn't like the conversation. Jen, on the other hand, took it in stride.

"That's just the con—"

"Convict!" Keith said. "The convict in me. No, it's not. The *convict* in me would just sit back and see what happens. That's because things that seem too good to be true—are usually not good at all."

"I meant nothing by it."

"Why would you say something like that?" Billy said.

Keith and Jen looked at him in surprise. Billy usually remained silent no matter the debate.

"Because I can be a bitch, sometimes," Jen said. "I just don't see it. Billy, you've been here as long as I have. Do you really think that they're not only going to shut us down but, as Keith put it in-screw us?"

"They're the government," Billy said in a matter-of-fact tone. "Besides, they already lied to us. Hell, they've been lying to us the entire time. They haven't come out and exactly spelled it out—but the writing is on the wall. This is and always was a military-based program."

"Only in part," Jen said. "What about the other members of the board?"

"Open your eyes," Billy said as he shook his head and looked around the cafeteria. "I became nervous when I found out the board had military people and a White House liaison. It struck me as odd. So, I guess my answer is yes. They will do something to screw us."

Jen was shocked but not surprised. She always believed Dir. Harrington held back information, but nothing nefarious. She even believed that there was a military application to the project, but the difference was unlike Billy, she would've still signed up. "Still, I don't believe they'll hold us, prisoner."

"They might not call us that," Keith said. "No, maybe they'll create some kind of reason that would keep us here locked in. I'm already restricted, but I bet you guys are now."

"Like what?" Jen said, still perturbed.

It was Billy who spoke up. "Something like 'due to changes caused by the last jump...certain complications could arise over the next few weeks, so until further notice all personnel will be confined to the Complex.'"

Keith smiled. "That's good. Probably true as well."

"I'm still not buying it," Jen said, thinking what if she was wrong. "Suppose you're right and there is some kind of, I don't know, conspiracy going on. What do you think we could change things or something?"

"I think we could blow it entirely out of the water," he said with a wide grin.

"How?" Billy said.

He looked at Billy, studied his expression and body language. Billy was down and ready to go. Jen wavered, and she was still on the fence. She's gonna need a little more convincing. "A jump."

"Jumps are suspended," Jen said.

"No kidding," Billy said before he nodded to Keith, "continue. I'm interested."

"The jump before last. I never completed the mission," he said, pushing his plate to the side. "In fact, I hid the disk but didn't know where I put it or what was on it. They pulled me back at the exact time I hid it. The director ordered you guys to pull me back at the same time I was hiding the disk, but I never got punished for it. They never brought it up. Doesn't that sound suspicious to you?"

"No, we can't do that," Jen said. "they could consider it an act of treason."

"How do we know that's not what I been doing," he said. "Who's the president?"

They stared at him, puzzled by the sudden question.

"Well?"

"I don't see—"

"Gerard Bushman," Billy said.

"What if I told you when I started the program, the president was a black man named Barack Obama?"

"Yeah, right," Billy said, a bit skeptical. "No way this country would've elected a black man."

"Yeah, I like to think it's possible," Jen said, "but I'm with Billy."

"Well, it's true, but that isn't the half of it. Every time I go back, this reality changes. You know I retain my original memories and the knowledge that comes with them. In other words, right now, I've got two dozen or more realities floating around inside my head. I never gave too much detail because I was afraid they'd take out of the program. But I know which are real and what the jump changed."

"I think you need to see Dr. Young," Jen said. "You might be having a psychotic break. If this is true, then why haven't you told any of us."

"Wow, you really don't listen," he said. "I just told you I was afraid of being taken out of the program, so I skirted around the issues that I was experiencing."

Billy took charge. "Tell us what you have in mind, and we'll decide."

"You send me back to the same time as the jump from two days ago. I will retrieve the disk from where I believe I hid it, but we need to be careful because they tried to kill me during the last jump."

"Oh, come on," Jen said, exasperated. "Now someone's trying to kill you. Are you sure you not a little paranoid?"

"Maybe I am," he said, "but, I'll tell you what...let's give it a few days. If nothing strange happens, I'll drop it, all right?"

"Okay," Jen said reluctantly.

"Whatever you want, Keith, I'm down," Billy said. "And I'm sure I can speak for the other techs as well. Either way, just give me the word."

"All right then," he said and stood up. "Let's get out of here."

Keith went back to his quarters and just hoped the board of directors showed their true colors. Unless they did, he wouldn't get Jen on board. He needed her. A jump would still be possible if Billy got the chamber techs on board, but there were too many variables.

Keith knew the plan brought serious risk. He'd never jumped back to the same day. Keith wasn't sure of the mechanics of such a jump. Though Jen told him that the same matter could not exist within the same time period, he believed that was different. Felt it in his bones different. Identical twins shared the same matter through their DNA.

He turned on his radio and lay on his bed. There's nothing else to do except wait-and-see. He just hoped he wouldn't have to wait too long.

28

They Didn't Disappoint: Jump Time

The next morning Keith headed to the gym. For him, nothing had changed, except not being able to jump. They were more people in the hallways—a lot more than usual. A small smile formed on his face. The folks he passed didn't look too pleased. He made it to the elevator and waited for a down car. On the quick trip down, he heard a couple of guys, in a uniform, he never seen, talk about some emergency.

Although Keith curiously piqued up at the word emergency, he wondered if there was another way to the surface. The elevator bank on the other side of the checkpoint was the only way out that he knew. To go floor to floor, one had to tap their ID, which acted as a tap card. He got off the elevator and made his way to the gym.

He came to the end of the corridor and turned left. More disgruntled people passed him. They built the complex to disorientate. Though you came down from the surface, he entered the complex from its first floor. It was a bit disorientating. The gym was just down the hall from the guard station. The only way out. A crowd formed outside the guard station and exit.

Keith stopped a woman walking towards him. "Excuse me," he said, motioning to the crowd. "What's going on?"

"Oh, nothing really," she said with a smile. "Upstairs had a fire, so we're not allowed to leave. Dr. Bell is going to make a formal announcement at 10 o'clock. It's not the first time. It's happened before."

He couldn't remember any fire. "I'm sorry, I don't recall the fire? When was that?"

"Oh, I don't know," the woman said, "about a year ago."

"Thanks, he said. The woman smiled and walked off.

Keith walked towards the crowd, which started to break up. He saw Billy first, who had a smile plastered on his face. Jen's face appeared next to him in the crowd. She didn't look too happy. Billy must've spotted Keith because he turned to Jen and pulled her towards Keith, pointing.

"All right, I believe you," Jen said, as they approached Keith, "come on."

"Where are we going?" Keith said, a bit confused.

"To get the chamber techs," she said as they walked. "This is probably the best time to do it. If we're gonna do it at all. You need to make this jump before I lose my nerve."

"I'm ready to go."

Several minutes 1 later, they found the two techs. It didn't take much convincing to get them on board. With the team ready, they went to the lab.

Jen used her computer to calculate the amount of CTE compound Keith needed for the trip. After they strapped Keith into the chair, loaded the CTE into cartridges, and brought it to the cleanroom where Keith sat in the chair. The tech took the Cartridges and loaded them into guns—they waited for Jen's order.

"All right, Keith," she said through the speaker. "You know the consequences involved in this jump. Are you sure you're ready to do this?"

"As I'll ever be," he said, shutting his eyes.

Jen looked over at Billy. "How's he doing?"

"He's good here. Vitals normal."

She looked at techs in the chamber. "It's a go. On my mark."

She watched her screen and waited for the red box to turn green. "Go."

A textbook jump.

If the project still operated when he got back, she'd be surprised.

"Good luck," Jen said into the microphone. She looked over at Billy, who looked nervous. "How long did you set the pullback clock?"

"He has eight hours to complete the mission."

"Hope that's enough," Jen said.

"Me too," Billy said.

29

The Bounce

Keith had known something had gone wrong long before he opened his eyes. His head hurt, and he felt like he'd just been bounced around the universe. When he opened his eyes, the room and the squishy feeling that was time during a jump felt off. He glanced around his bedroom. The same room he jumped to before, but something was different about it. He couldn't place the difference. *It would soon come to him.*

Slowly, he sat up in bed while searching for the clock. He found it on the nightstand next to the bed, covered by a martial art magazine. Keith couldn't suppress a smile, as he remembered his teenage years when he immersed himself in such things. He moved the Ninja Magazine—and jump back. Surprised to see the digital clock read 8:02 AM.

Instincts told him he was in the right place, but he didn't know if he was at the right time. He lived in that apartment for several years. The longest he lived in any one place besides prison. He left the bed and padded over to the mirror attached to one of the dressers in the room. The teenage face that stared back at him was the one he expected to see.

The time concerned him because he never woke up at any other time except 6:15 AM. However, his head hurt, so that he could've lain there since the correct time. He kept his eyes closed for a few moments, but who's to say those few moments weren't two hours. He had no way of knowing for sure. Then, to add to his concerns, he realized his memories of this time period never came forward. During the other jumps, it took no more than 30 minutes for his memory to clear.

Keith headed back to bed and got under the covers. He had a good idea of what could've happened. They tried to send him back to the same time, so maybe time bounced him to the nearest available time. It appeared the hypothesis about occupying the same space was true, even for him.

Frustrated, he lay with the pillow over his eyes. He thought about the mission and realized he didn't know the date. He sought out the calendar and saw his worst nightmare. The bounce had put him five days before he had the disk.

Since he couldn't jump to where he was, he figured he'd be pulled out within the next few hours. He didn't remember them telling him how long he had for the jump. However, he didn't know if it was the pain in his head or if they had forgotten to tell him.

Keith had an indeterminate amount of time to find a way to get his future self on the disk, but he to find it. The only way he thought of was the dream logs, but he saw nothing in them. Not really. He still had the belief that there was something there.

It was summer, so he didn't have to worry about going to school. An hour later, just after he got out of the shower, his friends came over to hang out. He got dressed and played PS2 in the living room. His mom had already gone to work. They ate breakfast together, but they didn't really talk—a normal day during his teenage years. Keith's enhanced memory finally kicked in, which was a good thing since his friends had come over.

He would now know what not to say. More to the point, he'd know what he was supposed to say. He saw the consequences of that already. It was weird knowing the word you were going to say, especially if the words were wrong. The advice was terrible.

He took one last look in the mirror. "Smooth as ever," he said with a little chuckle before going to the living room. His boys were no longer playing PS2. Instead, they were watching TV. BET, to be exact.

"Bout time?" Adam said. "Chicks take less time than you, damn."

"Look at you. Pretty as ever," Sean said and then winked.

"So, what you clowns' want to do?" he said. "Because I just feel like chilling."

"That's cool," Sean said.

Adam put his feet on the ottoman. His way of saying it was cool.

Keith found it a little nerve-racking, but it was his main source of information. It allowed him to figure out what to do. He would know what everyone in the room was going to say as long as he experienced it before. When he altered things, that's when he would be on his own until he got back on the path that reconnected his heightened memory.

When he said something different, he'd feel disorientated. Not every time, but enough to know better. The memories were there but unavailable. Denied access. He had to get back on track to regain access.

Adam started clicking through channels until he stopped on a local news station. Keith knew everything that was going to come on the screen. A breaking-news story.

As soon as the thought hit his brain, it appeared on the screen. It gave Keith an idea. He played the state lottery quite a bit: scratch tickets, the games with the big winners. If he had a bit of extra cash, he'd play something. He reached into his pocket and pulled out a five and a twenty-dollar bill. Now, he had to make it all work.

30

Joey and the Disk

Keith's eyes went wide as his memories played catch up. The download was quick and lucky for him, painless. After the images passed in his head became less groggy, he tried to look around. Always white. It took him a few seconds to realize that a sheet covered him. He didn't expect it to be there. He chuckled. The restraints were loose, and he easily escaped them.

He pulled the sheet off himself. The chamber was dark, but the lab was brightly lit. An attempt, he figured, hiding him.

There was nobody at the controls. It was just him. The place remained on lockdown, so in the back of his mind, he expected they would be there when he woke. Movement caught his eye. He removed the leg straps and quickly stood up. He could easily see into the lab.

He looked into the brightly lit lab. Jen, Billy, and the two techs kneeled on the floor. Dir. Harrington stood in front of them and appeared to be yelling at the top of his lungs. The glass petition stopped all sound.

Several men in black military uniforms stood around his friends. Two more armed men guarded the exit. The door opened, and Dr. Bell entered, looked at his team, and continued to Director Harrington. The two men stood there yelling at each other. Keith wished he could hear, but he stayed quiet despite knowing they couldn't hear him. He wanted nothing to give away his position.

Not sure what he should do, he walked back to the chair and sat down. As he did so, he noticed a loaded injection gun. He picked it up and turned it in his hands before he looked for the other one. The other one was also ready. *Why were they ready?*

Any minute, Dir. Harrington's men would search the lab for him. *Fuck it.* It's better they find him asleep. He grabbed the two guns. One in each hand then injected himself in each arm. He placed the guns down and leaned back before shutting his eyes, letting himself fall backwards through time.

Keith sat right up and looked at the clock: 6:15 AM. The calendar now hung on the mirror. As he looked at it, he smiled. It was the day after he hid the disk. He waited for his memory to come into focus.

An hour later, Keith walked over to the calendar and ripped it off the mirror. Taped to its back was the disk. With the disk in his hand, he went across the hall to his neighbor's house. The kid that lived there was named Joey, and he had a computer. He knocked on the door. The kid answered.

"Hey Keith," Joey said, smiling. "Wanna play video games on my computer?"

"No, but I need a favor," he said. "I need to find out what's on this disk. Can you find out for me?"

"If it's not password-protected," Joey said. "Come on in."

He followed Joey into his room. The kid was the neatest boy he'd ever met. He didn't like hanging out with the kid too much because he thought Joey was too much of a nerd and wanted no part of that. He laughed at the memories. Keith was about making money and having fun doing it, but the joke was on him. Joey grew up to be one of the richest men in the world. After developing a unique networking website, Joey became a multibillionaire.

Joey booted up his computer and inserted the disk. A few seconds later, after the computer made some chirping and beeping sounds, he looked up at Keith, who stood behind the kid watching the screen.

"It's got a password?"

"Can you still get access to it?"

Joey smirked. "It might take me some time, but I think I can."

"All right and try. I really need to know what's on this disc."

"I'll do my best."

He walked to the bed to sit down, but suddenly got dizzy. The room spun. *Time's up*, he thought. He tried to fight it off as he headed back to his apartment. "Hey Joey, I'm not feeling well," he said. "Do me a favor. Once you open it, hide it for me. I'll be back."

Joey mumbled something under his breath, but he didn't understand. He just made it back to his apartment before he collapsed onto the bed as they pulled him back.

31

Under House Arrest

Before he became fully conscious, Keith still felt his body being dragged and moved. He opened his eyes as the download took place. Two guards half-carried him off. He eventually put him in the chair and pushed him to his quarters. Keith shut his eyes for a moment, and when he opened them, he was in his bed. He got up and went to the door and tried the knob. Locked.

He walked over to the desk to read his dream journals. He looked through them but paid attention only to the ones with no dates. Nothing. No entry. He picked up the jump journals and found something interesting. He found a passage with no date. It simply said: JOEY in all caps. How was he supposed to get to Joey now? He knew Joey had an office somewhere around the same area the complex was located. It was in Boston, and it was close to downtown. *Could it be in this very building?*

He stared into space as he tried to come up with some kind of plan. He needed to find Joey—could he really still have the disk after all these years? He hoped.

The door opened, which pulled Keith from his thoughts. Keith sat up as two guards with machine guns entered with Dir. Harrington.

"Ah, good to see you're awake," Dir. Harrington said. "I'm sorry for all the security, but it's for your own good. You see, you were being duped into a treasonous act by Jen and Billy." Keith protested, but Dir. Harrington held out his hand. "I know it's hard to believe. I couldn't believe it myself. Now, they tell me you didn't know what was going on. I'm not so confident that I believe them, but I just need to know where they sent you back. What was the mission?"

"Mission," he said, surprised. "There was no mission. They sent me back because I asked him to do it. Something isn't right. I hid something, but I have no memory of what it was or where I put the damn thing. History changed because of it. Do you know what's going on? You ordered them to pull me outright when I went to hide it."

"No, Keith, I'm not sure what you're talking about," Dir. Harrington said. "Um, maybe you're confused. The jumps can do that, right? However, I agree with you. Something is amiss here, and I'll find out what it is. But I know nothing about a disk you supposedly hid—and you don't know where it is?"

Keith had to suppress a smile; he never mentioned the something was a disk. Give someone enough rope, and they'll hang themselves every time. Guaranteed.

"No, I lost it," Keith said, feigning disappointment.

"That's too bad," Dir. Harrington said. "Now, so you know, Keith. No more jumps. The program is suspended for the next month, all right?"

"I understand."

The director went to leave and turned back. "One more thing, you're confined to your quarters, so don't try to leave."

"No problem," he said with a small smile. "I'm used to prison, remember?"

The director shook his head and left.

Now, how does one get out of a top-secret government facility located under an office building in the middle of Boston?

32

Joe Co.

Confined to his quarters, Keith racked his brain, trying to come up with a way to escape. No luck. He sat in his swivel desk chair with his eyes shut and spun in slow circles. The problem had to be solvable, but how?

On the checklist of things he needed to do, figuring out the location of Joey's office sat at the top. *The Internet*. He spun 180 degrees and went over to his bed to grab his laptop. He set it on his desk and plopped back into the chair. It had a low battery, so he plugged it into an outlet. *Time to get to work.*

Keith had been locked up long enough to forget that everything could be found on the internet in today's society. He typed Joseph Cohen in the search bar and got a million hits. Joey became a billionaire, so going that route would be nothing but a nightmare.

He tried Joe Co, and the company's website came up at the top. Joseph Cohen had been at the top of technological advancements for well over a decade. Keith found the address under the contact info.

Keith entered the address into Google and images of a five-story glass and steel structure displayed on the screen. There were lots of pics of the building.

The building couldn't have been any more familiar, considering they trapped him underneath it. He wondered if Joey had something to do with the program. Not one to believe in coincidences. He hoped not.

He figured using the cell phone they gave him for his weekend trips either wouldn't work or was just a plain bad idea; he searched for free Internet phone service. He found one and waited while it downloaded.

The phone connected on the third ring, and an operator answered the phone. He asked to speak to Joseph Cohen; the operator patched him through to his office.

Joey's secretary asked if Mr. Cohen expected a call from him today. He told her no but insisted Joey would take the call.

With a bit of reluctance, the secretary disappeared and came back a few moments later. "I'll patch you through now."

"Keith, is that really you?" He said, surprised. "I thought you were locked up or something. Wow, I didn't expect to hear from you."

"I didn't expect to call," he said. "but away...do you remember...when we were kids, and I gave you a disk. By any chance, do you still have it?"

"In short, yes, I know where it is," Joey said. "In my safe, where you told me to keep it."

"I told you to keep it," he said, more to himself. "When was this?"

"After I showed you what it contained," he said, confused. "Are you all right?"

"No, not really," he said. "My head's in a fog. I don't remember a lot of things lately."

"Do you need it?" Joseph said. "Because if you do, why don't you come over and get it. You know where the office is."

"I do?" Keith glanced up to the ceiling as if he was trying to penetrate tons of concrete to see up into Joey's office with his vision. "Sorry, Joey, I really don't remember."

"Keith, you're worrying me," he said. "Of course, you know where, shit, you were just here a couple of weeks ago."

"But you just asked if I was still locked up?"

"Because you said you were kind of," he said. "You said they let you out, so you could be part of a rehabilitation program."

"Well, you see, that's why I need your help?"

"Of course, whatever you need," Joey said. "You know I'll help. Hell, you're my partner, aren't you?"

Keith found it hard to believe what Joey just said. His partner? What did he mean? Business partner perhaps, or was it a remark from them being friends as kids? Keith didn't know.

Keith did the calculation and figured he could have jumped back to one of his vacations. He was in real-time, and he'd gone to bed early one night. It had to be when he went back, but from what time in the future? He had trouble with a few things. He had no recollection of the disk's contents or telling Joey where to hide it; it appeared he would be very busy in the future. He also knew that at some point, he found a way out of the complex. Something as complex as the things he's about to do would comprise many jumps. It encouraged him. Boosting his confidence.

"I have a question for you," he said. "How long have you been at that address?"

"Keith, I'm really stunned and believe you need to see a doctor," Joey said, sounding concerned. "We rented the space together about 10 years ago. It was right before you disappeared off the face of the earth. Though that wasn't unusual to me. You've done that ever since we were kids—it was weeks before you asked about the disk after you gave it to me. I even asked you if you wanted to see what I found on the disk because I was so excited, but you looked confused and told me you didn't want to see what was on the disk—and then a few days later, you came by wanting to see what was on it. My entire life, you've been a confusing dude, but you been good to me, and we're partners."

"What's on the disk?"

"You know what's on it," Joey said. "And it was you that suggested we keep it for ourselves. Protect it. Hell, it's half the reason why I give half of my profits away every year. Besides, you know I'd say nothing over the phone. You need to come here if you want to discuss this."

"I can't."

"Keith, what's going on?" he said. "What aren't you telling me?"

"Remember the experiment I told you about?"

"The reason why you're out."

"Yes," he said. "Well, I'm not out. I am in an underground complex. The project went wrong somehow. I'm not sure what happened, but they shut down the project and confined us to our quarters."

"What?" Joey said, not sure whether to believe him. "I thought it was some kind of project to give you a second chance. A form of rehabilitation."

"I lied," he said. "I'm not allowed to talk about the project or its true purpose. Besides, you wouldn't believe me if I told you."

"Try me, forget all that. Where are you? Do you even know?"

"I know where I am, but you won't believe that either. I have one other question for you."

"Why did you pick your office space in that building?"

"I didn't pick the space, dammit," Joey said beyond frustrated. "You did. Not only did you tell me about the space, but you suggested I buy it when it went on the market."

"Why would you do what I suggested?"

"I can't take much more of this, Keith," he said, tapping something loudly on his desk. "You going crazy or something. You're my silent business partner. You're the one that gave me the money to start Joe Co. Technologies. Whatever they're doing to you has fried brain. Where are you?"

"Thanks, Joey, that explains a lot," he said, trying to sound as calm as possible. "As to where I am, about nine stories below you," he said. "I'm in a secret government installation that is called the Complex."

"You're underneath the building?" Joey said in disbelief. "How many people are in this Complex?"

"A few hundred, but I really don't know. At least on the levels the project is on, but there's three levels on this one— and there may be more.

"Our company occupies most of this building. There are only a few tenants. Would I not have noticed people coming and going?"

"No," he said. "Most live here. Besides, the entrance to the Complex is located inside the Sleep Study offices. Random people come and go all the time. It's their cover."

"This is crazy!" Joey said. "It's hard to believe."

"So, you don't believe me?"

"No...I didn't say that," Joey said. "After seeing the technology on that disk, I would believe anything, especially if you were the one telling me."

Static crossed the line.

"Find me a way out," he said. "I'm losing you."

Keith looked at the screen of his laptop. A flashing red block appeared. UNAUTHORIZED USER. The line went dead, and the computer went black. Keith stared at his reflection in the black screen.

He quickly removed the headset and stuffed it inside a drawer. Within less than a minute, his door jerked open, and two guards stepped inside.

Dir. Harrington just behind them. "Give me your laptop? There is no outside communication while we're in lockdown."

He picked up his laptop and handed it to the director.

"Your cell phone as well?"

He handed it to him. "I was only surfing the web," he said, shrugging his shoulders. "Shit, I was bored. Even in prison, we get rec-time."

"It's not a problem," the director said. "I should've removed it when you were brought back here. Did you talk to anyone?"

"No, I was just searching porn sites," he said with a smile. "I've been locked up for a while, you know."

The director shook his head and left with the guards. Keith was confident the two guards were still outside his door. *Now what?*

33

Mystery Code

After being confined for three days, Keith's quarters had become cluttered with notes, leftovers from the meals they brought him, and a stench that could only be described as shower time.

He figured they got tired of bringing him his food and smelling the rancid odor that found its way to the other side of the door. Smell so bad that the hallway outside smelled just like—well, like him.

Upstairs decided to let him out. He had access to the cafeteria, which would not be appropriate until he showered.

The three days of confinement consisted of him moving from desk chair to bed and back again. He spent more time in the chair than he did in his bed, which resulted in very little sleep. He thought long and hard over his problem and came to a conclusion.

The answer should've been obvious to him the moment he talked to Joey. Though obvious, at least to him, it wasn't. Not at all. It should have been. However, Keith resorted to his default process—use violence to escape. Not very practical in a locked facility several stories underground, so he pushed on and thought of other possibilities. He had to use his head and not his fists—what he needed to do but couldn't was jump.

How? They had already admonished him. He had no access to the lab or any other place besides the cafeteria and showers.

If there were some way he could get the guns preloaded with the correct amount of CTE compound, he'd be able to jump from his quarters. If he was only prepared for the situation, he could've stashed two guns preloaded with the compound.

He shook his head and smiled. The thought jumped into his head as quickly as a jump to the past. Joey had told him when he jumps to the past, so he knows he does it and when.

The jump would have to be under orders from the director because he restricted Keith from the lab. They said if he went to the lab, they would send him back to prison ASAP.

Keith was sure it wouldn't be the same prison he left, probably not one on any map. He thought about all these things as he strolled back from the cafeteria to his quarters. He showered and then went to get something to eat for breakfast.

The director sending him back on a mission or trip back in time seemed improbable. Why would he do such a thing? Keith wondered if there was another way. One yet to have crossed his mind.

No matter how he got there, Keith would have to assume he hid things he needed. He walked back to his quarters with a little more pep in the step.

Inside his cell quarters, he lay on his bed. Exhaustion took over every cell in his body. He shut down. He lay there for few moments, perhaps even hours. He looked at the clock: 11:30 AM. Lunch would be 30 minutes. With no reason he could think of, he got out of bed, moved away from the wall, and pushed on one end of the metal panel that was partially hidden by his bed. Nothing. Frustrated, he kicked it, and the panel popped open with a sealed hiss.

The space behind the panel, which was a vent of some kind, had been sealed up. Keith figured it was for his account, so he wouldn't be tempted to escape. At that moment, he still wasn't tempted. A foot into the shaft sat a box. He reached into the space and pulled it out.

The contents of the box held no surprise. An ejection gun and three sets of cartridges. They labeled each pair of cartridges with a number and a year. He loaded the ones marked with a number one. There also was a handgun inside the box, but he left that there and put the box back into its hiding space. After he pushed the bed back against the wall, he lay down and put the gun under his pillow, deciding it would be safer to jump at night.

The hours ticked by in slow motion. He tried to watch TV, but nothing could distract him from the countdown. He skipped lunch but ate dinner. In the cafeteria, he saw no one from his team. The restrictions weren't just limited to where he could go but to whom they allowed him to have contact.

8:00 PM came around, and he decided there was no time like the present. He normally would go to sleep around 10 PM, but he'd been up for three days. He was sure the guards outside knew he'd been up for three days and would not be surprised to find him asleep early as a result.

He checked off everything on his mental checklist and went over the plan several times in his mind. He even pictured removing the cartridge and loading the other.

The gun was cold in his hand. Keith was sure he could do it, so he took a deep breath. Loaded the cartridge. He injected himself in the right arm. He removed the cartridge and inserted the other. He pressed it to his left arm and squeezed the trigger. As he did so, he had an overwhelming feeling he forgot something. Keith barely had enough time to stash the gun and empty cartridges under his pillow before his head crashed on top of it—on his way. *Jump time.*

•

Keith opened his eyes and looked around and saw he was 16-years-old again. He looked at the clock and saw the familiar 6:15 AM appeared in a bright greenish light.

He took a shower, then got dressed before going across the hall to Joey's house. By the time he knocked on the door, it was 8 AM. Joey answered the door. Keith could tell he'd been awake all night. "Don't you ever sleep?"

"Not lately," he said. "What do you want?"

"To see what's on the disk, what else," he said, pushing past Joey entering the apartment. "And before you say anything, I'm sorry flaked on you the other day. I almost forgot about the disk, for real. Like I never knew it existed at all. What did you find? Anything good?"

"What do you think's been keeping me awake," Joey said with a big cheese smile. "It's amazing. The disk contains lines of code—of which I have never seen. There's nothing like it anywhere. I wrote down a piece of it and brought it to this guy I know. He has never seen it before either."

"Code?" He said a bit puzzled. "Source code cryptography?"

Joey cracked a smile. "Well, it's not cryptography, but they encrypted it. But I got around that in a week. I believe the information on this disk is an advanced alphabet for a new computer language or program, but I can't be totally sure."

When they entered the room, an icon flashed and spun on the computer screen. A huge Bald Eagle in front of a clock face appeared in the center. The logo for the project. He had only seen it on the computer screen and nowhere else at the Complex.

"...I could get a small portion of it to play."

"I've seen that symbol before."

Joey stared at him for a moment. "Yeah, that was all I could get so far because the info or rather program is too large. We need hundreds of megabytes to run this program. It won't open."

"So...does this mean you can't open it?"

He shrugged his shoulders. "I'll give it my best shot, but I have to build a computer with a lot more speed and storage space that doesn't exist. I'll check some newsgroups to see if anything already exists that is close."

Joey pressed a button on his computer, and the printer started printing. Reams and reams of paper stacked up next to the computer.

"What's that, Joey?"

"Stack of paper represents code written out; you can see how big it is."

"I assume that's a lot for a program."

"Considering that is maybe one percent of the program, I believe it's a lot."

"That's a lot for this, then, right?"

"I think this is a new type of program. I've seen nothing so big. If I can figure out the code enough to understand it, I may be able to modify my computer to get it to work."

"All right, I'll let you get back to work, but before I go," he said with a long pause, "we need to keep this to ourselves. Careful who you ask about anything, okay? And don't come asking me about the program anymore in front of my friends. I'll come to you when I need to know something about it, okay?"

"Yeah, I guess," Joey said. "You just don't want your friends to know you're smart. I get it."

"No, it's not that."

"It must be me then," Joey said, looking a little defeated. "Look, I know I'm a nerd, but hell, who cares."

Keith smiled. "You got me. Being smart and cool, so you keep my secret?"

"Of course, I'll keep your secret. Why wouldn't I?"

"Never thought you wouldn't, still had to ask," he said, heading for the door.

"Hey, there's one more thing though I'll need?"

"What's that?"

"I'm gonna need some money to buy parts to build a new computer."

"Can we upgrade that one?"

"I don't see that happening, so money to build a new computer from scratch would help."

"Okay, that's where I'm going," Keith said, "don't worry, Joey, I got you. We're partners from here on out."

34

The Lottery

By one in the afternoon, Keith was in tune, which meant full control over the day's memories. Ever since Keith was a young boy, he watched the numbers drawing and bought scratch tickets. He purchased at least one scratch ticket every day. His reasoning was he would waste the dollar, anyway.

Adam and Jimmy sat on his floor playing video games. He checked his pockets and found a $10 bill. He always hustled money one way or the other. He knew; however, the $10 bill came from someone who owed him money for weed.

"Come on, you all," he said as he stood up. "Let's go to the store."

"Sounds good to me," Jimmy said.

"Yeah, screw it," Adam said, putting the controller down. "This game's wack anyhow."

"So ain't you," he said, shutting the PlayStation off, "but nobody's complaining about that, now are they?"

Adam mumbled something under his breath and pushed Keith as he left. Keith just smiled. He had to wait for the memory to tell him what was gonna happen and how to respond, or he'd talk like the way he did in his present time.

The heightened memory served him well—and off to the store they went.

Though his speech pattern wasn't entirely perfect, he didn't speak with the same idioms and slang as he did as a kid. College taught him to transcend words and speech and project what you wanted people to see about you. He saw this with the old-school cats while he was locked up. Though many of them had very little education, they spoke with finesse and articulated their words in a manner that made the listener feel at ease. Well, he had no doubt that these guys were very good con artists back in the day. They cared about what they said and how they said it. Everything was measured.

Keith and his friends clowned around the entire five-minute walk to the store. They pushed and shoved each other. Called each other names and rank on each other's clothing. The good old days. When they got to the store, he asked if they had any money. Adam stared at him blankly.

"I got five bucks," Jimmy said.

"You do," he said, as he and Adam looked at him in shock. "Who'd you steal that from?"

"My mom's boyfriend," Jimmy said. "You all know my mom ain't giving me no money, that's for sure."

He smiled and shook his head as he entered into the store.

"Hey Adam, get us something to drink...and junk food," Keith called as he walked up to the counter and started talking to the clerk.

While they went off to get snacks and stuff, Keith got down to business. It was time to exploit his daily habit.

"What do you need, Keith?" The clerk named Cathy said.

"Anyone win anything lately?" he said, leaning on the counter.

Cathy rattled off which ones won that day and the day before. She even told him which book it was from and the number of the ticket.

As he was going through what seemed like the normal routine, his mind was doing things that were far from normal. He searched his memory and look for a ticket. The winning ticket for that day. He found it. No, there were two winning tickets—one for $500 and another for $800.

Kathy was still talking to him when he regained focus back on the conversation as she finished. "So, what do you want, honey?"

"What's the number on the dice game," he said, pointing to the card. "And the one next to it?"

She told him. "I'll take five of the dice game," he said. "I don't like the number on that one, but I want that game?"

"What number you want?"

The other game was about 20 cards away from the winner. Even with the $500 he was already set to win, he still didn't want to spend 24 extra dollars he didn't have to spend. "175, but it's too many cards away, C—"

"Don't worry about it," Kathy said, ripping the 25 cards off the roll. "Here you go, honey. Good luck!"

Adam and Jimmy came up to the counter and set the items next to Keith as he scratched the first two tickets—both loses.

"You ain't gonna win nothing on them things," Adam said.

"You never know, cuz," Jimmy said. "My mom won two thousand dollars before."

"And she probably smoked that shit up to?" Adam said, clowning.

"Now, we're not talking about your mama, now we?" Jimmy said, pleased with his comeback.

Keith scratched the third one and was surprised when it showed he hit $100. "Well, I just got a hundred, so there you go, Adam."

"See, Adam," Jimmy said, "just never know."

Keith scratched another loser, then hit again. "Oh, shit, I just hit for $500."

"Yeah, right," Adam said in disbelief.

"Look," Keith said, tossing it on the counter with the other hundred-dollar winner.

The four other customers in the store walked up to the counter to see if Keith's luck would hold out. Keith enjoyed the moment. "I got three matches, but I just need one more," he said, as he scratched faster. "Oh, no way! You all are not gonna believe this shit. I just hit...for...let me see... $800. Can you cash these?"

"Let me see if I have enough money," she said. "If I do, it will be no problem."

The store clerk brought the cards over to the lottery machine and checked her till. "Yeah, I can do it. I just have to double-check these tickets." She did. Then she handed Keith $1400. "You did good, Keith," she said, handing him the cash.

The other patrons congratulated him on his luck, as well. Keith wondered if any of them would believe it wasn't luck at all. Time travel was weird enough for him, and doing it along your timeline could be a little disconcerting at times.

However, it explained all the gaps in his memory as a youth. Those times throughout his life he had full conversations but no memory of it because he was sleepwalking. All of it now had an explanation.

"Thank you," he said, pushing all the groceries towards the register. "I'm paying for all his and—" he looked around at the four other regulars he always saw there scratching tickets. "Their stuff as well, and I ain't taking no for an answer."

"You won't hear no for me," one of them said.

Everyone laughed.

They headed home, goofing off, laughing, and having a great day, as they celebrated Keith's luck. Adam and Jimmy tried to get money off Keith, but he already had it spent. That unexpected hundred-dollar winner, though, allowed him to give his friends $20 apiece. It wasn't much considering how much he'd won, but it made his friends happy, nevertheless.

Back at the house, his friends tried to tell him what he should do with the money. He told him he already had plans for it, and they knew better to push the issue. At 16 years old, Keith already commanded respect from those around him, but he wondered if it was borne more out of fear than anything else.

After Keith's mother came home, he told his friends they had to go. He didn't need to tell them not to mention Keith winning any money because they knew his mom would take most of it, saying something like, "I'll put it up for you because you know you're not good at holding onto money." The problem was Keith would never see it again. Ever. In truth, she wasn't good with money. However, if he brought it up, it would always end up being his fault and lots of deniability.

After his friends left, and the real reason he asked them to leave, he went across the hall to give Joey the money.

"Wow," Joey said. "Where'd you get this, it's...it's...a lot?"

"I won it," he said. "Besides, it's only $1300."

"I'm sorry that's a lot," Joey smiled, "but I'm not complaining. This will buy most of what we need. My mother will give me the rest."

"All right," he said, "it's in your hands now."

Joey didn't even notice Keith leave because he was still too busy counting the money. He glanced back at Joey one more time before we went to the door and shook his head. Joey was in awe of $1300, but later in 7 years would be worth billions. Keith found it humbling and yet ironic.

Bedtime came quick, and it was at that moment he realized he was tired. He hadn't thought about being pulled back one time. He thought once the compound wore off, he'd be pulled back, but that wasn't how it worked. Shit, would he be stuck in the past until they pulled him back?

The stress made him feel dizzy, and the room spun. *Maybe I was wrong.*

35

Doc's In

Keith opened his eyes once the download was complete. Everything was a rush of movement as two armed guards yanked him to his feet and dragged him out of the room. He was already cuffed with his hands behind his back. The crash was slight, and he only felt as though he just woke from a deep sleep. His body and mind getting used to jumps.

Dir. Harrington stood close as he observed Keith. "It seems you were telling the truth, after all," he said as he reviewed a tablet in his hands. "Take him to the interview room." The guards dragged him out into the hallway. "Keith, don't you worry about a thing...believe me...you will talk."

Through the haze of sleepiness, Keith looked up at Dir. Harrington. "I have nothing to talk about, so good luck with that," Keith said with a wide grin. "Besides, as far as I can tell, I'm not the one who has explaining to do. We both know who should be the one talking, don't we?"

"Get him out of here!"

Two more guards appeared. Dir. Harrington ordered them to search the room for anything and to remove all of Keith's belongings. He wanted them brought to his office, so he could personally go through them.

Dr. Bell stepped into the room. He heard the verbal exchange between Keith and the director. He still had his clearance, which enabled him to speak to the five members of his team who were being detained in their quarters. After they stripped his room bare, Keith would be brought back to his quarters. A desk and a bed, but nothing else.

Dr. Bell was also sure they would torture Keith. During the exchange of words, Dr. Bell noticed a cloud of fear pass over the director's face.

The director finally noticed him. "What, Dr. Bell?" He said, contorting his face into a mask of anger. "You got something to say, then say it, doctor?"

"Why so you can lock me up as well, no thank you," he said in a soft, calm tone. "After you dismissed my team the other day, you and the Board of Directors told me there was a likelihood Keith would have to make another jump. What do you think the chance of that would be now, director?"

"We have other options, Dr. Bell," he said, his turn to smile. "There are others whom you're not aware of who can jump. Besides, do you think you were the only game in town? We laid out Keith's missions, and he has done them, so Doctor, he is expendable as well as you and the rest of your team. Be grateful you still have a team—and Keith may still have one more jump yet to make." To his death, the Director thought.

"There're more jump programs?" Dr. Bell asked, shaking his head in disbelief. "I don't believe you. How is that even possible? Unique candidates with the same gene and protein as Keith. You couldn't have used the kid. And please tell me you didn't use the lunatic? That would be insane on your part. Never mind irresponsible."

"Not any less than sending a convicted murderer back, now is it?"

"It's not the same, and you know it."

"It doesn't matter, doctor," Dir. Harrington said. "We've got at least a dozen jumpers. Because of Keith's exploits in the past, we were able to get a sample of Keith's blood and pass it on to a handpicked select few."

"Keith's right, isn't he?" Dr. Bell snapped. "Something was changed...by you."

"No, Dr. Bell, I changed nothing that our president didn't sign off on," Dir. Harrington with a shrug. "And... You don't need to know. Now, if you'll excuse me, I have a prisoner to interrogate." He nodded towards the doctor. "Good day."

The director left, leaving Dr. Bell to shake his head in Keith's soon-to-be empty quarters. He'd been so naïve the whole time. Jen had been right. She never trusted the Board of Directors, especially Dir. Harrington. He watched the men tear apart the room for a moment. *Torn apart like his life right now.*

Dr. Bell went back to his office, shut the door, and locked it. He walked over to his bookshelf, pressed the button hidden on one shelf—a recessed middle shelf slid over, disappearing into the wall behind. In its place was a safe. He opened and removed the entire contents of the safe.

He then retrieved his keys from his pocket and pressed the button on the fob on his keychain. A hidden door in the back of the safe popped up with an audible click. The space was small. Customized to fit the package it contained. A package he wanted to open for many years, but the young man who gave it to him made him promise he wouldn't until it was time. The doctor asked the man when that would be, and he only said, "When you have doubts, doctor. Serious doubt."

The time had come at this very moment. He'd never doubted the program. The directors or anything. He wasn't even sure why he never opened up the package all those years ago. Even after the young man appeared on his doorstep eight years ago, he knew the man at least heard of him. The young man's face had been on the cover of many magazines.

The kid was a billionaire by the time he was 24 years old. A year after he received his master's at MIT. Today Joseph Cohen's name was known worldwide. His company was bigger than Microsoft. It had far fewer legal issues than any of them, including Facebook and Amazon. He somehow knew about the project and told him he was asked to give him a package. One he wouldn't need to open for a long time—he was sure the time had come.

He set the package down on the cadenza. After he decided not to put the stuff back in the safe, he brought the package over to his desk. He sat down in his leather chair and took a deep breath while he stared at the package on his desk. Dr. Bell hoped he was ready for what the envelope contained. He picked it up and removed its contents. It only contained two things: a note and a compact disk, which KAO made. A company that went out of business in the 1990s. Dr. Bell inserted the disk into his computer, picked up the letter, and read it as the program on the disk loaded onto his computer.

Dear Dr. Bell,

I really hope you waited to read this letter because it is very important things happen the way they are supposed to happen, but I suspect you of all people understand that this more than anyone. I am the first successful jumper you find, and my name is Keith. If you waited, you know this to be true.

What you don't know is that a small government fraction has taken over the program at the highest level—the White House. The president himself is calling the shots. When I first jumped, the president was Barack Obama, a black man. Not the man you know as the president of the United States of America. He was one of the original backers of the project. Well, the project is known as SCP. In my reality, not yours.

I'm not sure exactly what is going on here. I'm not even sure if the president isn't just coincidental. At least on that end, but I don't know. One slight change could change the world. You'll find the information on the enclosed disk very interesting. I'm sure you'll know what to do, good luck.

Oh, one more thing. If you're reading this when I think you will be, I will be in one hell of a predicament. Probably being interrogated as you read this. Don't worry about me; I'll be okay. Afterward, this jump occurs when they send me back on a suicide mission—one that will backfire because of you. Thank you in advance. I don't need to remind you to remain calm and check out the disk. Before you do anything all right again, good luck, my good friend.

Your friend,

Keith

As if the computer knew he finished, it beeped, and a box popped up on the screen asking him if he wanted to continue. He clicked on yes as the program ran. Dr. Bell stared at the screen with an awful expression on his face. He'd been around technology for years, and he was even overwhelmed.

Two hours later, after reviewing the entire contents of the disk, he knew what he must do. He removed the disk, unplugged the USB drive, slipped both items back into the envelope, and returned it to the safe. After returning all the items to the safe, he sat back in his chair and checked his computer to make the Complex's security team didn't discover anything. Sure he wasn't compromised; he shut down his computer.

It made him angry to know something of this magnitude happened under his nose, but he had a cure for that—justice.

36

The Good Doctor Does His Part

Keith felt like he was in an awful movie. Besides the bright light shining in his eyes, the room was dark. Shadows moved about beyond the light's perimeter. Though it seemed like many hours had passed, thanks to one of his torturers wearing a wristwatch, he knew an hour and 32 minutes had passed.

They beat him and hit him with things while they asked him questions that made no sense. Questions for which he had no answers. Hard to answer something you didn't know. At about the time he looked at the watch, they switched up tactics. Since the physical didn't sway him too much, they just sat there in silence. Occasionally, they asked him a question or two. But no more. The one constant irritation was the damn light. An ever-present light that shined on his head. Sweat rolled down his cheek. His head felt fuzzy and heavy-a migraine forming scared him more than what they were doing for torture.

They obviously had orders not to beat him up too bad. He had a feeling that he would take another jump, but not one that he would like. They started back up with the torture and added an element—every few minutes, they'd douse him with water.

"One more question," Dir. Harrington said. "Who did you meet? Who approached you during your jumps? Someone must've?"

"No one," he said, as he struggled against the straps that secured his hands to the chair. "Not that I'd tell you fuckers anything, anyway."

The director didn't reply, but along with his men, he left. The darkness amplified the intensity of the light that shined on his sweaty face. With no fear of being doused with water, he closed his eyes. Sleep soon followed. A dreamless...black...sleep.

Something sharp pressed against his skin. He opened his eyes but instantly shut them. Defending himself from the bright assault from the light. Another sharp pain erupted in his other arm. He squinted against the harsh light, trying to see who was there. He heard an unfamiliar voice with a blurry face to match. He heard two people having a conversation that he could not understand. He closed his eyes again as sleep overtook him.

Director Harrington stood over Keith and looked over to the man in the room, who nodded.

"He's on his way then?" Dir. Harrington said. "Back to the year, I asked you to send them to?"

"Yes," the man said, moving into the light. His facial features coming into view. "I sent him back to 1992. I'm not sure why you sent him so far back; he couldn't be any use to you in that year. Not at all."

"Exactly," Dir. Harrington said, "here, he could escape and be a problem, but back in 1992, he's trapped. A prisoner of his past...quite literally. We will keep him there until we can check on what he's confirmed."

"I'm sorry," Dr. Bell said. "I can't believe he some sort of time terrorist."

"He admitted to it," Dir. Harrington said. "So, it's out of my hands now. But I'm sorry I had to tell you that. I know it must hurt. It just goes to show you, Doctor. You should never trust a convict. They'll always try to take more than you give them. If for nothing else, I hope we at least learn that lesson. A criminal is and always will be a criminal. Never to be trusted."

Dr. Bell was proud of himself for keeping a straight face. He couldn't wait for the moment he could tell this pompous asshole where he could go. The man was full of shit. In fact, the only person who could be trusted was the so-called convict strapped down in the chair. Keith will get the last laugh.

Dr. Bell injected Keith with the CTE compound but wished he was awake. Dr. Bell still tried to warn Keith, whispering in his ear about the other jumpers. Though it all made sense to him now, Dr. Bell wished to heaven he'd seen the disk sooner.

He understood it was his own conceit that blinded him from the truth. Once he told him about the disk, the black president, and freaking everything else, he should've listened, but Dr. Bell thought it was a byproduct of the download and crash.

Two guards came into the room pushing a wheelchair. They flop Keith into the chair to take him to his quarters.

"Post guards and check on him every 30 minutes, understood?"

"Yes, Director," one of the guards said with a salute and pushed Keith out of the room.

Dr. Bell and Dir. Harrington walked out of the room. As he left, he stole a glance back at the man who he knew would save the world, literally. A world he never knew. He wondered if he really could set things right, and if he could, what would happen to this world? Would it continue on or simply never exist? He wished his friend good luck.

37

Mother and Son

Keith opened his eyes while he clutched his head and noticed a sheet covered him. He pulled the sheet off his face. His vision…blurry. Head still groggy. The bastards must've beaten the crap out of him. His vision started the clear, but he still could only make out shapes in the darkened room. At least the light was off. The more his head became clear, the more he felt pain in other places sprouting up like vegetation. He closed his eyes and lay absolutely still.

He raised his hands to his face, rubbing his eyes and temples. Migraine? He hoped not—he didn't need to be anymore debilitated. He opened his eyes, and one of his hands came into focus—a small, young-looking hand.

Keith bolted straight up.

He looked around the unfamiliar room as he swung his legs over the side of the bed. His toes just passed the mattress, never-mind touching the floor. He somehow jumped, but how and where was he? Ignoring the clock, he ran to the mirror and looked for the calendar. He also needed to see his face. A habit that formed after waking from a jump.

The way they had decorated the room gave him a clue. However, his reflection told him he wasn't 16. Not even close. The top of the dresser with a mirror attached was covered with all kinds of junk. There had to be one, and he searched until he found it—a calendar. A small one buried under some ninja magazines.

It was opened to the month of June: the year was 2004. Keith was 14 1/2. He was proud of those halves as a kid. Not so much now. He liked it when people thought he looked like he was in his mid-20s, if not younger. Only off by a decade, but it made him feel good. He took care of himself, and it always felt good to hear it paid off.

Confused, he went back to the bed and sat down. What the hell was he supposed to do in the year 2004? It could've been a mistake or something. He tried to figure out the situation, but he had no answers. The last thing he remembered was the freaking bright light and someone whispering. *What was that all about?*

Why was he here? The only question that plagued his mind. He climbed back under the sheets and covered his head. He really didn't feel well. His body ached. He wondered if the pain had anything to do with the beating they gave him. Could that travel back through time with him? Some say pain was as much in the mind as it was physical, but he wasn't so sure.

The more his head became clearer, the more he understood it wasn't from the beating. He felt sick. Nausea welled up in his throat before he pushed it back down. He closed his eyes and fell asleep. An hour later, he woke up and went to the bathroom—a date with the toilet God. He puked more than his body should have been able to contain. He was grateful for the fluids that he must've consumed. *Damn, he hated being sick.*

He repeated the pattern of sleep and toilet, praying about every hour for the rest of the day. Keith's mother came into check on him throughout the day. Around dinnertime, Keith no longer felt nauseous. He remembered what it was on his fourth trip to the bathroom. The heightened memory hadn't yet kicked in, but he knew he had a severe case of food poisoning. He'd been sick for four days. The worst he'd ever been ill until that point.

Shortly after he woke, just after dinner, everything seemed to catch up—the heightened memory of the time period and what happened before the jump. Parts of the interrogation were a bit spotty. His mind not wanting to deal with it. He had always been good at blocking things out he didn't want to deal with at the moment. It would all come to him sooner or later. He just preferred sooner.

Although the Illness abated, his body was still racked with pins and needles, which just made him lay there. After another hour, his mother came in and doted on him. She sat with him and caressed his brow. He cherished the moment, and it made the grown-up Keith inside the boy want to cry. He couldn't remember the last time his mother told him she loved him. However, she'd occasionally show her love through her actions and not words. A tear rolled down his right cheek.

His mother saw the tear and thought it was the pain of being sick, so she took him in her arms and hugged him even tighter. It made Keith want to cry more, but he didn't. At that moment, he decided he needed to write his mother when he got back and apologize to her for all the shit he'd done. Looking back at this moment and many others like it, Keith realized with all his mother's faults—she still tried to raise him the best she could. Despite everything he believed, she did a good job. Only he was accountable for his adult actions. In no way should society hold his mother culpable.

Even now, Keith knew he would do it all again, but they were many things he would not have done. He also believed that if he graduated high school or got his GED back then, things would've turned out a lot different.

As it turned out, life is much more complicated than he first believed. After talking to Joey, he found out he was a silent partner in one of the world's biggest companies. Joey was like the fifth richest person in the US, just behind Mark Zuckerberg. Random thoughts jumped into his head. He now wondered how much he was worth since he was a silent partner. Was he a billionaire? If he were, he'd make sure his mother was taking care of for the rest of her life. Wouldn't she be surprised? Another tear rolled down his face as he thought about all the fucked-up shit he'd done in his life.

"Ma?" He said, his voice quivered. Pull it together. He was such a big baby when he was sick, and that would never change.

"Yes, baby," she said, pushing him away so that she could see his face. His mother always looked into his eyes when she talked.

"I love you, Ma...and...I know sometimes it don't seem so, but I really do. You're the most important person in my life. Right now, and when I am old...like 40."

"Well, 40 is not that old, baby," she said with a broad smile, "but that's the most beautiful thing anyone has ever said to me. And this isn't an excuse for bad behavior, Keith. You're a teenager, and you're going through a lot of emotional stuff right now. You know I was a teenager once and not all that long ago, so I understand. I may not approve of some choices you make, but you'll always be my son. Remember that, all right?"

"Yes, ma'am," he said, as he closed his eyes and fell back asleep.

38

Hanging out in the Past

Keith woke up at 8:30 the next morning. It reminded him he never checked the clock the morning before seeing if it read 6:15 AM. According to his heightened memory, he went right outside to hang out with his friends, but his mother offered to make him breakfast: eggs, bacon, sausage, and her home fries. He liked his mom's home fries the best. He thought they were better than most restaurants. *What kid didn't like his mom's cooking?*

He soaked up the mom time while they ate. After an hour, he went outside. Since he hadn't been pulled out, he figured they must have placed him there to keep him out of the way. A prison made of the past. He was two years away from when he needed to be and too young to go too far. He was young, but at least they didn't send them back to 1992. The furthest he'd gone back but had yet to be on that jump. His mother gave him five dollars, which was rare, but it made him smile.

As he wandered the neighborhood, he decided to head to Christie's Market. It was 10 AM and hot. Keith needed a cold drink. When he arrived at the store, his heightened memory informed him his friends had all gone swimming. It also told him the name of the lottery ticket that would when that day, and it would be number 202. It would hit four a thousand dollars at 11:30 AM. He also knew another winning ticket would hit at the 7-Eleven down the street. What a day. He roamed the store before he decided on a sprite in a pint of ice cream. Then he realized he had changed the past by spending time with his mom and not going swimming with his friends. But yet the heightened memory stayed; it never did that before, and it confused him quite a bit.

Keith went to the counter, put his items down, and asked what number of the ticket of the game he liked. He bought two tickets. It would seem the winning ticket would sit for an hour and a half before it won in the original timeline, but not this time.

There was only one other person in the store. He scratched the tickets and hit for $1000 on the second ticket. The additional ticket was for five dollars, which made Keith chuckle.

Cathy was happy for him, but she didn't have enough in the drawer to cash the tickets. She told him she was working a double, so he should come back later that night. She knew no one but her would cash the ticket for him. Keith knew Cathy believed her coworkers were just full of hate, making him like her even more.

He left the store and wandered around until he bumped into his friend Carlos Gomes, whom everyone called Carly. They hung out as they roamed the streets of Boston and stopped at the 7 Eleven. It was time to grab the other winning ticket; this one hit for $500. He knew the Indian dude behind the counter wouldn't cash it for him, so he stuffed it in his pocket unscratched.

"You're not gonna see if you won something?" Carly said, a bit surprised.

Keith normally would scratch the ticket on the spot, and apparently, everyone knew it. "Naw, not here. They won't cash it even if I win something." They stood outside for a second as Keith paused. "Hey, you want to go downtown?"

"We can check out the hip-hop stores on Winter Street."

"Sounds good to me, and then we can go look at all the jewelry we can't afford."

They got off at Downtown Crossing, and it was busy as usual. The sun was now higher in the sky, and it was hotter than hell. He checked his wristwatch, and it was just one in the afternoon. They walked to the corner mall where Keith scratched the $500 ticket and acted surprised when he won. Carly couldn't believe it. They dipped into a small convenience store Keith knew would cash the ticket. He bought a couple more tickets and then went to the food court and got their grub on.

It wasn't very often that he had a lot of money in his pocket when he hung out downtown. He made good use of the extra money, bought a couple of Adidas sweatsuits and a pair of white and blue Shell Toes to match. Even gave Carly $100 to buy whatever he wanted and told him he could spend it all.

While Carly tried on a pair of shell toes, a group of girls walked into the footlocker. One of them noticed Keith and walked over to him. His memory informed him he'd only seen her around school and downtown, but he didn't know her that well. He figured he'd help his younger self out, not that he would remember it. He just thought he could at least get his younger self in the door. The girl who Keith instantly recognized as the one he'd been on the beach with two years later looked almost the same. In his mind, they would be at least friends for that long.

They would date, and she would have his first kid and then move on, saying he had no goals. He did now; only he couldn't tell anyone. He thought about his daughter and her mother and wished he put them first.

"Hey, Keith, what you doing?" She asked and introduced him to her friends. "These are my girls: Tina, Breanna, and Tenisha."

"Hi," he said, pointing to his friend. "This is my boy, Carly."

They all exchanged greetings. Keith asked what they were up to. Well, he asked Kristin. She said they were about to go get something to eat but saw him inside Footlocker and wanted to stop to say hello.

"We already ate, but we'll go with you if you don't mind?" Keith said. "You ready?"

"Yeah, sure," Carly said, stuffing his old shoes in the box, "just let me pay for these."

Since they entered the store, an employee who'd been watching them approached Carly and accused him of trying to steal the sneakers—never given him a chance to even try to pay. Carly was so shocked when the guy laid into him. When the guy finally stopped, it was Keith who spoke. Just in time for the manager to hear what he was about to say.

"Excuse me, he wasn't trying to steal those; he's wearing them out, meathead. What, you don't think we got money or something? Yo, Carly, show 'em your cash."

Carly did. The man looked shocked, but he didn't know what to say. The manager came to the rescue and apologized to them, and threw in some sneaker cleaner for free. After Carly paid the sales clerk, they bounced. They laughed all the way to the food court.

They all scattered to buy what they wanted and met back up at a table. The food court was enclosed. One set of windows in the back and an eating area downstairs near the bathroom. They ate upstairs in the back room next to the window. The window opened up to a small alley that led to Winter street.

The incident at Footlocker still amused Keith and Carly. Kristin, who got food at the same place as Keith, talk to him until her girls came to the table. Keith couldn't help but try to hook Carly up with Kristin's girl Tenisha, who wouldn't give the poor kid a glance. It was funny to Keith because, in a few years, they would date—and the last he knew, they were happily married with three kids. Right now, she wasn't feeling my little homie.

A couple of boys sitting off in the distance caught Keith's attention. He noticed they were watching him and his friends. At first, he thought they were checking out the girls or wanted beef, but they were a couple of years younger than Keith, so he figured it was something different. What struck him most as odd was that they turned away every time he looked in the direction.

Then he remembered what Director Harrington had said about him not being the only talent in town. Then there was that whispering he heard. The more he thought about it, the clearer it became in his head, and it was Dr. Bell's voice "beware of the other jumpers—you're being watched—be careful. I believe in you. I believe you."

Keith looked over at the kids again and did the math. If the kids were 10 or 11, they'd still be old enough. Shit, they could be 6-years-old and still be part of the project. The only thing that puzzled him was that he thought he was the only one able to jump. It was a big deal that they had him go on the first mission, but it seemed like the other jumpers had always been there watching. *Nothing added up.*

The rest of the day went by quick and with no trouble. He even got Kristin's number. He just hoped his 14-year-old self would call her. He knew he would but hoped it happened sooner. He tried to remember the date they met and couldn't. His enhanced memory was clouding his own. *That's odd; he'd always been able to remember the present.*

It looked like something had changed.

Back on the block, Carly hung out over Keith's house. He only lived a couple of streets over. Keith's mother interrogated him about where he got the money to buy all the stuff he had. She seemed doubtful when Keith explained he bought a scratch ticket and won. He had $200 left and some change. He kept about $30 and offered $200 to his mom. To his surprise, she didn't take it all. Just $100. Keith thought she would take it because it was her money that bought the ticket in the first place. Besides, he still had the thousand-dollar ticket in his pocket. He wasn't about to tell his mother about that one.

"No, baby," she said, "it's your come up, not mine. Enjoy it." And with that, she went to her bedroom.

He and Carly hung out in the living room, playing video games for a while until they went outside. Carly asked Keith if he could walk him home because his mother wouldn't believe him where the sneakers and stuff came from. He was right. They walked to the door. She didn't believe Carly at all, but she believed Keith. He found it amusing because Carly was a good kid who wouldn't steal a thing, even if you put a gun to his head. He'd still say no. However, back then, Keith was getting in trouble. It just seemed to follow him around.

After he left Carly's house, Keith went to Christie's Market again and had Kathy cash the ticket, as she promised, and then left. Back at the house, he hid the money in a hiding spot he knew would still be there in a few years. He then went into his room and lay on his bed. Not sure what to do, Keith just thought about possibilities like if he could only make himself go back, but he couldn't. It wasn't possible. And even if it were, he wouldn't know how, so he rode it out in the past. Although he felt trapped, it was still the most freedom he'd experienced in a while. Physically and mentally.

Besides, while he was stuck in the past, he could keep winning money and stashing it for Joey. Joey did tell Keith that the funds to start Joe Co. came from him. He just wished he knew how much he had to come up with.

39

Woke in the Dark

A bright sun hung in a cloudless sky as a light breeze blew onto the beach where Keith, Adam, and Carly laid out their towels. Jimmy couldn't make it because he had to go see his grandmother. Family first. Sean couldn't either because they moved out of the blue to the South Shore. Keith's mother brought them to the beach. As far as he could remember, this was his first visit to Revere Beach.

Kelley's Roast Beef and a crowded beach full of bikini-clad ladies. Keith chuckled at his 14-year-old memories. Girls, food, and girls. Typical for teenage Keith. But adult Keith wished he was older, so the Revere Beach's memory included the arcade game parlors, amusement park games, and the rickety old wooden roller coaster. The beach was packed now, but only the sidewalk on the beachside showed activity. There were fewer open businesses now, and Keith knew that the vacant lots and many of the remaining buildings would be turned into fancy beachside apartment complexes within the next twenty years.

Keith's mother played volleyball with her new boyfriend. After his father left, there had been a parade of them. Most were complete assholes who saw Keith as an inconvenience, but not all. They fit the small category of men who were genuine in their love for his mother and him. Although Keith's adult mind knew no matter how good Dave was, she had a knack to chase the good ones away. With amusement, he watched his mother and Dave play volleyball. Dave asked him and his friends they wanted to play, but they all declined.

He and his friends played in the ocean for a good hour and a half until exhausted from the sun. They lay on the towels and soaked up the rays as they enjoyed the cool breeze coming off the ocean.

Keith continued to watch the volleyball match. Adam and Carly played chess, and to his surprise, it was Adam who brought the chessboard. Adam was pretty good at chess. Keith never thought of him as a strategist. Quite the opposite. Adam even beat Dave once out of several games, but Keith never could. Not then or the next year. Dave won every game until he left for good. Every day, the things learned go without notice, unless you're older, watching things unfold through your own youthful eyes. It felt strange but enlightening. Keith lay there feeling good about what he had learned over the past few weeks he'd been stranded there.

The gift of knowledge was an amazing thing. He'd never take memory for granted again. The longer he stayed, the easier it was to find winning tickets. He found he had full control of the memory record for the day. He no longer had to wait for things to take place with a heightened memory to kick in. The memories of the winning tickets, though, changed; he saw himself winning the ticket instead of being told about the winner. The first time he won and his intentions must've changed the timeline.

He thought about the jump and wondered about what was happening in the present or with the other jump teams that he now knew existed. It scared him, and not much did. They couldn't kill him while on a jump because they needed him to send the first message, but they certainly could keep him out of the way. However, someone tried to kill him, but he didn't think it had been the director.

The only thing that mattered at the moment was the 22 grand he stashed away. It had been way too easy. He still got memories of tickets that were potential winners that Kathy told him or he heard about, but life-changing money he wouldn't take. However, he wondered if the $1000 or $500 in the year 2004 weren't life-changing to someone. He just hoped that in his need to accumulate the money, it didn't wreck someone else's life.

Keith scanned the packed beach and searched for anyone watching him. Yesterday he'd seen a kid on a BMX-style bike watching him at the park. He'd swear he'd never seen the kid before, though he played basketball at the park almost every day. The kid took off when Jimmy thought the kid was staring him down and wanted to fight or something. Jimmy yelled at the kid and asked him what his problem was—the kid didn't bite. He just calmly rolled off. He continued to scan the area and became pleased that so far, not a single person looked out of place. *Thank God.*

The sun was too hot, and it made Keith feel tired. He lay back, covered his eyes with his sunglasses, and fell asleep. He felt himself spinning into dreamland, but he saw nothing but blackness. As the blackness pushed against his vision, he felt the chill. Keith woke with a start as he still stared into a void of nothingness. Without warning, a download came, and he knew what had happened. Pulled back. He waited for the guards, who never came, to snatch him up.

The familiar feeling of the pillow beneath his head made him relax. Despite the sheet that covered his head, he knew he awoke in his quarters at the Complex. He removed it and saw the room was dark. They removed the surge protector that cast his room in calming blue light. After his eyes adjusted, he saw the room was completely empty. Desk and bed remained. But no chair to sit in. All his personal effects were gone.

Keith sat up, surprised he was alone. Still a little groggy from the download. A tube stuck out of his belly. How did he get back? Who helped him? Was it Dr. Bell, again? With no way of knowing the answers to any of his questions, it comforted him to wonder. His head ached, so he lay back down and tried to get some sleep. As much as he wanted to be back, he wished he could have finished out the day with his friends and family at the beach. His mom looked the happiest he'd ever seen her on that day. He wondered whatever happened to Dave. He hoped the man had a long, happy life. He didn't have any kids of his own, but Keith thought he'd make a hell of a father.

40

Complex Escape

The room was dark as a black hole. Keith tossed and turned throughout the night. When he woke, he was hungry, almost on the verge of starving. Somehow, during the night, he pulled out the feeding tube. Director Harrington, it appeared planned on him being in the past for quite some time. Tucked away somewhere safe. Keith became convinced it wasn't supposed to have been the summer of 2004.

He got up and turned on the light. As he suspected, he trashed his room and removed everything. They pulled the bed away from the wall and didn't put it back. There were even two unopened boxes of ivory soap. He chuckled. Sometimes prisoners would hide small things within the bar of soap. Keith checked the hidden panel. The gun was still there. He secured the panel back in place and put the bed back against the wall.

They had taken everything from him: radio, computer, chair, and his journals. He sat at the desk, using his bed as a chair, and wrote with a pen and a pad of paper they left him. He wrote the next entry of his jump log, which they also took. He hoped that neither of the journals or the jump log would be much use to them. He wasn't worried about what they would find, despite knowing that he himself had inserted coded messages at some point in time. He felt it was in safe hands, seeing he didn't even have the key to decode it. He hoped they could not figure it out either.

The room reverberated with the slightest movement. The lack of belongings and stuff made the room feel more like a cell and induced tiredness. After Keith wrote a three-page entry into his makeshift jump log, he lay back down. The weight of the empty room crushing him back to sleep. He stared at the ceiling and thought about his next move. He wondered if they would check on him. He was sure they would, so he reinserted the feeding tube. It wasn't that difficult since all he had to do was reinsert back into the coupling. He lay there in the dark with the tube in place, waiting for them to come, and fell back asleep.

Keith awoke as the bolt in the lock turned. Not a muscle moved except his eyes. He played possum. The door opened, and he heard one of the guards, who was talking, say something unintelligible to the nurse as she came into the room. Bright light filled the room. Keith fought the urge to close his eyes even tighter.

The nurse checked his vitals and replaced the feeding tube. After she was done, she left the room. The process took only five minutes. Keith waited what he assumed was 10 minutes before he got up. He pushed the bed back in place and then crawled under the bed to the vent. He removed the gun tucked in his waistband before he grabbed two extra clips and stuffed them in his pants pocket. Then, he remembered the injection gun and the other unused cartridges marked 2 and 3. Where were they, or did he change something that made that an alternate memory? He tried to pull it up, but nothing came.

Keith crawled through the small space into the ventilation duct. Once his body cleared the opening, he pushed the panel shut with his feet. The shaft continued several uninterrupted yards before he came to a T split. Left or right were the two choices. He turned right when he noticed a familiar symbol and arrow etched into the metal. It pointed back to the left. He backed up and went the other way. He had to follow destiny, right? The symbol 신 was used in Taekwondo for divine, but it also meant god, spirit, and such. Keith smiled at the thought because the word was pronounced as shin but spelled sin.

He followed the labyrinth's sinuous route. The symbol marked the way. Keith wondered of its origin and if he had put it there in the past, but it looked like it was stamped into the metal. If the events of the past several weeks taught him anything, it would be nothing was set in stone. He'd left many clues for himself and wondered if this was just another one.

The ventilation shaft ran through the complex, providing him with many views of the rooms near his quarters. However, the ones that held Keith's interest the most were located on the floor of the duct, not its side. The vents he had crawled over occasionally would allow him to glimpse the level below. He came across a rather large room. The room resembled the lab, but instead of one chair, the chamber contained 20—each one occupied by a jumper.

The room was obscured a bit from his vision because of the recessed ceiling vent. The sight of the chairs and jumpers elicited have more questions. Just knowing about the location was important, though. He wondered if the place was ever empty or did those jumpers have replacements. It could be his only way to jump again.

Although it was good to know what he was up against, Keith was afraid that he couldn't help but look over his shoulder every second during the next jump. And that could be detrimental to the mission of the next jump. They couldn't kill him. He was first. His brain worked quickly to deduce possibilities. It was Keith who held it all together, and he knew it, but something still nagged at him from the furthest tips of the tendrils of his consciousness.

The duct continued on until he reached what appeared to be a dead-end. However, a symbol had been etched into the metal with no arrow. When he reached the end, Keith saw the duct went up at a 90-degree angle. The shaft above him was unclimbable, but there was a symbol, so he became confused. He paused, sitting at the base for a moment. There were no ledges or outcroppings that could be used as hand-holds to climb.

He sat with his back against the wall with the etching carved in it, exhausted from the crawl. Symbol no arrow. What could it mean? He grew frustrated as he looked up at an impossible shaft above him and elbowed the wall behind him hard. The loud bang echoed throughout the shaft. *Damn stupid.*

He may as well have just screamed, "I'm right here! No, of course, I'm not trying to escape. Why would I do that?" He turned around quickly and pushed on the wall to absorb the sound, but it was too late. It was already vibrating down the shaft from which he came and up into the shaft above. He could absorb some of the sounds, but not nearly enough. He looked at the placement of his hands and noticed something wasn't quite right.

He was so stupid. No arrow. He couldn't climb up. It could only have meant one thing. It was a panel like the one in his room. If only he could discern the meaning of the symbol before he made all the racket. He didn't have time to ponder the subject any longer. He pushed on the panel with both hands and opened the trapdoor. He crawled inside and shut the panel with an audible click.

Inside the new section, the air changed. It was obvious he was no longer inside the ductwork. The floor was cold cement. He looked around but could see nothing. Pitch black. No vents to cast the low light he had in the ductwork. However, here he could climb to his feet, so he began checking the wall for a way out.

After stumbling in the dark, for what seemed like an eternity, he found some pipes. Some were cold, and some were hot. He burned himself twice. Once he figured it out, he could feel the heat that emanated from the pipes. He no longer had to touch them. He came to a wall with something metal and elongated but was cool to the touch. A similar piece of long metal was below it and one above it. Convinced he found a ladder, he climbed.

One rung at a time, he climbed in complete darkness.

He counted each rung he stepped on and determined he'd gone 20 rungs, which were about a foot apiece. He had to be careful now. A fall from that height in the dark could be deadly. He reached the top after he counted 30 rungs in total. Above them was a 2' x 2' diamond-plated hatch. Keith found the handle and twisted it to unlock it, and then pushed it upwards. Bright incandescent light flooded the dark space— blinding him for a moment.

He climbed into the lush light as he squinted and crawled onto the tiled floor. He shielded his eyes with his hand as he looked around the room—an office of some kind. Keith shut the hatch to the utility room tunnel and stood up. His eyes adjusted, but his vision was still blurry as he took in the space. Where was he? He was sure he wasn't in the office's space used as the cover for the Complex.

Keith remembered the symbol. The symbol he was sure he'd put there himself, along with the box of Ammo and the gun. Did Joey have offices on the first floor? Did he have an office on the first floor? He found a light switch and flipped it down, sending the office into a semidarkness. The only light came from the floor-to-ceiling windows. *That's better.*

The subdued light helped his eyes adjust. He went to the desk, snatched the nameplate off it, and found what he thought he would—his name in the title. Cofounder and Cochairman. He walked around the desk to his chair. One he didn't even know existed. He was worth billions and never knew it. He looked around for something. Anything. Keith wasn't sure what he was looking for, but he was sure he'd know it when he found it.

His desk had a glass top and a calendar underneath the glass. After searching what was on top of the glass and steel desk, he began searching the drawers. He pulled the calendar out between the glass. A piece of paper fell out of the calendar and floated to the floor. He returned the calendar to its place underneath the glass and bent over to retrieve the paper that fell.

The paper turned out to be several pages stapled together. The top of the first sheet caught his eye. The Altered States Project. TASP. Keith scanned about 10 pages and could not believe what it contained or what it sanctioned. It even told him that SCP stood for the Special Censure Project.

There was more on TASP than he originally believed. A lot more. The different president in the present was just the tip of the iceberg. Keith wasn't so sure he could change it back. He did, however, believe it all began with him. Therefore, only he could change it. One thing he knew for sure was that he needed to take out those jumpers. They tried to take him out twice, and he can't have them watching him go off the timeline, but he wasn't so sure he could do anything.

The last several pages contained a list of hundreds of dates, names, and addresses. Keith wasn't sure what it meant. There was no explanation, but it wouldn't have been included if he thought it wasn't important. Obama, the name just jumped in his mind. He scanned the list and found it at number 19. Barack Obama. 1989 Somerville Massachusetts. 4/29/2006. On the date, everything started to go crazy.

Keith knew for certain he was gonna need Joey's help. He looked at the names on the speed dial and found Joey's, which was number two. He wasn't sure who number one was. He picked up the phone and pressed Joey's number. He picked up on this first ring. Keith told him he was in his office and asked him to come down. He hung up the phone and leaned back in his chair, and shut his eyes as he waited.

41

Joey Sees the Complex

Light tried to shine through the office windows. He sat in his chair with his feet on his desk and explained to Joey what was going on. The brilliant billionaire paced back and forth during most of the two-hour story-time. Conspiracy theories Joey could handle, but the incredulous expression that spread over his entire body when Keith mentioned time travel meant it was gonna be harder to convince him existed than he first thought.

The person who pioneered many technological advances—years before anyone should have—being skeptical made Keith have to hold in a smile. *Where did he think the programming he reverse-engineered came from?* Didn't he ever find it interesting no one ever questioned him about his advancements? Keith knew it would be easier for Joey to believe it was Alien technology than time travel. Although Joey was listening intently, Keith could still see the doubt in his facial expressions.

Joey exhaled heavily. "It's a little hard to swallow."

"Well, the truth is stranger than fiction most of the time."

"True enough, I suppose, but time travel. You know much energy it would take to bend space-time? It can't be done."

"I agree right now we don't have the technology available to do it that way, but I didn't go that way either."

"You have been back in time, but not that way?"

"'Everything is connected in the universe, and we have everything we need to do anything we ever need to do.' That is what you said to a packed audience at MIT?" Keith said with a smirk on his face. "The way I've been doing it, so I know it works, but we'll have this discussion about time travel on a different day. I don't have time to argue with you. What about the Complex below your building?"

"There's no evidence of any such structure underneath us," Joey said as if he was talking to a child with delusions. "I don't know what happened to you, but whatever project you were involved with has made you…I don't know…a little delusional or something. You're my friend, and, indeed, you've never lied to me. I just think you're a little confused, is all."

Keith took his feet off the desk and sat up in his chair, and swiveled in circles. "Yeah, I'm crazy as a loon, so how do you explain that I'm here in front of you and not in prison where I'm doing life?"

"Oh, I believe you're involved in a project, and they release you from prison for it, but a conspiracy involving time travel. It's a little hard to take."

Keith smiled at his friend's responses because it was apparent Joey was just concerned. He never knew him as someone to hold any kind of malice, just not something he was capable of possessing. Unfortunately, he would get nowhere unless Joey was on board, and judging by the fact that Keith was sitting in his office via a hidden doorway that led to a ladder in his office confirmed Joey gets on board, but how was the question.

Time was counting down, and he knew he had to get back to his quarters soon. If he was not there during the next check-in, he was sure he'd never be able to right the timeline.

"I got an idea. I need to get back to my quarters before I'm discovered, so come with me and see the Complex for yourself."

Keith got up from his chair and walked over to the utility tunnel's entrance that from this side was hidden underneath tiles. It blended right into the floor and would not be noticed by anyone. In his hand was a suction cup grip holder he found in his desk drawer. There were two of them, but he figured one would suffice. He walked over to the concealed lid, attached the suction cup near the edge of the section, and pulled.

"I didn't know that was there," Joey said. His world crumbled. "It's a utility shaft, right, so it probably leads to a room. It doesn't mean it's a complex."

"Shut the fuck up and listen," he said, standing over the gaping hole. "This is how I escaped. Don't you find it a little interesting that I suggested this building, and I begged you for this space for my office? If memory serves me right, wasn't this the maintenance room?"

"It was the maintenance room, but that doesn't mean—"

"Come on, I have to get back before they discover me missing, so let's go. It's the only way you'll believe me. Besides, what you got to lose?"

"Nothing, I suppose, but this is crazy." Joey shook his head, got up from his chair, and stood over the gaping hole in the floor. "All right, let's get this over with before I change my mind."

Keith nodded and then climbed down the ladder into the shaft. On his way down, he noticed two rubberized buttons. A black and green one. He pressed the green one, and the shaft slowly filled with incandescent light. Light blinking on one at a time. Keith made the mistake of looking down, forgetting the shaft was 30 something feet to the bottom. He decided it would be better to climb with the lights off, as he got a touch of vertigo when he looked down.

Keith looked up at Joey. "Don't look down because it's a 30-foot drop," he said as he began the descent into the shaft. "What are you waiting for? Come on?"

"I'm coming, but heights and I don't get along very well."

"Before you climb down, detach the handle and drop it down the shaft. Once you're on the ladder, hit the green button that will shut the lights off and then hit the black button next to it. I believe it closes the hatch."

Keith continued to climb down to give Joey some room, and then he stopped. He looked up in time to see Joey climb into the shaft, leaving the trapdoor open. Once Joey was fully on the ladder, he continued down a few rungs and hit the black button, and the hatch closed by itself.

"Why is this so deep? It shouldn't be, should it?"

"Kill the lights, and let's get going."

At the bottom of the shaft, Keith found the buttons like at the top. He hit the green button, and the lights came back on.

"That is a long way up; I still don't understand."

The sound of belief creeping into Joey's voice was like a beautiful song on a crappy day. He could see it already started to not add up inside the mega computer-brain Joey processed. The calculations did not compute.

"You haven't seen shit yet. Just wait," Keith said, walking over to the exposed ventilation duct.

Joseph watched with fascination as Keith opened the panel, and it swung on its hinges. Keith could practically read Joey's thoughts: *hinges on air duct, maybe Keith wasn't going crazy.* Keith laughed at his reflection and also knew Joey was trying to figure out why the ventilation shaft went down there in the first place. Thirty feet below ground.

"Hinges, but...why is there a ventilation duct down here, anyway?"

Keith looked at him like he was the stupidest guy in the world. "The Complex; it's the ventilation ductwork for the Complex."

In silence, they crawled into the vent. They were careful not to make too much noise. Joey followed Keith back the way he'd come. They passed a couple of rooms on Keith's level. Joey seemed surprised because he didn't know the Complex existed. It was still good to see it because Keith didn't know who he could trust. Billionaires weren't quite at the top of his list, but he never thought he was one either.

When they had to crawl over vents that showed the level below, especially the room with the 20 or so unconscious jumpers, he knew Joey could've turned back right then a believer that there was a secret base under his building.

On the way, Keith pointed out the symbol he needed to follow to get back out. Once they reached Keith's quarters, Joey looked around the room and got nervous, so he decided to leave. Before he could, Keith heard the key in the lock. Quickly Keith pushed the bed against the wall, and Joey hid beneath the bed. He could've climbed into the vent, but Keith knew he wouldn't dear out of the fear of making any noise.

In a rush, Keith inserted the tube and then pulled it out, realizing they'd find a full bag. That wouldn't be good. They'd both be caught. He hoped Joey didn't try to escape, at least not yet. The door opened, and the nurse walked in with the guard from earlier just behind her. She checked the tube and muttered something to herself about cheap equipment. She reinserted the tube and then left.

Joey propped out from under the bed. "All right, I'm in. Shit, I was in when I saw the first set of rooms. This is crazy. I had no idea something of this size was under my building. No matter what you said, I would have never believed you, and you were right to get me to see it to believe it."

"I guess that's why the government calls them secret installations."

Joey laughed but tried to stifle it as soon as he came out. "Sorry, but it's true. Now tell me what you need me to do?"

42

Decode the Journals

The Tag Heuer watch read 5:30 PM. Joey gave him the watch before he took off back through the ventilation system. Keith had given him instructions on what to do. Joey seemed not to understand why it needed to be done. Keith assured him it was part of a larger plan and that he needed to trust him. He was also sure Joey would do what he asked. Once again, he stared at the ceiling for the second time that day.

He found it interesting that Joey wore a $200 watch when he could've worn a $200,000 watch. The man was worth $42 billion, and if nothing else, he was practical.

Sounds came from just beyond the door—voices in the hallway. Keys jingled as they inserted them into the lock. The door opened, and Keith closed his eyes, pretending to be on a jump. The footfall told him it wasn't the nurse. Another person entered just behind the new walker. This person barely made a sound.

"Excuse me, that'll be all," the familiar voice said. "I'll be a few minutes. You may want to lock the door. I'll call you if I need any help, which I doubt I will."

The guard left, and Keith heard the door close, then lock. Keith believed he knew who stood by his bed. He needed to be sure, so he looked up at the man through slitted eyes. Dr. Bell stood over him and held an ejection gun in his hand. Keith wasn't sure what it would do since he was ready awake, but he didn't want to find out either.

There was no way of doing without startling Dr. Bell. He just hoped the man didn't scream. He opened his eyes and grabbed the doctor's wrist of the hand that held the ejection gun. He sat up while holding his finger to his mouth, telling the doctor to be quiet.

The doctor still jumped back about five feet and made a noise to boot. Dr. Bell looked shocked. "How did you get pulled back?"

"I'm not sure," Keith said. "At first, I thought you did it or Director Harrington, but after I awoke and nobody came in to check on me for quite some time, I figured they had to be another reason."

"Well, Director Harrington hadn't been here all day, and it wasn't me. I'm not sure of the reason, but here you are."

"I think I somehow brought myself back, but I don't know how that's impossible."

"There's a lot we don't know about jumps or how to control them, but from my data, I'm not sure that's possible. You need the CTE compound to jump and a mixture of adrenaline to pull you back."

"I guess it doesn't matter. You shouldn't be here. If Director Harrington catches you, you'll—"

"Director Harrington knows I'm here," Dr. Bell said, "but he thinks I'm checking up on you."

"But if that's not what you're doing, then what is?"

"You have places to be, my friend," Dr. Bell said, holding up the gun. "You sent me a letter through a trusted friend. It contained important information. I am to send you back to prison. Why? I don't know. The only thing I know is that you have a list of important jumps you need to make."

Keith reached into his pocket and removed the handwritten list. He wrote an hour ago. It contained the years he needed to jump to and nothing else. "If you gonna send me back, you may as well do it now."

Dr. Bell nodded and sent Keith on his way.

•

The uneven wop-wup sound of the fan told him his location and about when. He checked his watch, which he had in prison. 6:15 AM. Everything normal, at least on this front. He closed his eyes until he heard the CO call five minutes to count. He got up and put on his scrub pants, walked over to the sink, and washed his face. A few seconds after he finished, a CO yelled, stand for count.

Keith stood at the front of his bed until the CO passed his door. Even though there was a slight fog that is the jump, if Dr. Bell hadn't told him where he was sending him, Keith would've thought it was all a dream.

However, reality didn't come with heightened memory, but he knew where he was and why. The what and how was a different story. He was sure he'd be stuck there for at least a few days, so he figured he had plenty of time to figure out what the hell he was there to find.

He sat on his bed, turned on the TV, and watch the news. After it was over, he lay back down until the CO called chow.

Keith had an hour until that would happen, so he thought about what he saw in the news and other things. He grabbed his journals and started going through them. Maybe that's why he was here? Time to break the code. Could he have hidden the key to the code in his cell? Anything was possible at this point. The ability to time travel caused too many variables. If he hid the key in his cell, it would be somewhere that would be obvious to him and him alone.

"Obvious to him" kept repeating in his mind. Over and over. He looked around his cell. He came across his cosmetic shelf, but what about the shelf? Something. What? The bar of soap. The Ivory Soap was still in its package. He'd been saving it, but he couldn't recall why.

Keith went over to the shelf and opened the package. He removed the soap and studied it. A very fine line crossed the soap. It was more like an impression that was barely noticeable to the naked eye. He took his toenail clippers because they were flat and wide and pushed it into that slight impression. The soap split easily. *Jackpot.* Hidden inside was a folded piece of paper. He quickly unfolded the paper and found what he was looking for—a cipher key. Without it, he couldn't decipher the passages in his journals.

He was glad he was in a single cell because he could pull out the box that contained all his journals and place them on his bed and go through them using the key. He had a feeling that he couldn't read the journal straight through, that he would need all of them because the key would send him to different journals.

The breakfast call came quick, and he didn't go down to eat. He'd eat later. Besides, he had plenty of oatmeal that he could make his own breakfast.

With the key in hand, he got to work. A couple of the other guys stopped by to check on him. It wasn't like him to miss a meal. They wanted to make sure everything was cool.

After they saw he had all the stuff out and he was going through it, they figured he just got caught up and didn't come down. Once they saw he was okay, they took a left, and he got back to work.

The first few passages only contained a couple of decoded words. Serving more than practice than anything else. By the time Keith finished decoding the fifth passage, he had accomplished two things. He became acquainted with the key and coded the first sentence.

Behold the pale horse, Keith, and keep going but be watchful of those around you.

After the dinner, Keith went back upstairs to his room. He stayed up most of the night decoding ciphers hidden in the journals. He fell asleep just before 5 AM.

When the CO called for them to stand for the count, Keith jumped up—dazed and confused. Still somewhat sleepy. His body performing the routine while he wasn't yet fully awake. His eyelids heavy as sleep called him back to dreamland. Once the guard walked by, all Keith wanted to do was go back to sleep.

Instead, he walked over to the sink and turned on the hot water faucet. He plucked a regular tea bag out of the box and dropped it into his cup, and stared at the sink as the steam rose. He turned down the water and filled his cup. He let the tea steep for a few minutes before he pulled out the bag and tossed it into the toilet. He added some honey and stirred the tea until satisfied. He picked up the sheet of paper he had been writing on all night.

Behold in the pale horse, Keith, keep going. But watch those around you with diligence. You'll find what you seek. The time you have to succeed is short. Use your awareness, for there are many things you need to discover. Stay the course, physical and mental, as well as use the key. It is a treasure to be found—two in prison and one in nineteen ninety-three. There is one thing you must know. In a jump, you cannot die. You are in control. Likewise, this means you cannot kill others who jump. There are ways you can change the course. Please use extreme caution because they can do the same. They're many, a force to reckon with. Since you cannot die, do not think twice. What you do is for the good of the world, so hold your course and stay true.

The weird message concluded, but he didn't know exactly what it meant. He knew this was only one part of the cipher. Something that said enough so someone would think, *this is it.* He read it again and repeated it several more times.

Stay the course and use the key. It is a treasure to be found. He checked the key and concluded it could only be used one way. He then looked at the decoded passage. He knew there had to be another message hidden inside the passage. There was only one way to find out.

Like he did with the original words, Keith had to count the total amount of words in the passage. 146. Next, he had to scan the list of key numbers that had to match the total count. The number was jumbled, but that wasn't important. It was only used as an identifier. As long as all the numbers were there, it was all that mattered. This particular key was 43 numbers along, which means the passage contained as many words.

The first number was two. He wrote it down—the second word (in). The next was one, so he wrote down the first number after the last decoded word (the). Then the seventh word after that was (watch). The fourth number he counted 17 from the first word of the passage. This is where he needed to pay close attention because the following three numbers were 161, which told him all five words were in a row finishing the first sentence: *in the watch, you'll find what you seek.* He repeated the process until he was complete.

On a separate piece of paper, he rewrote the passage and used the key.

Behold *(in the)* pale horse, Keith, keep going. But *(watch)* those around you with diligence *(you'll find what you seek).* The *(time)* you have *(to succeed)* is short. (Use) your awareness, for there are many things you need to discover. Stay *(the)* course, *(physical)* and mental, and use the *(key).* Is a treasure to be *(found).* Two in prison and *(one)* in *(nineteen)* ninety-three. *(There is)* one thing you must know. In *(a jump you cannot)* die. You are in *(control).* Likewise, this means *(you can)* not *(kill others)* who jump. *(There are ways)* you can change the course. Please *(use extreme)* caution because they can do the same. They're many a *(force)* to reckon with. Since you cannot *(die)* do not think *(twice)*. for *(it is for good)* of the world, so hold your course and stay true.

He wrote out the decoded message and stared at it for an eternity.

In the watch, you'll find what you seek. Time to succeed, use the physical Key, found in 119. There is a jump you cannot control. Though, you can kill others there. Use extreme force. Die twice it's for good.

He'd carefully read the message; it started to make sense to him. He picked up his watch and held it in his hand as he thought about what the message said. He used to live in cell 119, but that was on another block. And he wasn't sure how he'd get inside it to look for the key. A physical key. *Is it a real key?*

The CO called that morning's chow, and he went downstairs. He strapped on his watch as he headed to chow and wondered how he would get into the watch after breakfast. He checked the watch and then figured out how to get in the block 8-1 and into cell 119.

43

USB Drive

After breakfast, Keith went back up to his cell. No time like the present. He got to work on the watch. Not having the correct tools made it a slow process, but he got the cover off with prison ingenuity. Attached to the underside of the cover was a tiny piece of folded paper. He removed the piece of paper and unfolded it with care. From sitting inside the watch for a long time, the edges became crisp, and he was afraid to tear the thin paper.

He held up the paper and looked at it in awe. Tiny writing covered both sides. The smallest writing he'd ever seen. The only part that wasn't covered was the fold and crease. He set the paper down and looked at the watch one more time. On the backside of the cover, etched into the metal, was a series of numbers—another key.

Laughter and loud talking in the hallway brought him back. He glanced towards the door. His heightened memory intact but foggy since he changed a couple of things with the watch. The more familiar heightened sense came back to him—the feeling of being on constant alert. Prison life.

Keith copied the number sequence onto a random piece of paper to read more clearly. The tiny writing on the back of the metal was clear but close together, making counting the digits difficult.

The unfolding piece of paper was more rectangle than a square and measured 2" x 2.5". This, too, needed to be copied down and made larger for the same reasons as the string of numbers found.

As he wrote, the note read like a crazy person's rambling about the coming Apocalypse. The message hidden within the apocalypse rhetoric, he hoped, would sound saner. It took nothing to decode tiny passage, and it revealed a short and concise line of text: Inside your cross. *His cross.*

The cross was large for a pendant, but it was the weight that made him wear it. It stayed in place and didn't move too much. Besides his sneakers that he walked in with, it was the only other thing they allowed him to keep. Though he didn't wear the pendant much, the chain hung around his neck. He kept the cross safe in his locker. He was never really one for crosses or a huge jewelry fan. It just seemed to get in the way when fights happened.

Although he wasn't sure why he wore the cross to court on the day he got convicted, someone brought it to him, that was it, but he couldn't remember who brought it. Joey, he thought, maybe Adam or Jimmy. The only thing he knew for sure was he didn't own it beforehand. He wore it that day because he figured it couldn't hurt.

Keith found the gold cross, with Jesus nailed to it, inside a small box wrapped up in toilet paper. He sat on the bed as he removed the cross and discarded the box, tossing it onto the bed. The charm was heavy as he remembered. *Too big for his liking.*

The cross's length was easily 2 1/2 to 3 inches, and its crossbars were more than an inch. For prison, it was huge.

Thick, too. The cross Jesus was nailed to was maybe a shy less than 1/2 inch long. He examined the cross. Twice. It appeared to be solid.

Whether it was instinct or some forgotten memory, Keith tugged the bottom as he pushed the two ends of the crossbar inwards. The bottom came off to reveal something he would have never expected to find: a USB drive.

When he got back to the future, he would need two things—the computer in his office and the cross in his belongings. He put the cap back on, as the CO calls five minutes to count. Time for lunch, and he was hungry.

Chow came and went. Keith went out at the next movement and walked the yard. He did his best thinking when he walked the yard, especially the quad. He needed to find a way to somehow get inside 119. The people came and went from that block; he wasn't sure if he knew anyone he could trust to do it for him. Besides, Keith wasn't even sure where the key would be found. Something small could've been hidden anywhere, but where would he have hidden the key?

It bugged him he couldn't remember. He didn't remember the watch or the cross either. There was only a blank space where those memories should've been. Though he remembered most things, some were vague at best, just at the edge of remembrance.

Though most things have a way of working themselves out, he had his doubts. He felt like something was missing. A part of the puzzle that was never included. It had to work out, right? Why else would he be there? It had to be to accomplish this task. Keith had to believe he hid the key in a place that he could easily gain access at the appropriate time.

A cool breeze swept through the alleyways. It was a nice spring day, so the birds were out and singing. The flowers that were planted in front of every unit started the boom. I packed the two main yards with people trying to forget where they were and enjoy the day. Keith found himself on the quad where there were the most flowers.

He was lost in thought when his friend Harry called to him. He stopped and waited for Harry and the person who was with him to catch up. He didn't recognize Harry's friend.

"What's going on?" He said as the pair caught up to him. As they came closer to Keith, he recognized the other person. "Oh, shit, when you get here?"

"Yesterday morning."

"Damn Dave, it's good to see you," he said as they continued to walk. *Got to keep it moving on the quad.*

"Yeah, when I saw him," Harry said, "I told him you were here."

"What you doing for time, nothing serious, I hope?"

"Nah, three years, that's all," Dave said, "...I got a little more than a year to go."

Keith nodded. "Where they got you?"

"The eights," Harry offered.

"Yeah, eight-two."

"You wouldn't happen to be in 119, are you?"

"Damn, I am," Dave said, shaking his head. "Why you ask?"

"Used the be my cell," Keith said, holding back a smile, "but we have a lot to catch up on. So how have you been?"

The three friends caught up on old times and things they missed until the yard closed for dinner count. Keith made plans with Dave to meet up at first movement the next day. At 8:30 the next morning, he would talk to him and ask him to get the key if he could figure out where he hid the damn thing.

44

Find Treasure

The housing unit settled down for the night. His side of the floor became ultra-quiet. His cell was next to the stairwell that divided the floor in two. Each side had a door to the stairwell that locked, but the individual cells didn't lock on his block—at least not the two cells he'd been in since being classed to the unit. He stayed up late trying to figure out where he hid Key in 119.

The morning came fast and was another nice day. Where could he have hidden something like a key? The only answer was in plain sight—the best place to hide anything. The how and where he'd hide something like a key in plain sight was beyond him, but it's what he would've done. Keith would've left nothing up to chance, so he just needed to remain calm and think it through. There would be no guessing. It would be absolute, a no-brainer. So, what was he missing? The missing puzzle piece floated just outside his conscious memory.

It seemed like there were a lot of things missing lately, but he didn't know why or how. It felt weird that he could have changed things and have no memory of it at all, but he lived a whole secret life through those blank spots. Keith knew he didn't remember because he didn't remember the days that were changed by a jump.

Just after breakfast, Keith wondered if the note contained another message. He only had the one code, but the message seemed too long to produce a three-word line result.

He wrote down the key and added up the numbers. Nonplussed at what to do, Keith added three more numbers. The numbers were derived from the three words that resulted from the first solving of the key. He wrote down the key backwards and set out to re-decode the message.

Once he completed the task, Keith found what he was looking for and more.

•

Around the quad, he went at a quick pace. His speed walking wasn't to be trifled with. Under normal conditions, he wouldn't slow down for anyone and make anyone that wanted to talk to him keep his pace. It was how he slowed unwanted conversation. He checked his watch and headed over to the Westfield. They'd call the 9:30 movement shortly.

It wasn't a bother that Dave didn't come out at 8:30 as planned. Things didn't always go according to your daily schedule in prison. Dave came out, and they continued to walk the Westfield. It was the most private place to walk.

After they caught up some more, Keith told his old friend he needed a favor. He told Dave that he wouldn't have asked him if it wasn't for two reasons: he needed someone he could trust, and they needed to be living on block 8-2 in cell 119. He then told him where he hid the key, and it was right in plain sight, all right.

The key was hidden in a clever spot. Keith had cut a rectangle 2.5 inches by 3.5 inches out of the cardboard from the back of one of his notepads. Then he cut the center out, roughly in the shape of a key. He glued paper to one-side that matched the size of the rectangle and placed the key in the hole, and then glued a half-sized sheet of typing paper piece to the other side. He then placed a small square towards the wall in a shallow indent and attached it just beyond the head of his bed where there was a space. He acquired some paint to touch up the walls and used it to cover his hiding place as well.

Dave went to his cell at the next movement and came right back out, claiming it wasn't there. Keith insisted it was there, and Dave reluctantly went back inside at the next movement since it was the morning's last movement. They planned to meet back outside at 1 PM.

Dave and Keith met on the quad, and Dave slipped the key into Keith's hand as Dave gave him dap.

"I had doubted the thing was there," Dave said. "I'm not sure why, but I was looking for something bigger. It was almost impossible to see. It blended seamlessly with the rest of the wall. Nobody would've thought that was hidden on a cement wall. I'll have to remember that tip if I ever have the hide something that small and flat."

"Be my guest," Keith said as they walked past the school building to the right in the original movement gong to the left. "I'm just glad you showed up because I've been trying to figure out how to retrieve the key for some time now."

"No problem, anytime, my friend."

"Don't worry, I might have something else for you to do for me when you leave, but not sure yet."

"If it's something I can do, I got you, brother."

Keith nodded as they continued walking at high-speed. He wasn't positive because he wasn't sure his cross was in his property back at the Complex. If it was, it sat in the director's office, but he could change its location, right? He didn't see why he couldn't. He had the power to change the past. This much he knew.

"Thanks for grabbing the key for me," he said, patting his friend on the back. "It's really important. I owe you one."

They continued to walk around the quad and get reacquainted some more. At 2:30 PM, the next movement, Keith went inside. He needed to be alone so we could think. He had possession of both prison treasures. But now what? Now he had to figure out how to keep them safe until he could leave.

Keith lay on his bed and thought about not just the keys she the memory drive but everything. As his mind filled with the possibilities, Keith twirled the key between his fingers. "What does this open?" He asked aloud to the empty room. And got no answer.

Keith examined the key and saw the only identifying mark was a set of numbers on one side of the key, and the other wasn't exactly blank, but whatever had been there was no longer visible. He had a discarded lens from a peer of eyeglasses he used to magnify things. It only magnified things about two times, but it was better than nothing. Prison was filled with a lot of nothing. It didn't help much at all. He still couldn't make out the writing. Keith wrote a grocery list of ideas until he came upon one that might work. Emphasis on might.

He removed the blue folder from his locker, and inside were drawing supplies. There were two lead pencils and a box of colored ones, along with a bounty of typing paper, which was good to draw on. What he was after was tucked behind the 20-pound typing paper, a couple of sheets of what looked like tissue paper, but a tiny bit heavier. He removed a pencil and a sheet of paper and set to work.

He placed the paper over the flat blank part of the key and lightly shaded it with the pencil. It took Keith doing it a few times before it showed a visible impression of a logo. One of a bank that no longer existed, but the place was still a bank, and he wondered if the key would still work. *A safe deposit box key?*

In the end, Keith knew exactly what to do, and it didn't involve a single person he knew. Just the US Postal Service. He recalled the address to Joe Co. Technologies, so he grabbed an empty soapbox and stuffed it with tissue paper, then covered the box with typing paper. Once it was wrapped up, he addressed it to himself and made sure he put the correct postage amount on it before placing it on his desk. Ready to be mailed. After he mailed the package, he thought he tried to pull himself back if he could. There was no time to waste.

45

The Disk

The trip through the ventilation system took less time this go around. Knowing the way made all the difference. Keith wasted no time when he got back, thanks to a minimal download and no crash. He crawled under his bed and through the opening. He checked his watch upon arrival. It was just a shy past two in the morning, so he felt confident that nobody would bother him until morning.

He closed the panel to the duct and bounded up the ladder. Once in the comfy confines of his office, he headed straight for his hidden safe that not even Joey knew about. There were only a couple of items in the safe: a key, a gold chain with a big cross on it, and the stack of cash. He removed only the key and the cross. He wondered why he didn't just get to it earlier when he was in the office. He could've, right? It should have been there. He placed the two items on his desk.

The office wasn't completely dark due to light coming from a flood lamp outside. He sat down in his chair and turned on the desk lamp. It provided just enough light for him to examine the items. He picked up the key—something about it looked somehow different. A smile slowly crossed his face as he flipped the key over several times. His eyes widened as a serious laugh escaped from the bowels of his soul. Nothing was ever simple. Not in his world, and not now. The key that he held in his hand wasn't the one he sent with the chain. It was different. The key looked brand new like they cut it yesterday. Somehow Keith knew it wasn't, but he now had a better idea where to find the lock to the key. He just hoped he was right.

Outside his floor-to-ceiling windows was nothing but black sky. Some faint rustling at the top of a few trees' yards away. He stared in that direction only for a moment, then went back to his computer. He turned on his computer, and once it was ready to go, he inserted the thumb drive that was hidden within the cross into the USB port.

When it prompted him, he entered his password and called up the drive. A screen popped up—this one attached to the memory drive and asked for a password. Without thinking, he typed jump-man. Another box popped up—PASSWORD ACCEPTED...

The USB drive contained several items. The third on the list piqued Keith's curiosity because they simply named it The Disk. He clicked on it, and an enormous program loaded. He just hoped his computer could handle it, even though he knew it would.

Another screen had popped open that contained a status bar for the loading program. Despite its size, it loaded fast. It didn't sit right with him. The program was on its own drive and should have opened with ease. He watched the bar creep up to 100%. Then another box popped up declaring the computer was safe. Now it made sense. The drive held a program to sweep and clean any computer to which it was attached. It was a very smart idea, and probably Joey's. If he weren't sitting in an office of one of the most advanced tech companies on the planet, he wouldn't have believed it was possible. Keith had been living a secret life his entire life and kept it from himself.

The computer beeped.

He looked at the screen, and a familiar logo with the three letters SCP spun on the monitor. He clicked on the image, and the program commenced.

Screen after screen contained data—highly classified data—of a secret program called the Special Censure Project. SCP. They billed the program as the latest archaeological tool ever invented. Every detail of the program was in this file. It showed proof of the program's ability. Proof time travel was possible.

An eerie thought passed to Keith's mind. *It all started with him, and it will all stop with him.*

46

Retrieved the Key

The morning traffic was light. There seemed to be no cars in sight, but the foot traffic was the opposite. It was unusually heavy for a Saturday morning. Early morning at that. Though summer was ending, which meant back-to-school shopping had begun, even in a downturned economy. Back to school, shopping was a must.

Keith crossed Tremont Street as he headed for downtown crossing. The acrid smell of asphalt and the tangy taste of ozone permeated the air. Noise that only a big city could make added to the mix. Over 650,000 people called Boston home. Although he didn't know the exact number, many thousands more worked there and visited for shopping and tourist attractions.

Downtown Crossing was a shopping district that had seen better days, but it was still the place to shop. Keith walked down Winter street and turned left onto Washington, passing the Corner Mall. It was early. Boston was just waking, but people were everywhere. It had only been several years since he had been there, and it had changed dramatically. The world moved on, he supposed. He'd read that somewhere, but he couldn't place where at the moment.

Keith continued up Washington Street, headed to his jeweler—Boston Jewelry. A smile crept onto Keith's face. Kal was gonna be really surprised to see him when he walked through the door.

A few minutes later, he entered Boston Jewelry. He expected Kal to look at the door and see him come in, but his back was facing the counter so that he could remove a chain from a display for a customer. He helped the young brother pick out a chain for a rather large medallion. As it got closer, he saw the medallion had an equally large W8 on it. The entire piece sparkled. Iced out for sure.

Keith approached the counter, and Kal had yet to see him approach. He waited patiently as the young brother picked out a chain. When he finally decided on one, Kal turned to face them with the chain in hand—at that moment, he noticed Keith and smiled.

"Keith?" Kal said, surprised and confused. "You're not on the—"

"Don't worry," he said, holding up his hands. "I didn't escape and nothing."

Kal held up his finger. "Let me finish with this guy, and I'll be with you in a moment. It's good to see you."

Kal picked up the necklace and handed it to the young man with the huge pendant attached.

"Take your time, Kal. Time is one thing I have plenty of at the moment."

"Oh, where are my manners? Keith, this is Damien," he said, then to Damien, this is Keith. He's a good friend. A real good friend." He let it hang in the air. "Damien is from the South Shore."

"Nice to meet you," Damien said. "I'm sorry if I sound rude or anything. My friend José was murdered a few days ago, and I'm going up to see his family now. This was for him, but I never got a chance to give it to him." He traced the name

José on the medallion with his finger. "I'm sorry for being so blunt, but I hope you understand."

Kain nodded, knowing no words were necessary. He also saw the kid was wearing the same medallion. His instincts told him it was going to be hell to pay for whoever killed his boy. He felt he was an excellent judge of character, and the young man who stood before him was a killer if he ever saw one. Calm, cool, and collective on the outside. Polite and charming, but he could see it in his eyes.

When Damien decided on a chain, Kal took several more off the rack. He then reached down and pulled out a box. He opened the box to reveal several more medallions and carefully placed the chains into the box. The kid paid the bill with an American Express Black card and left.

Keith looked up at Kal. "There's gonna be death in that boy's wake, my friend. Serious death."

"You're not kidding," Kal said. "It's too bad because Damien's a good kid. He's been a customer of mine for a few years. You'd never guess who brought him to me?"

"Who? Keith said, knowing he must know the person.

"Kain," Kal said. "That kid's like Kain's son."

"See, I knew I was right."

"So why are you here?" Kal said. "What you need?"

Keith held up the key in his hand.

"You know," Kal said, taking the key. "I've wondered when you'd come for your box."

Keith smiled. "I guess now you know."

Kal shook his head, smiling. "It's in storage. I put it there when you went away."

"No need to explain, Kal, I understand."

"It will take me a minute, but I'll be right back," Kal said as he left his booth and headed for the door. He told someone to watch his stuff. If Keith's memory was right, the guy he asked was his brother.

The jewelry store was busy. Kal returned five minutes later with the box in hand. Once Kal was behind the counter, he placed the box on his display case. The box looked similar to a safe deposit box, although smaller. Kal was more than his jeweler and friend. In some ways, he was also his bank. When you dealt with a lot of cash, you couldn't use certain institutions, so many in the game used their jeweler. Kal didn't hold everyone's money, just a select few. There was no interest and no fees. Kal expected that he'd spend some money in the store.

Kal pulled out another key and inserted it into the dual keyholes. He then turned them together. Like a safe deposit box, it couldn't be opened without both keys. He opened the lid and removed a small cardboard box. Something like a watch would come in. He had a sense that opening the box would change everything. He picked up the box and removed its top. An elaborate platinum skeleton key stared back at him. Keith removed it from the box and held it up by its sleek chain.

"I hope you like the way it came out?" Kal said. "Let me show you how to open it?"

Keith nodded. He assumed the key was hidden inside of the piece, like the thumb drive hidden within the cross. Kal showed him how to open the cross to reveal the key hidden inside.

"How much do I owe you?"

"Nothing, it was my pleasure."

Keith put the chain around his neck—it felt like the only thing to do. The two friends caught up on old times before Keith left. He had to get back to the Complex before being too late.

47

Change in the Game

The trip back to the Complex had almost been uneventful. Keith made it back to his quarters. Along the way, he felt like a set of eyes followed his every move. One to trust his intuition, he took a circuitous route back. He made it back to his quarters around 1:30 PM. He pushed it by staying out so late, but Kal didn't open until 11:30 AM.

Keith's head just touched the pillow before he fell fast asleep. In truth, his body got a lot of rest, but his mind and consciousness needed to break. Sleep was equally important for the mind, and he welcomed it. He could always think better after a restful slumber.

Keith stirred when he had a weird suspicion they had moved him—transported to a room with bright lights. Though he was acutely aware of this, he couldn't wake himself up.

He woke up with a start and found himself strapped to a bed. He looked around. Doctors and nurses filled the room. His head swam. Vision blurred. The room spun. Stopped. And spun again.

A woman in a white coat stood over him. He believed her to be a nurse and not a doctor. She turned and called for someone.

Another woman in a white coat came over. Although this one…was…not a nurse, but a doctor.

"He's coming around," the nurse said.

"How are his vitals?"

"Stable," someone from behind him called.

"Come on, Keith, wake up!" She said, urging him. "Come on. You can do it." She turned to address a man who just entered the room. "Dr. Bell, he's waking up."

Although he woke up, but not for another three hours, he opened his eyes to find the entire team there. Dr. Bell, Jen, Billy, and the two techs. Everyone. The room looked like any hospital room one ever encountered. However, beyond the hospital-like doors, he knew led to the Complex. *Home sweet home.*

"What the fuck happened?" Keith whispered, his head coursing with pain.

His friends all stood and rushed to his bedside.

"About time you woke up, big guy," Billy said with genuine concern in his voice. "It wasn't looking good for a while."

"How are you feeling, Keith?" Dr. Bell said.

Keith had felt like he was on fire. Severe pain course through his body. He winced at the pain. Someone, but he couldn't recall who showed him the button so he could self-medicate. He pressed the button. Almost instantaneously, the pain went away. Keith wasn't sure how long it would last, but every second the pain was gone, it allowed him to focus.

"Besides the pain," he said with another wincing, "I'm doing okay. Just fine, Doc. Could be better, but can someone tell me what the fuck happened?"

Dr. Bell took a deep breath and stepped forward. "Your brain…couldn't handle the last…Jump. It just stopped. Refused to work. I guess you could say it went on strike, but there's more to it than that, I suppose," he said, as he told his friend what happened. Keith suffered a severe brain injury—one that was almost fatal. If the director hadn't checked up on him, he'd be dead.

"Wait a minute," Keith said, batted and confused. "Doc, I wasn't on a jump. I was in my quarters taking a fuckin nap. It gets tiring doing nothing all day. Shit, weren't you...all of you...not getting tired of being restricted to your quarters? I know I was—"

"Restricted to our quarters?" Billy said, a bit confused. "We weren't confined to quarters, neither were you."

Keith looked at Billy with wide eyes. One's big as saucers. "What do you—" Keith stopped himself, realizing what must've happened. Somehow while he was in the past—someone—change the future. Who? Another jumper? He didn't know, but he also admonished himself for not noticing the feeding tube was gone. However, he had no answers. Could another jumper change something, causing this alternate future? He missed something but wasn't sure what it was or when.

Instead of saying another word, Keith shut his eyes as he lay back down. He had set up to protest but suddenly felt drained. His friends thought nothing strange about his behavior because of what they say he just went through. They wished him well, and moments later, he felt the familiar moving feeling he experienced earlier. This time when he opened his eyes, he knew he'd be in his quarters.

48

Reality Check

The cafe was busy, and the sound reverberated inside his head. Keith brought his hands up to his face, rubbed his eyes, and then his temples. He looked around the busy cafeteria through slitted eyes. Keith had severe migraines as a kid, and this felt like one of them without nausea.

Everything seemed to hurt his head, which made him wince in pain. Light being the worst offender. It made him want to go back to his quarters and hide under the covers in complete darkness. A place where it was quiet and the lights not so bright. However, he promised Billy and Jen he'd come out for coffee and regretted it.

"Damn, Keith," Billy said, staring at Keith as he sat directly across from him, "you look like shit? We could've done this another time."

"Thanks, I feel like I should've too," Keith said, with a low laugh. "I want to kill you guys for—"

"Kill who?" Jen said as she approached the table and set her tray down to Keith's left. "Now, what were you say—" she stopped short when she noticed the pain on Keith's face. "Oh, guess it's me you want to kill. You do look terrible. I'm sorry you're in pain, but you had to get out of that damn room. You'd been holed up in there for the past two weeks."

"I'm not mad; it just hurts," Keith said, still massaging his temples. "Damn, memories inside my head are so confusing, and nothing adds up."

"All right, you win," Jen said as she handed Keith his order. "Take your sandwich and drink, and we'll walk you back to your room, but tomorrow we're going outside."

"You have no choice," Billy said with a smile.

"All right, you got that," he took his food and stood up.

A few minutes later, he was back in his quarters. It felt more like a prison cell than ever. The headache went away about an hour later. His lights were dim, and it was quiet. Dark and quiet, along with his fan, always helped.

Keith sat at his desk feeling a bit better. His friends left him and told him they'd come back in the morning. He ate the food that he brought back to the cell. He hoped to see his friends in the morning but knew we couldn't involve them. The timeline had changed. Reality changed.

Keith believed there was one person who knew about the change: Director Harrington. He hoped he had until morning because he needed to jump. But to where, he wasn't sure. He had an idea that the contents of the hard drive hidden in the cross would at least contain a hint.

He had to consider all the things that led up to this moment, such as the disk and key. He believed the key needed to be used in this reality and not the correct one. No, it was more like a feeling—intuition. It was his intuition that he could always rely on, and it made sense. He found the key in this reality, after all, and not the last altered one.

His head still not yet 10 percent. The key was safe in the key pendant that he'd locked in his safe before climbing back through the ventilation system. He had to find the lock for the key, but he had nothing else to go on. Keith made his way up to the office above ground and got to work on the computer. He wasn't too surprised to find what he was looking for on the first try, but he had, and he needed to use the key first. Whether or not it was intentional—this was where he needed to be. In this reality, as strange as that might sound.

In fact, this would be the third reality that he had experienced where the world was different enough to be noticed. The key itself was an interesting item. Keith laughed out loud. A big belly bellow. He couldn't believe where he had to use the key. Just couldn't believe it, but he was sure of one thing for sure—shit was about to hit the fan.

49

Altered State One

Back in his quarters, Keith pondered what he believed to be the next move. On his way back through the ventilation system, he stopped at the vent that allowed him to see into the level below. Into The Altered States Program. TASP. The jump chamber wasn't full as the last few times he saw it. Most of the seats were empty. Three of the jumpers who appeared to be sleeping, Keith recognized. He was sure they were the ones who had been watching him during his jumps. He couldn't help but wonder where they were and when at this very moment.

After he got back to his room, he wrote down the time and how many jumpers there were. Of course, on paper, it was a time and number. Nothing specific. He now had the way to get into the chamber but had to figure out when he could execute his plan. He laughed at himself because it seemed like a suicidal mission. Why wouldn't it? He had no idea where he needed to go, and not to mention, he was seriously outnumbered.

He was sure of one thing: it would be that they armed TASP jumpers. They weren't like him. Shit, they even armed him once or twice. They had a cocksure military presence one had while still being active. *Him against the world.* He could take on the world. Why not? He recognized the look as false hope. He came across a good deal of ex-military types in prison and came to one conclusion: all men are created equal—but it was the heart that truly counted. *Nothing more.* It boiled down to who wanted it more, and in this case, he believed it was him. The jumpers below were just following orders while Keith was trying to save the world.

It didn't take him long to formulate a new plan. All he had to do was follow it through. He'd have to wait until later that night to do it, so he patiently waited. The jumpers below worked 24 seven. The overnight seemed like the shift with the fewest men. He still had a couple of hours till sunrise, but he still decided to stay awake. He'd sleep after he hung out with his two friends and then wait for nightfall to execute his plan.

As Keith lay there staring at the ceiling, he wondered what it was they did to him. He was more than sure it wasn't from any jump. His head swam with altered realities. They did something to the timeline, but he felt they also did something physical to him, and he knew for certain it wasn't good. Whatever they did, prompted another question—why? Did they know he left the Complex? If they did, how did they know? He remembered and swore. Fuck, he'd been so damn stupid. The GPS tracker was implanted under his skin for when he went on vacation. He'd forgotten all about it. With all the altered realities swimming in his head, it seemed like such a long time ago. Not several months, but years. A lifetime away from him. *Fuck.*

"That changes everything," he muttered under his breath, "but it still needed to be done."

He gave it some serious thought before realizing he was several stories underground, so the GPS shouldn't work. He wasn't positive, but it was something he remembered reading.

Either way, it made him feel better to continue with the plan. The reality he was in wasn't his, but this wasn't a jump, so he needed to make whatever plan he could come up with work. He wasn't an immortal. No, in this world, death is death. If he dies now, the Altered State's—changes made—would not be corrected. Game over.

Grateful, this was not some Hollywood sci-fi movie where the main character dug the GPS out with a spoon. He hoped his assumption was correct. Feeling more confident, he worked out. He had less than two hours before his friends would be at his door, so you might as well work up an appetite.

50

Altered State Two

The sun started the fall in the cloudless sky. It had been a wonderful day. Keith was glad he got to spend it with his friends. Before he knew it was 8:30 PM, and he said good night to his friends.

When they came back inside earlier that day, he had to go see Dr. Bell for a checkup. He chatted with Dr. Bell for a little while and then met back up with his friends. Except for that one time apart, they were there together the whole day. They hung out until around six when they ate dinner at the Complex. They hang out some more in the café after they finished eating. After, they walked Keith back to his quarters.

He looked at the clock one more time and shook his head. He was exhausted, but there would be no time for him to try to sleep. He figured if he tried to sleep, he wouldn't wake up until morning and miss his opportunity.

He had a lot to do in such a short time. Being overly tired would not help, so he started earlier than he originally planned. He hoped no one came to check on him. The first stop on tonight's mission was to go back to the office. He wanted to make sure he missed nothing, and on the way back, he would stop to check on the level below.

Part of the plan would also be to check for other vents that would give him better access to TASP. He hoped there was because dropping into a den of 30 or more soldiers, regardless of whether they were on a jump, was something to be concerned about.

About 9 PM, he snuck out through the ventilation shaft. He stopped to check on the level below and saw chaotic silence. All the seats were occupied, at least the ones he could see. Whitecoat lab technicians moved about—from jumper to jumper—in silence. Keith noted the time. 9:10 PM and moved on. He'd look for another way into the lab when he came back.

Twenty minutes later, he was in his office and went straight for the computer. He found something that would help with his plan. He smiled. Before him, displayed on the computer screen was a complete map of the level below that TASP occupied.

The room where he needed to use the key was surprisingly close. Two rooms south of the East exit. But it wasn't all good news. The diagram of the jump chamber was huge—and it showed the jump room contained 100 chairs. Jumpers. *A fucking hundred.*

The computer file even had blueprints of the lower levels. It showed other ventilation grates that accessed the lower level, but none were close enough to be useful. At least not for going in, but one might work for his escape. The one he would use to get into the lower level of the Complex had a 15-foot drop.

Dropping to the ground would be easy enough; the hard part would be getting to his destination unseen. He'd be back in his quarters, if everything went according, under 30 minutes.

Before he closed the file to go back down, he came across the TASP jumpers' schedule, and it was dated for now. He found the current week—to his disappointment; he discovered after tonight the TASP jumpers would be around the clock. 24 seven. Keith had no choice but to do it that night.

At midnight, Keith was at the ventilation grate to the lower level. The light below was poor, and the room cemetery quiet. He could see the two jumpers who occupied the chairs below the grate. He removed the grating and put it off to the side. Earlier, he'd gone back to his quarters to retrieve the 40 Cal semiautomatic handgun that was left for him along with the three extra magazines. The gun had no silencer, though it was equipped with an extended threaded barrel. Too bad. Invisibility would have to be his top priority, so using the weapon would be in a last-ditch effort to escape.

Keith secured the gun in his waistband before he took a quick peek outside the grate. Not seeing any movement, he lowered himself into the hole. He hung from the vent then let go, landing as silently as he could In between the two chairs. He scanned the area—no white coats. The jumper in the chairs didn't move. Not that he expected them to do anything but sleep.

Most of the hundred chairs were empty. Keith counted 25 jumpers. The exact number the schedule said would be there. He made it 20 feet from the exit before he heard voices accompanied by approaching footfall. He ducked behind a large filing cabinet. One that stood about 6 feet. He watched as the two people walked into the chamber: a white coat and an armed guard. The guard held an MP5. The same gun that the Coast Guard used. The technician checked on her charges and exited through the door on the far end of the room along with the guard.

He wondered why there was an armed guard with the technician. Were they expecting him?

He bolted to the door and stopped. After making sure the coast is clear, Keith stepped into the hallway and turned right. He memorized the path to the room he had to go to, but he wasn't sure if this level had security cameras. The path he followed was the only way to the room, so he'd have to deal with the outcome of being spotted by the cameras, if there were any.

He entered the next corridor and still saw no security cameras. Two more corridors, and he arrived at his destination. The office door was locked. He removed the key from his necklace and inserted it into the lock. The lock turned, and he entered the room. *Now what?*

The key contained markings on it. On one side, a five-digit combination of numbers had been etched into the metal. Keith found the safe that was in hiding very hard in the left corner behind the desk. He entered the digits, turned the handle. An audible click told him it was open.

Inside the safe, the contents made him laugh out loud. He covered his mouth and looked around. He remained still for a moment to make sure nobody heard him. The safe contained a couple of files and some CD jewel cases. Also, sitting on the top shelf all by its lonesome, which was the reason he laughed, was a silencer. One that threaded easily onto his weapon. Keith grabbed what was inside the safe and left the office.

At a brisk pace, he walked to the end of the corridor. Two choices, right or left. Left led to the way out. He slowed as he bounded around the corner only enough to make sure it was clear. The next right and another left, he'd be home free.

The corridors were awash in incandescent light. The silence made their buzzing loud and crisp. Doors lined each wall; Keith moved as fast as he could without running. Five feet from his next and final turn, everything went wrong.

At that moment, two armed guards turned down the corridor—headed straight for him—he slowed his pace. There wasn't much more he could do. If he were any closer, they would've run him down. The guys didn't react. He nodded to them as he passed, and they did the same. He just turned the corner when they called for him to stop. He could see the door he needed to go through up ahead.

"Stop!" One guard shouted. He didn't know which one it was, but his mind's eye saw them raising the MP5s in his direction. "Stop!" The same voice repeated.

Keith did the only thing he could do. He stopped.

"Turn...around...slowly and hurry up," the other guard called as they approached.

Keith did as he was told, except hurrying.

He smiled as they approached him. "What's the problem?"

"Where's your ID?" The taller guard said. He had black hair and piercing blue eyes. The other guard was shorter but somehow looked a hell of a lot meaner.

"Are you a jumper?" The other one added. "Where are you going?"

"No," he smiled again. "I'm a guy who just broke into a secure secret facility that's several stories... underground." He slurred the last part for effect. "I'm just waiting for you to get closer...so I can...kill you."

The two guards smiled. They glanced at each other and laughed. Each guard grabbed Keith by the arm and walked him back the way they had come. Away from the door, he needed to escape.

"Come on," the tall one said. "Let's get you back to your quarters."

"So, what you name, so we can do that? The short and mean guard asked as he pulled out a device.

"Dom Shidts," Keith said, still feigning drunkenness.

"What?" The short one said, letting go of him to use the device.

Keith wasted no time and took the chance. He brought up his left arm and clasped the taller guard's shoulder, and simultaneously grabbed his hand as he pulled. With quick speed, he brought the guy to the ground. The guard's weapon clattered away across the tile floor. The other guard spun to react, raising his gun but dropping the device as he did so.

Keith stepped in towards the guard. He grabbed him in a way to give him leverage. They struggled. Keith spun the man around and strangled the man with the MP5's strap slung across his chest. He pulled the strap hard, cutting off the guard's airflow. The man barely hit the ground when gunshots—rang loudly—as they reverberated off the walls.

Keith darted back around the corner and pulled his weapon. He peeked around the corner and saw Guards had stopped halfway through the corridor. One of them shot at him. Drywall sprayed in his face as several slugs ripped the corner apart. That was close.

He took a breath and stepped around the corner and took four shots—two apiece. Keith hit one in his chest, and he just took it. Bulletproof vest. The other slug hit the other guard in the throat, and he died before he hit the ground.

He saw more guards come around the corner, so he ducked and bolted for the exit. A blaring alarm sounded as he passed through the door. It's Blarnt! Blarnt! Blarnt! ear piercing sound broke the silence. The vent was in the back of the room. The grate gave him little trouble, but it pulled off. Without haste, Keith entered through the small hole and pulled the panel closed behind him.

He made his way through the maze of ventilation ducts. He stopped only once to replace the grating he used to enter the TASP complex. Once he was in his room, he spun around, while still under his bed, put the gun on top of the box along with the extra magazines and the stuff he just retrieved from the safe. He hoped he made a clean getaway. He replaced the panel and slid out from under the bed.

Keith set up, opened the notebook he kept on the desk, paused, looked at his clothes to see if they were dusty. They were, so he pulled them off and put on a fresh T-shirt and a pair of shorts. He quickly flipped through his notebook pages until he found the letter he started writing earlier—just in case he needed a cover.

Before he could finish writing a hundred more words, guards rushed into his room. They handcuffed him, then brought him out into the corridor. Keith glanced around and saw they were doing the same to others as well. A few moments later, the guys that went into his room came out.

"It's clear," the guard said, coming out of the room. He looked over at Keith and the guard next to him. "You're all set. Let's go."

Keith watched them leave and enter another room.

51

To Kill a President

Keith entered his quarters and shut the door, and leaned on it. *Damn, that was close.* He shook his head in disbelief. The space before him was a mess. Thorough. It made his quarters feel more like a cell. They turned his bed over with the mattress tossed on top of it. The bedclothes were scattered about. All his clothes were dumped into a pile. They also scattered the several boxes of his prison belongings about. The place was trashed. It was obvious they were looking for something. And by the looks of things and the sounds in the hallway, they hadn't found it yet.

He crossed the disaster that was called his room and quickly removed the panel. Everything was still there when he left it. He replaced the panel and began cleaning up. His adrenaline was high. Better not to waste it.

An hour past and he could still hear them in the hallways on his floor. He opened the panel, sure they wouldn't come back, and removed all the items he stashed there. Better to be safe than sorry. He stuck his head inside a ventilation duct and listened for a moment. Satisfied, he closed the panel. He picked the items off the floor and placed them on the desk. He pushed the bed back with his hip. He put the box that contained the guns and ammo on the floor. And he focused on the files. The disk would have to wait until he could go back upstairs, which he'd have to do by morning.

The files themselves looked old. The corners were dogeared, and the manila folder had turned grayish. He flipped open the one that was on top of the pile. The stapled packet of paper within was as old as the aging folder. The paper had turned yellowish. The ink had faded and, in some spots, became almost translucent. Photographs were attached to the packets. Each photo was of him in various stages of childhood. The first folder's information was about the first mission Keith executed and the outcome of said mission. He flipped through the pages of the file. Open another folder and did the same. This was the proof he needed. He got to the last folder, which looked newer. He opened it and smiled a wide I-know-some-thing-you-don't smile. *Got him.*

The hardest part was trying to figure out to whom and where he could bring the file. The conspiracy went all the way to the White House in two time-lines. Maybe the information was on the disk as well. He had the laptop they gave him, but the place was on alert, and he wasn't sure what spying soft-ware capabilities they had. They caught the phone call from before, despite that being in a different reality. He assumed it was top-of-the-line. He glanced at his watch, which was 3:30 AM. *No time like the present.*

He made his way to the office. As he went, he thought about the information in the folder. It contained a complete mission file for an upcoming event. One that would change the power of the US government over to a select few. It started with changing events so—Barack Obama didn't become pres-ident. The memo was dated March 16, 2000. Twenty years ago. He smiled because it was eight years before he got elected to become the first black president. It was also before Keith got arrested, so it made him chuckle. He laughed at the damnedest things. It would appear the year 2000 was his next stop unless he found something different on the discs.

It took him an hour to go through all the files on the disks. There were more mission files. Each disk label top-secret and was encrypted. The thumb drive contained a decryption program that could decode the files. It was more of the same. A lot of what was on the USB drive, being encrypted with the government's techniques, provided print proof that some kind of tampering was being done to the timeline.

He would have to find someone that knew about the program and bring them the information. Who? Would have to be someone that wasn't part of the conspiracy.

He shut off the computer and put everything he brought back with him to the office into the safe. He hoped that was the best place for everything he had, including the gun. He hoped he would not need it.

His adrenaline waned, but the rush of events made him forget time—everything blurred together. The trip back to his quarters felt like mere seconds. He lay down and easily slipped into a jump. The year 2000 firmly displayed in his mind as he went—March 16th, 2000.

52

Recon 2000

Keith awoke in the apartment that he lived in just before they arrested him for the murder of Dougie and his crew. Although he'd awoken in many different times and places by now, he knew this would be the hardest. He had the power to kill or not to kill. The whole detailed event could be put in his dream journal. Without a doubt, he'd take it as a fact and avoid it. Change would only put off the inevitable. No matter how many changes were made. He ended up in prison then to the Second Chance Project, as he liked to think of it, or should he call it a Special Censure Project. He usually settled for SCP. There were at least a few dozen different versions of reality floating around in his head. In all of them, prison and the project were always there.

Keith realized that when it came to things related to him, he only postponed the events related to his life off for another time. He believed this was bigger than life itself. Other people's lives could be changed, but not his own. The end result stayed the same. The untold prophecy he was meant to fulfill. An unlikely hero in this story about an antihero that didn't want to job. He'd see it to the end—his end—if that was the case.

He'd never seen himself as a hero of the story and still didn't think he was one. He felt he was just a good patriotic citizen doing the right thing. Let's face it. His ability to get the job done by any means necessary made him perfect for the job. He didn't need to be liked or thanked, but he thought no one would find out about his heroic deeds anyhow. Besides, a true hero does things when no one's looking.

If someone ever said. "You're gonna save the world some-day." Keith would have laughed and said something like, "only if I killed the person who would someday destroy it, and I don't see that happening, so pass the blunt." Normal people think like that, don't they? *It can't be us.*

Keith believed the forces that control the world were far bigger than everyone. Anything was possible. Anyone can be a hero at some point in their life, even the most un-hero of us all. A broken clock still told the correct time twice a day. There would be no praise for him. Who the hell would believe it anyhow—time travel alone is hard to swallow, never mind a convicted murderer saving the day?

Keith milled about the house most of the day in a state of utter confusion. He did not know who to contact and how to prove what was going on. All he knew was something that happened on this day, March 16, would change the course of an election eight years later. The only thing he learned from the information he had read was that it would take place in Boston on this date. Weird that it was a date that would include Boston. He may have to pull out and try again. As he was trying to figure it out, there was a knock at the door.

Keith assumed it was one of his friends. He looked through the peephole. It wasn't. Instead, he found a paperboy, and he wanted to be paid. Keith was about to protest because he didn't order any newspaper, but then he realized if he didn't, then who? Him, that's who. A better question would have been when? The answer—a different when.

He reached into his pocket, pulled out a 10 spot, and gave it to the kid.

"Thanks, Mister," the kid said before taking off down the stairs to the building's exit. Keith shook his head and tucked the newspaper under his arm as he reentered his apartment and shut the door. He brought it over to the table to read. He had a feeling the newspaper held the key to this trip. The mission at the kitchen table. He sat as he carefully read the newspaper—front to back. The newspaper was the Boston Globe, but Keith liked the Boston Herald better because it was easier to read, but they both rags in his opinion. Keith skipped nothing as he read.

After several pages, he stopped to make a cup of green tea. He'd been drinking green tea since he was a teenager. Once he made his tea, he went back to reading the newspaper.

"Aha, there it is," he said to no one. There it was, a small article. If he read the newspaper the way he normally would have, he would've missed it entirely. He recognized a name that was now familiar to him. But if he hadn't realized it, it would all be for nothing.

The second paragraph of the article mentioned...Harrington's name with no title. Just his name. The other names that were mentioned were well-known generals and politicians.

The article talked about a summit that would take place the next day. The summit would cover the safety of our borders and what these men believed we should do. The suggestion was to set up an agency called Homeland Security. Keith smiled because, after 9/11, these boys got what they wanted. He believed it would be this agency that stripped America of what made it so great—freedom.

The sun shone outside as spring approached. The sound of children playing outside came through the window he kept open a crack. Keith knew no matter what, he'd see this through to the very end. It was his destiny. His alone. It started with him, so it must end with him.

He knew nothing terrible would happen on the 16th, but he'd go to the Park Plaza Hotel, where the summit will be held tomorrow. That's where a secret meeting was to take place that would alter history, and he needed to know who the players were. Hopefully, they didn't already know who he was, at least by sight. He knew they had controlled life since he was very young and manipulated it to their needs, but he's in control now.

53

The Park Plaza

On the way over to the hotel, he picked up some accessories, just in case he needed them. The bellhop that assisted him with his luggage brought more than a lot of clothes up to his room. Keith dressed to the nines thanks to a suit he found in his closet that was brand new. When he called to make a reservation, he found that there was one room available, but he would not need it. Halfway through booking the room on the phone, the clerk asked him if he would still need his other reservation. The clerk assured him they based it on address, phone number, and the same credit card's last four digits. Keith explained it must've been his assistant who booked the room months in advance, and he had forgotten to place it on his calendar. The room was rented for the week, but the summit was only for a day. Another clue perhaps that a longer, more secretive summit would take place over the week.

The bellhop escorted Keith up to his room as he lugged the several bags on the cart. They entered his room, and the bellhop put the luggage where Keith directed it to go. Keith looked around the suite—a presidential suite. The place was enormous and came with a complete kitchen. He tipped the bellhop handsomely and escorted him out of the room. He opened up one of his bags—the one that contained equipment: Headphones, a strange-looking dish, and a plastic box that contained several guns. Keith didn't know what to expect, but he certainly came prepared.

Keith had most of the equipment and guns already had in a storage locker in another city. The firearms with silencers were thanks to his man, Dex. The listening equipment he had in his possession for some time. It was used for a job when one of his crew members got robbed. He tracked down the people and used the listening device to determine when the place was clear. He retrieved the stolen goods without harming a soul. His preferred outcome of a mission, unless someone tried to kill one of his guys, then payback's a casket.

The Park Plaza lobby, with its tall columns and marble floors, was a sight to see. On this day, it was filled with a sea of bodies from one set of doors to the next on the other side. Secret Service men were everywhere in the hotel. Yes, they swept the rooms for guns and stuff, but unlike the movies. People have pistol permits, and guns are more prevalent than one believes. The grand ballroom in the other rooms on the mezzanine was where the real lockdown took place. He'd come down to the front desk because he had received some mail.

It would appear at one point either Keith set it up at a future date or recruited some help in the past. The envelope contained credentials and a ticket to sit in the summit. He went back up to his room and passed several Secret Service men on the way. He nodded to them as he passed. They nodded back. At least they weren't rude, he said to himself. He believed manners were the key to peace. He chuckled at the thought and entered his room.

After seeing the chaos in the lobby, Keith determined the listening device that used a discreet wireless earbud may be too much of a hassle. He didn't put it in when he went down to retrieve the mail. After seeing the blinking light on the phone and checked it, he was glad he did not use the earbud. The Secret Service was one problem. He was sure that they would be on the lookout for such a thing. The other problem was the crowd. There were over 200 people crammed into the lobby downstairs, but it was now check-in time, and he was glad he opted for early check-in. There were far fewer people when he arrived just a couple of hours ago.

'Ihe gun would have to stay in the room until needed, as with the listening device, unless he came up with a better idea of how to use it. He figured once the crowd thinned out of the lobby and the guest went into their various rooms and whatnot, the device would be better utilized. Keith headed downstairs to get a drink at the bar. The summit wouldn't start until 8 AM the next day.

Keith stood in the lobby once more and took in the crowd. Under normal conditions, Keith would've looked out of place. Not for the color of his skin, but the clothes he wore. He didn't see one person over 15 wearing Rocawear clothing or Sean John. He took it back. As he saw her, one person rocked out in Rocawear, and boy did he look out of place. Keith, however, wore a tailored suit, the one he found in his closet. He watched the cat in the Rocawear clothing move about the lobby. Two Secret Service agents were watching him from two different angles. They moved when he moved. Profiling at its best, but he had to give credit to most of the agents there because they watched many people and focused on a few. Several other guys were being followed the same way, and Keith went to follow them.

At the bar, Keith ordered a shot of tequila and Corona. He chatted with those to his right and left. He introduced himself with the credentials that were mailed to him. The credentials said he was Keith Richards, a journalist for Black Business

Magazine. He got some double takes because his name is the same as the musicians and because on the black side of things, he could pass more for white than he could for black.

While at the bar, he devised a plan on how to use the listening device. He'd roam the hallways and try to avoid the Secret Service, seeing him too many times on floors that he did not belong. Though he dressed the part and could speak it as well, he already saw racism be used in profiling. He grabbed the device from his room, but instead of using the earbud that came with the device, he put on his beats. This way, they would assume he was listening to music.

He had to find Director Harrington and follow him. He decided the gun would still stay in the room because he had an overwhelming urge to kill the director. However, he felt it wouldn't stop anything but only postpone it. He was sure that the program had been in play since he was a child. They had been watching him his entire life, and he believed they guided him to prison.

The core doors were somewhat busy around 6 PM. He walked around his floor first and then went up to the sixth floor and worked his way down. Twenty minutes later, he reached the lobby. A couple of false alarms; the person wasn't Director Harrington. Not even close.

Keith became hungry, so he got something to eat at the hotel restaurant. And that was when his luck finally changed. Keith was about to dig into his dinner of steak tips, mashed potatoes, and asparagus when Director Harrington entered the dining room. He sat about seven feet from Keith, and though the man looked around, there was no recognition when he looked in Keith's direction. He walked to a table within air shot and sat down. Five severe-looking men sat at the table. One was black. Director Harrington sat down at the table, and the men seemed pleased with the future director. The thought of killing him crept back into his conscious thoughts.

The men held their glasses up and toasted the newcomer. Keith didn't even need the listening device. The arrogantly confident men began discussing their plans, with no concern whatsoever as to who may be listening, right at the table in plain sight. Keith's table was the closest occupied one, and to these men—he must have looked like a fool in a $2000 suit, eating alone. A lonely but nicely dressed slob.

As if he planned it, Keith's cell phone went off. He quickly answered the call. It was Adam who only wanted to know if he wanted to go clubbing. He told him he couldn't because he had something important to do—and he'd catch up with him tomorrow. Keith hung up the phone, shaking his head, feigning disgust, even checking the time on his watch. He tried hard to make it look like his date had just canceled, and he was furious. Keith didn't believe he had to do it for the men at the table because they barely knew he existed. However, he noticed three Secret Service men in the restaurant, and his display was more for them.

The six men started discussing how they could set their plan into action. He could hear them clear as a sunny day looking over the ocean. He couldn't see them because his back was turned slightly to the table. He could see a couple that sat at the table, but the one that sat directly behind him he couldn't see at all. Director Harrington sat just out of his limited view.

With no thought as to why he picked up his phone and went to his contacts to call a woman who had been begging him to go on a date, he called her, and she was more than willing to come to meet him. She was a little surprised at the place, but since she dressed nice, Keith had no doubt she'd turned heads when she walked in. Besides, she was the only chick he knew who wouldn't look out of place. Angela was the only rich college girl he knew.

After he hung up, he moved to the opposite seat to see the dining room entrance. He placed the cell phone on the table as well. He called the server over and ordered a bottle of champagne. Cristal. It was early 2000. He then asked him to take the plates away.

In the 20 minutes it took Angela to arrive, Keith overheard a great deal of information that he could use. It turned out Director Harrington was important. More important than Keith even realized. This was the inner circle of the money men behind the project. They openly talked about who needed to be placed—and who—needed to be diverted.

They talked about making sure that an up-and-coming Democrat didn't get a chance to speak at the DNC convention in 2005. They even laid out a sketch of what was to be done. Director Harrington removed a folder from his briefcase and passed it around. Keith smiled. He recognized it as the one he took. If it wasn't the one he had already read, he was sure it would contain the same or more incriminating evidence than the one he already had. As he concentrated on the conversation, one of the men looked up, smiled, and blew a soft whistle. *Angela had arrived.*

•

The morning sounds of Boston could be heard through the open window. Keith lay on the bed listening to the sounds while reviewing last night's events. Angela had left a few moments ago. He had to admit that it surprised him she wanted to come upstairs to his room. It wasn't part of the plan but ended up working out for the better. They had a pleasant dinner. Angela said she had a wonderful time. Keith wasn't entirely sure how seeing as he had paid most of his attention to the other table. In any case, he was pleased with the outcome.

After dinner, Director Harrington and one of the men from the table went to the cocktail lounge. Angela wanted to go to the club and, in the end, settled for a nightcap. Angela made him get up and dance to what the pianist was playing. Neither of them knew the song. It was slow and intimate, and he couldn't have asked for a better viewpoint of the two men. Keith wanted that file. No matter what it took, he'd get it. He then would stash it somewhere and jump back.

The unknown man left first, and Director Harrington sat at the bar for 20 more minutes. Keith and Angela followed Director Harrington out into the lobby. Harrington waited near the bank of elevators. Keith suggested to Angela they call it a night, but she wanted to go up to his room. The elevator doors opened, and they fold Director Harrington in. Angela and Keith hugged close, making it obvious of their plans for the rest of the night. Director Harrington didn't look at Keith once, but he stole a glance or two at Angela. Director Harrington pressed floor number four, and Keith pressed number three.

He didn't want to blow the tale by going up to his room floor where he had no room. Keith fixed the shirt in the mirror and put on his jacket. He left the room and headed towards the elevator. Only one person waited for the elevator, but Keith took the stairs. The corridors were virtually empty. Some maids cleaning rooms and a straggler headed down to get breakfast. Using his listening device, he walked around the floor until he heard Harrington's voice.

It surprised him he passed not one Secret Service agent or many people at all. The route to his room had been virtually human-free. He stayed in front of the door to the room like he was waiting for someone to come out. The listening device picked up sounds beyond the solid oak door. He listened to see if Harrington was alone in the room but couldn't tell for sure. *Fuck it*, he thought, then knocked.

A man's voice called for him to wait a minute. Keith drew his weapon and stood in a way to conceal the gun—which he held against his thigh.

A moment later, the door opened, and Harrington stood before him.

Before Harrington could utter a single word, Keith raised his gun, silencer attached, at him urging the startled man back into his room. Once inside, he shut the door using his foot. The door slammed hard. Director Harrington already began pleading.

"I...don't have...much money," he said, then pointed at a low hatch. "But what I have is over—"

"Shut the fuck up," Keith shouted. "Get over there on the bed, now!"

Director Harrington went to protest after he sat down but saw the look in the man's eyes and stop. He was sure it was a robbery. The man must believe he was rich or something. Harrington hoped the man would just take his wallet and other belongings in the hutch. When the man grabbed the items and stuffed them inside his jacket pocket, Harrington felt relieved. The feeling was short-lived. The gun remained pointed in his direction the whole time, but it was the first time he noticed the silencer. He believed someone sent the man to kill him. A new sense of pride welled up inside of him the way it does when a man believes death is inevitable.

"Who sent you to kill me?" he said, not as confidently as he hoped. "You can't stop it. No matter what they told you!"

Although unexpected, Keith's interest peaked, so he looked at the man. "Stop what?" He barely finished the words when he noticed a briefcase sitting next to the nightstand. "Hand me the briefcase—slowly. Unless that is you want some extra breathing holes. And answer my question. Stop what?"

Director Harrington picked up the bag, and with a steady slow movement, he handed it to Keith. He said and thought of throwing the bag at the intruder and Rush him, but the thought went as quickly as it came. "There's nothing of interest to you in there. It's just papers for work—"

"I'll be the judge of that," Keith said, taking the bag from director Harrington. "Now, answer my question."

"Killing me won't stop the consortium from setting legislation for the Homeland Security Bill. It will happen. Nothing can stop it. It's already in motion."

Keith nodded as he backed away from the man into the door. His gun still pointed at director Harrington who would become the director of SCP. When he was a safe distance away, he looked into the leather briefcase. Several files stared back at him. He saw two light-colored ones and pulled them out, but only enough to see them before he slid them back.

He looked up at Harrington. "'Thanks, he said with a smile." And left the room. He ran to the stairs and back to his room. He changed quickly back into his suit and then sat on his bed and removed the files. He was afraid the briefcase had a tracking device, so he brought it to the window and tossed it out.

The briefcase contained 11 files, and eight of them were color-coded: two blue, three red, one gray, and two yellow. Though it was the tan-colored ones he was interested in, he spread out the three folders and flipped them open one at a time. The second folder was the one he hoped to find, the folder he'd stolen from TASP. Keith smiled because he knew eventually they would recover the file, just in time for him to steal it, but that wouldn't be for some time.

The file contained what he expected to find, except the stapled packet. Though this he knew wouldn't be there, seeing it was dated 2006. Satisfied everything was in order, he closed the three files, stacked them together he then picked up the stack of color-coded files flipped open the blue one on top. He smiled. *Jackpot.*

He closed the files and got his bags. Once everything was packed, including the files, he called the front desk to tell them he would check out early. He'd originally rented the room for seven days. He told him his meeting had been postponed and needed to get back to Chicago. The woman at the front desk told him a bellhop would be up in a few minutes. He thanked the woman and hung up.

Twenty minutes later, he was in a cab that took him back to his house. He grabbed the cab several blocks away from the Park Plaza Hotel, just in case, Director Harrington reported the theft. Though in hindsight, it would seem director Harrington never reported the crime. After seeing the other files, Keith wasn't surprised.

The cab pulled over in front of his building. Three young teenagers hung out on the stoop and came quickly to his aid. The teens were no fools—they knew he was a serious player, and more importantly, they knew he tipped well. Money talks, bullshit walks, especially in the hood. Once he got back into his apartment, he put all his toys away and stashed the files behind the false panel in one of the kitchen cabinets. Keith went to lie down. While he stared at the ceiling, Keith went back to the present. There was something he needed to check on. He shut his eyes, and the world spun and melted together.

54

Complex Reality

Groups of guards roamed the corridors like worker bees. A buzz of activity. Keith walked the most circuitous route to the cafeteria, free as a bird. Thank God for small favors. The reality seemed to be the same as he left it—no further changes, as far as the download was concerned.

He stole the files, so he knew he had changed something, yet the present still became altered. A very important thing came to mind—he now understood—in order to fix things, he had to change the past before the change had occurred. On some level, he'd already come to this conclusion. However, there was a greater concern: what about the changes that he had no memory even happened?

He only knew about the change in this reality because maybe he jumped simultaneously as another jumper completed their mission. He didn't see the other jumpers as evil; they probably thought they were doing good—just following orders for Uncle Sam. Unfortunately, they were unaware Uncle Sam had been kidnapped, and someone else now gave the orders. Orders that so far, to his knowledge, changed the presidential election. He had changed little things on his own missions, but he was sure that the other jumpers piggybacked his missions. How did they exist before he entered the program? This was the information he needed to find.

Keith noticed, besides the roaming patrols, they posted other guards at various points along each corridor. The beefed-up security didn't surprise him. Why would it? An unknown man did breech a top-secret government installation without so much as tripping an alert. To make matters worse, after being discovered, he disappeared into thin air. Keith figured they also knew by now what he had taken.

With nothing to do, he went to the lab like a normal day. Even though of some questions to ask, as if he was unaware of what was going on. He hated lying to his friends. It didn't matter that he protected them. Dr. Bell, he hoped, had answers to some questions. Before they changed the reality, Dr. Bell had helped him in a big way. The importance of what he needed to know outweighed the risk. How does the past affect the future? He needed to know how to change things back without screwing everything up in the process. Was it even possible?

Keith turned down the corridor to the lab where two guards were posted just outside the door. When he approached, the guards asked for ID; he showed it to them, and they let him enter. Everyone was present, including the two technicians, whose names he never could remember, which was weird and in of itself.

Dr. Bell was engaged in a conversation with Jen. He looked over as Keith entered.

"What's with all the security?" Keith said as he scanned the room.

"An intruder broke into the complex last night," Dr. Bell said, shaking his head. "They took some files, and until they find out who it was, there will be tighter security."

"What? You mean, they don't know," he said, feigning incredulity.

Dr. Bell shook his head. "Not a clue."

"I find that a little hard to believe," he said as he shook his head from side to side in what seemed like slow motion. "This is a secret installation. Isn't there a protocol for this kind of thing?"

"They assured us there was strict protocol, but I'm starting to believe they were relying on the secrecy of the space and not security procedures."

"Before I get any more depressed," Keith said, "are we jumping today?"

"No, we've been shut down until further notice."

Keith sat in Dr. Bell's chair and put his hand to his forehead. "Hey Doc, now my head swims with even the slightest change made during a jump.?"

"That's to be expected," Dr. Bell said, "but it could get worse with stress. How are you feeling in general?"

"Well, I keep feeling like I made a mistake on the first jump, maybe even all of them."

"What kind of mistake are we talking about?"

"Do you think there's a way I could correct them?" He said, pretending to ignore Dr. Bell's question.

"I need to know what you did?"

"My friend Adam died shortly after I went back," he said with a pause as he glanced downward, "I made it, so he didn't die. I planted the seed in his head that changed his life. I thought it was for the better—but as it turns out—it wasn't."

"A simple vocal encouragement was enough to alter things in our present severely?"

"Yes, I believe that it did," Keith said, "unless other jumpers are mucking up the past besides me."

Dr. Bell stared into space for a few moments. "Well, there's nothing we can do about it, at this moment—"

"Because we're suspended?"

Dr. Bell nodded. "But when it's possible, all you have to do is go back to the beginning and change it? Take it all back."

"But I can't jump back to the same time because I already have been there."

"You could go back to the day before or somehow make it impossible for you to be where you were at."

"Ingenious, Doc," Keith said, holding back a smile, "I'll keep that in mind for when we're able to jump."

"Keith, your good man...I sensed it on the first day we met. You were just at the wrong place at the right time. I'm glad I met you."

"Thanks, Doc, it means a lot."

"When we're able, we'll correct what you did? Must've been hard to come to me and admit the mistake, especially after we repeatedly told you not to do what you did. That took courage—something I believe you're not of short supply. I'm just glad you're on the good side."

"Me too," Keith said as he thought to himself. *You have no idea.*

55

Douglas

The TV in his quarters cast a bluish flickering light. Keith stood, a rainbow silhouette, as the blues and greens flickered onto the walls and himself. Although the TV was on, Keith paid little attention to the screen. The doctor's words filled his head. It engulfed him to the point where all his focus went to what the doctor had said.

After seeing what happened to Adam and how changing the past moved up his own incarceration, Keith was sure the doctor was wrong. He knew he couldn't jump back to the same day because he was already there, and the doc's idea that he went back before the event happened and stayed three days would only move the day up or backward today when he was available. He witnessed this already with what happened to Adam and himself.

He thought about leaving himself stranded far away but didn't want the consequences that would result in a confused and dazed Keith of that time period. He had a feeling that he would die before he opened his eyes in the present.

He saw the files for a reason. Before he stashed the files away, he took another look. Each person involved in the consortium had a file. It seemed Director Harrington didn't trust anyone. He put together a dossier on each of the members. One of the men would become the president in the altered future that he currently called the present.

The files contain dossiers on not just his friends and allies but of his enemies as well. It would explain why he kept it with him at all times. The blue and yellow marked tabs were of his opponents. One of them, in particular, was a guy named Jonathan Douglas, who had become a roadblock in getting the proper legislation passed to set the mission in motion. He was the chair of the oversight committee for the SCP and one of the men who sat on the Board of Directors but never spoke.

Jonathan Douglas could be an ally or a shark in tuna's skin. What choice did he have? Douglas, however, had been very vocal in his opposition to the project. According to the files, it was due to its too tempting military applications. He was against such possibilities. Somehow, they got him to change his mind, or did they? There had to be a reason that not only SCP became active, but TASP as well. Does Douglas know about TASP?

Something on the television caught his eye. The news-caster just reported that the president signed a new bill into law that would allow the government to use any method to find any threat to the American way of life. Keith laughed. The threat was ready in office. The new president was already shit-talking Iran, which hinted at more war. He didn't like the way things were going in this reality. Keith shook his head in disgust as he shut the TV off, lay back on his bed, and shut his eyes—and jumped.

He now knew what needed to be done.

•

Outside, the weather of March tried to usher spring into being, but to no avail. Snow covered the ground, only a couple of inches, but enough to cause problems. Boston was not a great place to park and drive without snow. However, a couple of inches wouldn't stop him. But people came to Boston from all over the globe to go to work, school, and live. Some drivers on the streets shouldn't have a driver's license. He heard kids playing outside while he went over the files.

Noon approached fast, and he stopped to make some tea. He sat in his living room with the cup in his hand as he looked at the files scattered over his coffee table. According to the files, Douglas would be in his office today. Tuesdays and Thursdays.

The 20-story glass and steel building before him contained government offices. Jonathan Douglas had his office on the 18th floor. Keith headed for the café across the street that had outside seating. As he crossed the street, several drivers leaned on their car's horns. One of the drivers was a business executive in a Benz who yelled a few obscenities his way. Money doesn't make one civilized, does it?

The cookie-cutter café had an upscale appeal. The chain had cropped up in major cities across the US in the past three years. He placed his tea and sandwich on the table and removed his laptop from his backpack. Remote workers were nothing new in the city, so he blended right in. The table he picked sat near the corner of the building. He chose it for two particular reasons. It was in the shade, and two, it had a great advantage point of the front doors to the building where Mr. Douglas's office is located.

The foot traffic, albeit heavier on this side of the street because of the shops and an alley cut through, made for a suitable cover. The light traffic on the other side allowed him to see the entrance unobstructed most of the time. The file also stated that Douglas never left his office earlier than 4:30 on the dot, and only on the rare occasion had he left later.

Keith scanned the area back and forth. He wore sunglasses so as not to look too obvious. A habit he picked up while in prison. Inside, it was never good to let people see what you were doing. Because if you did, they might catch you sleeping, and then you'd be laying in a puddle of your own blood wishing help would come. Keith saw nothing out of the ordinary. However, Director Harrington had a file on this guy, and he knew someone had to be watching him. He took a sip of his tea and continued to enjoy his sandwich and decided a bowl of Broccoli and Cheddar soup would be a great complement to his lunch, but instead, he stayed in his seat and watched the doors.

Two teenage boys sat at a table in direct sunlight. Under normal conditions, this would not have attracted Keith's attention, but they both sat in a way to see across the street. He checked his watch, and it read 4:25 PM. The teenagers were between 14 and 16, which would make their present ages old enough to be part of TASP. They were typical teenagers. Nothing about them stood out. Average height. One had black hair and tan skin. The other had blonde hair and a tan that looked paid for. The black-haired kid scanned the area on this side of the street. He seemed satisfied because he then engaged in conversation with the kid across from him. Although Keith didn't concentrate on him as much as the other, he was positive the blonde kid scanned the opposite side of the street. Keith checked his watch again, and it was time. He'd know soon enough. Douglas exited the building and crossed the street toward Keith, and straight into the café.

He glanced over at the kids as they got up from the table, threw away their stuff, and picked up their skateboards, which Keith didn't see at first, and then went to the side of the building where there was an alley and started doing tricks. He wasn't surprised at all when Douglas came back out of the café with a drink, and a small bag went into the alley himself. Douglas walked slow. A methodical pace. A man who enjoyed taking in everything around him. Keith watched the kids up ahead skate and stop. Do a couple of tricks more and stop. Clever tail. His technique required less ingenuity—he stayed back about a block and waited for an opportunity.

The foot traffic picked up as they walked along. Keith had to pick up his pace. He lost him for a moment. A couple of blocks up, he saw the kids stop and start talking. They knew something Keith didn't, and sure enough, Douglas entered a newsstand. A fitting place called Dugs News. Keith caught up and had to stop himself. He tied his shoes. Douglas came out with a couple of magazines and a newspaper and went into the bar next store. Lady luck showed on her face. Keith walked into the bar, never breaking his stride, just another business person blowing off some steam after work.

Because of the no-smoking laws in Boston, the air was clear but thick with the pungent smell of alcohol. One room opened space with a no-nonsense bar off to one side. Keith spotted Douglas and sat in the empty seat next to him on the right. He sat down as the bartender, a pretty dark-skinned beauty, served Douglas his drink. Keith brought two files with him. The one that contained information on one Jonathan Douglas and the other about an unofficial project called TASP. The bartender asked Keith what he'd like, and he told her. She made it right there and then left to see to her other customers. Up close, Douglas looked like he had drunk too much already, but the drink before him most likely was his first.

There were several other people in the bar, but he felt nothing. His instincts said the coast was clear. He slipped the folder out of the satchel he'd been carrying and slid it in front of Douglas.

Douglas looked at him. "What's this—"

"Don't talk, just review," Keith said as he took a sip of his drink.

He watched the others, and nothing appeared out of place. Douglas looked up twice to say something, then thought better of it. He closed the file, and his face told Keith he had questions and wanted answers.

"Who are you, and where'd you get this?" He said, scratching his head, "what do you want?"

"My name is unimportant at the moment," Keith said, "but I stole this from Harrington, the director of the SCP."

Dr. Douglas shook his head in disbelief. "The bastard's keeping tabs on me?"

"Yes, there're two teens outside, and they've been tailing you since you left work."

"The kids with skateboards," Douglas laughed. "They're too young—"

"Not for SCP, but they're not part of that program. They're part of Harrington's other project called TASP."

"TASP? I never heard of it."

"It's the military version of SCP."

"You seem to know her lot about this?"

Keith slid the other file over to him. "Everything you need to know is there...Keith stood to leave, including my cell phone number, but I don't need to tell you that your phones may also be compromised."

"No, you don't," he said and looked at the file before him and glanced at Keith. "I'm sure I'll be in touch if what I believe is in this file."

"I'm sure you will," he said. "They're copies, so destroy them if you need to, but if you want the originals, they are safely tucked away."

Keith turned to leave.

"One thing before you go..."

Keith looked at the man who bore the weight of the world on his shoulders and probably did.

"Who are you?"

"Read the file, and you'll figure it out," Keith said as he tossed a ten-dollar bill on the bar and left.

56

The Call

Darkness settled in as Keith turned down his street. Kids played Relievo, a form of two-team tag. People hung out on the stoops—kids and adults alike. As he made his way to his crib, a few people remarked on his clothing. He doubted anyone on the block had ever seen him, king gutter himself, wear a suit, never mind a nice one, except for court, of course. It must've been a shock to their ghetto system. Don't get it twisted. People in the hood wore suits, but they were usually a bit older than he.

As he climbed the stairs to his building, he said, what's up to some kids who always hung there. He made it up to the third step when his phone rang. He stopped on the porch, fished the phone out of his pocket, and answered it without looking at the screen.

"Hello?" Keith said into the phone.

"Is this the person I talked to earlier?

"That depends."

"This is Douglas," he said and then paused for a moment. "I'm on a payphone in a bar I never go in, so it's—"

"It's never safe," Keith said, "so don't ever lie to yourself again. To answer your first question, yes, I am."

"I found the material you gave me to be very interesting," Douglas said. "Of course, I now have many questions."

"Later," Keith said. "Right now, I want you to go out the back door and then go buy a prepaid phone. Use this Social Security number: 026-15-2368 in the name David Rockwood born 10/1/88."

"I won't remember all that," Jonathan Douglas said. "Okay, I got paper, so can you repeat that?"

Keith repeated the information three more times.

"When you get the new phone, call back this number," he said and then hung up.

After borrowing his neighbor's car, he drove to the nearest place one could buy a prepaid cellphone downtown. Keith knew Douglas would walk five blocks from the office. In a city like Boston, it was easier to keep track of people around you while on foot, so he knew Douglas would walk or take the T. Keith arrived before Douglas and parked across the street in the shadows. Douglas walked into the store, talk to the clerk, and walked back out with a box in his hand. While Douglas made that transaction, Keith watched the area for anything odd. Nobody followed him, but just because he didn't see anyone didn't mean they were not. Satisfied, at least for now, he brought his attention back to Douglas, who now stood outside the small building with the phone plugged into an outside outlet with the new cellphone held in the air. The man wasn't wasting any time. Keith laughed and went back to watching the area. A few minutes later, his phone buzzed across the car's dashboard. He looked over to the side of the building. The phone still attached to Douglas's air. He answered, "yeah?"

"It's me, but this phone isn't fully charged. I have the damn thing plugged into the side of the building. "

"Listen," Keith said, "don't worry about it. I want you to walk down the street towards the Dunkin' Donuts and stay on the phone."

It was New England. Dunkin' Donuts was everywhere.

Keith watched as Douglas left the store across the street as he headed to the Dunkin' Donuts. He could hear the man's breathing—heavy and ill regular. The man wasn't used to exercise. Douglas kept muttering to himself. After watching the area Douglas left, Keith was now satisfied nobody followed the man. Although that seemed odd, Keith picked the guy up.

"Turn right down the next street—"

Keith observed Douglas through the windshield, looking around. "Are you here?"

"—Just take the next right."

"Okay. Okay," Douglas said.

"Relax, we'll talk in a moment. I just need to be sure you haven't been followed."

"I understand...fully."

There were two cars in front of Keith and several behind him. Keith passed Douglas, turned down a side street, and pulled over. He rounded the corner seconds afterwards. Douglas almost passed him until Keith lowered his window and called to him.

Keith looked over at the G-man after he got in the car. "That wasn't so bad, was it?"

Douglas smiled. "No, quite painless—for a moment anyhow. But I have a feeling it's going to get...really bad."

"There's no doubt in my mind," Keith said as he turned onto the expressway.

Douglas looked around. "Where are we going?"

"Nowhere," Keith replied in a calm voice. "I figured it would be safer if I just drove around."

"All right," Douglas said, "you're one of them, aren't you? A jumper?"

"Yes," he said, his face expressionless. "I'm a bit more than that because, without me, the program wouldn't exist."

"You're not—"

"No, I'm SCP, not TASP."

They drove south on Route 93 in light traffic. Keith answered Douglas's many questions, and the ones he couldn't answer he left alone. Keith explained things could be corrected, but not until after he gets back. Everything had to happen the way it did.

The plan was simple: all Douglas had to do was keep tabs on Harrington and the other six men of the Consortium. He already gave Douglas a copy of the files. All he had to do was go along with the program, pretending to be in the dark while compiling a case against the treasonous deeds.

An hour and a half later, he dropped Douglas off a block from his apartment building. He then drove back to his apartment in his parked the car on the street and stopped as neighbors to thank him for that and to use the car and return the keys. He also gave him some money for gas. Keith went up to his apartment crashed onto his bed exhausted, but something inside him said it was time to go, so he closed his eyes and thought...*homeward*.

57

Death Distraction

A loud bang woke Keith up—he looked around his room and listened. He was still in the jump. It wasn't a bang, but someone pounding on his apartment door. He threw on pants and bounded for the door to stop the banging. *This couldn't be good.*

"Who the fuck is it?"

"It's Jimmy, dawg," he said from the other side of the door. "Come on, let me in."

Keith unlocked the door to let his friend inside. One didn't need to be a psychologist to know something bad had happened. Jimmy paced back and forth as his arms flailed about. He told Keith what had gone down. The usual scenario. One of his boys—in this case, Ricky—got into a fight with someone, probably to save face, and after Ricky kicked the dude's ass, the dude shot Ricky in the face. Another friend dead. Another funeral. For no reason but to protect one's reputation.

During Jimmy's explanation of the situation, Keith stuffed his gun in the front of his waistband and pulled down his T-shirt to cover it. Jimmy sat down and went silent. Keith went into his bedroom and quickly came out with another gun and handed it to Jimmy.

"This what you want, dawg?" Keith said. "You sure you want to do this?"

Jimmy nodded as he stood up, and they left the apartment in silence.

They walked to Jimmy's car—the neighborhood crawled awake. Worker ants on their way to work or school. Many just stood on their stoops. Word had already made its way back to the block. Everyone knew what was about to go down. He saw people on their porches. Some poured out their liquor. Paying their respects. Keith nodded. The kids on the stoop nodded and gave their respects as he passed them on the stoop steps. He looked over to see how Jimmy was holding up.

Jimmy glances around in a frantic motion before he looked over at Keith. "They know what's about to happen—don't they?"

"No doubt," Keith said, getting into Jimmy's Accord, "they can smell it in the air."

Keith's mind was light-years away, though. He never thought he'd be in this type of situation again—though he wasn't, really. It had already happened. Keith knew how the entire night would play out. Most of it, anyway. The next morning, he'd wake in a hospital room, missing an enormous chunk of his memory.

Keith knew anything that connected back to him couldn't be changed because it already happened. He didn't know why it only affected him. He knew enough now to play by the rules, whether or not he liked it. There would be no changing things now. Not for his timeline—it must play out the way it's supposed to.

"Yeah," Jimmy said, getting behind the wheel, "the smell of death." He turned the key and pulled off—set for revenge with murder on his mind.

Everything slowed down, as if in a dream, which it kinda was for Keith. One that was dragged out but still knew the conclusion of it ahead of time. Although Keith knew what was coming, it all felt so new. On some level of his conscious mind, he experienced this event for the first time.

The temptation to alter the coming events bloomed in his gut until pressure burned its way into his brain. He pushed the feeling back down as if it was bile tried to force its way up his esophagus. The consequences were too great to risk letting the thought take hold. Bending to the impulse to change the forthcoming events would be no different from what he was trying to prevent because he couldn't foretell what the future change would bring.

The streets on which they drove became a blur as he got lost in his memory. He couldn't remember when he pulled the gun out of his waistband and held it on his lap. Yet, he knew it was there, and it was locked and loaded. *Ready to go.* Keith looked over at his boy. At some point, he did the same because the gun he gave Jimmy was resting on his lap as well. He looked up and out through the windshield, everything still and that disconcerting slow-motion. A group of people, mostly teenagers, were laughing outside in front of a triple-decker...

"That's the spot, dawg."

Keith nodded; he needed little information to know the place Jimmy meant. The events of that night would remain ingrained in his brain for the rest of his life. Eventually, it would set the course that brought him to prison and then to the SCP. He really wished it was something he could change. A tear rolled down his cheek for the pain and suffering he'd about to cause to some poor family. He said a silent prayer for his soul and looked at Jimmy one last time because they were about to change this family's lives forever, as they took loved ones away from them.

They pulled behind a cargo van, a couple of houses before the house. The street, a popular shortcut over to the next main parallel main street, saw a lot of unfamiliar cars, so one more wouldn't be noticed.

They left the car running while they exited and crossed the street between a Honda Civic and a U-Haul truck. Something caught his attention—three young children walked in their direction. A boy and two girls who were maybe 10 or 11 years old. Keith wondered what they were doing outside so late and shook his head. The kids didn't even notice the guns in the two man's hands.

Their pace was quick, their strides long, as they approached the crowd in front of the house. One man, obviously amped up from something, sat at the top of the stoop talking shit. Jimmy told him, as they closed the distance, that was their man. The man stepped onto the porch, which was maybe 5 feet higher than the sidewalk. Though they had a clean line of sight, the crowd concerned Keith. Jimmy raised his gun and unloaded it. Keith did the same.

The rest of the night was a blur. After they lit up the dude and watched him fall, they fled the scene. A few people in the crowd pulled out weapons, but Keith shot one in the head as they opened up on the crowd. They made it back to Jimmy's car and took off. They sped through the streets of Boston as they headed back to Keith's neighborhood. A block from Keith's Street, tragedy hit.

"Slow down!" Keith yelled. "Ain't no one behind us. Fuck, slow your damn ass down."

"I got it."

The last thing Jimmy said before he ran a red light and a semi with a trailer slammed into the driver's side of their car. The big rig crushed it into a mangled mess. Keith was lucky to be alive. When he saw the news on TV the next night, he wished he died as well. A recap of the shootout was on the news. He turned it up to listen. The man who they shot was dead, so were three children who got caught in the crossfire. The same three kids that passed as Jimmy, and he walked to the house. Keith shook his head and shut up his television.

He closed his eyes and forced himself out of there and into a jump back home.

58

Future Stop

Two dots stacked upon each other blinked through the darkness. It took a minute for his eyes to adjust. Numbers appeared on both sides of the blinking colon. The familiar 6 and 15 followed by the letters AM. *Keith blinked.* His heart rushed as his head spun a bit. It had to be a coincidence.

He got out of bed and padded out of his quarters and down the hall to the bathroom. Though it was a communal bathroom, it was better than having one next to the bed. The automated lights didn't turn on, and it was eerily quiet. Not completely abnormal, but enough to raise an alarm. The base would awake soon, and along with that came people crowding the corridors. Jumps may have been suspended, but most of the other workers still had jobs to perform.

The corridor still quiet five minutes later made Keith pause. He passed not one person in the hallway as he walked back to his room. Were they on lockdown again? He didn't think so because there were no guards. The magnetic pole of curiosity tugged at him as he lay back on his bed. He tossed and turned for five minutes—until curiosity won.

The gun and other stuff were still in the vent, so too much couldn't have changed. He removed the gun and placed it in his waistband, and let his sweatshirt fall over it. He figured someone had to be at the guard station. Keith saw signs of life. A couple of people were ahead of him. A man and a woman. He watched them as they turned into the café. They wore yellow hospital scrubs. He could see a few more people in the cafeteria. They were also wearing colored scrubs. Some royal blue and red uniforms as well.

Keith kept it moving, past the café, down the corridor, and took a right at the end. The guard station came instantly into view. Two guards stood outside the elevator doors on the other side of the thick, foolproof glass. Another stood on the other side of the protective glass wall. Another was holed up inside the glass box between both sides. The only one with the power to let anyone leave. They controlled the gate and the elevator from this level. The lone guard on this side looked at him as he approached.

"Good morning, Mr. Richards," the guard said, "will you be leaving?"

"No, I don't think so—"

At that moment, he realized he had had no type of crash or download of any kind. And not one memory had changed. That wasn't normal. *What the fuck was going on here?*

"Have you seen Jen or Dr. Bell this morning?"

"Dr. Haskell is in her quarters, I believe," he said. "As for-ah-this Dr. Bell, I'm sorry...I'm not sure who that is, sir."

"Never mind," Keith said, as he read the guard's name tag, "Brooks, it was an important, anyhow."

"No problem, sir," the guard said. "Have a good day."

"You too," he said, as he walked back the way came. A few minutes later, he stood in front of Jen's door. The guard had called her Dr. Haskell. Did she get married? He knocked on the door, and a few moments later, a familiar female voice asked who it was.

"It's Keith."

The door opened with force. The woman before him looks like an older version of Jen. She was in her mid to late 50s.

"There you are," she said, wrapping her arms around him. "Where've you been?"

"What do you mean?" he asked, confused. "Jen, is that you?"

"Of course, it's me. Who else would it be," she said, smiling, as she then pushed away from him and looked deep into his eyes. "It's finally happened—you've gone senile on me. I knew it was only a matter of time."

"Senile?" Keith scoffed. He brought his hands to his face, and when he did, he stopped and looked at them. Examined them. They seemed somehow different. Older. It hit him. "What year is this?"

Shock lit across her face like a fire. "2030," she said, now concerned.

"Jen, I'm not getting senile," he said as he walked into her room. "I somehow jumped into the future. I've always known it was possible. What a shock to your system when you're not expecting it."

"Please sit down," Jen said. "How long ago—when did you jump from?"

"I was in a self-induced jump before I was about to experience severe pain for the second time I bailed and ended up in this when. It was several months, perhaps a year, into the program."

She smiled. "I've been waiting a long time for this," she said as she held his hand. "There is much you need to know. They shut the project down. Dr. Bell, unfortunately, got killed trying to save your life. The rightful president was restored in your correct present in 2008. You saved a lot of people. You will save many more."

"How, there's no way to set things right. I can't go back and change it. I already jumped on that day."

"There is a way, but it only fixes the presidency," she said. "Your friends had been thoroughly surveilling the man who was to replace the real president. And in doing so, they caught him in a compromising position—it was all caught on film. It involved children. The local news network received photos after they publicly announced their support—he resigned quietly, of course, citing health and family issues."

Jen's quarters were large but very utilitarian. He saw no boxes and only a couple of mementos on the desk, along with a picture of Dr. Bell, herself, and Keith. He doubted she lived there full time. He took a breath, confused by the whole situation. Once he realized he was in a jump, he hoped for his enhanced memory to clue him in. Nothing. He had many questions, but the one that made it to the top was about Dr. Bell.

"Dr. Bell died saving my life?" He said, picking up the picture of the three of them. "When?"

"Just before you set things right," she said. "You returned from a jump. The director at the time—"

"Harrington?"

"Yeah, that was him. Well, he rushed into your quarters. He had no guards with him or anything. Dr. Bell saw him and followed him to your quarters. The good Doctor wasted no time when he saw Harrington with a gun pointed at you. He tried to stop him. As they struggled, Harrington regained control of the gun and killed Dr. Bell. By this time, the guards showed up. The director tried to spin it around and told them he stopped Dr. Bell from killing you. They almost believed him until your friend showed up to arrest him."

"Who is this friend of mine?"

"Jonathan Douglas."

At the hearing of Douglas's name, Keith knew he was on the right track, and I had to get back to his time. His when. So we can set things right. He looked at Jen. "Thank you, but I got to go, so I can make sure everything happens as you say it does."

She hugged him and kissed him on the cheek. "Be careful, all right?"

"I will," he smiled. "There isn't anything else I need to know about, is there?"

Jen shook her head.

"Good," he said and left her quarters.

59

Back to Normal

Since he awoke at 6:15 AM and crashed, it had been a whirlwind of the medical test followed by meetings. According to the updated information inside his head, the presidency was reversed back to normal. He thought he would have to tell Douglas, but it apparently had already been set into motion by Keith's own actions. However, there were still unexplained things swimming around in his head.

Keith sat through the last of the mission debriefings. He had a jump in two hours. During the last four meetings, he had been brought up to speed. Director Harrington explained that one package had never made it to the attended party. And that one contact, a young woman, had been killed in an accident. He also explained to Keith how they believed an assassin was trying to terminate him.

"But why would someone want me killed?"

"I'm not sure," Dir. Harrington said, "Keith, you need to be watchful during these missions. Believe me, when I tell you, many would like to see this program fail. They're waiting for us all to fall flat on our face."

"Well, that ain't gonna happen. I'll make sure that I'm fully aware of my surroundings."

"That's all I wanted to hear."

"Is there anything else?"

"No, you're free to go."

Keith got up from the conference table and exited the room with Jen and Billy close on his heels.

"Hey, big guy," Billy said. "What do you suppose that was all about?"

"I don't know, Billy."

"Do you think there's really someone trying to kill you?" Jen said.

"That's nothing new," he said with a laugh. "You read my file. I've been shot, stabbed…shit…you name it. So many times, I'm on a first-name basis with everyone in the emergency rooms across the city. Yes, I believe it. Someone had been trying to kill me for years, but they've never been able to accomplish the task. So far, I've survived every time. And trust me, it's not a good thing because you start the think your Superman or bulletproof, which of course, I'm not. Surviving all those near-misses made me worse. The attempts didn't stop after I went to prison. Several times new cats tried to stab me."

Billy hung his head. "Well, in that case, big guy, be…be careful…all right?"

"All right, that's something I can do," he said, as he turned the corner to his quarters, which were now in sight. His friend's concern for his safety didn't surprise him, but he was a little taken aback by Director Harrington's. Why would he want to keep him alive? Wouldn't Harrington rather Keith be dead? Maybe he still did. With the presidency back to normal, Director Harrington needed him—to make it happen. Wherever things went wrong, Keith was supposed to go back and fix it.

All-day, he tried to sort out the fresh memories. Nothing stuck out as important, but he knew some things were different, even from his original memories. Things still have not been fully restored. Besides, future Jen said Dr. Bell saved Keith's life by giving his own, and Jonathan Douglas arrested director Harrington. He wondered more and more if it ever would be fixed—would be back to normal. Was this the new normal?

His friends walked him to his quarters and then left. He checked the vent, and everything was still where it belonged. He sat on the bed, glanced at the clock, which read 3:30 PM. He had an hour and a half to the next jump, but they wanted him in the lab in half an hour, so there was no time to jump on his own. He would like to have jumped on his own first, but he wasn't even sure when he was jumping to, anyway. No scouting. Whenever it was, though, he'd be ready.

60

Kill Douglas

It felt weird going to the lab to jump. Keith had gotten used to doing it on his own. He asked several times where he was jumping to—he wanted to know what year he was going to? It really didn't matter they didn't answer him; he'd find out soon enough. Instead, they strapped him in and sent him on his merry way.

When he awoke, Keith knew he was in his 20s, and it was right before he killed Dougie and his crew. The surprises kept coming. By noon, he walked among eerily familiar skyscrapers. He picked up the package. Before he even broke the sale, Keith knew the envelope contained at least one item: a gun. It also contained a photo of a man.

Though Keith had known about the military connection for a long time now, it still surprised him they wanted him to kill somebody. And if it went wrong, they could deny it. The envelope contained a gun and a picture. What else could it mean? Keith found a payphone and called Jonathan Douglas.

"Hello?" Douglas said.

"Jonathan, it's me," he said, "and I ran into a slight problem. A potentially disastrous one."

"I see," he said. "What kind of problem, and is it solvable?"

"I don't know. Everything was corrected in my present," Keith said. "However, he sent me back to correct a mission that went wrong. I picked up a package, which contained a picture and a loaded gun with a silencer."

"Who's the target, and when did they give you hits?"

"You," he said, "and I'm standing at a payphone a block away from you."

"You're here in New York?" The question was rhetorical, so Keith didn't reply.

After a moment of silence, Keith said. "What do you suggest I do?"

"I guess you have to kill me," Douglas said with a slight quiver in his voice. "Put it in the center of my body. I'll be wearing a vest."

"What kind?"

"Why is that important?"

"It could, but it depends on the manufacturer."

"Hold on," he could hear the receiver being placed down on a hard surface and then some rustling sounds. "It's an ArmorTech vest."

"That's good. I don't know of any defects with that maker."

"When does your intel say I leave for the day?"

Keith looked at his watch. "20 minutes at 4:30 PM."

"You do believe you're being watched, correct?"

"Yes, though I see nothing strange at the moment."

"My friend, just do me a favor?"

"Sure, what's that?"

"Don't miss."

●

Twenty minutes later, Keith walked down a busy sidewalk towards Douglas's office building. When he reached the corner of the building, Douglas emerged from the lobby entrance. Never changing his pace, Keith approached. Two unknown men accompanied Douglas. Once Keith was in range and had an unobstructed line of fire, he removed his gun in a quick and fluid movement and shot Douglas twice in the chest. He disappeared around the corner of the building before Douglas hit the ground. One of the men stayed with Douglas, and the other unsuccessfully searched the area for the assailant—Keith.

•

Police cruises screamed past the bus Keith rode on. He watched out the windows as several went by the bus. Keith exited the bus at the next stop and walked about a block until he found a small alley. He ducked down the alley, found a drain, and dump the weapon into it. He covered the drain with cardboard boxes that were lying about. He returned to the main thoroughfare, where Keith healed a cab to the airport.

Keith made it back to his neighborhood by 11 PM. A bus dropped him off at the corner of his street. He made it halfway to his house when someone in a black hoodie rushed out from between two apartment buildings. Before Keith could duck for cover, the assailant fired four shots in quick succession. One round hitting him in the abdomen. The other missed him by inches and struck two nearby cars. Car alarms pierced the quiet, cool night air as the gunshots rang out. He collapsed to the ground as the shooter jumped into a car and sped away. Keith lay on the sidewalk, staring up at the streetlight as everything spun.

61

Good to Go

The two technicians jumped back when Keith screamed out in agony. He sat up, looked around, and fell back into the chair. Nausea caused bile to rise in his throat. The world spun, even with his eyes closed. The moment he opened his eyes, the download brought him back to reality. Still strapped to the chair, he vomited on himself.

The two technicians rushed to upright the chair to a sitting position so Keith didn't choke. One technician unstrapped him while the other pushed him forward, hoping to let all of it out. Keith straightened, wiped his mouth with his shirt, and shook his head.

"Can't take me anywhere," Keith said, gesturing to his clothes and the mess on the chair and floor. "What the ride."

He glanced around the room while he searched his memory, pushing the other timelines back at the same time. He noticed nothing out of the ordinary in front of him or within his memory of the current timeline. *It was as he had last left it.*

He could see Dr. Bell and Jen beyond the glass at their stations. They smiled at him, but he could discern concern just under the surface.

He'd stood on wobbly legs. "Before you ask, I'm fine. Just glad to be back."

"We're glad to have you back," Dr. Bell said through the microphone.

Keith walked to the other side. "Where's Director Harrington?"

"On his way," Jen chimed in.

"He wants to debrief you himself," Dr. Bell said, approaching Keith. "He said this mission had to do with national security, and it was important. Was it a success?"

"I believe so," Keith said, hoping Douglas was all right.

Jen also walked over to him. "Everything all right?"

Keith shrugged. "So far, yeah. No crash, so I am happy."

"I'm confused," Jen said, "why were you screaming, and what caused the vomiting?"

"You sent me back to the day I got shot," Keith said, still seeing the images in his head. "It happened right before they pulled me back."

Dr. Bell and Jen exchange looks.

"What?" Keith said, sensing something wasn't right. "What is it?"

"We didn't pull you back," Dr. Bell said, rubbing his hands together. "You came back on your own."

Keith took a deep breath. The right words escaped him. He shook his head, not knowing what to say. He'd been jumping back and forth for so long now he'd forgotten he'd told no one about his newfound ability. He had a memory of trying once, but nobody listened, so he gave up. However, he decided it was best to keep the secret and pose a plausible hypothesis.

"I guess the shock from getting shot sent me right back," Keith said. "Is that possible, Doc?"

"It's as good a hypothesis as any, I suppose," Dr. Bell said, mulling it over. "I'm impressed, Keith, that might have some teeth to it."

They continued with the normal questions upon return as they waited for Director Harrington, who showed up as they finished up with their own inquiry.

Keith stood to meet Director Harrington. "How did it go?"

"Come over here with me so that we can talk privately," Dir. Harrington said.

Keith followed Director Harrington over to an unused workstation across the room that was out of earshot of the others. Keith didn't recognize any trouble in the director's mannerisms. No red flags.

"First, I like to apologize on our part," Dir. Harrington said. "We didn't know exactly what orders you'd be carrying out. With that said, you did well, Keith. You hit your target with a double-tap to the chest. A nice cluster. You showed great skill; unfortunately, the target was wearing a vest and survived."

Keith looked down as if he failed and was disappointed. "Who was he?"

"Some terrorist planted high up in our government," Dir. Harrington said with an air of authority that almost made Keith believe his words. "Don't worry about him. The mission was a total success. You may not have terminated him, but the simple act of shooting him changed history. You're a hero, son. Be proud, for you did something good for your country."

Keith allowed himself to smile. Director Harrington just tried to blow some serious patriotic smoke up his ass. They had been no changes in history. Nothing discernible, but Keith had to go outside to be sure. On an earlier trip, the memories weren't triggered until he went outside. However, he now had better control over the download and sorting out the memories.

He also knew Jonathan Douglas wasn't a terrorist, far from it. He worried about the man, and as soon as he could sneak back up to his office, he'd call him to make sure everything was all right. He hoped Director Harrington and his powerful group of men didn't get rid of Douglas somehow. He was the only connected man Keith had in his corner.

The rest of the debriefing went quick. The Director allowed Keith to go back to his quarters. Director Harrington seemed too interested in the fact that nobody pulled him back. Keith reminded him about the attempt on his life. Director Harrington apologized emphatically and saw the attack as a plausible reason why he came back. If the memory of that night hadn't been part of his original history, Keith would've sworn Director Harrington tried to have him taken out.

At about 2:30 in the morning, he snuck back up to the office and dialed the prepaid cell phone number that belonged to Douglas. He picked up on the sixth ring.

"Hello," the groggy voice said.

"Who is this?" Keith said in a stern tone.

"It's me…Douglas," he said. "Is everything all right?"

"I'm glad to hear your voice."

"In that case, I assume everything isn't good.?"

"No, not really," he said, and he explained what happened.

"That was a long time ago," Douglas said. "I've been waiting for your call for a very long time."

"Is everything still a go?"

"I ask because Director Harrington claimed the target was a terrorist placed high in the government and needed to be taken out before something major happened. He also told me that shooting the target, the attack never happened, and we change history for the better. If it had been, I would've known."

"So, you thought maybe they locked me up or something?"

"Yeah, that's about it," Keith said as he shifted in his seat. "I'm just happy to hear you're not."

"Well, have you corrected everything that needed to be corrected?"

"I don't think you can get any closer than the original."

"You're ready then?"

Keith concentrated on the memories inside his head. Nothing important jumped out at him. "Yes, I guess I am."

"Then get ready, Keith," Douglas said. "We'll raid the place tomorrow and arrest Harrington and the men behind him and close down TASP."

"Thanks for the heads up, but now I'm not getting get any sleep."

"You'll get plenty of rest after," Jonathan Douglas said. "Good night, see you tomorrow."

The line went dead.

As Keith made his way back to his quarters, he felt light on his feet. He could see the end in sight. *About time.*

62

Empty Nest

The next morning a page came to Keith's quarters. A meeting had been called, and his presence required. On the way to the conference room, Keith wondered what was going on. Could this be Douglas? He didn't know how he would get in with a small army.

The last attempt on his life invaded his thoughts. He concluded it had been Harrington, but the only problem was that it was part of his original memory—he now called first memory. He knew they had been following him his entire life so that it could have been him.

Keith walked into the conference room and took a seat with his team. The Board of Directors were there, along what a surprise. Douglas. Dr. Bell, Harrington, and Douglas were standing off to the right, in a far corner, having a hushed conversation. Keith got a sinking feeling. He feared that somehow there had been a turn of events. He watched the group of men as they took their seats. None of them gave any hint to what was going on.

"All right, let's get this meeting underway," Dir. Harrington said. "First let me introduce Jonathan Douglas, head of the

Oversight Committee that keeps us honest," a wave of stifled laughs made its way around the table, "he'll be sitting in on the meeting that was called because of a matter of wrong-doing made by a member of Dr. Bell's team." Harrington's gaze fixed on Keith and made him feel like he was under a spotlight. "One of the techs, a Will Rickerson, was arrested this morning for leaking information to an outside source."

Confused, Keith looked over at Douglas, then Dr. Bell, and to Director Harrington. Keith then leaned over to Jen and asked her who they were talking about. Keith didn't know, and Jen didn't answer him. At least he wasn't being duped. However, he still waited for the ax to drop.

"... And we believe Rickerson had at least one co-conspirator." Director Harrington paused as he scanned the table, looking at every person there. "We plan to send Keith back to find out, just to be on the safe side."

"When do you plan to send me back, sir?"

"Right after the meeting," Dir. Harrington said, "and with that, I will conclude this meeting."

Everyone got up to leave. Dr. Bell approached Keith with Douglas in tow. "Hey Keith, this is Sen. Douglas, the chair of our oversight committee."

"Nice to meet you, sir," Keith said as he shook Douglas, his hand.

"Likewise, son," Douglas said with a smile.

"Excuse me, will you?" Dr. Bell said. "Director Harrington needs to talk to me, but I guarantee, Senator. I leave you in very capable hands."

"I'm sure you are."

Once Dr. Bell was out of earshot, Keith got down to business. "What happened, and why are you here?"

"You gave me faulty Information. There was a problem with your intel."

"I don't understand. What problem?"

"Director Harrington had just given me a tour of this entire complex, including the level below this one, and it's completely empty. Not a single thing. Gutted right down to the bare concrete. Like nothing had been there in a long time."

"Empty?" Keith said as his mind searched for memories. "Impossible. They were there last night when I checked on the way up to the office building above us."

"Well, there is nothing there now, and that's all that matters," Jonathan Douglas said. "If we hadn't met the way we had...I would've already started having doubts, but I don't. Just get some evidence so that we can bring them down, okay?"

"Yeah, I can do that," Keith said, inching towards the exit. "I have a jump right now, so I better get going."

Douglas watched Keith leave the room.

Fifteen minutes later, after getting his instructions from director Harrington and looking at a photo, he was ready to go. It would be a short jump back—just a couple of months. Douglas watched from the viewing room, and it struck Keith that if Douglas hadn't met him in the past and proved himself, Keith doubted Douglas would believe the man who appeared to be asleep had slipped through time into the past. He'd be skeptical. Before Keith could formulate another thought, he slipped through time.

63

Rickerson

Everything was almost normal. He awoke at 6:15 AM, got dressed, and checked the calendar for the date. The date was familiar, but he figured because it was only a couple of months prior that took place. Still kinda fresh in his mind. However, it didn't come to him until right before he left on the mission. It turned out to be the day he jumps back to contact Douglas for the first time. He believed in coincidences until he started working for a program that could manipulate people's futures. Rickerson's accomplice had to be a misdirection. Keith felt another attempt on his life was much more likely.

On his way to the lab, he met up with Jen and Billy, coming out of the cafeteria. He walked with them to the lab. Once there, Keith found Will's station and waited for him to arrive. It was a brief wait. Keith recognized him from the picture he saw before the jump. He'd come into the lab with a couple of other technicians. Wilson "Will" Rickerson was 5'10" tall with dark hair and a complexion to match. In a crowd, Rickerson would get lost as unremembered. An errant thought jumped into Keith's mind. Did Richardson work with Douglas? He was sure Douglas would've told him if he had.

Keith sat on the couch having a conversation with Jen and Dr. Bell while keeping an eye on Rickerson. He glanced at the wall clock, which read 9:30 AM. Any moment, Rickerson should get up to leave. As if Keith was a mind reader and not a person from the not-too-distant future, Rickerson stood and made his way to the exit. Once Richardson left the room, Keith excused himself and followed him out. Keith knew where Rickerson was headed but didn't know if he would meet up with someone along the way. However, to Keith's dismay, Rickerson went straight to the records room on the Complex's second level.

The records room door had a large window, which allowed Keith to see most of the room. It appeared that Rickerson was alone in the room. Keith waited a few moments before he entered the room. Rickerson jump back a bit. Startled by Keith's entrance into the room. Keith closed the door and said hello. Rickerson looked nervous, obviously caught in a place where he knew not to be. Keith went to the last row of files, retrieved one he pretended to need, and brought it to the photocopier. He made several photocopies as he watched Rickerson, who scanned files from the second row. The man still looked nervous but tried hard to make it look like he was just confused. He didn't succeed.

"You look lost?" Keith said, giving him a way out. "This your first time in records? It confused me the first time."

"No, it's not," Rickerson said, "but it still confuses me."

"That's understandable," Keith said as he retrieved his copies and put the file back. Before exiting the room, he tried to take a peek at what Rickerson scanned.

Ten minutes later, Rickerson left the room and headed to the elevator. Keith, who watched him from the stairwell at the far end of the corridor, waited for Rickerson to press the button to call the elevator before he rushed down the stairs to the next level. On the main level, Keith casually walked to the elevator. The doors opened, and Rickerson exited, but he wasn't alone. A blonde-headed woman was with him. Keith had seen her around. She dressed expensive and attractive, but it seemed weird because he saw Rickerson as a social recluse, so seeing them engaged in full conversation stood out to him as odd.

Keith hit the call button as they exited the elevator and headed to the housing quarters on that floor. He could be married and having an affair? Keith followed them but kept his distance, Keith knew where Rickerson quarters were located, and they weren't headed to that section. They came to a door and went inside, and shut the door. Their body language gave no social cues for romance. She had to be someone important because only officers and officials like Jen and Dr. Bell had quarters in this section. *Could he work for her?*

Keith walked up to the mysterious woman's door and listened. Unfortunately, indistinct voices passed through the thick metal door. He knew many of the quarters in the section had two or more rooms, unlike his, which was more like a simple dorm room. Keith's stomach growled, so he looked at his watch and stopped off at the cafe to get something to eat. Keith looked around, but there was no place where he could conceal himself, so he headed to the cafe.

An hour later, as he finished up, Rickerson walked by the cafe, and Keith ensued as he headed for the exit. Keith had no doubt that he headed up to the surface. Keith waited to be stopped at the elevators, but he had full reign to go where he wished in this reality. The only plus side to the altered reality. Topside, he caught sight of Rickerson as he exited through the building's main entrance. He followed Rickerson into a picnic area on the other side of the building. A place Joe Co. employees liked to take their breaks. Rickerson sat at a table with his back facing Keith, who saw an empty table in the front and sat down. He took out his phone and pretended to be on a call. A few minutes passed by when a man in a business and sat down at Rickerson's table. The man looked familiar to Keith, but he couldn't place the face.

Rickerson put down the book he had been reading. The conversation seemed to be one-sided, with the suit doing most of the talking. Rickerson was a series of nods and head shakes. He didn't look too happy at all. Something Keith sensed had gone seriously wrong—but what—Keith didn't know. The conversation ended, and the man got up and walked towards the back-parking lot behind the building. Rickerson sat there for a moment as he stared off into space before picking up his book and resumed reading.

Keith had a bad feeling. He got up and headed towards the front of the building. When he reached the corner, he looked back at the table. It was empty. The only place he could've gone was to the back parking lot.

A small manicured green space dotted with trees, flowers, sculpted bushes separated the building from the back parking lot. The lot was quite large, with close to 500 parking spaces. Rare in the city. Keith traversed the green space quickly while simultaneously scanning the area. A few people occupied the green space on the right side, eating their lunch or playing Frisbee. A flash a moment to his right caught his attention. A person in quite a hurry headed toward the parking lot. Keith gave chase.

At the edge of the green, Keith surveyed the section of the parking lot. He scanned the lot and wandered through the parked cars while staying alert for the unexpected. Not a single person in the parking lot or had any car left while he stood there searching. Keith shook his head, dumbfounded, as he headed back towards the building. Where could Rickerson gone? Keith could only wonder.

The sun sat a tad bit lower in the sky than an hour before, still warmed the beautiful day. Keith looked towards the sky, enjoying the free air. Although he could have done the same back in prison, the air beyond the wall was much more enjoyable. The bad feeling from earlier came back. And it was too late when he recognized it for what it was—an image of a man chasing him with guns flashed before his consciousness.

He picked up his pace, crossed the asphalt to the path in no time. Without warning, a man appeared from behind a stand of elm trees. The man raised a semiautomatic pistol at Keith and fired. He dove over the waist-high evergreen bush and scrambled through his stand of trees and shrubs.

Bullets smashed off the bark of the tree as he passed—Keith's ears filled with zinging noise as bullets buzzed past his head. White-hot pain exploded on his back and spread like spilled ink on cloth. He kept running as more white-hot pain spread through his thigh, and he tumbled to the earth. Exhausted, Keith just lay still. People rushed over to him. He could hear people yelling something before everything went black.

64

Unharmed

Lights flashed overhead. Through slitted eyes, pain erupted every time he tried to open them. He lay on a gurney surrounded by people pushing him down the hallway. He couldn't keep his eyes open. He stole a glance downward and couldn't see past the bloodstained shirt. He closed his eyes as they brought him into an operating room.

The paramedics worked feverishly to keep him alive on the scene. He kept fading in and out of consciousness. The hospital staff rushed him into surgery. They transferred him from the gurney to an operating table. They stripped Keith of the tattered remains of what was his shirt and pants. The surgeon approached Keith with practice efficiency, ready to attend to the major injury to his side.

The surgeon cleaned the injured area and used suction to free it of blood to get a better look. He looked at those around him and shook his head. The Intake Report stated the patient suffered an abdominal puncture that went clean through exiting through the front. He became more puzzled as he wiped away the remaining blood. The wound was smaller than expected. He entered the cavity to repair the internal damage.

"The report said the bullet went straight through, didn't it?" The surgeon said, sounding puzzled.

"Yes, two rounds—into the back and exited the front," an assistant said, the report in hand.

"This didn't go straight through," he said. "The damage just ends...and there is no bullet." He worked feverishly to repair the damaged area. As he worked, he stopped in his tracks as he saw the tissue heal itself. "What the fuck?"

"What is it, doctor?" The same assistant with the report asked.

"I must be seeing things," he said, pulling out for a moment. "All right, let's try this again. Let me finish repairing the—" he paused and stared in disbelief. "That's impossible."

He pulled out again as the wound closed up on its own accord.

•

Keith found himself waking to familiar faces, yet again. He just hoped all the excitement of him ending up inside hospitals would soon end. He wasn't surprised to see the doc, Jen, and Billy, but he was very surprised to see the director.

After asking him if he was all right, Keith had to answer a barrage of questions. Why was he outside? Who shot him? And the million-dollar question Keith really couldn't answer. Why did his wounds heal themselves?

"I really don't know," He said. "Maybe because I'm on a jump."

"You're what?" The director asked.

Keith told Harrington and Dr. Bell everything while Jen and Billy waited outside in the hall.

Something in Harrington's eyes told Keith he already knew. With the skill of a politician, Director Harrington turned it around. Questioning whether it was something in Keith's past that was the cause. Rickerson had been under surveillance for a few weeks, and they were ready to arrest him, so at least that part was true. Keith questioned everything around him. The realization that nothing was as it seemed.

After they debriefed Keith, Director Harrington left to see to his release from the hospital. While they waited, he spent some time talking to the Doc, Jen, and Billy. He had many questions of his own, which now he bounced off the only people, he hoped, had the answers.

"I still don't understand why I'm still here," Keith said, waving his hands over his body. "The few times I experienced severe trauma—it has pulled me back. That didn't happen this time, and my wounds never healed this fast before. Ever. Not one time. Not even in a jump."

"I believe it has everything to do with the fact you're on a jump. The puzzling part to me isn't the superhuman powers of healing—but I agree you weren't pulled back as you had been before. Why?" Dr. Bell said while looking at Jen and Billy.

"Could be his body cannot expire while his future consciousness is in control," Jen said.

"Maybe, I suppose. It's a possibility," Dr. Bell said, "but why—is what I'd like to know?"

"I not known the reason myself," he said, as the door to his room opened, and Harrington entered. "Am I all set to go?"

"Yes, get dressed," director Harrington said.

Back at the complex, Keith, for the first time, had undergone testing while in the middle of a jump. He could tell Jen and Billy and even Dr. Bell was giddy for the data they were about to get. It was something they never thought about testing. Jen and Billy extracted reams of data, as Dr. Bell asked question after question. Two innocuous questions hit home: how did he feel during the jump? How did it feel?

Until Keith had been shot, and his wounds healed with miraculous speed, he felt the same. As he always had during a jump, like wading through water while looking through cheesecloth. However, as Dr. Bell reiterated with the next question, how did he feel? He had a realization; although he felt normal considering the circumstances, his environment had changed—at first, it had been foggy, unclear, like a dream. Normal for a jump.

Over time, the more he jumped, he had become acclimated to this new environment. It became clearer, vivid, and in some way more real than reality. Back in the present, he was assaulted with the altered versions of the past. A constant presence. It became a battle to sort and push back all the memories except the original. Sometimes one of the newest timelines would take hold and push the other back. He felt claustrophobic within his own head. It was too crowded. Being on a jump freed him from that feeling. Although he hadn't seen it or understood it before, he also felt stronger and more sure of himself than he did in real-time. In the present, he questioned himself at every move.

After testing, Keith left with a new understanding. A new secret. His power of intuition was only the beginning of his abilities he possessed during a jump. This realization also caused him to pause because if it affects a jump or—every jumper—would also have these gifts. The TASP jumpers would have the same abilities. And if the assassin is a jumper himself, Keith was gonna have one hell of a fight on his hands. He already came to the belief that a one-on-one confrontation with the assassin was inevitable.

<h1 style="text-align:center">65</h1>

<h1 style="text-align:center">On the Wrong Side</h1>

A storm raged the landscape outside the complex, but the destructive force had no match for the storm brewing inside Keith's mind. The revelation that, during a jump, he was immortal only brought on more awe and confusion. As long as the shock of an event didn't pull him back, his body wouldn't be harmed. The only problem he saw was the flip side of this revelation—the other jumpers would likewise be indestructible.

And to make matters more difficult, he couldn't talk about TASP soldiers also being indestructible to his friends. They were not aware of TASP, at least not in this reality—and the probability of ever returning to the reality where Dr. Bell sacrificed his life for Keith would be next to nil.

Almost being taken out again fortified his belief that Director Harrington and his people, now, wanted him dead. He was no longer needed, therefore expendable, especially in any time. After he made his first jump, if Keith had gotten killed, the only program to be ended would be the SCP. The Second Chance Project, he mused. What it was for him. TASP would continue unchecked—which would make them unstoppable.

After Keith finished the multitude of examinations, Dr. Bell told him Director Harrington wanted to see him in his office—he wanted Keith to elaborate further on his mission. Although Keith was 100% sure Harrington tried to eliminate him, he couldn't let his suspicions show. The meeting with the Director was brief. Keith was ordered to continue his mission until they pulled him back.

Director Harrington also asked if he had any memories of being shot before he came back to go on this mission? Keith said he didn't, but it didn't mean much because altered things got pushed to the edges of his consciousness. He would search for specific things and get inundated with every change, no matter how small. It was better for him to hyper-focus on individual things, so if he didn't know he got shot, he could check it. Shit, there was that time that he missed that the president had been changed, but he couldn't tell Director Harrington that, now could he? *Nope.*

The mission included a timeframe of seven days. Keith had three days left. Within that time, he needed to find out what Rickerson was up to while staying alive. Keith laughed to himself since the recent discovery staying alive was the least of his worries. Keith went back to his quarters to figure out some kind of plan.

The situation at hand called for things to be kept close to the vest. Keith appreciated he was secretive by nature so that this part would be easy. He kept a lot of knowledge to himself, but he believed it was for the better. However, from time to time, he wished he could share it with someone. Keeping the stuff in was too much of a burden for any person to handle for long. But the years in prison had prepared him for this.

The unscheduled jump into the future had in some way let him know that Jen and Dr. Bell could be trusted. They did not know of his abilities or the existence of TASP. At first, he believed it better not to involve his friends, but Keith was smart enough to know when he needed help. He couldn't do this alone, and trying to hadn't quite worked out very well. He hoped the decision wouldn't lead to Dr. Bell's death—and he still didn't know if he could trust Billy.

•

An hour later, Keith was in a company car waiting for Rickerson to leave for the day. According to the security log, Rickerson left after work on Friday and came back Monday morning. This wasn't so unusual since only the crucial employees to SCP stayed 24 seven at the complex. Jen and Billy even had taken a week off a few months ago. Out of the team, only Dr. Bell never left for any great length of time.

On schedule, Rickerson left the building, got into his car, and pulled off. Keith waited until Rickerson pulled out of the parking lot before following since he had planted a GPS tracking device inside his since trunk. He had to acquisition the car and GPS tracker with Director Harrington's permission. When he left, the car was waiting for him, along with the tracking device at the curb.

Rickerson took Keith all over town. He made several stops along the way: post office, Staples, candy shop, and finally ending his trip at an Italian restaurant called Anthony's. Keith followed him inside. The maître d' asked for his name for the reservation. Keith informed him he didn't have one and was told they were booked, but if he wanted to wait because there usually was a cancellation or two. Keith being the internal optimist gave the man his name. The man looked down at his log and looked up at Keith, puzzled.

"Excuse me, sir, but you are already on my list."

"But I hadn't made a reservation."

"This is true," he said. "You're on the guest list of a Will Rickerson."

The maître d' waved it off with his hand. "Please follow me."

The maître d' escorted Keith to Rickerson table. The man had an amused expression on his face as Keith took his seat. After the maître d' left, rickets and smiled.

"My car just left," Rickerson said in a smooth tone. A white Barry White. "To them, you must have decided to have dinner or at least give me a head start."

"Most likely," he said, "so why am I here?"

"Because me being caught is crucial to the success of your ultimate mission."

"And what would that be?"

"Look, I work directly for Sen. Douglas."

"I have many questions, but I'll ask them after you tell me what you're doing and prove to me you can be trusted."

"Fair enough," Rickerson said as he explained his mission to Keith. They had planted him to divert some of the attention off Keith. The information from Keith that got funneled down to Rickerson allowed it to look as though he had been causing all the trouble. He even explained that getting caught was part of the plan.

During dinner, which they ate, Keith surveyed the dining room, looking for anything he deemed suspicious. Keith wasn't yet convinced that Rickerson was on the right side. Director Harrington could've planted Rickerson to get information from Keith. Halfway through the meal, Keith excused himself from the table to use the restroom. As Keith hoped, a role of payphones lined the hallway to the restroom. Keith was pleased to see them since everyone had a cell phone these days. He picked up the receiver of the payphone and placed a call.

The phone rang several times before Douglas picked up.
"Yes?"

"Do you have someone unannounced inside the Complex?"

"Yes, has he been compromised?"

"If he's the person I'm eating dinner with, the answer would be yes."

"Hold on a second," Douglas said. Keith heard a click as Douglas went to another line. A few moments later, he was back. "I will not say his name for obvious reasons—"

"It doesn't matter anymore," Keith pressed. "I'm on a jump, and he's already been caught. My mission is to find out who, if anyone, was his accomplice."

"All right, Rickerson. Willson Rickerson."

"That's what I needed to know," he said but remembered something. "Who's the woman?"

Douglas laughed. "Another dependable agent," he paused. "Call her his accomplice."

"Well, if you're trying to draw them off me—it's too late. Someone has been trying to kill me, and they almost succeeded a few days ago, so your plan isn't working. If you want them turned over, that's what I'll do, though it looks like I'll have to, anyway. I believe Dir. Harrington already knows and is testing me, but it doesn't make sense to me."

"No, it doesn't. Not if Harrington knows, and he's trying to kill you, but there is, however, another possibility."

"Yeah, what's that?"

"Someone else wants you dead."

"Hell, there's a 100 people that want me dead."

"Rickson's okay," Douglas said, "but I'm going to let you go now."

"All right," Keith said and hung up, but he still didn't know what to do. Someone else wanted him dead? That's an understatement. But Douglas meant someone attached to TASP or something.

Douglas gave Keith a lot to think about, but he was sure the would-be assassin was a TASP jumper. Keith walked back to the table and considered the next move. He sat down and continued eating. Rickerson remained quiet for a few moments.

"Looks like you've got the world sitting on your shoulders?"

"Feels like it too," he said in between bites.

"I know you checked me out," Rickerson said. "Is everything all set?"

"Yes, you've been compromised. Dir. Harrington's taking you down."

"When?"

"Real soon. I'm not sure of the exact date," Keith said an obvious lie. "Although, he doesn't know who your accomplice is, at least, as far as I know—and let's keep it that way for now."

Rickerson stopped eating and put his fork down. "Okay, I got it. I'll keep her hidden."

They finished their meal and left. The valet brought Keith his car. On the way back to the Complex, Keith remained in heavy thought and didn't see the van pull up beside him on the expressway—or the man with machine guns until it was too late.

He glanced to his left in time to see the muzzle flash and heard the rapid succession of gunfire as they turned his car into Swiss cheese. He slammed on the brakes. The van kept going. Keith pulled over to the side of the road. He knew they had hit him, though it felt as though he'd been stung by bees. He checked he checked the wound on his left side and legs, but they were already healing. He pulled back onto the expressway and headed to the complex—he called Dr. Bell along the way.

66

What's up, doc? Does it Stop?

The ride back to the Complex was slow and steady. Two-inch holes dotted the side of the company car. Smoke escaped from the hood, billowing into the air in thick puffs. Dr. Bell and another man who held a fire extinguisher greeted Keith in front of the office building. Keith pulled over, popped the hood, and parked in front. The man with the extinguisher stepped towards the car, raise the hood, as a cloud of smoke, and engulfed the man before he sprayed the engine, putting out the fire. Keith got out of the car and met Dr. Bell at the curb.

"This is seriously getting out of hand," Dr. Bell said, a bit irritated.

"You think?" He said as he gestured towards the car. "There is of no more doubt, Doc. Someone is trying to kill me."

"Come on," Dr. Bell said, heading into the building. "Thomas will take care of the car."

The car didn't concern Keith. Not even a little bit. His life seemed more important somehow. They remained quiet until they reached the elevator that would take them down to the Complex. Despite him still being in a jump, and indestructible while there, he knew he'd soon be pulled back—he was running out of time. He wondered how long it would take before they realized their only option was to kill him in the present.

Keith stayed in the jump to take out the assassin.

"Are you sure it's not someone from your past?" Dr. Bell said as they entered the elevator.

"Positive," Keith said. "At least as sure as I can be, anyway."

Dr. Bell searched Keith's facial features for any clue. "You have someone in mind, am I correct?"

"Yes, but you might be surprised."

"Okay, who?"

"Our illustrious director," he said.

Keith watched Dr. Bell as the older man looked up at the security camera and then back to Keith, whose shoulders slumped. He looked at Keith with sad, knowing eyes. "Better not talk here."

Keith nodded, and then silence ensued. They remain quiet until Keith and Dr. Bell was inside Dr. Bell's quarters. Once inside, Keith explained everything. Well, almost everything. He still kept his other abilities to himself. When Keith finished, Dr. Bell paced back and forth for two minutes. The silence was too much for Keith, but it was Dr. Bell who spoke first.

Dr. Bell sat on his couch and stood again to pace some more. "This is serious business, isn't it? If he found out, we all could be in danger. Is there really another facility under this one?"

"Yes, and it's still there," Keith checked the night before, "but sometime from now until I make this jump, they move TASP out."

Dr. Bell shook his head. "This is so unbelievable. "

"Yeah, just like time travel."

They both laughed.

"Nevertheless, I am with you." Dr. Bell said as fear rose and spread throughout his body. "And I hope you know you can count on me. No matter what it is, I'll do it. Sorry, I got you into this mess—this is not what the project was supposed to be about. I still can't get my head around all this. It had to take years to manipulate the presidency in their favor?"

"Yes, they did," he said, "but there were many things that were put into motion—all because they sent me back on those missions. Believe me. I cannot wait until this is over."

"The thing I don't understand is that they've kept you under a microscope and watched every move. Why would they let you go back to prison?"

"I believed I had to follow the original course—maybe they believe they needed me to do everything that I did the first time and not deviate from my timeline. I think they wanted to be sure I become a member of the SCP."

"That can't be good to learn that they had manipulated your entire life to fit their misguided needs."

"Well, Doc," Keith said with a smile. "You must not forget. It isn't gonna be good for them afterwards. Harrington and the consortium will get what's coming to them. What worries me is this assassin. I'm safe while I'm on a jump, but I'm afraid that they'll try after being pulled back — and defenseless. As it is now, they don't know I have this ability, but Director Harrington suspects something, so it's only a matter of time before they do. It's why I have told you, after this last attempt on my life. I need you to keep your eyes open and keep me informed after this jump. Okay?"

"Understood," Dr. Bell said. "Is there anything else?"

"There is; I'll be pulled back soon, so this is what I need you to do."

After Keith explained everything he needed Dr. Bell to do, they sat around talking about anything that came to mind. At some point, Dr. Bell pulled out a beautiful old chessboard with exquisitely carved pieces. Dr. Bell explained he wanted to play Keith ever since he told him he could play. Unfortunately, they had been too busy, and he hadn't had the time. The two men played for an hour but stopped when Keith felt dizzy. Keith stood up and placed both hands on the sides of his head. He held them there as if he tried to keep himself in this time period physically. "I'm going. Not a word to me after I leave," he said and passed out.

67

Arrested Development

The moment Keith opened his eyes, he knew something was amiss. It was written on the faces of the team around him. The grave facial expressions of the team put them on alert. Just beyond the glass, Dr. Bell, Jen, and Billy stood off to the side. Another group of men stood outside the door beyond the glass wall. Keith waited for the download before attempting to pass through the door. Douglas was also there and accompanied by two men. The scene made no sense—until the download—as the alternate memories assaulted his mind, which resulted in a crash. He closed his eyes to the pain and took a deep breath. After a moment, he opened his eyes, stood, and walked to the next room.

According to the newly altered memory, Keith somehow became a traitor that should never have been involved with the SCP. Rickerson had turned up dead, and the last person to be seen with him was Keith. The day before, he made the jump. Was that possible? Where was he? He'd have to search his memory later when it wasn't so confusing.

He stepped into the room. "What's going on?"

"Keith, I'm Sen. Jonathan Douglas, the head of the Oversight Committee assigned to this project...and I'm sorry, but we need to place you under arrest. Guards."

The two-armed guards stepped forward and placed Keith in handcuffs. None of it made much sense. Keith looked over at Dr. Bell, who mouthed, "I don't know." The meaning was clear that Dr. Bell was also in the dark. Keith found it interesting that Director Harrington wasn't among them.

"Why are you arresting me?" He demanded as the guards maneuvered him towards the door, but he planted his feet into the ground. "What is going on?"

Douglas stepped to him. "You're being placed under arrest for trying to alter history to benefit yourself. As a traitor to this great nation," Douglas paused. "Now, get him out of here!"

The guards obeyed, leaving the room we Keith. Douglas then turned to Dr. Bell and his team. "I'm shutting the project down. My people will want to interview everyone in contact with Mr. Richards. Until that happens, we confine everyone to the Complex. Is that understood?"

They all agreed.

Douglas apologized for any inconvenience this might cause, but Keith was a traitor and had to be punished. Douglas left the lab, leaving Dr. Bell, Jen and Billy stunned.

The room where they held Keith was small. Confining The room contained only a plastic chair. Keith sat in the chair and stared ahead. Nobody had asked him any questions. Not that he had answers for them. He sat there in total silence—while he searched through his memories like one would search a computer database. After what seemed to have been hours, he found a fragment of what he looked for. He grabbed at it with his mind and focused on it until it became clear. As he was about to play it back—Douglas walked into the room.

Keith looked up at him. "I want a lawyer?"

"Dead men don't have any rights, Keith?" Douglas said,

tossing a file he held in his hand onto the table. "Guess you didn't read the fine print. Go ahead, see for yourself."

Keith flipped open the file. The release papers he signed were there. Sections had been highlighted in yellow. He quickly scanned the paragraphs and shook his head several times as he read. When he finished, he looked up at Douglas in disbelief.

"There's more in the next packet."

According to what he read, he agreed to sever all ties, which meant officially he died at the hospital due to medical complications. It specified nothing specific. He looked down at the open folder on top of the packet. The next packet had a bright yellow sticky note attached to the paper. Upon it was a handwritten note. Keith read the three sentences and smiled to himself.

The note was simple.

You're about to be compromised, sorry. This was the only way. TASP still had moved its operation, so we don't want to take them down unless we can close it down completely.

He looked up at Douglas as he closed the file and pushed it away. "In that case, since I'm already dead—then kill me," Keith said with a guttural snarl. Positive someone was listening from somewhere outside the room.

"Have it your way," Douglas said. Snatching up the file, he turned to leave. "We'll see how you're feeling in several hours."

Douglas left the room.

The message was clear: jump back and find out where they moved the TASP operations. He knew it had been there three jumps ago. All he had to do was jump to that timeline. He shut his eyes, and the world spun. It was getting easier with every jump.

68

TASP HQ

Once Keith opened his eyes, he rolled off his bed and made his way up to the office. The memory forecast was clouded—until about 10 AM. He had about three hours before he needed to be back to his quarters.

Sitting behind his desk, he searched the files on one of the disks. He looked for anything that may have been a clue that he left himself. A moment before he was about the cash in his chips, he hit the jackpot. He found a link that was hidden in the body of a photograph to a list of dates. After each date, there was a title. It didn't take long for Keith's mind to associate the dates and files into something more meaningful. Keith knew the dates were the days of all the jumps he had taken—hundreds of them. Most of which had not yet happened. He found the present date he was currently in and hovered the cursor over it. *Nothing.* He tapped the title. *Bingo.* He double-clicked the link. The page only contained one sentence: You must go back two weeks.

He wasted no time. After shutting down the computer and returning the disk to the safe, he went back to his quarters and jumped back. No sooner did he open his eyes, he shut them and jumped two weeks into the past. As he had in the prior jump, he went up to the office. He cursed himself the entire way for not checking the dates against the list. Now, he had to go find out what needed to be done.

The round-trip took about 30 minutes, and Keith was back in his quarters. He stuffed his gun into his pants and put on a uniform he got from his office's closet. The dated entry explained what he needed to do, and it included when and where to find the uniform. He checked himself in the mirror and was satisfied that he would pass. He went back to the grate that led down to TASP. He quietly dropped down into the lower level. *Back into the hornets' nest.*

Boxes had been stacked up. He dropped behind them. They were taller than Keith thought. They provided him with superb cover, except he couldn't see anything either—the things started off right. He saw gray uniformed men, dressed as he was, who picked up the boxes and carried them out of the room. Keith knew he had to do the same. He grabbed a box from the pile and followed suit.

He followed several men in front of him to what appeared to be a loading dock. Several box trucks and two caravan trucks waited to be loaded. He put the box in the back of the box truck and was ordered to go back for more. An hour and 50 minutes later, they finished and were ordered aboard the cloth-covered truck. The truck was a standard military issue. After he got on board, they closed the back drape and secured it.

When the truck stopped, he checked his watch. They traveled for 35 minutes. They could be 5 miles or 35 miles away, if not more. He was sure it was closer to the latter...because of how smooth the ride had been. They waited for another ten minutes until someone opened the drape and ordered them out of the truck. Once out of the truck, he surveyed the area as he unloaded the box trucks.

They were in a warehouse. Standard variety. From what he could see, which wasn't all that much, it was a giant open space. They took the boxes to a shed that was against the nearest wall to the left. Once the room was filled to capacity, TASP agents shut the double plywood doors and told them to stack the rest of the boxes outside the shed's door. Three people brought the last of the boxes. A commander who barked orders opened the shed doors. Keith smiled, but as he looked around, nobody was surprised to find it empty. He was glad he had stayed quiet. They loaded the remaining boxes and piled them into the shed before it went down.

69

Men in the Box

Once they delivered the boxes to the other installation, they came back for more stuff. Keith climbed back into the access shaft, back inside the lower level. No one seemed to have noticed an extra man among them. He also thought it strange no one talked. For a moment, he worried the others would ask questions. Where you from? What unit? Did I serve with you in Iraq? None of that was necessary because nobody said a word. They rode, worked, and ate in complete silence. He thought he joined the society of monks that had taken a vow of silence.

The only ones who spoke were the officers barking orders. He figured it was a security measure. It sure would be effective. Most people would be compelled to talk and try to make friends. However, it made Keith happy that he wasn't that type of person because he would have been discovered if he had been. Although he couldn't have been killed, it would've blown his cover—and in the present, death would have waited.

After they returned for more boxes, he snuck away and climbed into the ventilation system. He wasn't familiar with the ductwork—but soon found familiar markings. Divine was written like earlier, in the other shaft, in Korean. He followed the marked trail to more familiar surroundings and made his way up to his office instead of back to his quarters.

The stay at the office was brief. Keith changed his clothes and double-checked the mission on the computer before grabbing a handheld GPS tracking device. After he changed his clothes, he left the building. Dressed in an Armani suit, he walked to his car parked inside a special lot for executives. He would have been surprised to see a million-dollar electric sports car, but the jump log had already warned him. James *Bond, eat your heart out*, he thought, as he got behind the wheel and started it up. No sound. Just a computer voice that said ignition on, and he was off.

As he drove out of the parking lot, Keith noticed a cradle—he picked up the GPS device from his lap and placed it in the cradle. A perfect fit. He turned it on and followed the directions to the warehouse. It brought him to a warehouse in a small industrial park 42 miles outside of Boston. Afterward, he followed the jump log's entry to the letter. First, he stopped to get a bite to eat. Second, he headed to an address he retrieved from the log of another place he had gone to in Boston. Keith had no one idea why he was supposed to go there, only that it was logged. A scheduled stop.

The address brought Keith to the South End. An upscale section of the city that had seen rampant gentrification over the last two decades. The brownstone, in which Keith pulled in front of and parked, was four stories tall and a good 40 feet across. The only light on was the one next to the door. He got out of the car and walked up the three steps and pressed the buzzer—and waited. After a few moments, Keith was about to try again when the door opened.

The man who stood before Keith stood about 6 feet tall and heavyset. He possessed a friendly face with a brown complexion—though he could belong to any nationality. His ethnicity was hard to determine. He'd never met the man before—

"Keith!" The man said as he beamed. "About time you stopped to see an old friend. Come in, come."

Keith followed the man into the living room. A large room with a fireplace. Two armchairs and a large couch. The center of the space. The couch faced the fireplace. Photographs cover the walls. The man asked Keith if he wanted a drink. He said he didn't, but the man disappeared for a moment. Keith scrutinized the photographs. In each picture, a group of men stood before various buildings—a ribbon being cut in front of them. They had to be close to a hundred framed photographs in this room alone—all the same size.

The pictures all had one thing in common. His host was in every photo.

The man returned with a tray of cold cuts, small rolls, and drinks. He placed the tray on the coffee table in front of the couch. Keith turned to the man.

"Every time you come," he said with an honest smile. "You always look at those pictures. Find what you're looking for?"

"Not yet," Keith said, his turn to smile. He noticed the tray of food and walked to the couch, and sat down. Beside the tray, a brown paper-wrapped package sat on the table.

"I assume that is what you came for," the man said. "It's been waiting for your return for a long time."

"How long has it been, my old friend?"

"Well, let's see," the man said and raised his hand to his head—a gesture of being in deep thought. "I believe you were, what 13. It was a day I would never forget. It was winter, and I had yet to shovel the walk. I had come outside to get the newspaper...and wouldn't you know I slipped. I lay there for some time, splayed out in front of my stoop. I don't recall how long I lay there, but I do remember this tough-looking adolescent helping me up. He then asked if he could shovel the front of my house, and of course, I agreed. He came over every day for weeks—and then you just stopped coming.

You asked if I would hold on to that package for you the last time you came by. Said it was important, and you trusted no one else with it. I agreed, and it's remained unopened. I hope it's not contraband of any kind, just kidding. How you been?"

"Not bad," he said. It was the truth. "I'm not sure what's inside it. I only know, as you do, it's important. However, let's catch up first, so I liked these pictures back then?"

"Well, only the ones that were up at the time," the man walked over to the wall where Keith had been standing when the man brought in the tray. The man pointed to several photographs. "These were the ones you saw and asked about."

Keith got up and stood beside the man. "These right here?"

"Those are the ones," the man said. "I do miss playing chess with you—you are so good. I imagine you're better now. Things haven't changed much here. I still don't get many visitors."

"I asked about them?" Keith looked at the photographs and recognized one of the warehouses like the one he just left.

"Yeah," he said. "Interesting questions, if I recall. My father built those warehouses in the early 50s for a government contractor. I forget the name, but the company didn't last long."

"What kinds of questions did I ask?"

"The strangest of them all," he said with a smile. "You asked if it had a basement. Most of the warehouses, as my father built, didn't have basements though some had boiler rooms and steam tunnels, the interesting thing was this building not only had a basement, but it also had a subbasement. The town had height limits, so they had us build down instead of up."

"So, there're two floors in the ground?"

"No, five," he said. "Three regular floors plus a basement and subbasement."

"That is interesting," he said. "I think I should open the package now."

70

Cityscape

Car horns honked, and people packed the sidewalks. The nightlife came to life after dark. They slipped out of sight. Keith stood on the stoop for a second as he left the man's house. He still didn't know the man's name, but the guy didn't seem to mind. He did, however, seem to like Keith's company. Keith and the older man played several games of chess. The man was a superb player—Keith won one game out of six.

Although he wished he could've stayed longer, he had work to do. His heightened memory was intact, yet there was nothing about this guy. A blank spot. Had he found a way to block his memory so that the update didn't record certain elements? It didn't take long for Keith to know he liked the guy. Loyal and honest friends were hard to find.

Keith had asked him why he hadn't opened the package. The old man's answer not only was simple but made a lasting impression on Keith. "It wasn't mine to open," the man said.

The box contained twenty $100 bills, a folded note, and a key. *What's up with all the keys?* Keith wished he had made the puzzles and clues a bit easier to solve. Was it too much to ask? Well, he made it complicated for a reason.

The note revealed the next part of the plan. He pulled into the garage at the Prudential Center. He parked on the second level and took the escalator up to the mall. He cut through Center Court and down Back Bay Arcade and crossed over the bridge over to Copley Place. He could've parked in that mall's parking garage but believed where he parked was for the best.

He cut through the Copley Place Mall to the other side and crossed another bridge so he'd come out in Copley Square. He could've walked a straight line from the Prudential Center, but he wanted to check things out along the way.

He cut through Copley Square Park and walked past the fountain before crossing the street and going into a small store. The sign above the door said Shipping Pros.

Inside the store, he scanned the store's contents. He saw mailboxes and walked to them in the back as he withdrew the key and checked the number on it. He found the corresponding box and inserted the key.

The box contained a single piece of mail: a legal-sized letter. He removed the envelope and tore it open. He removed the single sheet of paper and looked at it. *Shit!*

"Thanks for the warning," he muttered. He quickly exited the store. He scanned the crowd on the sidewalk—hoping something clicked. The note said if he had made it this far, he's on the right track. It also said that he had been tracked by the GPS tracker in the back of his neck.

It had been the second time he had forgotten about the freaking thing. There was a hit team, according to the note, outside somewhere, getting ready to take him down. He found it interesting. Didn't they know he was immortal on a jump—and why did he feel the need to warn himself? Director Harrington should've briefed them on his newfound ability by now.

He crossed the street as he turned right onto Dartmouth Street and took a left into the public alley. He headed back towards the Prudential Center.

As he cut through the alley, which was as long as a city block with only two ways in and out, he passed a building that caught his eye. He could just see the back of the building, but it looked familiar. It resembled the one from New York—and his dream. *Fuck!* He turned, in time, to see a person step from the shadows with two guns raised.

The discharge lit up the area. He drew his own weapon to fight back. A slug hit him in his left breast. The searing pain hurt and caused him to wince in pain. He willed it away, which is easy to do now that he knew he would heal. Keith landed a couple of shots of his own, but it only pushed the assailant backward a little.

The assassin dropped his magazines and reloaded. He unleashed another round—Keith took cover behind an SUV. He reloaded the only extra magazine he brought and stepped out to face the assassin. The man stepped from the shadows. An emergency light from the building closest to Keith lit the man's features. He closed his eyes as if in a state of fright. He shook his head as if to wake himself from a nightmare.

"What's the matter, Keith," the man called as he walked towards Keith. "Looks like you've just seen a ghost?"

"Well, I know you ain't no ghost," he said with the gun pointed in the man's direction, "but you'll be soon enough. Shit, I killed you once, so I guess I can do it again."

Keith didn't understand how Dougie remained alive, but it sure added to the whole—they manipulated him his whole life—bit. This time, however, Keith aimed for the head and struck his mark. He stood there long enough to see Dougie collapse to the ground. He then passed out himself from his wounds. He lost track of time as he laid on the cold, smelly ground of the alley. He heard sirens in the distance—a small crowd gathered around him. He got to his feet and stumbled off, ignoring the protest that came from the passerby's.

71

Death Chase

The room contained a bed and a dresser. The phone next to the bed screamed hotel, as did the rest of the room. He got himself out of bed and stumbled to the bathroom. The boulder that sat on top of his shoulders felt heavy and unsteady. He didn't remember waking, but he knew the signs of a crash.

The pain lingered just out of reach as it waited for the right time to attack again. The pain caused by the crash resembled a migraine—and not the Excedrin Migraine kind. He stumbled over to the window and saw tall buildings but didn't recognize any of them. Where was he? He went over to the nightstand and looked for a room service menu. Sure enough, he found one inside the nightstand, under the Gideon's Bible. *A cheap hotel indeed.*

At the top of the menu, a laminated sheet of card stock, there was a circle with an old building with a garage in front of it. The script that elegantly scrolled around the outside proclaimed this was the establishment called the Bostonian. A Tony hotel overlooking Boston Harbor. He was on the 12th floor. Curious, he went to the room's door, opened it, and checked the hallway. Not a soul in sight. How did he get there? Had Douglas dropped him off there? No, it didn't seem to fit, yet there were no guards. He was sure Douglas kept up the appearance that Keith was under arrest. He went back into the hotel room and almost tripped over a small duffel bag. *This must be mine.*

He brought the bag over to the bed and emptied its contents out. A change of clothes despite the clothes he wore looking brand-new. A toiletry kit with an electric razor and a safety razor, which told him it was his doing, somehow.

He removed some more items along with a gun and two full magazines. He would need them now because he was in real-time now and no longer immortal. There was one last item, a white legal-sized envelope. He opened the letter. It was from Dr. Bell, and it said he had done precisely as I asked him—when the time warranted it. He believed now was that time. Keith couldn't agree anymore. Those were his exact feelings. Dr. Bell said he didn't know who to trust, and he wasn't sure if they had turned Douglas. He didn't want to take any chance—especially with Keith's life.

Now that Keith knew who helped him, he relaxed a bit. He took a shower. When he got out of the shower and got dressed, he put away the stuff that was scattered across the bed back into the bag. When he grabbed the bag, he noticed the front pocket bulged the little. Did he miss something? He opened it to find a wad of cold, hard cash. He counted it. $5000. That would do, for now, but he might need some more. But in the present, there was no enhanced memory to manipulate the lottery.

He finished packing the bag and ordered room service. An omelet and home fries along with a cup of tea and a glass of cranberry juice. Once he got dressed and ready for the day, he left the hotel, not bothering to check out. The letter said the room was in a false name and paid for the next two weeks. It was a nice gesture, but Keith wouldn't stay in one place for more than two days. Never mind two weeks.

Director Harrington's government goons were out to get him, so staying in one place wasn't an option. There was still the matter of the GPS tracker buried in his neck. The person outside of the Complex he trusted besides Douglas and Joey was Kal, the jeweler. He knew Kal could point him in the right direction. If anyone could point him to an off-the-books surgeon, it would be Kal.

Outside the hotel, he searched for familiar strange faces. He took in every face. That way, if you saw the face again later, it would register. He may not be in a jump at the moment, but his memory still worked fine. He walked to South Station and then cut up towards the shopping district. Ten minutes after he left the hotel, he arrived at the jewelry store.

When Keith entered the store, Kal smiled. "Back so soon, my friend?"

"Yeah, it sure seems that way," Keith said. "Kal, I have a favor to ask of you?"

"If I can, you know, I will help. What is it?"

Keith explained the deadly situation, and whether or not Kal believed him, his old friend still helped him out. It wasn't much thought will count to come up with a person he thought could help. Kal had asked him if he remembered that Kid he'd met the last time he'd come in. Keith remembered, but not the kid's name. Kal told him about Damien and also reminded him of who Damien's father figure was. The street legend Kain.

Kal gave Damien a call, but Damien didn't think he could help and thought they should try Kain. Kal called him and hung up the phone a few moments later.

"This is your lucky day. Kain is up this way."

Thirty-five minutes later, Kain walked in.

"It's been a long time, my friend," Kain said, given both men dap and Keith, a long hug. "I thought you were inside?"

Keith explained the situation in Kain, said it wouldn't be a problem, and then left.

72

Ally

The Bugatti Cruised through downtown and out into the suburbs. The car pulled into a driveway of an enormous house—one of Massachusetts's largest mansions and very old. The house dated back to the early 19th century and had been upgraded over the years. Kain pulled the car around a circular drive and parked in front of the door.

"We're here," Kain said as they got out of the car. "Come on, he's expecting us."

The massive doors opened as if they were automatic as they approached. A man in what Keith could only describe as a Butler's uniform greeted them.

"Gentlemen, please follow me," the butler said and walked off down the long hall with art-covered walls. "It's been a long time, sir. I hope things have been well?"

"They have," Kain said. "My company keeps me very busy these days."

They walked the rest of the way in silence. The hall was massive, and the art that covered the 15-foot walls was extensive. Keith believed he saw a Picasso and a Rembrandt but couldn't be certain. They took him right at the end of the hall and went into the second room on the left.

The room is exactly what one would think a Butler would lead them to—a library. A small one. Bookcases lined each wall from floor to ceiling. The small room had a cavernous feel because of its 15-foot-high ceilings.

The man who they came to see looked up from the book he was reading. He placed the book down onto a small coffee table, next to the window where he sat.

The man was humble, but his presence exuded confidence. He beamed as they approached. "My God, Kain, it has been a very long time. I hope I can be of some help to you."

Kim explained to Keith along the way that Dr. Burke had been a very successful surgeon for many years. Although he had been officially retired for the past decade, he had patched up various clientele—those who couldn't go to the hospital. The man was a keeper of many secrets.

"Doc, I'm sure you can," Kain said, "but I'll let my friend here explain the situation to you."

Keith went into full detail—two hours later, they left the mansion.

"Alright, where can I drop you off?"

Keith hadn't thought about where he wanted to go. "I really don't know. Anywhere downtown, I guess, would be fine. "

"They can't track you now," Kain said, "so why don't you come down to exurbia and kick your feet up. Relax a bit. There's no way in hell they'll find you at my place."

"That's probably true," Keith said, with a slow exhale. "But I get something I need to finish up here. Thanks for the offer, though. You were a huge help."

"I can Admire a guy who finishes what he starts. You're a good man, Keith, always have been. And if there's anything I can do, call me?" Kain said, handing him a business card.

"Well, you have already done enough," he said, his face looking tired, "and believe me, I appreciate it a lot."

The conversation lasted the entire 29-minute trip. Kain pulled over on Boylston Street near Emerson College.

"Is this good?"

"Yeah, this is fine; thanks again, Kain."

"No problem," Kain said as they clasped hands. "Take this, it's not much, but it should help you stay low a little longer."

Keith looked down at the large knot of hundred-dollar bills Kain had put in his hand. "You do—"

"Of course, I don't, but I just did. Be safe, my friend."

Keith shook his head in disbelief. Kain had always been a generous person. Always willing to help those he called a friend. "All right, I will try," he said before he got out of the car and disappeared into the crowd.

73

Listen to Himself

The city was crowded with lots of pedestrians, which made it perfect for Keith to wonder about. Despite the occasional puffy cloud, the day was bright and cheerful. Beautiful, sun-filled days always brought a smile to his mug. Tourists, locals walking about, joggers, and bicyclists enjoyed the day. Though Keith felt far from bright and cheery, he took it all in with a smile.

He stuffed his hands into his jacket pockets and felt the grip of his firearm resting inside his waistband. *A fugitive once more with no place to call home.* Not that he called the Complex or prison home, but the Complex there was a sense of normality, and he felt like he'd become part of something that benefited society. A placed he belonged.

He couldn't go back to the Complex, and Kain's place was too far away, but he needed to go to his office, which was located above the Complex. It was probably the safest place in the city because nobody knew it existed. Instead, he walked around the city out of fear that Harrington's men may spot him going into the building. Though Keith had never seen the Complex's security room, there had to be surveillance cameras, sensors, and sentry that protected the premises.

Keith had forgotten how difficult things could be in the present. He became too used to being in the past and having abilities to help him. *This was no jump.* He knew he left a clue for himself somewhere in case this happened. When it happened. Since he hadn't jumped back yet to lay out the clues for himself, there was reason to be hopeful.

He racked his brain as he went down the steps to Downtown Crossing Subway Station. The T station was somewhat busy. The crowd made him uneasy. Not knowing where to go, he jumped on the first train that came into the station.

Lost in thought, he passed several stops without noticing. He looked up and out the window—and noticed he crossed over the Longfellow Bridge into Cambridge. He exited the train at Central Square. Above ground, he walked walk down Mass Ave towards Boston.

Keith tried to come up with a plan but didn't know what to do. He stopped at Dunkin' Donuts in Central Square. Keith and his cousin Joe used to hang out on the Avenue all the time. Back when his cousin lived at Columbia Terrace. They were tighter than brothers back then. *That was a long time ago.*

They used to run all over the area. He remembered they always ended up at the parking garage next to the library. Without realizing it, he walked down the side street that led to the garage. A few minutes later, Keith wondered through the first level of the garage. He wasn't sure what he was looking for, but he believed this is where he would find his next clue. He searched each level. He checked out the cars, the people, and the graffiti on the walls. It was on the third level he found his clue.

On the wall, in front of a black BMW, was the same symbol that led him out of the complex. Divine in Korean. He walked to the front of the car. There was nothing on the ground, so he turned to look at the vehicle—a BMW 750. The car was beautiful, and it made him smile. The top half of the windshield had a son strip in the middle of the sun strip was the same Korean character. He walked to the driver's side door and tried the handle. The car chirped, and the door popped open. He must've implanted an RFID under his skin. A simple thing to do. He got in and drove out of the garage.

Inside the glove box, he found a Microsoft Surface, a gun, and a small stack of hundreds. Keith wondered why he would leave a gun when he knew he had one or the money since he knew Kain had given him some. Keith wasn't sure why he laid out the things as he had and couldn't wait to find out why.

He drove down Mass Ave, over the bridge, and into Boston. He took a left onto Commonwealth Avenue, then turned onto Exeter Street and found a place to park. The trees were in full bloom, and he was in a shady area parked under an elm tree.

He picked up the Surface that he placed on the seat from the glove box. He turned it on and a box popped onto the screen: Enter Password. Without thinking, he typed in divine. Although he didn't have the enhanced memory, as he did on a jump, his instincts picked up the slack...and he was grateful. He always trusted his instincts. Better than having nothing.

The box disappeared, and another screen popped up. It was a video of himself. Keith recognized the background as being in the car. He connected the Surface to the car through Bluetooth to hear it through the car's speakers.

His voice was smooth as it came out of the Harman Kardon speakers.

"'Since you're watching this, things haven't gone smoothly as planned. And you now find yourself in a heap of trouble. Whether you know it or not, you're on the backup plan. You also have come face-to-face with the one person who has been trying to kill you: Dougie. And I'm sure you have many questions as to how, why, and the like. The answer is simple—TASP. You'll find out more later.

"'Right now, you have more important things to take care of—like keeping us alive.'" On-screen, he picks up a gun. "'There are two of these in a stash box. Located in the dashboard. To access it, press the garage door button and hold it for 10 seconds. You'll hear password needed use the same password you used to get into the car.'"

He paused the video of himself and did as it said. A few moments later, he held two handguns and six extra magazines. The guns were new. He never heard of the brand, never saw one like it or its ammo before. He pressed play.

"'This model came out after you killed Dougie, and you never saw them before. They are Herstal FN 57s. It takes a 5.7 mm round. Each mag holds 20 rounds, and these particular rounds are armor-piercing.'" He placed the gun on his lap. "'I hope you're ready for what comes next. You're almost there—just a little longer, and this will be all over. Before I go, I'll leave you with this advice. *Trust no one.*

"'There is one more thing, and it's going to sound crazy, but you need to jump from the frying pan into the fire. I know how it sounds, but it's what you need to do. The money Dr. Bell gave you will be sufficient. Now this is what you need to do—'"

•

Nineteen minutes and 29 seconds later, the video ended. According to himself, the conspiracy goes deeper than Harrington and the Consortium. Apart from the deep pockets of the six men, there was another player. One of whom was richer than them all combined. A man with connections at every level of government, and if he didn't see the name uttered from his lips, he would never believe it was true.

Now, he had to go to the address, where according to the video, he would find another project—One with deeper pockets than any government. Controlled by someone who would reap billions of dollars by investing in the past. It was simple, really. All one had to do was make mistakes, then at some predetermined time, go back and fix them.

If one were to look closely at the last 10 years, they would find several companies that seemed to come from nowhere—causing a serious threat to big tech companies—only to be bought out for enormous sums. If they looked beyond the articles of incorporation and followed the money through the dummy corporations and shell Corporations, it would all fall to one company. One person. Joey. His partner. *Trust no one.*

Deep inside, Keith harbored some doubt. Could Joey really be behind this entire mess? It didn't seem possible. Keith being a billionaire didn't seem possible either, but he was. He was Joe Co's cofounder. However, it appeared on no public documentation by Keith's own order. They would've never been able to go public—not with his background—so at least he believed. Joey wasn't part of Harrington's plot. He did this on his own accord, and it couldn't be allowed. If it ever came out, Joe Co. Enterprises would be ruined, but time travel would be a hard thing to believe, so Keith needed to take care of this on his own.

He pulled up in front of the building, and it surprised Keith he found the space. It was Boston, after all. Parking had always been a problem. It happened when you mix lots of people together and add in tourism for good measure. He got out of the car and looked up at the building. Joe owned the entire building. He scanned the area as he headed for the entrance.

According to the video, Harrington also caught wind of this project. Hence, Keith needed to wrap up this mess before director Harrington connected the dots and tied this to the conspiracy charges against him. For now, Director Harrington only suspected that Rickerson was on to him.

74

House of Mirrors

Nightfall approached as Keith watched the nondescript building. It had been several hours, and not a single person entered or exited, at least not from the main entrance. After he arrived and checked the building for other entrances, he only found two—the loading dock at the back and side door with no handle.

He had seen no vehicles enter the sole street that led to the dock, so he felt confident nobody had come or gone that way. However, his patience waned as time went on. Keith entered the building through the main entrance. He was, after all—the cofounder of the company that owned the property. He exited his car and crossed the street.

Through the front doors was another set of double doors, which greeted Keith as he entered the building. He stood in the breezeway for a moment, which was approximately 10 square feet. Two cameras recorded his entrance. Next to the second set of doors, on the wall, was a card reader and the biometrics reader as well. Keith stepped in front of the cye scanner and put his face up to the reader. A moment later, he heard a beep and whirl sound. When the screen turned green, black lettering spelled out bio password accepted. He pulled on the door.

Beyond the second set of doors was a deserted reception area. The place looked deserted. Behind the reception desk was the only corridor. He walked down it. The automatic lights kicked on, sensing his presence, as he checked each room as he went. No sign of life. At the end of the corridor, he turned left and checked two more rooms for a total of five.

The last room showed some signs of life. The room, although small, had a door across from the entrance. A U-shaped counter blocked the way to the door. Tech equipment took up all the counter space. He didn't understand why the equipment had been placed there but noticed a little gateway that allowed people to cut through to the door. It must have been where someone allowed others through with the aid of biometric technology and wondered if he could.

Keith walked up to the petition and peered over to where someone would be seated and saw a card reader within reach, but he had no card.

He searched the rest of the floor and came back to the U-shaped countered room. He found nothing. Two other offices had locked doors with card readers. If the door behind the U-shaped counter held something important, Keith figured there should be a biometric scanner somewhere in the room.

A few moments later, he found it on the backside of the counter as you stepped through, but it was for a handprint scan. He placed his hand on the scanner. Nothing happened. No beep. No light. No, nothing. A few moments later, he found a switch that turned on the scanner. After he placed his hand in the scanner and it beeped and whirled, he entered the room.

The room resembled the others in size but not in contents. The lab equipment surprised Keith because it looked a lot like the chamber chair. However, this chair was of the high-tech variety. Keith circled the chair and wondered what it was for—to jump? He wasn't sure. He walked over to the observation area when the control panels faced away from the chair. One monitor brightened when he touched the screen. A box popped up on the screen asking the user to look at the screen for a biometrics scan. Keith obliged and placed his face in front of the screen. The screen lit up green as before. It then went blank. Before he could blink, a new screen took its place.

Diagnostic information scrolled past his eyes. What is this? At the top of the screen, there was a hint to the project. The letters spelled out R.E.A.L.I.T.Y. He wondered what the acronym meant.

He scrolled through data for a few minutes before he stopped. A box command popped up asking for permission to initiate the program. He touched the screen, hoping to get more information.

"I wouldn't do that if I was you," a voice from behind him said.

He turned to face the person. Yesterday, it would have surprised him to see the man before him, but today he wasn't at all surprised. "And why not?"

"Because it's not time yet," Joey said.

"Not time for what?" Keith said as he waved his hand around and followed with his gaze. "What is this place?"

"What's it look like?" Joey said. "Hell, you had me build it, so you tell me?"

"How convenient."

Joey shook his head. "I Couldn't access that," he pointed to the console, "if I wanted to."

"What are you talking about?"

"This lab is and what you think it is," Joey said. "It's not a Time Machine. You came to me a few days after I met you in your office, and you brought me downstairs. You gave me the diagrams to build this place. And told me to keep it off the books and off-line until you showed up again…here…now. So, I'm here. You're here, so that means only one thing."

"Yeah, what's that?"

Before Joey could reply, an explosion rocked the building. Klaxons sounded. Red lights flashed, which he didn't notice. Emergency lights came on right before the power failed. Overhead lights flickered like a raging battle until darkness won. The equipment and console stayed lit, probably because of a backup system.

Keith looked at Joey with a hundred questions.

Joe answered two of them: Backup generators and TASP.

Keith grabbed both guns from his waistband. *Ready*. He eyed Joey, not sure whether or not to trust him. He told himself not to trust anyone. Somehow TASP followed him. But he removed the GPS, so he was at a loss. It took the sound of something heavy pounding on the door to the room to take him out of his thoughts.

He glanced at the door and then back to Joey, who was now holding a gun of his own.

"If that is TASP, this will not be good," Keith said, breathing out slowly.

"It is. And it's not."

"You seem better informed than me, so what do we do?"

"That's simple," he pointed to the chair. "We use this for what you designed it to do. Their head of Jumper's with them."

Joey glanced at his watch.

"They think we've gone rogue or something, so am I to believe I devised this? Just another plan?" He rubbed his forehead and face with his left hand, exhausted. He wished he was on a jump. That way, he'd know exactly what was going on and who to trust.

"All right then," Keith said. "What does it do?"

"It gives them well a ride of their life."

"What the hell is that supposed to mean?"

Something heavier pounded on the door. The middle of the door buckled by the force. He figured they were now using a battering ram. He pointed his weapons at the door. It was a tough door. Ready to ride. If he was gonna die, so were some of them. He looked over at Joey, who still hadn't given him a straight answer. Keith threw his hands up and shrugged as if to say, "well?"

"It gives them an overdose of your blood. Well, of a protein that was extracted from it."

"My blood," he shook his head. Another dent in the door. "Why?"

"Your ability, it comes from your blood," Joey said. "That's why they need you because without you—time travel, at least this way, is impossible—"

Another bang. This one made a bigger dent. Voices yelled from the other side, and they could hear the scatter of boots from beyond the door.

"They're coming," Keith said. "Get ready!"

The two friends stood together with guns pointed towards the door.

"Shoot anyone that comes through, you hear," Keith said, in what almost sounded guttural like a growl.

Joe nodded as the place rocked from another explosion.

White light filled the room. Debris covered them. The door was no more. Red laser beams pierced through the smoke-filled room. Keith got knocked back, but he kept his ground. He looked in Joey's direction and couldn't see him through the smoke.

Figures filled the doorway. Keith wasted no time and unleashed his weapons. Round after deadly round. He heard more gunfire off to his right. Joey. More figures, this time, however, fired as they entered through the doorway. The battle began.

Seconds later, both guns breached. Keith dropped to his knees, releasing the magazines, as he did so, and reloaded.

He stuffed two more magazines into place with an audible click—he stood fired and repeated the process two more times. *Joe started screaming.*

"I've been hit! I'm out! I've been hit…"

Keith rushed to his friend's aid. Joey had fallen to the ground and blood-soaked the top half of his shirt. Bullets squealed by, narrowly missing Keith's head. His ears rang. He returned fire as more soldiers filled the room. A few more fell. But it was futile. More soldiers took up their place. There were too many men. His guns breached, and he was out of magazines—

A round tore through his shoulder, and losing balance, he reeled backwards, tripping over Joey, and crashed to the concrete floor. He closed his eyes—as he tried to ward off the burning pain in his shoulder. He opened his eyes and time to see a multitude of laser beams dot his chest and arms. Probably his head as well. Several soldiers stood above him, pointing their weapons. One of the soldiers stepped forward and smashed him in the head with the butt of his rifle. *Lights out.*

75

Reflection

Pinpricks of light lit up the darkness of his mind. He opened and shut his eyes as mental lights exploded into starbursts. The light sensitivity sent a shock wave of pain from his eyes to the center of his brain. Keith reached for his head but was stopped by the handcuffs attached to his wrists. The light in the room was too bright for him to open his eyes, but he could tell they handcuffed him to a chair.

After the pain quelled, he tried one more time to open his eyes one more time. The pain was manageable. He glanced around the room. Two guards stood a foot away with guns at the ready. A small group of soldiers and two men dressed in suits walked towards him. The pain would get so intense that he'd rest his eyes for a second. The next time he opened them, the group stood before him.

A heavyset man, one of the suits, stepped past the guards.

"About time you're awake, sunshine," Dir. Harrington said." Your friend over there," he pointed towards Joey, who was cuffed to a chair and looked pretty battered, "says this place is exactly what I think it is."

"If you say so," he said. "Truthfully, I have no fucking idea. The only thing I do know is you're a traitor. Changing the past for your own gain."

"Me," Dir. Harrington said. A smile broke out across his face. "Really, we've been trying like hell to fix what *you* did." He stressed you so hard spittle sprayed Keith's face. "We know everything, now. The both of you conspired to retrieve technology from the past to help propel his company, *your* company, into the stratosphere. You see, Keith, you're the trader...not...me! The best part is I have proof. My people have recorded your entire life. You thought you were so smart, but you didn't count on the fact you been under surveillance since you were a child—"

Keith remained silent because he knew Director Harrington would use this new discovery to crucify him. Keith and Joey were the perfect scapegoats. Keith was a bit confused. *Why would he set himself up?* He kept trying to recall his memory but remembered that he wasn't in a jump.

"Before I put you in a military prison with neither a phone call nor attorney privileges," Director Harrington said, "I need to tell me something."

"Forty-two, that's the answer, but you probably won't understand it, though."

"I don't need some random number," Dir. Harrington said as he scrunched up his face and tightened his brow. "I need you to access these computers, so my techs can check out the equipment. This technology is more advanced than our own. It's quite obvious you've given the process a few upgrades. How? I don't know. Now, get up and turn it on."

Keith didn't move. Couldn't move. A guard uncuffed him as the two more guards stood in front of him and pointed their weapons at his face. He stood and strolled towards the console. One of the guards pushed him onward, telling him to hurry up. Keith accessed the computer and powered up the chair. He didn't explain to Harrington that the chair did it all. No technicians are needed. Sit in the chair and program the date, and it will inject the compound, and off you go.

"It's all yours," Keith said with a smirk.

"Good," he said…and smiled. "Get in the chair and show us how it works."

Keith looked over at Joey, who was still out of it. It was his blood, so he didn't believe it could harm him. However, there had to be more to the chair, but what? The two guards pushed him violently towards the chair, who screamed at him to move faster.

They strapped him in the chair, and a tech stepped behind the console. A second later, Keith felt the sting of the needles and the burn of the CTE compound. Within seconds, he was gone.

•

Keith awoke to find himself inside a hotel room. A very nice one. He recognized it immediately, like the one he stayed in when they sent him on vacation the first time.

He wasn't sure why he was there, but he had some ideas. During this week, Joey said he visited the office, and probably at the same time, he put the gun and extra CTE compound in the event behind the panel. If the compound was measured specifically for this trip—he didn't have that much time. He figured the chair recognized him and overrode any command Harrington's tech gave it. *Clever.* He sprang out of bed as his heightened memory slowly took root—and set out to lay down the clues.

76

Things Revealed

The ominous bluish-black sky reflected his mood. Keith wasn't sure how the chair work or what it really did, but it bounced him through time like a pinball. With his heightened awareness, he could lay each clue precisely where he needed to go. The only thing that puzzled him was that this should've been done at the end, yet he saw no end in sight.

He stared up at the sky as a stomach reeled and his vision spun. He braced himself for what was to come.

They ripped him from the chair before his eyes became more than mare slits. He thought the two guards, with their assault rifles drawn on him, were back. They didn't drag him away. Instead, they told him to stand a few feet from the console. He guessed they didn't want him to wander off. He looked at his watch. *It didn't make sense.*

He jumped through several days…months even, yet only five minutes had passed. The chair was definitely more advanced than he was told. But maybe Joey didn't know of its capabilities. Keith assumed Joey was the one that built it, but he put the restrictions on it. He kept himself in the dark, so why not others?

Director Harrington walked over to Keith. "Well, you survived. You have a pleasant trip?"

"Could've been better," he said, as he wondered where Harrington thought he had gone. "The beach was fantastic. Not a cloud in the sky."

Director Harrington ignored him. "My men will test this machine, and if it works, as well as I suspect it will...we'll take it back to the Complex—"

"Yeah, but the one that is one level below, right? You traitorous motherfucker!"

"You need to tame that violent temper of yours," Dir. Harrington said in an incredulous tone. "Haven't you figured it out yet? No matter what you say, Keith. The only traitor here *is* you. Well, you and your partner. Lucky for me—under the Patriot Act—we can take you into custody without ever notifying a soul."

"Huh, that's good," Keith said. "Making me disappear means nothing. But Joey, the king of the tech world, is a known figure. How are you going to explain that one away?"

"Easy," Dir. Harrington said with a big smile as he leaned into Keith's face. "Lost at sea, seeing he's supposed to be on his yacht, right now. I'll make up something plausible, so don't you worry." He patted Keith on the shoulder.

Keith just glared at him.

The two men turned their gaze towards the chair and watched as Harrington's men each jumped for two minutes. Thirty minutes later, the last man stood up from the chair and approached Harrington.

"Any problems, major?"

"No, sir."

"Good, that your men and return to the Complex."

"Sir," the man said with a salute before leaving to follow the orders.

A group of men in coveralls stood near the door. Keith wasn't sure when they arrived. Director Harrington waved them over. As they got within earshot, Director Harrington ordered them to dismantle the place and bring it back to TASP not the Complex. The new place that Keith had discovered in the garage that the old man's father built in the 1950s.

Director Harrington turned to Keith. "This motherfucker Douglas has been up my ass, looking for some wrongdoing, so I have to thank you because I can serve him up you. On a silver fucking platter." He gestured to his men. "The men around you all believe in TASP and what it stands for. They know the risk. Since I got word that Douglas had it out for the program, and I discovered his mole Rickerson...I've been looking for a scapegoat."

"How original," Keith said. "I'm not your scapegoat."

"I also knew you would never join TASP. You may be a piece of shit murderer, but I knew you were too proud when I met you. Bet you like the country the way it is. Who cares if it's going to shit. It's the way motherfuckers like you like it. I'm right, aren't I? I've been looking for a way to get rid of you, and you just gave it to me."

"Is that why you sent Dougie to kill me?" Keith shouted. Director Harrington's men turned towards the commotion, but Director Harrington stood there smugly. "I just want to know how a man I supposedly killed still walks the earth?"

The two guards stepped towards Keith, raising their weapons. He got the message. They Already got their traitor. As far as they're concerned, they could kill him, now or later, it didn't matter. It was music to Keith's ears because it meant that Harrington had no clue about his connection to Douglas, which meant that the plan at least worked to keep his involvement secret. Keith heeded their warning and remained silent—and only smiled.

"Ah, a man who knows when it's time to hold his tongue," Dir. Harrington said. "I can't say I'm sorry because I'm not. You're a worthless murderer. True, you didn't kill Dougie because he and his crew never really existed. They were a small team of my men I put in place—to ensure prison was where you ended up. It worked out great. Since we now command the future and the past, we know what will transpire. The best part is that you delivered the message. But your part in this has ended."

Director Harrington gesticulated with his hands towards the guards. "Get him out of here."

The guards grabbed Keith and made for the door.

"His friend as well."

Another set of guys grabbed Joey, and he took the two men out the back and into a blacked-out SUV. The minute they were in, the Explorer guards hooded them—he figured this was as good a time as any to jump back to finish this once and for all.

77

Scapegoat

The room was a perfect square at six feet by six feet. A single heavy door broke the gray of the solid concrete walls. The room had a bed and a desk. They allowed him paper, pens, and pencils, but no mail. Keith knew he was not a prisoner of the US government but only of TASP. He assumed they'd hold him there while they could plant as much evidence as they could. It's just a matter of time. Whatever his plan—he hoped it would be executed soon.

Keith felt once there was enough proof, he'd be offered up as a sacrifice to the government—dead. At which point, they would arrest Director Harrington, not knowing Keith's involvement with Douglas. Keith rather, he remained alive to stop Director Harrington and the Consortium—*it was the least he could do.*

They allowed Keith nothing that could tell him the time, so there was no way of knowing whether it was night or day. He wondered about his life, which had been a lie because they had manipulated it since his childhood. They turned his gift against him—his love into hatred. However, everything comes full circle, eventually. There would be a time when he looked back, smiled, and thought—*he helped save the world now if he could only get his part done.*

Keith sat up and looked at the door. He heard keys. The deadbolt slid open with an audible click, and the door opened. Director Harrington stepped into the room. He took up most of the floor space with his size.

"Don't worry, Keith," he said, "your part in this is almost *over*." He stressed the last word. "You must understand that I do this for our country...and I'm truly sorry that it has to be this way."

"No, you're not," he said, smooth as ice. "Don't say you're doing this for the American people because that's bullshit. I don't believe society would want the military to have such power."

"The military. We're not military," Dir. Harrington said. "We're the people that will keep them safe, so they can enjoy the freedoms we provide."

"Who keeps them safe from you?"

Director Harrington echoed the question. "You need not worry about those things. In a few hours, we'll let you go—"

"Sure, you will!"

"—You'll have a few hours before we hunt you down. Call it a head start. The order from the president will be your death notice. Disappear if you can, or blow your brains out. Do whatever you think you need to do, but either way, in the end, the conclusion will be the same—"

"Ah, me dead," Keith said with eyes downcast. "You're so generous, at least, I have a choice, right? I already know what I'm gonna do."

"And what would that be?"

"You let me go, and I will find you and finish what you started,"

Director Harrington shook his head and left the room. He shut and locked the door behind him. Keith stared at the door for a moment. He hated to admit it, but Director Harrington had a good plan. Once he declared Keith enemy number one, he'd release him and hunt him down like an escaped animal on the loose. A bit unorthodox with the whole letting him go, but Keith understood the reasoning behind it. Harrington needed footage of Keith on the run. No matter where Keith went, he was sure he'd be in surveillance the entire time. Keith wasn't a praying man, but he prayed right there. Not only asking for forgiveness but liberation. *Come on, Douglas.* It's got to be part of the plan.

78

Rescue

Stuck in the cell with not much to do, Keith took a nap but was rudely awakened by the guards who rousted him from his sleep. He grilled them and pushed one out of the way as he got out of bed. "Guess it's time to go, huh?"

One guard handcuffed Keith behind his back before the other one he pushed ordered him out of the room and into a golf cart. One guard sat next to him, and the other sat next to the driver but faced Keith. They took no chances.

They had been watching him long enough, his entire life, to know what he was capable of doing. They knew all too well. The ride to an enormous garage at the back of the building took five minutes. They were still underground, but the cavernous room was packed with all kinds of military-style vehicles and blackout SUVs. There seemed to be only one main entrance into the base. A lit tunnel off to the left and big enough for the large military trucks must lead to the exit.

The golf cart stopped, and the guard next to Keith nudged him to get out. The guard facing him got at the same time with his weapon trained on Keith. The other did the same.

The driver pulled off and parked the cart next to several other golf carts. The two guards with Keith didn't wait for the driver. Instead, they pushed Keith towards one of the black SUVs. Keith scanned the area and took as much of the base in as he could. One of the guards opened the back passenger side door.

"Get in," the guard ordered his gun-waving Keith inside.

Keith climbed up with the help of a guard and sat down in the front row. The handcuffs tightened as he did. He grimaced at the biting pain. One of the guards pushed him towards the window and sat next to him. The other guard climbed into the driver's seat. The car started, and they waited. Keith assumed they waited for the other soldier. He looked around the SUV, looking for what he didn't know. He was sure he'd know if he found it.

An explosion went off in the distance. It was faint and almost imperceptible. Was that outside? Keith couldn't tell where it came from. But for the second time that day, Klaxons sounded. Red lights on the walls and ceilings flashed. *Sen. Douglas arrived. Had to be him.* A few moments later, a golf cart barreled into the garage with two men inside.

Director Harrington and a guy he'd never seen before got out of the golf cart and headed towards the SUV. One of the guards opened the door.

"Sir?"

"There's federal agents upstairs and soldiers, so let's go. We've been compromised. Time to move. I don't know how they found us, but they have. You to take care of him then catch up. Meet us at the Birds Nest." The next question was directed to his passenger. "You come with me."

"Yes, sir," they said in unison. The man in the golf cart followed Director Harrington along with another soldier to a different SUV. They got in and drove off. The driver turned to the guard next to Keith.

"Kill him and let's go." The guard reached over Keith and opened the door. "Get out."

Keith didn't move.

The guard drew his weapon, and as he did so, Keith managed a hip-check with his remaining strength, which pushed the guard into the door on the other side of the car. A gunshot rang out as the guard squeezed the trigger before it fell to the floor of the truck. The gun got stuck between the seat and the door. Keith raised his feet and kicked the driver as he turned back to see what was happening. Keith got punched in the head twice by the guy in the back with him but still slid out of the truck and ran back the way they came. He didn't have run too far down the wide corridor.

A group of soldiers met him at the entrance—guns trained on him. A man stepped from behind them. Keith instantly recognized the man in the blue suit.

"He's all right. Clear the area," Douglas ordered. "Now, go!"

Douglas had one soldier free Keith's hands. Keith rubbed his wrists and nodded to Douglas before he turned back towards the garage. He walked at a break-neck pace.

"Where're you going?" Douglas called.

"After Harrington," he said, as he pointed towards the tunnel, "he took off down the tunnel a few minutes before you came."

Keith jumped into the SUV he just came from. The two TASP men lay face down on the cement with their hands cuffed behind their backs. He guessed they wouldn't need the truck, so he hopped in, put it in the drive, and raced into the tunnel after Harrington.

He wasn't sure what Director Harrington had inside the leather briefcase but knew he had to retrieve the case. Director Harrington had to be stopped at all cost. Light up ahead caught his attention.

As he drove closer, Keith saw the end of the tunnel, giving way to a small parking garage. The doors were open, so he flew out into the evening light. The taillights up ahead had to be Harrington's. He stomped on the gas pedal.

The powerful engine pushed the big truck forward. He rocketed to the end of the street. As Keith pulled onto the main thoroughfare, he saw the SUV turn left at the next light. He did the same and quickly caught up to Director Harrington's vehicle. He tried to stay back and out of sight but had been spotted.

The SUV in front of him raced away and blew through three stoplights. They stopped for the fourth. Keith gave pursuit.

Harrington's SUV made it onto the highway, which was void of any traffic at the time of day. Keith caught up to Harrington with little effort. There were very few cars on the highway that wouldn't yield to his flashing blue and red lights. The two trucks had a clear stretch as they raced side-by-side. He checked the passenger side windows, but he couldn't see through the dark tint. He got his answer when they veered into him and pushed him into the next lane.

They sped off, but Keith regained control and sped after them. He pulled up alongside the SUV. He tried to maintain a speed where the giant SUV's nose was before the rear tire of Harrington's vehicle. When he felt confident, he spun the wheel, smashing into the rear quarter panel. Keith tried to spin the heavy SUV with no luck. The driver swerved and lost control, but only for a moment.

Up ahead, Keith saw two big rigs with trailers and another opportunity. He floored it and passed the Director. The highway had three lanes, which included the breakdown lane. The two trucks were practically neck to neck. Keith drove in the breakdown lane; as he did so, he called Douglas for backup. With back up on the way, all he had to do was slow Director Harrington down. Bright lights reflected in his rearview mirror.

Director Harrington's headlamps grew brighter as they got closer to Keith's rear end. Keith realized that slowing down would not be in Harrington's plan...and he wasn't about to let Keith add it to the plan, either. An instant later impact. Anything loose, suspended in midair, as everything slowed down for a moment. In an instant, everything resumed, and stuff flew to the front. The nose of the truck dipped.

The SUV swerved, and Keith barely maintained control. He almost hit the tractor-trailer to his left and then the guardrail to his right. He regained full control of the SUV in time for Director Harrington to swipe the driver's side rear quarter panel.

The big truck Spun as he turned in into it but couldn't straighten out. He took out several yards of guardrail as he smashed into it and flipped over to the other side. The truck flipped several times more before resting in a ditch. Keith stayed strapped in but lost Harrington.

79

Chase

A young man in his early twenties helped Keith out of the wreckage. The stranger helped Keith back to his car, a hooked-up BMW M5. Keith smiled when he saw such a beast of a machine—he pulled out his cell phone called Douglas, who answered on the first ring.

"Your backup will be there shortly," he said. "You... Everything all right?"

"The fuckin bastard ran me off the road. I lost him momentarily, but I'm about to commandeer this kid's ride. It's a hooked-up BMW M5, and the vanity license plate is X CON," Keith said, as he smiled to himself at such an appropriate vehicle for him to take down a traitor. "He's not gonna be too happy about it, though."

"Don't worry about him," Sen. Douglas said. "Find Harrington, and support will squash any problems. We'll let the state and local authorities that a federal agent is in pursuit of a suspect. But, Keith, be careful."

"Sure, no problem," he said and hung up.

The loud whopping noise of a helicopter made Keith look up and saw several filled the sky above. He jumped into the driver's seat of the BMW with the kid rushing over to him, protesting. Keith quickly explained the situation, and the man seemed doubtful, but Keith could tell the man thought he was being duped. An ex-con can spot another ex-con a mile away, but he somehow convinced him that the people approaching in the helicopters would verify everything. He shut the door and raced off.

He pushed the BMW to high-speed's. This time Harrington would not get away, not if he could help it. *Not this time.*

The BMW sped along the highway, weaving in and out of traffic. A dark blur to the vehicles as it passed. The split to Boston or the South Shore approached fast, and Keith had to decide which way to go. His cell phone rang.

Keith answered it, putting the call on the luxury car's hands-free system.

"Keith, you there?"

"Yes, I got you on hands-free."

"Good, keep this line open," Douglas said. "Harrington's SUV was spotted headed to 93. It looks like he's headed towards the city."

"Good, that makes my decision a lot easier," he said as he pushed the car even faster. The speedometer ticked up. Under normal conditions, the BMW would cut off at 155 mph, but Keith was sure this ride was capable of far greater speeds. Although he didn't see any evidence, he wouldn't be surprised to find out if the car had Nitrous oxide. If it had NOS, Harrington wouldn't stand a chance. "Sir, can you do me a favor?"

"What's that?"

"Ask the owner of the BMW if it has NOS?"

"You just did. We're all connected."

"This is Rogers...the man says it does, and I'll let him explain how to access it."

"It's not that complicated," the owner said, "it's like accessing a stash spot."

"Does that mean I need to turn on the radio and flip on the high beams or something?"

The owner laughed. "No, look at the console, just below the radio. Do you see those blank spaces?"

"Yeah, what do I need to do?"

"Simply press the first and last at the same time and hold for 20 seconds and let go."

He did as he was told while trying to keep his eyes on the road. The cars on the street started thinning out as he took the split up to Route 93. He let go, and he wasn't disappointed. The five panels moved inward and were replaced with five labeled switches. Two switches and a red button were grouped together. Keith was sure the switches went to the NOS tanks. However, he wondered what the other switches on the right did.

"What're the other switches do?"

There was some muffled arguing, and then Rodgers said. "Unless he is promised he won't get into trouble, he isn't saying a thing," Douglas reassured the man he was helping his government. One that would be most appreciative. The man spilled the beans, and Keith smiled like a Cheshire cat.

"You got to be fuckin kidding me," Keith said with a deep laugh. "What's the odds of me getting into this ride."

"Yeah, I'm starting to wish I didn't stop to help you," the man said with a laugh.

"What's the odds," Keith said and flipped the switch to prime the first burst. The button glowed red a few moments later, letting him know it's ready. "All right, boys and girls, I won't be talking for a while. Wish me luck," he said and pushed the button.

A second later, the MPH needle pinned, and Keith was forced back into the seat. Even at these extreme speeds, he could handle the precision-made machine. It was better than any carnival ride he'd ever been on. Douglas and the support team heard his screams of joy—and then silence.

The silence persisted for several long minutes until Keith spotted the SUV. "I see the fucker; I see him." He slowed down to a more normal, albeit fast, speed. Harrington was passing the gas tanks when Keith caught up to him.

"I'm a couple of cars behind him now," he said as he checked the highway. "It's pretty busy out here. I'm not sure where all these cars came from, but there's a lot of them, so I'm just gonna fall back and follow him for now."

"That's fine, just don't lose them again," Douglas said. "And you sure he's carrying sensitive information?"

"Definitely, no doubt in my mind," Keith said as he tried to maintain his distance from the SUV up ahead. "We're passing the old Boston Globe."

Keith stopped talking and concentrated on keeping the distance. The Ted Williams tunnel came up, and they didn't take the exit, so he was very pleased that he didn't have to chase him through a long ass tunnel. He hoped they would get off and go through the city. When Harrington passed the last exit before the Tip O' Neil Tunnel, he wondered if he'd get off an exit or head to the Tobin Bridge.

"We're going through the tunnel. See you in a few minutes. I might lose signal…"

Keith watched the SUVs' brake lights as they entered the tunnel. The SUV switched lanes to the right, and he knew all the exits were on the right. "He might get off the highway," he said aloud. "Harrington's vehicle past the first two exits."

At first, Keith thought Director Harrington would continue up RT93 and over the Zakim Bunker Hill Bridge, but he was mistaken—as he watched the big vehicle take the next exit. *Why would he go that way?*

Keith took the exit when he was able, and it brought him to the right side of the Rose Kennedy Greenway. They were just north of South Station, and Harrington's vehicle was up to head in the left lane and stopped at a red light.

Harrington's vehicle turned left once the light turned green and then right. Was he reversing direction? Harrington headed back the other way. He tried to maintain some distance, but traffic was too light. Twice he thought he got too close and got spotted, but Harrington's vehicle showed no signs that they knew he was there.

For a second, Keith thought he was gonna get back on the highway and head south, but he saw the right blinker go on and take a turn. When Keith got to the Street and turned—the Director's vehicle disappeared. Keith continued down the street. He glanced right and saw the Director's vehicle at a light a few blocks down.

He followed him but lost him momentarily when he passed Summer Street. Downtown is a maze of one-way streets, so Keith had to be careful. He went straight and let the road lead him. Twelve minutes later spotted the car abandoned in a public alley. The rear end of the vehicle stuck out into the street so that Keith couldn't miss it. He hoped it wasn't a setup. He slowed down as he drove past.

As he did, the sound of a jackhammer dotted the length of the car. The passenger side windows exploded and showered Keith with glass. He had been spotted and being shot at. He stomped on the gas, and the BMW pulled away. The rear window exploded, and the car listed to one side momentarily like a ship about to sink. The BMW, however, was up equipped with run-flats—so it was good as long as he didn't have to go too fast. Never one to back down from a fight, Keith spun the car around and headed back towards the gunfire.

This time ready.

The two soldiers stood at the foot or so in the street and fired their assault weapons at Keith. People in the immediate area fled the scene. People were screaming. It was pure chaos. Keith stopped as the bullets ripped through the car. With no more time to formulate a plan, he checked the 40 Cal he had taken out of the trunk and smashed a gas.

The BMW careered towards the men. The first jumped out of the way but not completed in time. The front right fender clipped the man, sending him spiraling into the ear. *That'll be a rough landing.* The other step beside the truck, as Keith crashed into the back of it. He put it in reverse as the man raised his gun and aimed it at point-blank range. The front of the car got held up—stuck to the back of the truck, so he mashed the gas to pull away. He looked up at the man in time to see two scarlet color dots of blood blossom on his chest before he fell back. Over the grind of the two vehicles, Keith didn't hear the helicopter hovering above. Though now he could hear the car's owner.

"My car's totally fucked," the man said.

"It sure is," Keith said, "and Director Harrington got away."

80

Loss

The extra guards, provided by Douglas, walked the corridors of the Complex in pairs. The debriefing took all night, and Keith and Dr. Bell were tired. Jen had already left with Billy, who also turned out to be one of Douglas's men. They kept him in the dark as the rest of them. No surprise there. Billy's job, as it turned out, was to keep Keith safe. Not that he could have—since most of the danger happened while he was on a jump. He could, however, protect Keith's unconscious body, so no one else could kill him while he was on a jump.

Keith mused about how most of the attempts on his life happened while he was on a jump and therefore immortal. For the most part, it was all over. He broke up TASP and shed light on the shadow government that operated in the dark. Although, it wouldn't be over until they captured Harrington and the project's info returned. Lost in thought, Keith didn't hear Dr. Bell, who was walking beside him.

Dr. Bell placed his hand on his shoulder. "You in there?" he said with a chuckle. Keith glanced at him and nodded. "Good thought I lost you for a second. I haven't seen my house in months, so give me a lift, and I'll buy breakfast."

"Sounds like a plan," he said, as they approached the exit and had their belongings over to the guard and stepped through the tank, called the petition they had to enter and retrieve this stuff on the other side before they could enter the elevators. Douglas gave all the SCP employees the next few weeks off but reassured them the project would continue but under new guardianship. The doors to the elevator closed. *Going up.*

An electric sports car met Keith and Dr. Bell at the curb. Joey sat on the hood as they approached.

"It's good to see you're still alive," Joey said

"Same to you," he said. "That mine?"

"Sure is, don't you remember—you're a multibillionaire, don't you know?"

"Oh, that's one thing you don't forget once you find out. I had gone on for too many years thinking I was a pauper when I was a prince. It's time to live a little."

Joey pushed off the car and stepped to Keith, and hugged him. He stepped back away. "Don't ever lose touch with me again, you hear? You're the best friend anyone could have." Joey said before he headed back inside.

"Something tells me that's a two-way street," Dr. Bell said as he watched Joey go back into the building.

"Yeah, that's the truth if I ever heard," he said. "He's a far better man than me, but he just doesn't know it."

Dr. Bell nodded and got into the passenger side of Keith's car. Keith got behind the wheel and put it in drive, and took off.

Bright and fluffy cumulus clouds drifted across the sky, except for the direction they were headed. The doctor lived in the South End. The same place the old man lived in a section that had seen gentrification over the past few decades. The doctor lived in a renovated brownstone on a quiet side street.

The drive didn't take long. The Complex was only several blocks away. They passed the Prudential Center and could see the former John Hancock building as they turned onto Dartmouth Street and waited at the intersection of Columbus Avenue when his cellphone rang.

Keith's phone was attached to the hands-free system, so he pressed the phone symbol on the steering wheel. "Hello?"

"Harrington has been spotted," Douglas said. "Is the Doctor still with you?"

"Sure is, and he can hear you. I got you on hands-free."

"It's good to hear you're a safe driver," Douglas chuckled. "But I'm afraid you're both not gonna like what I'm about to say.... My technicians have been working all night to find out what exactly it was Harrington had taken."

"I assume they found out?" Dr. Bell said.

"Yes, and more." Keith could hear the reluctance in Douglas's voice. "It's been confirmed. He took off with every bit of the project's knowledge. *All of it.* They also found detailed plans that Harrington thought he erased of his mission should things backfire."

"He had a backup plan is what you're telling me."

"Oh, it gets better. His plan is rather simple. Go back and kill you when you're a child and take your blood."

"But he can't," he said as he glanced at Dr. Bell.

"Yeah, he needs your blood, so yeah, he could." Dr. Bell said. "Kill you, and he'll have all of it, but it would be a limited supply. The reason why they kept you alive until now is that they have been taking your blood since you were a child and had boatloads of it."

"And I thought being the first protected me," Keith said with a nervous chuckle. "Wouldn't killing me erase everything they have? No blood for TASP jumpers."

"It would stop this deviation of the original timeline. He'd have to have set up this contingency within the lifetime of their oldest jumper, which may be Harrington himself."

Their plan was a long time coming, and it made Keith sick, but Keith could see why the program waited for things to play out as they were told. Thirty-three years, they took his blood and used the supply to make jumpers. There could be thousands of jumpers still out there.

"All right, where is he?" Keith asked, understanding the urgency of the new information. "Do we know when he's going back?"

"He's in Lynn," Douglas said. "Drop off Dr. Bell and head up there."

"All right, I will—"

"No, don't drop me off," Dr. Bell said in a stern voice. "I'm going with you…and that's that."

"Any problems with Dr. Bell going with you?" Douglas said.

"None that I can think of," Keith said, remembering future Jen's warning. She said Dr. Bell died to protect Keith. But she said it was after he came back from a jump, so maybe everything would be okay. Manipulating the future would never be a good idea. Keith turned left and headed to the highway and over the Tobin Bridge. He took Rt 1 to Lynn.

City of sin. They wrote a ditty about it. "Lynn Lynn, city of sin, you never come out the same way you went in—and neither would Harrington." Keith laughed at the thought.

The twenty-five-minute ride there was peaceful and the sky clear, but now a dark, ominous cloud sat above the city. The two men didn't speak until they crossed the city limits. The doctor asked Keith if he knew where they were going. Keith said he did as they crossed the bridge into Lynn. They passed several car dealerships, a grocery market, and a Walmart. They came to light and turned left and follow that. They were in a commercial district. Warehouses surrounded them.

The warehouses gave way to a residential neighborhood. Keith stopped at a stop sign, picked up his gun, checked to see if there was one in the chamber, and placed it on his lap.

"This isn't exactly a nice his neighborhood, Doc. Don't let the houses with the white picket fences fool you, all right?"

"Believe me…it didn't," Dr. Bell said.

Keith shook his head with a bit of laughter. "All right, as long as you know."

He turned at the stop sign and continued up the street. A few moments later, Keith pulled onto another street, and Keith pulled over and parked three houses before the address where Harrington was spotted. The address brought them to a small warehouse, which probably was a garage. Keith and Dr. Bell got out of the car and headed towards the building.

The street was well-traveled by both cars and foot traffic, but it was early morning, so only a few people were walking about, and most of them were children headed to school.

A group of teenagers, he believed to be gang bangers, sat on a stoop right before their destination. As they got closer, Keith noticed one of them tapped another on the shoulder and pointed in their direction. Keith prepared himself for confrontation.

They continued to walk towards the group in front of the warehouse. They had to pass a group of teenagers to get to the destination. There is no way around it. When they were about 10 feet away, one of them got up and stood in the middle of the sidewalk.

After the situation with Dougie, he wouldn't be surprised if these guys worked for Director Harrington as well. The revelation that Dougie worked for Harrington had changed his whole perspective.

"What's up, cuz?" The man said. "Nice car you all have. Got a dollar I can borrow?"

"I'm afraid I don't," Keith said, knowing the game. Ask for some money and when it's given, ask for more. A lot more, and when you refuse, they'll try to take it. "We got some business to take care of right now, but maybe on the way out."

They passed the men and made it a few feet before the man shouted. "Hey, Keith, where you going, son. We got business to take care of right here."

Once he heard his name, he couldn't help but look back at the gang bangers—in time to see the kid draw his weapon and aim it in Keith. The other five on the stoop did the same. Two more teens on the porch produced assault weapons. An AK-47 and an AR-15. He pushed Dr. Bell out of the way into the clear.

He didn't remember pulling the 40 Cal from his waistband, but he had. The man on the sidewalk had to be the leader. This would not be good. Keith wasted no time as he leveled his weapon and shot the two men with the assault weapons.

The others stood up as the leader shot at Keith and the doctor. Dr. Bell dove behind a van that was in the parking lot of the warehouse. He covered him from behind a pickup truck parked on the street, drawing the fire away from Dr. Bell. Keith stepped back out and squeezed off some more rounds.

He felt dizzy, and his vision blurred and out. He shot the first person he saw, and it wasn't the leader, just a member of the crew. After noticing the doctor was unconscious with his back against the van's front tire, he ran to the doctor's aid, checked his pulse, and found none. "Fuck no!" he cried in a guttural animal-like sound. Two magazines left. He inserted one into his 40 Cal and walked right up the sidewalk as if he owned the place. He took out the four remaining men with ease. The leader's gun breached open, and Keith shot him in the head.

He hobbled back to the doctor. Several slugs had ripped through his own body, but he only cared about the doctor at the moment. Maybe he took the pulse wrong. He called Douglas to have an ambulance come.

The door to the garage was locked, but it took very little force to open it. He felt like an ass leaving Dr. Bell laying in a parking lot, probably bleeding to death if he wasn't already dead, but the mission had to be completed, or whatever happens to the doctor would be in vain.

81

Confrontation

The door slammed shut behind him with a loud bang that reverberated throughout the space. Nothing like telling the person you're sneaking up on that you have arrived. He scanned the room before him and found it smaller than he expected. The room contained several vehicles, a boat, and not much else. One vehicle had government plates. The intel had been correct. It was time to put a stop to it all by capturing Director Harrington.

There was a door at the back, so he checked it out and hoped his blundering with the racket he just made didn't make Harrington take off. Gun in hand, he traversed the 50 feet towards the door with caution. The stale air of age, rust, and oil made became overpowering as he walked towards the door.

Since this was in a perfect world, he didn't make it to the door. Keith got caught in the open as gunfire lit up the darkened garage. Streaks of metal-lightning screamed all around him. Keith knew he'd just been ambushed. There was more than one shooter. He dropped to the cement floor and elbow-crawled several feet toward the truck.

A sharp pain seared through his leg. He stifled a scream. Fuel to keep going. Eye on completing the mission. The future depended on it.

A faint light filtered into the garage from a window in the distance. Two barely perceptible shadows moved across the floor. Keith ejected the magazine and placed it on the ground before he fished out another and inserted it while holding it close to his stomach in an attempt to muffle the sound of the click. He pulled back the slide and chambered a round.

He didn't get a good look at the men shooting at him, but he saw the silhouettes. Neither of the men looked like Harrington. Keith figured Harrington had men stationed here, so he would find more than the two who have him pinned down at the moment. He had to take these two guys out and see what else Harrington had in store for him next.

He just needed a fighting chance. If he could get them before they used all their ammo, he might get it. He tore a part of his shirt off and wrapped it around the wound on his leg. His leg kept bleeding, and it hurt like hell, so he needed all the concentration he could muster.

The boat on the other side of the truck gave him an idea. He crawled under the truck while keeping an eye on the shadows. The gunfire had ceased for a moment. The shadows grew.

The boat had a stepladder at the back. The 40-foot-long yard also had a swimming platform beyond the stepladder. As quiet as he could, he climbed the ladder into the boat. He looked around the deck and saw nothing—so he moved on to the cabin.

As he quickly searched the boat, he found several items picking them up as he went—a spool of heavy fishing line, bug spray, and a grill lighter. The boat had two sleeping quarters, and inside one, he found a tackle box. He removed some flies and several hefty weights. He also found a gutting knife with its talon-like claw of a blade. Confident he wouldn't yet be found, Keith sat on the bed and improvised a couple of weapons.

The weights, flies, and fishing line made a makeshift version of a Bolo or weighted chain like manriki-gusari. After he found a roll of electrical tape, he taped the extend-a-lighter to the can of bug sprayer. He tested it to make sure it worked. He left the cabin moments later and still felt like he didn't have half a chance, but he was going to give it his best shot.

As he quietly snuck off the boat, he noticed the room took on an air of silence that could only be described as deadly. He climbed down and checked the ground—he could no longer saw the silhouettes of either assailant. A sudden sound, like someone kicking a can, came from his right.

He headed in the sound's direction with a knife in one hand and a gun in the other. He passed the truck and turned right— and confronted a stack of boxes. He moved around the boxes, and he noticed several blue barrels with the path straight down the center. The barrels were stacked two high and several deep.

The corridor went on for about 15 feet, and at the end, light filtered through the same large window that provided the silhouettes. The closer he inched towards the window, the more his stomach crawled with a thousand spiders. Despite his gut telling him this was a bad idea, he pushed on, wincing from time to time from the wound on his leg. He stopped, listened, and continued on, stopped listened again, but this time he heard footfall, so he waited.

Keith picked up speed as the footfall got louder. He glanced side to side as he moved down the blue barrel lane at high-speed. He was about there, just another few feet away, when a figure dressed all in black appeared at the end. The filtered light made the person appear to be nothing more than a silhouette. A deadly shadow. With barely any thought, he threw the knife—its odd-shaped blade spinning through the air on its deadly trek.

The black-clad shadow raised its assault weapon across its chest. The knife clattered loudly off the weapon to the floor. Keith moved swiftly towards the shadow as it raised its gun. *So much for not attracting attention*, he thought as he squeezed off several rounds from his own.

Three of the four rounds found their mark and hit the shadow dead center, while another missed its head to the left. The last one caught the shadow in its left eye. The shadow collapsed to the ground. Keith ran as fast as he could. He made it to the assailant, grabbed the shadow's weapon. Released the magazine and checked to see how many were left. The 30-round mag only had about 15 more rounds. The assailant, who turned out to be a man, had a sidearm on his right side. Keith removed it along with an extra magazine he found on the guy's belt, but there were no extra magazines for the assault rifle.

Keith never heard the other assailant approach. Powerful hands grabbed his shoulders—and pulled him back with extreme force. Keith landed on his back hard, which forced the air out of his lungs. The assault rifle clattered across the ground. Pain wracked his body, but it wasn't time to rest. His flight or fight response kicked into overdrive—to kill or be killed.

The force of the fall made him shut his eyes, but he opened them in time to see a boot crashing towards him. White light exploded through his skull in a million bright shards as the foot smashed into his face. The foot moved to his throat and held him in place.

Keith cursed himself for not hearing the other soldier approach from behind. He fought the pain as he opened his eyes and stared up at his assailant. White dots, which made it hard to see, obscured his vision. It was too disorientating, so Keith closed his eyes. He tried to remain calm as the assailant pressed his foot harder on his windpipe, cutting off much-needed oxygen.

Keith fished the can of bug spray out of his jacket pocket. Dizziness set in. He could hear a man's voice telling him he was going to die. Consciousness waned. The assailant then applied even more pressure. Keith fumbled one-handed with the extend-a-lighter taped can. He brought it up as high as he could and aimed at the man and squeezed the trigger—fiery liquid sprayed the man's clothes and ignited them instantly.

The man stepped away from Keith to put out the flames. Keith gasped. The flood of oxygen almost made him pass out. He fumbled, he fumbled for the gun he dropped. After he found it, he picked it up and emptied the rest of the magazine into the man set ablaze.

There could be a dozen more of these guys, and the thought made Keith wince in pain. He stood on shaky legs and looked down at the dead man—and hoped there weren't anymore. He feared Harrington escaped again. He ejected the magazine and let it clattered to the ground. The new assailant had two on his utility belt. Keith grabbed one and inserted it into the weapon.

On shaky legs, Keith made his way to the door. On the other side, a short hallway led out to the back of the building to a fenced-in parking lot. Three doors were facing each other along the hallway. Keith approached the first one, opting to open the right side first. It was empty, as was the one across the hall.

He crossed the hall in a zigzag pattern to the third door and repeated the pattern until he made it to the exterior door at the end of the hall. None of the rooms were occupied or showed any signs of inhabitants.

He went through the heavy steel door and found himself in an anteroom with another steel door on the other side. Someone had turned the large hallway into a makeshift office with two desks cluttered with paperwork and office equipment. He figured this was the room Harrington used because of its quick exit.

The makeshift office was organized. Everything seemed to have its own place. Keith glanced around the room and believed the room had a purpose. It wasn't a safe house. It was something more. It could have been Harrington's remote office. The place where he could do the paperwork that needed to be done. Something about it was off. Too perfect.

For a moment, he thought about searching the computer but decided not to—Harrington was far too smart to leave anything there. If he found anything on the computer, it would probably be misdirection. Something that would lead Keith farther away. He found nothing useful, so he exited through the back door.

He stepped out into the sunlight and glanced around the parking lot for any signs of Harrington. He believed he must've got away. A saltwater breeze wrapped around him and sent a chill up his spine. His leg wound suddenly conspiring with his head and made him dizzy. He went back inside.

The feeling something wasn't right wouldn't shake. He stood by the door and tried to figure out what he missed. He only encountered two men inside. Two. It didn't sit right with him. There should've been more men. Not once did he see Harrington? Was it possible this whole thing was a misdirection so that Harrington could disappear? *Damn.*

The sudden thud—thud *whack* sound of a helicopter broke his concentration. He looked up to see it hovering above him. His cell phone buzzed in his pocket. He headed to the front of the building, as he removed and answered the phone.

"Keith, it's Douglas. I'm landing now. Where are you?"

"Inside the location, but there's no sign of Harrington," he said, anger clear in his voice. "But I'm not done searching—I must've missed something."

"All right, I'll call back after I squared things away with the locals. Where is the doctor?"

"Unfortunately, he didn't make it. Gang bangers killed him outside. They knew my name—they were waiting for us."

"That definitely changes the situation, doesn't it? Find that cocksucker before he makes off with—"

"I know...and...I will," Keith said, frustrated.

He researched each room, but the second time around, he noticed an abnormality. All the rooms were shaped the same—all equal size, except the second room from the front. The slight irregularity with the wall that separated the garage to the office like all the other rooms were pancled. The walls hadn't been changed since the 1980s. He knocked on it to see if it was hollow, but he was rewarded with a solid thud. No hollow space there. He banged again angrily with the bottom of his fists—and the panel popped open, revealing a small elevator.

"Going down?" Keith said, relieved he found something.

The elevator went one level down. It opened up to a long passage that led away from the building. He followed it to the end. There were no doors along the passageway, but he must have missed something.

Two men with assault weapons entered the passage from the door in front of him. He opened fire and cut the two men down. Machine gunfire erupted from behind him as bullets whizzed past, and some tore through his flesh. He ran forward, over the two dead men, and through the door. On the other side, he collapsed his back against the door. *Probably not the safest place to rest.*

Keith scrambled in the darkness away from the door, found a wall, and placed his back against it. He raised the machine gun and waited. The two newcomers stepped into the room or hallway, and Keith dropped them. He got up and went over to the door, using the light from the hallway to determine whether it was a room. He found the light switch and flipped it.

It was a room that had four doors. Cameras were installed above each one. Before he could decide which one to take, the one behind him burst open, and a single gunshot rang out. He felt the pain from inside and grabbed at his side as he spun in the intruder's direction.

"Looking for me!" Harrington said as he raised his gun again.

Keith went to raise the assault rifle, but it was gone. He must've dropped it when he grabbed the side. He went for the 40 Cal inside his waistband. It was too late. A bullet hit him dead center in his chest and sent him crashing to the concrete floor. Air whooshed out of his lungs as he hit. Pain wracked his body. Harrington stood above him with the gun pointed to his head.

"You're like a damn cockroach," Harrington said, "you just don't want to die, but you will."

What with all his strength, he gritted his teeth through the pain as Keith stretched out and swept Harrington's legs, bringing the man down to Keith's level. Harrington's weapon clattered across the room, out of reach. Keith looked for the weapon, but it was just beyond Harrington's back. The two men wrestled on the ground. Keith, the stronger of the two, easily pinned Harrington down, but Harrington wasn't without resourcefulness. He poked and prodded any place he saw blood—he found Keith's leg wound and squeezed.

Keith released him and scrambled for the 40 Cal. He picked it up and leveled it at Harrington—and squeezed the trigger. Two coupled crimson dots appeared in the middle of Harrington's torso. He collapsed back against the wall and didn't move. Keith moved up against a different wall and watched him the entire time. He stared at the Harrington's motionless body until everything around him darkened. His cellphone rang, and he answered it and, in a daze, he told Douglas about the elevator before the darkness overtook him.

82

Just a Dream

Every time he opened his eyes, he questioned the reality. The same old shit as of late. His mind filled with false memories. The last thing he remembered was watching Director Harrington collapse to the ground with blood pooling around his body. He kept his eyes closed for as long as he could. The bright light beyond threatening to assault his eyes. It happened every time he awoke in a brightly lit room—the light hurt through closed lids, never mind if he opened them.

He opened his eyes after gaining some strength and saw some kind of plastic thing over his face, nose, and mouth. He tried to move his head but couldn't. The only thing he could move was his eyes. His vision was out of focus, but he could see white, green, and something that looked like Walt Disney threw up. The colors swam around him and slowly turned into people. A nurse, a doctor, and someone off into the distance. He must be in the hospital.

A woman in a white coat, Keith realized, talked to him, but he could understand what she was saying. He tried to say as much but was unsuccessful. The mask obstructed sound, but he wasn't sure if he could speak at all. He watched them as they stood over him. He closed his eyes again, but only for a moment. Answers were needed. He stared at the woman he couldn't understand and pleaded with her with his eyes for her to help him. His vision blurred and faded to black until there was nothing.

•

Rousted by the sound of a female's voice, Keith became conscious and somehow knew it was the same woman he pleaded with but couldn't understand. He stirred within his bed. He forced himself to open his eyes—to regain full consciousness. The sheer act of doing it was strenuous and made his eyelids feel like they weighed a ton. Light slowly crept in as the darkness faded as he entered into the conscious realm of the living.

The woman leaned over him and asked him if he was all right. He nodded or at least believed he did. He felt a smile form and was happy he could understand her. He gathered all his strength and managed to ask. "What happened? Am I okay?"

The woman smiled and told him to rest and that he needed to relax. He closed his eyes because he believed she was right. It was something important about the woman, but what? He didn't know. Again, he faded off to the dark world of unconsciousness.

•

"No, don't go? I need answers," Keith screamed as he sat up. He awoke again from the same nightmare. It seemed so real. He glanced around the room, and everything was normal. It was exactly where he was supposed to be. In his cell at MCI-Norfolk. He was glad he didn't have a cellmate because he had been waking up from nasty nightmares for the last two months. Ever since he had gotten back from the hospital. The dreams seemed real. Strange, but fantastic at the same time.

He got up and started his morning stretching routine. He had been in the hospital for several months. He was lucky the lab caught it in time. The tests at the hospital were conclusive—he had a serious problem. They diagnosed him with a word that not only had 20 letters in it but was impossible to be uttered by mere mortals. He believed it was a lost word of the ancients.

As he exercised, he thought about everything. The dreams were only part of the issue. Because of them, he didn't know what to think. Was he going nuts or what? He asked himself 100 times. Keith had always been proud of his health and state of mind, but now all that seemed to be in question.

They gave him a mountain of paperwork that said he was at Mass General, but was he? Foreign memories flooded his conscious mind. Memories that couldn't possibly be true. A different president. One that wasn't the current one in the White House. A million-dollar car that belonged to him, but yet he was broke and incarcerated.

After he finished stretching, he did a couple of hundred push-ups. Nothing too strenuous. At the end of his workout, he put water on for green tea. He also went into his locker to get his medication. The only meds he'd ever been on were for migraine. Now he took several pills: two right after he woke up, then he'd have to go to the med line in the afternoon.

The pills kept his mind healthy, so he took them. However, fleeting thoughts of doubt into his mind on occasion. What if his memories were really his? No, he had to stop thinking that way. It was bad enough they wanted him to see the psychologist as it is, but he had refused the request so far.

Since as far back as he could remember, he has always been able to rely on his gut instinct for better or worse—it has always been on point. Unfortunately, it now told him something wasn't right. He made his tea and sat on his bed. He glanced at the sole letter on his desk. Stared at it for a few moments before he reached for it and opened the letter from his friend Joey. The letter didn't help one bit—Joey sent him money. He knew why, but none of it made any sense.

They had been friends as children and lost touch over the years. Joey had found him after he got back from the hospital. Joey's letters were cryptic, but the money was not. Joey had written to him seven times over the last two months, and Keith's canteen account had grown exponentially.

The money Keith welcomed a lot, but the last letter said something about his case being turned over. That he had people working on it and knew it would get done. He didn't know what Joey was talking about. Sure, he had an appeal going, but he didn't think it would be successful in any way. It was kind of impossible. He killed somebody.

The CO called chow. Breakfast time. He made his way downstairs, and everything seemed brighter. Clearer. He made his way through the chow line, got his breakfast, and brought it back to his table. On his way back up the stairs, after he ate, the CO stopped him.

"Richards, pack it up. You're being released today."

"Get the fuck out here," Keith said, thinking it was a joke. "I'm doing life."

"I know, but not anymore, you're not," the CO said.

He went back to his cell in a fog to pack his belongings. His friends dropped by to wish him luck at the surprised release. It had to be some kind of mistake. *Didn't it?* If it were, he would soon find out. After he got the stuff ready, he went back downstairs to ask the CO if you could call booking to make sure it wasn't a mistake. It wasn't. But he had to sign some papers. Release forms of some kind. They asked him if he needed a ride, and he did, so he called Joey.

I'm going home, he thought in total disbelief.

83

Haunted Release

Everything moved too fast, but he didn't complain—quite the opposite. Joey, who was close by, picked him up at nine on the dot and whisked him off to the city. Joey told him he'd take him to his house. A picture of a brownstone popped into his head. Though he wasn't sure if it was the place in question, he didn't care. He was free.

Joey had picked him up in style. Keith had never been in a Lamborghini Aventador before, and Keith enjoyed the moment. What a way to start your day being free. He floated on the proverbial cloud nine. Joey said something, but Keith missed it. "What's up?"

"Nothing really, but you seem to have slipped away on me for a moment," Joey said with a bit of concern in his voice. "You sure you're okay, right?"

"Yeah, nothing really. I'm on top of the world right now," he said with a smile. "You taking me to the brownstone?"

He wasn't sure why he said it that way, but he had.

Joey glanced over at him and smiled. "So...you do... remember?"

"I didn't lose my memory," Keith said with a bit of disgust. "Just get confused. My head's filled with false memories—several for the same dates. It makes no fuckin sense at all."

"Memory can be a funny thing," Joey said. "It's like a string. If you focus on all the memories associated with the brownstone, maybe that'll help."

"Yeah…I don't know," he said, shrugging his shoulders a bit while he scrunched up his face, "but I guess it's worth a try."

Since returning from the hospital, Keith had tried many things to understand. To sort the memories out. Nobody had any answers as to how one could have multiple memories. Ones that couldn't possibly belong to one person. The mental health department insisted he had dissociative episodes because of the fragmentation. He felt his release was bittersweet because now he was home free but mentally imprisoned.

"Well, do you want to get something to eat or go straight home?"

He liked the sound of the word home, but he could tell Joey wanted to hang out, and food that didn't have any involvement with a prison sounded fantastic. "Food sounds good right now."

"Any place special you'd like to go?"

Keith couldn't think of any. "No, why don't you pick someplace?"

"Don't worry, I got you covered," Joey said as they rocketed to his Boston. "Sit back and relax."

Keith smiled because he liked the sound of relaxing. He leaned back in the seat and stared out the window. His head, at least for the moment, seemed clear. He found himself focused on the brownstone and connecting the dots of the memories attached. The first associative memory was difficult to find, but it got easier with each new find. Excitement made him smile. Some myriad memories were fantastic and couldn't possibly be true, but Keith still pressed on. Before he knew it, they parked outside of the restaurant.

"We here, my friend," Joey said, opening his arms wide as he parked.

He pulled himself away from his memories and looked around. The smile that still plastered his face got wider. Because the restaurant Joey picked was one of his favorites. At least the memory attached to the brownstone told him so—several others also told him so.

"I like this place," he said, realizing something, "isn't this place new?"

Joey smiled. "It sure is, and I know you like it, which is why we're here."

"How could you know that? I'm not even sure how I knew I like it here."

"One step at a time, my friend," Joey said in a reassuring tone. "There's a lot I need to tell you."

Keith went through his bag for his medication the hospital had given him. He was late taking his pills, and he figured now would be a good time as any. Joey watched him.

"You take meds?" Joey asked, surprised. "Since when?"

"Since I got back from the hospital for my condition," Keith said. "These right here for anxiety and these bad boys help clear my head up—?"

Joey grabbed the clear plastic bottle of pills.

"—What are you doing?"

"These have to be the reason why your memories are so muddled. The double-crossing son of a bitch. He had them drug you. It had to be Douglas."

"What are you talking about?"

"Keith, you weren't in a funking hospital. You were recruited for a secret government project. Hell, you saved the fuckin world, as we know it."

"Damn, thought I was losing it."

"Forget about it, for now, let's go eat. After I have someplace, I need to take you. Maybe it'll jog your memory."

With a bit of reluctance, Keith agreed, yet he had the same doubts. Though he didn't tell Joey, Keith had some insane and improbable images flood his mind and 100 false thoughts since returning from the hospital. There had been several unexplainable events. One, in particular, woke him up from a dreamless sleep to discover a message written, somehow, he knew by his own hand, in the dust on his TV screen.

The message was short and simple. You're not going crazy. Find it. Take control. When? Why? He didn't know. So, I think Keith knew for sure his hand wrote the note—but he didn't remember doing it.

Halfway through lunch, he told Joey he believed him. They had a good time reminiscing about the old days when they were teenagers. As they talked, a certain string of memories fought their way to the surface of his consciousness. The more Joey talked, the more connections formed. There was no time like the present to get in some questions of his own.

"About earlier, I believe you. There's this one certain string of very persistent memories. The more you talk, the more it becomes clearer."

"That's good."

"But I need you to look at it from my point of view."

"I don't understand, but go ahead. Help me understand."

"My head is swimming with, what feels like, 100 distinct memories...and it's not only confusing but claustrophobic. Our mind is supposed to be a place where we can escape to, but not mine. How is it possible?"

"I can only tell you what I know," Joey said, "are you ready to listen?"

He put his fork down and stopped eating. "I'm all ears."

"First off, you need to stop taking those meds, agreed?"

Keith nodded. "If that's what it takes to get answers, and it's done...please continue."

An hour later, Joey finished bringing Keith up to date. He didn't handle it very well, but it intrigued him. It was a lot to process. "Could you take me home, now?"

"I can."

"I just have one other question. Do you own an electric sports car? If so, how do I know?"

"The answer is you have several expensive sports cars, and one is electric, I believe. You bought many with the large number of shares of Joe Co. Technologies stocks you own as my cofounder.

"I am your what?" Keith said with an incredulous look.

"It is what it is," Joey said, then called the server for the check.

He left the restaurant and ride to Keith's townhouse in silence. Keith spent the ride silently looking out the window but not seeing anything beyond the glass. He was lost in thought—focused while he searched and remembered. He followed the stack of memories to its root. The further he examined his errant memories, the more relaxed and calm he felt. The realization that this string was his reality overwhelmed him a bit. No matter how fantastic it all seemed—he knew it to be true. As he came to this epiphany, they pulled up in front of his house.

Keith felt reassured for the first time since returning from the hospital, and his head felt clearer. Only one set of memories were prominent. At least for the moment. And that was all he could ask for. Though he knew he could call upon others if he needed to, he didn't see the need.

"Thanks for the ride, Joey," Keith said, "and the answers. You're a good friend, and I want you to know I appreciate it very much."

"No problem, that's what friends are for," Joey smiled. "You want me to go in with you?"

"No, I remember this place," he said. "My head cleared, at least for the moment, and this was the old man's place. The man I used to visit as a kid, right? We played chess."

"Yes, I believe so."

"All right, let me get going," Joey said.

He got out of the car and watched Joey pull off into traffic and drive away. The city here smelled good. It smelled well, free...and that was all that mattered. He was free.

410–DÉJÀ VU

"Yes, I believe so."

"All right, let me get going," Joey said.

He got out of the car and watched Joey pull off into traffic and drive away. The city here smelled good. It smelled well, free...and that was all that mattered. He was free.

Author Note

December 10, 2020

Dear Reader,

Thank you for giving a schlep like me a chance. It means a lot. I value your time and feedback. Please leave a review whether good, bad, or indifferent. It's taken a long time to get this out to you, and I hope you enjoy it; and if you didn't, I apologize—if it's my writing please let me know and if it's an editorial issue please let me and my publisher know.

In 2006, I wrote the first draft to Déjà Vu: The Domino Effect. Certain things changed like dates and period Easter eggs, and events had to involve other folks. The original vision of this series was a superhero story arc where Keith is a superhero while in the past. Though elements of this still exists, I see Keith as an Anti-hero with a newfound gift that can right the wrongs of the immediate past while hunting down any remaining TASP agents that are still out there. Also, he's not the only one with the gene, we know there are at least two others and they'll both need to make appearance in the series.

I'm a situational writer, so I come up with a question and throw a character into a situation to see how s/he reacts. Keith will be more affected by the multiple timelines in his head. I will be sure to be more immersive with the emotional and physical consequences. My question was simple, "How would you react if you had this dream?" My answers were drastically different than Keith's and Keith's ideas won out. The dream led to time travel and this version of the story.

This is my first author's note and I am not sure what to write. I want to give some insight into my process and into the developement of the story, but mostly I just want to share my thoughts with a potential new fan. Thank you again for reading my novel and please send ffeedback—I would love to hear from you.

Sincerely,
John Gates

Author Bio

John Gates lives in Boston and summers on Cape Cod. He has had many careers over his lifetime but creating worlds from words is his most favorite. The next title in the Time Walker series should be out sometime this year.

•

You can connect with John gates on Facebook or send fan email to j.gates@npgbooks.com.

•

Check out his publsiher for updates at www.npgbooks.com.

www.ingramcontent.com/pod-product-compliance
Lightning Source LLC
Chambersburg PA
CBHW061347190726
48288CB00005B/1625